HOUSE of ROOTS and RUIN

ALSO BY ERIN A. CRAIG

House of Salt and Sorrows

Small Favors

The Thirteenth Child

A Land So Wide

HOUSE OF ROOTS AND RUIN

ERIN A. CRAIG

ROCK THE BOAT

A Rock the Boat Book

First published in the United Kingdom, Republic of Ireland and Australia
by Rock the Boat, an imprint of Oneworld Publications Ltd, 2026

Text copyright © Erin A. Craig, 2023
Cover art copyright © Marcela Bolívar, 2023

The moral right of Erin A. Craig to be identified as the Author of
this work has been asserted by her in accordance with the Copyright,
Designs, and Patents Act 1988

All rights reserved
Copyright under Berne Convention
A CIP record for this title is available from the British Library

ISBN 978-1-83643-165-7
eISBN 978-1-83643-162-6

Interior art used under license from Shutterstock.com
Printed and bound in Great Britain by Clays Ltd, Elcograf S.p.A

This book is a work of fiction. Names, characters, businesses,
organisations, places and events are either the product of the author's
imagination or are used fictitiously. Any resemblance to actual persons,
living or dead, events or locales is entirely coincidental.

No part of this publication may be reproduced, stored in a retrieval system, or transmitted,
in any form or by any means, electronic, mechanical, photocopying, recording of otherwise,
or used in any manner for the purpose of training artificial intelligence technologies or systems,
without the prior permission of the publishers.

The authorised representative in the EEA is eucomply OÜ,
Pärnu mnt 139b–14, 11317 Tallinn, Estonia
(email: hello@eucompliancepartner.com / phone: +33757690241)

Oneworld Publications Ltd
10 Bloomsbury Street
London WC1B 3SR
England

Stay up to date with the latest books,
special offers, and exclusive content from
Oneworld with our newsletter

Sign up on our website
oneworld-publications.com

For Paul—in a world of catfish, you have always been my arapaima. I love you so.

1

THE PAINTBRUSH WAS TOO WET.

Pigment concentrated through the boar-hair bristles, sluicing out in irregular blots and smudging the line I'd wanted crisp.

"Hold still," I murmured, barely moving my lips as I dabbed the brush on a rag, lest I somehow jar the moment before me and lose its magic forever. "Just one minute more."

The corner of Artie's lips trembled as if fighting the urge to break into a grin.

"I'm almost finished," I promised. "Just . . ." I flicked the brush across the canvas, capturing the gleam of impish merriment brightening my nephew's eyes. "There. It's perfect."

"I want to see! I want to see!" Artie exclaimed, falling out of his carefully arranged pose and tumbling over himself as he dashed behind the easel. His eyebrows fell. "That's not what I look like. Is it?"

I studied the rendering with a critical eye before glancing back to the little boy before me. Thick waves of dark hair like mine, like most Thaumases, but with his father's button nose. "I think it's a fine likeness."

"Very fine," a voice affirmed from the doorway behind us.

"Mama!" he cried, racing off to give his mother a hug. "Am I done now?"

Camille raised an eyebrow at me, seeking confirmation. I set down my palette and nodded.

"All done." Camille pressed a swift kiss to the top of his head before he was off, racing down the hall, breathless with pent-up energy.

"How was he?" she asked, entering the Blue Room to study the portrait more closely. Her amber eyes missed nothing. "This arrived for you this morning," she said, handing me a thick envelope. It was marked with several palace seals.

Mercy.

"A little squirmy but that's to be expected." I ran my thumb under the flap, ready to rip open the envelope and dig out my sister's letter, but I paused, watching Camille take in the painting.

"It's a lovely painting," she complimented. "I can't believe he's five now. Where have the years gone?" My sister brushed a strand of burnished auburn hair from her face and her fingers fluttered over the corner of one eye, feeling at the nonexistent lines she worried were beginning to creep in.

"*My* birthday is coming up, you know," I mentioned, keeping my voice as light and casual as I could.

She frowned as though I'd accused her of something. "I wouldn't forget that, Verity."

"I didn't mean— Only . . . maybe we could talk about what we should do this year?" I turned on my stool, looking up. "I thought perhaps we could go to the mainland? To the capital? Mercy said—"

"It's not Mercy's place to say anything," Camille said, glancing at the envelope in my lap. I could see she wanted to snatch it up and read the missive for herself but instead she stepped forward, squinting at a brushstroke.

"She said that I *could* still be presented at court, if we wanted to. Eighteen is a little older than most girls, but—"

Her sigh stopped me short. "I would have loved to take you at sixteen. You know that."

"Only I was at Hesperus, helping Annaleigh with the baby," I supplied, knowing her excuses by heart. "But last year—"

"Last year we were in the middle of the east wing renovations. It was hardly the time for a long, extravagant trip."

"I know," I said, tucking a bit of hair behind my ear. She was bristling for a fight, and if she started snapping, I knew it would be impossible to sway her. "I know, I know, I know. But now . . . the house is all done. The children are old enough to travel. I'm sure they'd all love to see Arcannus."

Camille shook her head, backing away from the canvas, her eyes drifting around the room as if looking for something to improve. She approached a chaise and plumped a down pillow until it stood on its own like a tuft of meringue. "Oh no. The children would never come with us to court. They'd stay behind with their governess, of course."

I took a quick breath, hope reaching high into my chest like a man drowning at sea and grasping for a life raft. "But we . . . we could go? Oh, Camille, think of how fun it will be! We haven't been to the mainland since Mercy moved to court. Annaleigh could come, too, and I'm sure Honor would join us. Foresia isn't that far from the capital, and perhaps even Lenore . . ." I stumbled to a halt as I always did whenever Lenore came up.

My third oldest sister was a complete mystery to me.

"Lenore is Lenore. I doubt she'd . . ." Camille ran a quick hand over her hair again, as if assuring herself that everything was still in place. "All of that does sound . . . It could be quite agreeable," she allowed. "But your birthday is next week. There's no possible way we could have everything ready by then. The travel alone is a full day by our fastest clipper. Perhaps we could arrange something this fall? Before Churning."

My face fell.

We wouldn't.

The weather would grow bad.

The twins would get sick.

Camille would have half a dozen excuses by then, none of which I could argue against because she was older and wiser and a duchess and you might be able to lead a spirited debate if it were simply the first two but her title was as formidable as a citadel high atop a hill. Bordered by a barbed stone wall. And a moat.

Camille crossed to the giant windows overlooking the Salten cliffs. She made a beautiful silhouette in front of the dramatic landscape, and my fingers itched to sketch her. I could envision the first long lines, gently curved to indicate the flow of her mauve skirts. It would be the perfect juxtaposition for the thick, short spikes I'd use for the cliffs.

"We *should* do something festive, though," she mused. "What about a party?"

I was too surprised to respond. Once Camille fixed her mind on something, trying to budge her from it was like prying a barnacle off the seawall.

"What do you think?" she asked, turning back to me, the weight of her stare cool and steady.

"I think . . . that sounds wonderful! How many people could we invite? Mercy said the princesses have been wanting to visit. Spring would be the perfect time for them to see Highmoor. And if Beatrice comes, you know Phinneas will too, probably. Oh! The Crown Prince! At my birthday!" My heart fluttered as I recalled Mercy's descriptions. "He's supposed to be madly in love with dancing. Perhaps we could make it a ball! Not a terribly formal one, of course. I know how much work they take but maybe—"

"Enough!" Camille said, breaking through my haze of ideas like a battering ram. "You've overexcited yourself, Verity."

"I haven't," I promised, feeling the heat in my throat even as I protested. My imagination had the tendency to run ahead of me, like a young colt racing after its own legs.

"You're flushed scarlet," she pointed out. "I'm sorry, I didn't mean to mislead you with thoughts of a large affair. I only meant a family dinner. Something cozy and intimate. Cook has been eager to try out some new recipes with the spring vegetables. It would just be us. And Annaleigh and Cassius, of course."

"Oh . . . of course," I said, feeling small.

She wandered over to the shelves of books before pausing at a small portrait of all our sisters.

Well. Most of our sisters.

Back when there were eight of us.

We'd originally been twelve strong but our three oldest— Ava, Octavia, and Elizabeth—passed away in quick succession after our mother died giving birth to me.

Then, years later, Eulalie followed after them, slipping from the same cliffs Camille had just been in front of. The triplets died months after—two of them anyway—another tragic accident. Rosalie and Ligeia. They left Lenore by her lonesome, like a set of silverware missing its fork and knife. Though I was six at the time, I don't remember their deaths, only the fallout. Lenore retreated deep inside her mind, a living ghost, eyes blank, lips forever drawn into a grim line.

Then . . . Papa and Morella, my stepmother. There had been a fire, a terrible one that nearly consumed the entire manor. I should be able to recall that night—I'm told there was a snowstorm, one of the worst our islands had ever seen—but there's nothing in my recollection of it.

My very first memory is of a sunny afternoon on Hesperus, a little spit of land farthest west in the chain of Salann islands, where my second oldest sister, Annaleigh, lives, tending the lighthouse. My other sisters, Honor and Mercy, and I lived there for part of our childhood as Highmoor was rebuilt. Camille insisted on using as much of the original structure as safety warranted. The rest she faithfully re-created, keeping everything exactly as it had been. Soft gray walls soaring four stories high and topped with a blue and green gabled roof. Two sprawling wings. A solarium filled with koi ponds and palm fronds. A great hall used for feast days honoring our patron god Pontus, king of the seas. A grand and glittering ballroom, almost never touched. All of it exactly as it had been in my early childhood, though I couldn't recall a single instance of it on my own.

Camille and Annaleigh say it makes sense I'd not held on to the memories of that dark time of grief. They wished they, too, could discard those thoughts, those reminders of how painful life could sometimes be. But nothing about it feels natural to me.

Their faces—my father, my mother, so many of my sisters—haunt me, though I've no memories of them alive and whole and here. Their portraits remain, scattered throughout the manor, hung on walls, tucked onto shelves, desks, and bureaus. I should not be so familiar with Eulalie's easy, winning smile or the dazzling russet hue of Rosalie's curls, but I could sketch them in an instant. I've memorized every curve of jaw, arch of eyebrow. I know how Papa tilted his head while deep in thought, how Mama's eyes sparkled, but I do not remember the sounds of their voices, nor how they took their coffee. Did Papa and I ever while away afternoons on the lawn, staring up at clouds? Did my sisters swim in little eddies of surf down by the north shore, their limbs long and white against the black sands?

This house has always felt full of ghosts to me—not of spirits in white sheets and chains, nothing as clichéd as all that—but of memories snatched away. Memories I'll never be able to claim as mine.

Camille adjusted the framed painting before clasping her hands together, decision reached. "So. A family dinner. What do you think?"

Her hope was palpable, written in the crook of her lips, all the way down to her fingertips dancing lightly over the velvet chaise before her.

I couldn't find it in myself to let her down.

It's why at seventeen—almost *eighteen*—I was still at Highmoor, running after my nieces and nephew, watching them grow, watching Camille's life proceed on ahead of her while mine seemed to be withering away in the wings. She needed me. She needed me here. And so I tried to tuck away my dreams of travel and adventure, my ambitions and desires. They didn't go down easily. They were always there, always part of me, asking, begging, beseeching for more. More than this house, more than these islands.

Pontus help me, I wanted more.

"All right," I agreed, forcing my lips into a smile.

For her.

For my sister.

2

"HAND ME YOUR BRUSH, WON'T YOU, DEAR HEART?" Hanna asked.

It was that rare moment of quiet in the house, hours after dinner when the children were mercifully put to bed, their chatter stilled. The days were growing longer and I'd already drawn my curtains closed against the lingering light. The velvet drapes softened the air in my room, shrouding it into a deadened silence.

I sat in front of my vanity, dressed in a long nightgown of ivory batiste and my favorite silk robe, tightened securely around my frame. Hanna, my nursemaid, my friend, and my closest confidante, had been bustling about behind me, tidying the room, turning down the linens. Next would be hair brushing, then tea. We'd had the same evening ritual for years.

Hanna removed the comb holding up my dark tresses and began working her crooked fingers through the waves, seeking out any last remaining hidden pins. Those clinked in the catch-all dish at my right, a clamshell Artie had found on the beach last summer. He'd carefully polished the concave surface till it glowed and presented it to me, his round cheeks lifting with unmistakable pride.

"Mercy wrote," I mentioned, leaning forward to remove the envelope from the drawer I'd cast it in before dinner.

"And how is the young ingénue?" Hanna started brushing out the ends of my hair with practiced strokes, careful not to tug on any knots.

I broke the wax seal and withdrew the contents. There was Mercy's letter, soft and sinuous curves scrawled across just a single page—short this week—and a second envelope bearing my name in an unfamiliar hand. I flipped it over and studied the seal. Intricate floral vines cascaded over a heart aflame.

"Do you know this crest?" I asked, holding it up for Hanna to inspect.

"That looks like the People of the Petals. In Bloem," she added.

Bloem was a tiny province near the heart of Arcannia. The people of the region worshipped Arina, goddess of love, beauty, and the arts, and Bloem was known for being the most refined and cosmopolitan area in the country, even putting the capital to shame. Its streets had as many fashion houses as they did theaters and salons.

So I'd read.

I ran a thoughtful finger over the seal. The wax had a deep purple hue, a sign of nobility. "I don't know anyone from Bloem, do I?"

Hanna frowned. "Not that I can recall. Perhaps Mercy's letter will explain everything."

Nodding, I set the envelope aside and picked up my sister's missive.

"'Dearest Verity,'" I began, reading aloud for Hanna's sake.

"'You missed the most marvelous party last night. There were so many guests in attendance. My dance card was never empty but I still managed to take a turn about the room with Princess Beatrice, though of course we pretended it was nothing more than a laugh. Still. Sometimes I think that girl shall drive me mad with her charms.

"'Two of the guests were the Duke and Duchess of Bloem, Gerard and Dauphine Laurent. They have a grand apartment in Arcannus, as well as their family estate in the country—Chauntilalie. Beatrice, Euphemia, and I stopped there on summer progress last year. It's beautifully decrepit and wistful. Lavender fields and so many little hills and dales, truly a bucolic dream. You would love it.'"

I stopped, briefly wondering what it would be like to simply go on a tour of the kingdom. Mercy seemed to spend half her life traveling with the court, a companion to the princesses, and she never made it sound like the awful lot of work Camille claimed it to be.

"'Dauphine surprised me by visiting my suite yesterday afternoon and we caught up over tea. She was quite enamored with a series of your paintings I have on display—the little one of the sunrise over Selkirk, the tide pool with that darling crab, and of course, the portrait you did of me. She wanted to know all about them and was delighted to hear how well I know the artist.'"

"Look at that," Hanna said, the brush now at the crown of my head. "A duchess fancying your work!"

I closed my eyes for a moment against her gentle ministrations before continuing on.

"'I was seated next to the duke at dinner—such a dear old

soul—and he asked if I might relay this letter to you, from Dauphine. Apparently, they'd like to offer you a commission, little sister. What fun! You should absolutely accept, of course, and make sure your travels involve a stop in the capital. I miss you and can't wait to show you off to all my favorite friends. Please come soon. Your dearest, Mercy.'"

"A commission," Hanna echoed. She set down the hairbrush and began dividing up sections of my hair to braid.

"How odd," I murmured, burning with curiosity. I'd never received a letter from someone who wasn't a relation, and my fingers traced the lilac seal once more before I broke it.

Thick and creamy and edged with a glint of rose gold, the paper inside was far nicer than Mercy's usual stationery. The duchess's hand was a refined copperplate, written in a shocking shade of orchid ink.

"'My dear Miss Thaumas,'" I began, bringing the letter closer to me. A cloying bouquet danced in the air. The paper had even been sweetened with perfume! "'First, I wish to introduce myself to you. My name is Lady Dauphine Laurent, Duchess of Bloem. I'm an acquaintance of your sister Mercy and hope to become a friend of yours. Second, I wanted to commend you on your obvious talent as an artist. Your work is exquisite and fresh. I've greatly enjoyed your portrait of Mercy and admire the style in which you captured her.

"'My son, Alexander, turns twenty this year and my husband would like to mark the occasion with his first adult portrait, as is the tradition for all Laurent heirs. As you may know, Bloem boasts of several academies and conservatories. In the last month I've looked through so many portfolios of work, I feel as though my eyes have crossed and I honestly can't remember a single piece from them. But there was something in yours that stayed with me.

"'To be short, I want you to be the one to paint my son. We will obviously pay you for your efforts and would be more than pleased to host you at Chauntilalie while you work. Please respond to my request at your earliest convenience. Alexander's birthday is in just three months, and I know it would please my husband to unveil the portrait on his special day.

"'Yours most earnestly, Dauphine Laurent.'"

"They want you to go all the way to Bloem to paint?" Hanna mused, tying off the braid with a ribbon in dark blue. She tapped the top of my head, work done.

All the way to Bloem . . .

My heart quickened. My first real adventure!

I stood up quickly and my knee bumped against the edge of the vanity, jarring the taper candle. I caught it before it could clatter over, spilling its foul wax upon the marble tabletop. Every year, Annaleigh gave me a case of candles for my birthday. She had them made up especially for me, claiming I'd been fond of the scent as a child. It was a horrid mix of sea salt and sage, and as much as I detested it now, Camille made sure the candles were used, claiming them to be too extravagant of a gift to be stored away and forgotten.

"I should write her back at once," I decided, turning to the little desk near the fireplace. I sat down, pulling out a sheet of parchment and my inkwell. A silver octopus, the Thaumas sigil, wrapped its arms around the container. My stationery was nowhere near as fine as either of the letters I'd received. Camille bought my supply from a shopkeeper in Astrea, made from the pulp of harvested kelp. It was grainy, with irregular blots of fibers, and had a slight tinge of green. It had always been more than suitable for my purposes—letters to my sisters, silly doodles for the twins or Artie—but I paused now, tracing the bumpy surface and wondering if I ought to find something nicer for my reply.

"Are you sure that's a good idea?" Hanna asked, busying herself with the tea cart. "You know your sister is going to have an opinion about that. About all of that."

"I'm sure she'll have many," I said, setting pen to paper with a decisive flourish. The paper wasn't important. The message was. "She usually does."

Hanna brought a cup of cinnamon tea and leaned against the back of my chair, reading over my shoulder. I could feel her eyes on my neck like a physical weight. "Well?" she prompted.

"Well . . ." As I signed my name, the nib of my pen scratched the page, sounding deeply important. "I'm eighteen next week. An adult. Camille doesn't get to decide absolutely everything in my life for me anymore. If these people—these kind and respectable people—want to invite me to their home, if they want to pay me to paint, then I'm all for it. I can't live at my sister's house forever."

"It's your home too," Hanna reminded me. "It always has been."

"Not exactly. Not since it became Camille's. I don't even recall what it was like before it was hers," I admitted, though Hanna knew all that.

Most nights she'd tell me about my childhood, from the time before I could remember. We'd sit on the love seat, drinking tea, while she spun another story. I was her only charge at

Highmoor—Marina, Elodie, and Artie had their own nursemaid, a much younger woman named Callabeth. Camille had confided to me once, after the twins were born, that she didn't want them growing fond of Hanna, already so old and frail, and marring their childhood having to mourn her.

Looking back at our youth, it made sense, wanting to shield your children from the pain that had marked you. I was also more than happy to keep Hanna all to myself.

"Just think of how nice it will be without me here for a while," I said with a false brightness. What *would* she do to occupy her time? Camille had kept her on because of loyalty. Since my return to Highmoor, Hanna had only ever looked after me. Mercy and Honor had declared themselves too grown to need fussing over. I wondered if Hanna was hurt I'd leapt into this commission without talking it through with her. "You can kick up your feet and finally get around to that sampler you've been talking about."

Hanna loved to sew, and her needlework had always been a source of pride for her, though I often kept her too busy to ever work on it.

"I'll be back in no time," I promised. "It's not like it will be goodbye forever."

She sniffed and turned back to the cart. "I suppose not. Now that your letter is all done, shall I tell you about the time Annaleigh snuck an army of sea turtles into the bathtub downstairs?"

"Sea turtles in the bathtub?" I echoed, following her over to my sitting area. I'd heard this story a dozen times before but always pretended as though it were the first. "Why on earth would she do a thing like that?"

3

"I THINK THAT'S EVERYTHING, MRS. BENNETT," Camille said, scanning her long list of supplies. Her fingers ticked over the last items, satisfied. My sister treated every rare shopping trip off Salten as if we were going on a yearlong expedition through jungles unknown.

"Oh, actually," I said, looking over my small stack of items. "If you have any more of the large sketchbooks"—I pantomimed the size I was after—"I'd love to get another of those. And a pack of charcoal pencils, too, please."

Camille nodded toward the shopkeeper. "Once you've tallied it all, Mr. Stammish will arrange for everything to be taken to our boat."

With a quick bob of her head, Mrs. Bennett began a list of her own, writing up my sister's invoice. Roland Stammish, Camille's valet, stepped forward and soon they were deep in discussion about how to best pack all the boxes for transport to the marina.

"I'm famished," I said, turning to Camille hopefully.

She studied a display of wooden toys in the shop window.

When she picked up a little sailboat, I knew she was thinking of Artie. She hated leaving the children at home, but the twins had bickered all through breakfast. Elodie finally sought to end the argument by hurling a scone at her sister, but she'd missed the mark, striking a silver pitcher and splattering cream all across the table. Camille's fury had been sudden and swift.

"Camille?" I prompted. "Lunch?"

"What?" she asked, drawing her attention away from the toy boat. "No, not today, I think. We ought to be heading back. Roland will be wanting to—"

"Please?" I begged, spinning a colorful disk. Small dolphin figurines leapt out of painted waves. "It's been ages since we've had a meal together, just the two of us. We never do anything together."

"We're together here. Right now," she pointed out. She replaced the boat back into the display and brushed her fingers.

My lips twisted, on the verge of pouting. I'd planned out exactly how to do this and she wasn't going along as I'd envisioned. "There's that tavern down the road. William says you always go there when you come to Astrea."

"Well, yes," she allowed. "They have a very good chowder."

"That sounds wonderful. All this shopping has left me so hungry. Aren't you?"

She glanced at the sparkling silver watch encircling her wrist. William had given it to her for an engagement gift before they were married, promising to always honor and respect the time she needed to run her domain. I suspected the only reason she'd wed him was that he was the only suitor to never challenge her authority. Her sigh wafted out like a slow leak. "I suppose we do have the time. Mr. Stammish," she said, raising her voice. "My sister and I will be at lunch. You'll let us know when you're ready to leave."

It wasn't a question. Few things ever were with her.

I fought the urge to clap my exuberance. I'd been aching to tell Camille about Dauphine Laurent's letter all day but hadn't managed to find the opportunity.

Hanna was right. Camille was unlikely to immediately accept. She would have to be convinced, coaxed. And if that didn't work, coerced. I'd sealed my fate earlier that day, dropping my acceptance letter into the post when my sister wasn't looking. I had no reason to suspect that Camille riffled through my correspondence, but I didn't want to leave a single thing to chance.

I was getting away from these islands.

We were seated in a booth far larger than a party of just two required. It was at the back of the tavern, in a secluded corner far from the rest of the open floor, and as Camille carefully tucked herself into the farthest side of the table, hidden away behind a wooden screen, I understood that this was her table, where she always sat. As the duchess.

We rarely went out in public together on the islands—she usually brought her children or husband along with her on visits to Vasa's shipyards or to bless the beginning of the fishing season with a grand ceremony at Selkirk. She left Hesperus to Annaleigh, certain she could manage the lighthouse all on her own. Our family all attended the Churning festival on Astrea—

a weeklong celebration thanking Pontus for his benevolence—and as I pondered over the past year, I realized that was the only time I'd been off Salten with her.

"Why did you want me to come shopping with you today?" I asked after a barmaid brought us great sloshing mugs of cider, leaving them unwiped to create a galaxy of sticky spheres and rings across the thick oaken table.

"Hmm?" she asked distractedly. She'd been watching the room beyond our booth, studying the faces of the townspeople present.

"We never go shopping together. It's always you and Roland for supplies for the manor or you and the children when it's time to order new clothing. The last time I went out with you . . ."

I wracked my memories. There must be one instance . . .

But I came up short and shrugged.

She dragged her gaze from the bar, glancing down at the table between us. "I hadn't thought attending fittings or pricing out new shingles would be something of interest for you."

"I mean, probably not but . . . it was a surprise when you asked me to come with you this morning. A nice surprise," I allowed.

Her lips rose in an approximation of a smile and she took a small sip of the cider. I had the distinct feeling she was trying to come up with some bland course of small talk to fill the time and knew I needed to act now if I wanted to say my piece.

I took a breath, the words I'd been preparing all morning heavy on my tongue, but as I opened my mouth, something else entirely fell out.

"Is it me?" I asked, and then was unable to take back the question because her eyes were upon me, finally meeting mine.

"You?"

"You seem distracted or uncomfortable or . . . something. I just . . . I get the sense that you would rather be anyplace else in the world than here with me, right now, and I just wondered—"

"Is it you," she said, supplying my next words.

I nodded, waiting for her denial.

She traced a ring of spilled cider with her middle finger.

"It's not . . . you," she finally said, but there was little assurance in her tone. "You know I love you very much, Verity, and you know how much I treasure having you at Highmoor with us, with me. All of us do. William thinks of you as his little sister. The children adore you."

"Then what is it?"

Camille winced silently as the barmaid returned, carrying a large tray. She set down bowls of chowder and a basket of crackers before us. Cutlery clattered to the table.

"Anything else, milady?" she asked.

"Thank you, Wynda. I believe we're quite all right."

With a nod, Wynda bustled away to check on another table before making her way back to a stool at the bar.

"We're fourteen years apart, you and I," Camille said briskly, dropping little rounds of crackers into the chowder. "I'd like to spend more time together, just the two of us, but . . . we're at very different stages in our lives. We always have been. I'm a wife, a mother. I have an estate to run and affairs at court. There are so many obligations that you'll never need to know or worry over. And you . . ."

"And me," I echoed, knowing there was nothing in my life that could ever match the mantle of importance placed on Camille's shoulders.

She reached out and squeezed my hand. "I am so, so wonderfully glad you're here, that you live with us. Highmoor will always be your home, you know that. Perhaps I've not shown you how much I appreciate you being there. I need to do better. I . . . I will try to be a better sister."

"Camille, I didn't mean to insinuate that you—"

"I will be better," she promised.

"Well . . . actually . . . there's something else I'd hoped we could talk about," I said, slipping the duchess's letter from my pocket. There was something horrible in the way Camille had said Highmoor would always be my home. The words themselves sounded lovely but their implication made me bristle. Staying at home meant I never went anywhere. I never learned anything new. I wouldn't find a suitor, a calling, *myself,* if I never left. Camille was bound to Highmoor, she was called to protect it and the islands, but I . . . what purpose did I serve behind its stony walls? "I . . . got that letter from Mercy yesterday."

She took a small spoonful of the broth, rolling it around her mouth while she contemplated what I wasn't saying. "Oh?"

"She's made friends with a duchess, from Bloem—"

"Dauphine Laurent," Camille cut in, nodding.

My head bobbed in time with hers. "Yes, well. The Laurents have a son—"

"Alexander," she interrupted again, taking more crackers and crushing them into her soup.

"Alexander," I agreed. Each time she broke my train of thought, my nerves mounted, growing from my middle like a bramble of tangled vines, reaching up to strangle me.

"He's a lovely young man," she said, glancing out across the room again. "I can't imagine being in the duke's position."

"Position?"

"He's an invalid, you know. Alexander. Some nasty fall or childhood malady, I can't remember which . . ." She shook her head as if it wasn't of importance. "He hasn't the slightest bit of movement in his legs, has to go everywhere in a wheeled chair."

"How awful," I murmured, picturing how it would look in painted form, a small, forlorn figure seated before a looming old manor, the grounds chock-full of overgrown greenery, threatening to swallow the boy whole.

Camille took another bite. "Do you not like it?" she asked, gesturing to my own bowl. I still hadn't touched it.

"I was just . . . letting it cool for a moment."

"So, let me guess. Dauphine is after Mercy to visit Chauntilalie, isn't she? She's obviously trying to set up some sort of arrangement with the pair of them behind my back. And Mercy wrote to you to . . . what? Get her out of it?" She rubbed at her temples with a sigh. "I swear, she's such a baby sometimes."

"What? No."

But Camille was already playing out her imagined scenario, too intent upon it to hear me. "Mercy," she snorted. "Dauphine must be scraping the bottom of the barrel. Anyone with one eye can see that that girl has already pinned her heart to—" She cut herself off abruptly, glancing sharply toward a couple who'd passed by closer than she liked. She swallowed. "Well. You know."

I did.

"That isn't why she was writing," I said, carefully bringing out the duchess's letter and setting it down on the table between us, now a sodden mess.

After giving it a wary look of disdain, she opened the wrinkled pages. I watched her eyes dart back and forth, scanning the bright ink. She read it once, twice, a third time, then put the letter back down. "No," she said without preamble.

"What do you mean no?"

"No, you won't be going." She downed a long swallow of the cider as if seeking fortitude.

Normally I would have nodded and followed her wishes but her earlier words still echoed uneasily in my mind.

Highmoor will always be your home.

Always.

It will *always* be my home.

My home will *always* be here.

But why should it?

Had she ever once asked me what I wanted out of my life?

No.

She just assumed she knew best and went around making sweeping pronouncements like that. Like she always did. Like a duchess always would.

I took a sip of the cider myself, then another. "I don't recall asking permission."

Camille's eyebrow arched sharply. She seemed too stunned to reply.

"I'll be turning eighteen next week. I'm more than old enough to be making my own decisions."

"Eighteen is hardly—"

"You let Mercy go to court at sixteen."

"The king requested it. What was I to do?"

"Honor left at seventeen," I continued, keeping my voice level. It had been a double blow, both my closest sisters leaving within just months of one another. I'd felt abandoned but tried to stay hopeful, knowing that only in a few years' time, I too would be old enough to join in their adventures.

Only that had never happened.

They were out there. I was still here.

Always.

"Honor became a governess. She had a job."

"So do I," I said, glancing at the letter.

"That's not . . ." She trailed off and closed her eyes. "That's not the same."

"I already sent her my acceptance."

There was a quick flash of amber as her eyes opened, narrowing at me. "You what?"

"I wrote back, saying I'd be delighted to accept the post. I mailed it off this morning."

She took a deep breath. Her cheeks burned brightly and I noticed her hands trembled with rage. "Then you will write her back and say it was a mistake. You'll have to apologize, of course, but—"

"There's nothing to apologize for. I *am* going."

"You're not." Her voice was terrifyingly calm. She'd not raised it once, keeping every word crisp and deliberate.

"I don't understand. Everyone else has left. Annaleigh, Honor, Mercy, even Lenore! You let all of them go without a fuss. I only want what they did. It's time for me to find out who I am, who I'm supposed to—"

There was a crack in the veneer of her face, just a small glimpse of the thoughts swirling in her mind that she desperately tried to hide, but as I spoke, it grew bigger, splitting the mask into tatters. "Dammit, Verity," she snapped, striking at the table with the palm of her hand.

It was as shocking as a slap. My breath caught in the hollow of my throat, unable to understand her reluctance, why there was such fury in her eyes.

"You're not them. You're not like any of them!"

She struck the table again, and the bowls and mugs trembled at the force of it. Before I could say anything, Camille swooped off the bench and was out the door. It swung shut behind her, striking against the frame with a resolute finality.

I sat frozen in place, staring at the food before me. I didn't have to look around the tavern to feel the eyes of everyone in the establishment staring at me, wondering what had occurred. Camille always presented such a calm, dignified façade in public. She must be mortified at the scene she'd caused. I was certain she would quickly return, making up excuses for her out-of-character antics.

A minute passed.

Then another.

And another.

And still she did not come.

I sat in the booth, unable to leave, unable to stop my short grasping gasps for air.

What had I done?

I'd wanted her to see me as I truly was now. Her sister, grown up and ready for the responsibilities of adulthood. Ready to fly from the nest. Ready to make decisions for myself. I wasn't a little girl any longer.

I hadn't guessed she'd react like that.

Against all odds, my stomach let out a loud gurgle. I dared to look over at the customers. A few people quickly glanced away—they *had* been staring—but some offered sympathetic smiles.

Another barmaid, different from the woman who had served us, came over, her steps tentative as if she wasn't sure her presence would be welcomed. Her skin was a dark copper and her black hair was cut short beneath her mob cap.

"Are you unwell, Miss Thaumas?"

"Oh, no, I'm fine. Just fine," I said, trying to believe it was true. Every minute that passed without Camille's return increased the dread building in my chest.

"You're crying," she observed, and pushed Camille's unused napkin toward me.

I snatched it up, patting at my eyes. "I hadn't even noticed."

"Sisters can be difficult, can't they?" she guessed, her eyes darting toward the door as though Camille had suddenly stormed back in.

She hadn't.

"They can be," I agreed.

"I have three," she said, ducking into the booth, sitting in Camille's spot. "All older. It's hard being the baby of the family."

"It really is." Despite my misery, I smiled at her. "I'm Verity."

She took my extended hand, shaking it with her cold, calloused ones. "Miriam."

"It's nice to meet you, Miriam. Thank you for coming over. I . . . I'm not exactly sure what I ought to be doing and everyone was staring so."

"Not everyone," she said, tucking a lock of dark hair behind her ear. "There's that gentleman over there, seated with the lady in green. She's been giving him an earful about some new hat she saw in the shops and I don't think he even heard your sister leave."

A bit of laughter burst from me. "Well, that's very good to know. And here I was, worried we'd caused a scandal."

"Oh no, miss," she said, her face drawn with mock gravity. "If you want to know a true scandal, look at that couple sitting over there—the man who has the big gold ring . . . and the lady whose fingers are decidedly bare."

I studied the pair she spoke of. They were leaning in toward each other, whispering and looking as if they were the only two people left in the world. "What's so shocking about that?"

Miriam's blue eyes twinkled; her smile was sly. "See that woman over near the bar, in the purple dress?"

I spotted her, studying the couple with barely concealed wrath. I ate more of the chowder, expecting something to happen.

"That's the gentleman's sister-in-law. He's not yet spotted her, but it's obvious she has him."

"Scandal indeed."

"Feeling better?" she asked, gesturing to the half-empty bowl.

"I am," I admitted. "I still don't know what to do, but—"

"Verity."

I jumped, startled by Camille's voice. I hadn't noticed her return or approach, and judging from the color leaving Miriam's face, neither had she.

"You're back," I said.

"Yes, well . . . Roland has the boat loaded. We ought to be getting home."

"Don't you want to finish lunch? Perhaps we could talk about—"

"We need to leave."

"Camille, this is Miriam," I said, feeling terrible my sister had not even bothered to acknowledge the girl in front of us. "We were just talking."

Camille's gaze drifted over her, never settling upon her face. An angry red crept out of the ruffles of her collar, staining her neck like a bloody handprint. "The tide waits for no one," she said, her eyes fixed above Miriam's head. Without a goodbye, she turned on her heel and was out the door, never once looking back to see if I followed her.

4

LATER THAT NIGHT, I TAPPED ON THE DOOR OF Camille's parlor.

"Come in," she bid, her voice light and welcoming. I feared she thought me William or one of the children.

Entering, I spotted her seated before her vanity, removing the day's finery. I watched her face sour in the mirror's reflection and knew I'd been right.

I turned, glancing out the windows at the setting sun as it painted the world crimson. Camille and William's suite of rooms took up nearly all the fourth floor of the west wing and offered the most spectacular views. I could even see the flash of light from Old Maude tonight and wished I could somehow will myself back to those golden childhood days on Hesperus.

"Dinner was lovely," I started, trying to mend this horribly broken fence with the empty compliments Camille usually drank up like water.

"You didn't take a bite of it."

I *knew* she'd been watching me over the rim of her goblet, assessing my every action.

She tilted her head and plucked off a fat teardrop pearl earring, then placed it in a silver dish.

"Camille . . . can we talk about this afternoon? Please?"

She removed the other pearl and rubbed her earlobes, massaging them. "I don't see the point, but you do seem determined to have your way in all things today, so fine. Let's talk about it. Let's talk well into the night, till we're both hoarse and exhausted. I have a council meeting at seven on Vasa tomorrow, but I'm certain the men will understand if I'm not at my best. I'll just tell them Verity wanted to talk."

"Camille . . ."

She spun around on the little tufted stool, her eyes sharp and fierce. "What?"

Faced with her wall of fury, my resolve crumbled away. I felt as though I were standing on the cliffs outside Highmoor. One wrong step and I would fall over the edge, careening toward my end.

Eulalie's painted smile flashed in my mind and I winced.

"I didn't . . . I didn't mean for it to go the way it did."

"A small reassurance," she said, turning back to the mirror. She took off her necklace, laying it out on a dazzling midnight-blue cloth. As she folded up the little square of velvet, I noticed her cuticles had been picked raw.

"I'm sorry," I said, wanting to take a step toward her, wanting to kneel next to her like I would have when I was younger, pressing my forehead against her side. She would have reached out to comfort me then. She'd have rubbed small circles between my shoulder blades, placed a kiss on the top of my head.

"For what?"

Her words stung like acid and I pushed away the thoughts of what she used to do. There would be no such comfort today.

"I didn't mean to upset you. I don't want you angry."

She sniffed. "Well, you've failed spectacularly at that."

I swayed back and forth, uncertain of what to do. It was clear she wasn't in the mood to talk—this conversation would go nowhere—but I also knew if I were to turn tail and retreat, the incident would fester between us, growing and spreading like the black rot of a gangrenous limb.

"I just . . . I just don't understand." Her admission was soft, a stark contrast from the earlier barbed assault, and I almost didn't hear it. "I've given you so much over the years."

I glanced about the room, not understanding the dramatic shift between us. "I know."

She took a deep breath, looking at her reflection, her stare vague and unfocused. "I was nineteen when Papa died. In the course of one evening, I inherited his title, a smoldering estate, and the sudden care of my five younger sisters." When her eyes rose to meet mine, they were watery with bright tears. "I've made sure you were clothed and fed. Educated. That you felt loved and cared for. I wanted—always—only the best for you. I've made this home as comfortable as I could. . . . Why are you so hell-bent on leaving it? On leaving me?"

I hazarded another step closer to her. "Camille, it's not you I want to leave. . . . It's not even Highmoor."

Her sigh quavered. She looked on the verge of sobbing. "Go on and do it. Everyone else has. It was a delusion to think you'd be different."

In an instant, I was at her feet, throwing my arms around her legs. The expression on her face had wounded me. I'd never seen Camille so vulnerable. So alone. "The others didn't leave you either. They just . . . they have their own lives to start."

"I always thought our lives were meant to be here, the Thaumas sisters, sisters of the Salt." She swallowed. "They've all gone so far away. . . ."

"I won't," I hastily promised. I pushed back every notion of my grand adventure. Pushed and stamped and trampled it into the dust beneath my feet. Anything to remove that dreadful look from my sister's face. "I . . . I'll write to Lady Laurent tonight. It will go out with the post first thing in the morning. I'll make whatever excuse you want me to. I'll stay, Camille, I will."

There was a long moment of silence. I couldn't see her face, couldn't tell what she was thinking, but hoped, hoped, hoped that somehow I'd made the situation better. I hoped my sacrifice had reassured her, had stopped her tears. It was terrifying to watch my sister—any of my sisters—cry.

"Thank you, Verity," she said, running her fingers over my hair, tickling the back of my neck like she used to. I closed my eyes and tried to sink myself into that act of forgiveness.

I didn't know how long we stayed that way, each trying to comfort the other from an impossibly uncomfortable position, neither of us seeing the other's face, just trying to make our earnestness felt. Finally, Camille broke away and picked up a small cloth from the vanity.

I straightened, sitting on the back of my legs, and watched her remove the stain from her lips, slipping back into her duchess mode, always self-possessed, never inefficient.

"Now that that's settled, you should be off to bed. You'll want to write that letter tonight and we could all use a good sleep. Hmm?" She tweaked my nose, but the motion felt off, a shell of affection.

"Of course," I said, fumbling to my feet. She'd won this battle and was already eager to move to the next task on her list. All of us were little ever more than an empty box in need of a check. Already I regretted my impulsive oath. "I could have Hanna bring you up a cup of tea, if you want. It always helps me sleep well."

Her lips settled into an unreadable line. "You can take one of my candles if you want," she volunteered, ignoring my offer and gesturing to the tapers flanking either side of the vanity. Even she was using Annaleigh's stinky gifts.

"That's all right," I said, and gave her a swift kiss on the cheek. "I've never been afraid of the dark."

༄

I waited until I was on the back staircase, heading for the second floor, before I broke apart, giant gasping gulps of breath bringing me to my knees. I flushed hot, my cheeks scalding even as my fingers quaked with cold trembles.

"It's only for a little while," I cried, making promises to myself that were beyond my powers to keep. "She can't expect you to stay here forever. She can't."

I shuddered, wanting to let loose a torrent of tears but I was wrung out, a sail without wind, a fish on dry dock, screaming to breathe in its airy surroundings. I stifled back floundering sobs. They wracked through me, curling my spine inward as I drew my knees to my chest, trying to hold myself together however I could.

"Look at that," someone whispered on the landing a floor above me. Their voice carried down the stairwell, echoing and repeating over itself.

"Who's there?" I called out. My fingers clawed at my sides, panic spiking through me like an ice pick.

Someone had overheard my distress. Someone had witnessed my breakdown, and rather than come to my aide, come to comfort, they'd watched, cruelly judging me, mocking my angst.

"So many tears."

Who was that?

Who were they speaking to?

I leaned out over the railing, straining to find the figures in the darkness above me. Oh, why hadn't I taken Camille's light?

"So much sorrow," murmured the companion.

Uncurling myself, I sped up the stairs as silently as I could, intent on surprising the voices. Was it a pair of idle maids? Camille and William traipsing after me to make sure I'd really gone to bed? Who?

But the landing was as empty as it had been when I first passed it. I peered down the third-floor corridor, certain the voices had fled when they heard my approach, but it, too, was still and dark.

Then . . . a flash of red.

A ways away, near the other end of the hall. There one moment, then gone the next, slipping around the corner.

"Lenore?" I asked incredulously.

It looked just like her hair, worn loose and long, a sparkling curtain of russet against the low glow of the gaslights. The children's rooms were on this floor, and the lamps were kept burning through the night to stave off bad dreams.

I followed after her, confusion swirling within me. "Lenore?"

Had she come home? For my birthday?

We'd wanted her there, of course. I would have sent her an invitation myself, but I'd not known where to address it. The last time she'd contacted any of us had been months ago, penning a short note to Camille.

"I'm fine," she'd promised at the end of the missive. *"Everything is fine."*

She'd tucked a small flower into the envelope, pressing its strange red petals between a bit of wax paper to preserve its beauty.

And now she was here.

I hurried after her. It had been years since she'd left Salann. Years since I'd seen her face.

"Lenore," I tried again. "Wait for me."

Why wouldn't she turn and greet me?

"Tears," she whispered, and her voice carried strangely down the hall. For a moment, I could have sworn it came from behind me, familiar lips pressed directly to my ear.

"Sorrow," her unseen companion agreed.

"Tears."

"Sorrow."

They repeated the words over and over, their whispers rising to hisses, like steam released from a kettle too hot and ricocheting through the corridor to form a horrible melee of noise so loud I was surprised the children could sleep through it.

"Lenore!" I cried out, racing around another corner to watch her descend the main staircase. "What are you saying?"

"Tears," she repeated, pausing on her tread to look up at me.

I could clearly see the second figure now, standing beside her, their hand gripped tightly around my sister's.

I blinked hard.

I wasn't seeing clearly.

In fact, I was seeing double.

But neither of the figures was Lenore.

They stared up at me, concern marring their pale and lusterless faces.

"Sorrow," my dead sister whispered, and then I began to scream.

5

WHEN I CAME TO, I WAS IN MY BEDROOM, STARING AT the canopy above my bed.

Beside me, the mattress was dented in. Someone was sitting on it and for one terrible moment, I couldn't see who it was. Another scream tore from my throat as I envisioned Rosalie and Ligeia flanking me in sleep, their long dead limbs reaching in to cover me like a shroud.

"Stop that. Stop it this instant."

That hiss of command, of seething disappointment. It wasn't my not-so-recently departed sisters.

Only Camille.

"Drink this," she said, pushing a small glass of amber liquid into my hand.

I sat up, swaying as my head dipped, listing back toward the pillows. Back to the bed and unconscious sleep where I could pretend I'd never seen my two lifeless sisters walking through the corridors of our home.

But Camille's insistence kept me in check.

The brandy was strong, biting and sharp. My eyes watered

as I swallowed the fiery spirits, but oddly it helped. My mind focused on the present, the now. On Camille, sitting at the edge of my bed, a rose-colored robe cinched around her waist.

Rose like Rosalie . . .

No.

I kept my eyes on Camille as I finished the wretched drink and tried not to notice how the angle of her cheekbones, the curve of her eyes, even the way she held her head now, tilted with unchecked curiosity, were exactly the same as Rosalie's. As Ligeia's.

Why did we all have to look so agonizingly similar?

"Who did you see?"

I licked my lips, considering the careful phrasing she used. She'd asked *who*, not *what*. "What were they?"

"The triplets, then," Camille said thoughtfully.

I imagined Lenore joining their ill-fated duo and shuddered. "Sort of."

"Sort of," she agreed unhappily.

"Camille . . ."

Her eyes met mine, dark as the rosin Elodie used on her violin bow. She looked so lost. "I . . . I'd always hoped that somehow, Pontus willing, we'd never need to have this conversation."

I waited for her to go on, but she didn't seem to know how, so I went ahead and said it, said the one word that was guaranteed to crack her silence wide open. "Ghosts."

She nodded.

"Our house is haunted," I continued. "With ghosts."

She shook her head. "Not the house . . . just you."

She grabbed my empty tumbler and made a beeline for the

little cart of spirits someone had brought in. Hanna, most certainly. I wondered if she'd helped Camille take me downstairs or if it had been Roland who'd carried my listless form down the long halls.

She poured herself a glass, then added another finger into mine. "If we're going to do this, we should at least be comfortable," she said, dropping onto the wingback chair and leaving the chaise for me. "Verity?" she prompted, holding out the tumbler.

With reluctance, I left the bed, took the brandy, and sat down, facing her. My stomach heaved as she gestured for me to begin. "I thought it was Lenore at first. I saw her down the hall and went after her. But . . . but it wasn't her."

"I know."

I straightened with interest. "You've seen them then? You've seen them too?"

"No." She sighed. "I guess it would be best to start at the beginning of everything. It's just . . ." She pressed her lips together, reluctance clouding her face. "Ever since you were little, you've seen them."

"Rosalie and Ligeia?"

"Not just them. All sorts of them. Of . . . ghosts." She visibly shivered and took a large swallow of the brandy. "Annaleigh noticed it first. . . . You had sketchbooks full of our older sisters. Ava and Octavia. Elizabeth. You were too young to remember them but they were drawn with such detail, such painstakingly accurate features. . . ."

"I don't remember," I said, pushing against that gray fog of lost memories. "Where are the sketchbooks now?"

"They burned in the fire. There's so much about that time

that you don't know. It would take more than one night to explain it all but for now, please trust me when I say it's better that you don't remember. After the fire, after . . . everything . . . you went to Hesperus. Annaleigh said she thought you were better, that everything you'd seen before had just been part of those . . . nightmares. But then you started telling her about Silas. . . ."

I squinted, dredging up the memories from my time at the lighthouse. There'd been an older man there, with craggy features and soft tufts of hair. "The Keeper of the Light," I said, remembering. He'd shown me the best ways to polish the curved glass windows of Old Maude. He'd taught me how to tie knots, spot constellations I'd never heard of, and ways to predict the weather. I frowned, my words echoing in my mind. "Only . . . that can't be right. Annaleigh is the Keeper. . . ."

Camille nodded. "Silas died the night of the fire . . . or sometime before. I don't know exactly how it happened. But he was dead."

"A ghost."

Her stare confirmed it.

"But he didn't . . . he didn't *look* dead."

"They never do," she said, fidgeting with the ties of her robe. "Not to you."

I looked down into the tumbler, studying the way the lines of cut crystal refracted shards of light through the brandy. I could feel Camille staring at me, on the edge of her seat with concern.

When I dared to meet her gaze, I kept myself as still and small as I could, bracing myself for the storm to come. "I don't believe you."

Her mouth fell open. She'd not expected that. "Why would I lie about something as grave as this?"

I ignored her poor choice of words. "Because you want to keep me here. Because you'd say anything—*do* anything—to keep me at Highmoor." I frowned, trying to remember the pair of girls on the stairs, trying to recall every detail as it had been, not as my tired mind had guessed at in the dark. "Those weren't ghosts. Those were maids, dressed to look alike, dressed to look like our sisters." A bitter laugh bubbled up inside me, bursting free like a boil popped. "No. Not maids. I bet you brought them here, hired them just for this. Actresses. To fool me. Oh, Camille."

Her eyebrows drew together into a single worried line. "You think me capable of something so twisted?"

Slowly, I nodded.

Camille was the oldest.

Camille was the duchess.

And a duchess always got her way.

I'd been challenging her authority for months, slipping off on unsanctioned visits to the other islands, sending away for applications to Arcannia's best art conservatories, begging to visit Mercy at court. She knew I wanted to leave and had concocted a plan to keep me here.

Yes. She'd do that. She'd do that and more to keep me from undermining her.

"You want me to stay here forever, a scared little girl jumping at shadows, because you need someone to take care of," I said, triumph coursing through me as I began to see the threads of her motives woven throughout this entire mess. "You need to feel big and important, to hear people fawn over you for your benevolence."

She snorted. "You don't get it. You don't get it at all."

"But I finally do. This was never about me. It has always, *always* been about you. Your need for control. Your need to be admired. And look at the lengths you'll go to get it."

Camille set her tumbler down on a side table, staring off into the distance as if she couldn't bear to look in my direction. "Everything I've done has been for you. Do you know what would happen if you ever left the islands by yourself? If you did go to court, go to school, go wherever? You . . . you . . ." She trailed off in a groan, balling her hands into claws of frustration. They trembled with pent-up kinetic energy, wanting to lash out and strike something. The table, the glass, maybe me. "You see them everywhere. Everywhere," she repeated darkly. "When I came back for you at the tavern today, there you were. Introducing me to a serving girl who wasn't there. I shudder to imagine what had happened before my return. What people thought. What people said. What they're saying now."

I remembered her strange avoidance of the girl, of Miriam, acting as if it was beneath her to acknowledge the server's presence. I thought Camille had just been overplaying her role as duchess. But what if . . .

"Do you know how strange you look, speaking to them, carrying on entire conversations overheard as one-sided? You look mad, Verity, as though you've entirely lost your mind. If I wasn't there, if you weren't here, under my protection . . . you'd be taken away, thrown into an asylum. No one is going to believe a girl who talks to thin air."

An icy line of worry trickled down my spine. For a moment, I could see it happening, could picture my hands gripping filthy iron bars, hear my cries for release. "You'd get me out, though . . . wouldn't you?"

"To what end?" she spat, her anger rising. "News of your confinement would spread across the kingdom. Think very hard on how you'll go on after that. No one is going to want a mad little fiancée, for a mad little wife, issuing out mad little children. You'd be ruined forever."

I tried the brandy again but my throat felt too thick, too sick to swallow. It lingered in my mouth, burning.

"And then . . . it would all come back on the rest of us. People would talk. People would wonder. What do the rest of the Thaumas girls see? Do you want that on Mercy? Honor? Marina and Elodie? Everything we do always comes back round to those who love us. Think about them, Verity. Think about their futures. Please."

I felt myself begin to nod, begin to acquiesce as I always did, but caught myself. "You're the one who's mad," I whispered. "This whole scheme is insane. Those weren't ghosts. They weren't spirits come to warn me of impending doom. Things like that don't exist."

Camille watched me warily, as if facing down a wild animal capable of destroying her. "But they do."

"How would you know? You say you can't see them. If I'm the only one who can and *I* can't tell they're ghosts—" I started to laugh again. The absurdity of the conversation had gone too far. It sounded as though we were actors in a badly written play, our dialogue too outlandish to bear. "You'll have to do better than two girls in red wigs running about in Lenore's old nightgowns. If someone was truly being visited by ghosts, they would *know* it. There would be no question of it."

Her body bristled and her stare had turned cold. "You're so very sure of that?"

I nodded.

"Roland?" Camille called out, raising her voice.

Her valet entered my chamber, still wearing his suit despite the late hour. "Madam?"

"I wondered if you could go and fetch Hanna for me, please?"

He cocked his head, squinting. "Madam?"

"Hanna Whitten? Our old nursemaid?"

"I . . . I remember who she was, madam." Roland made no motion to leave and find her.

His words struck me like a bolt of fire from the sky. *Was* . . .

Camille was not to be stopped. "Could you go get her, please? For Verity?"

Roland glanced uneasily between us. "I don't understand, milady. Hanna Whitten has been dead and gone these last twelve years."

6

DRIP. DRIP.

Drip, drip, drop.

Water plinked into the tub, sending ripples across the surface to lap against my bare skin.

I wasn't sure how long I'd sat in the bath, naked and shivering. The water was cold now, beading against my skin like icy diamonds, the bubbles long gone.

As I sat in the water, hunched over my bony knees, the drip echoed against the glazed jade tiles and lulled me into a dissociative trance.

Far from Roland and his ludicrous pronouncements.

Far from Camille.

Far from ghosts I wasn't fully sure I believed in.

Far from Highmoor.

Far away to a place where it was just me.

Me.

Me and the water.

Me and the leaky faucet.

Drip. Drip.

Drip, drip, drop.
Drip. Drip.
Drip, drip—
Creeeeeeeeeeeeeeak.

I froze, my muscles tensing into a painful rictus of dread as the sound ripped me back into the present. Back where it was too cold and too dark and anything could have been hiding away in the shadowy depths of the bathroom. Watching. Waiting.

Waves of pebbled gooseflesh rose and every bit of me stood at attention as I noticed the burnished seahorse doorknob turn, listing to the left as someone on the other side fumbled with it.

Was it my long-dead sisters, come for a late-night visit? What would they look like up close? I imagined ghoulish faces and fanged grins, tendrils of red hair running down their bodies like rivulets of blood, clouded eyes as white as milk.

The seahorse dipped all the way around and the latch clicked, releasing the catch. I sucked in one sharp breath, cringing as the door slowly drifted open.

For a moment, it seemed no one was there.

"Ro . . . Rosalie?" I dared to whisper, fear staking my throat too thin. I could feel my heartbeat ricocheting through the veins in my ears, its pulse drowning out any answer from the other side.

The Other Side.

But then Hanna bustled in, carrying a tray of hair soaps and oils, a fresh bath sheet hanging over her arm.

"Did you say something, dear heart?" she asked, her voice clear, her figure unmistakably present and solid.

Echoes of Roland's absurd statement lingered in the back of my mind and I wanted to laugh. How foolish did he and Camille think me? They probably planned to let Hanna go first thing in the morning, taking away my one solace as they plotted how to best carry out this ridiculous claim.

"I thought I'd find you in here," Hanna said, setting down the tray and arranging the items along the marbled countertop. "I heard about the . . . argument . . . and went to your rooms to see how you were coping. When you weren't there, I knew you'd either be down at the shore or in here."

She turned and dipped her fingers in, *tsk*ing at the temperature before turning the faucet handle, coaxing hot water back into the tub. I jumped at the metallic screech, my teeth sharp against one another.

Roland's words, however preposterous, had set me on edge.

"Whenever something's troubling you, you always turn to the water." She ruffled the back of my neck and wet strands of hair clung to her wrist.

My dark curls against her crepe-paper skin unreasonably cheered me. A ghost couldn't do that. A ghost couldn't do any of the things she'd done.

"Hanna . . . ," I started, then stopped. For one strange, horrible moment, she flickered in front of me, like a candle on the verge of sputtering out. Had I blinked, I would have missed it.

"Yes?"

She flickered again.

I scrunched my eyes closed and sank into the bath, letting it muffle the sounds of her chatter. I was struck by the sudden and horrifying notion that when I emerged, she'd be gone.

She'd be gone because *Hanna Whitten has been dead and gone these last twelve years.*

Roland's words rang louder now, amplified by the water surrounding me. I stayed under as long as I could, my lungs burning and screaming at me to just come up and breathe. Breathe!

"—don't you think?" She blinked at me, waiting for my response to a question I'd not heard.

"What?" I managed.

"I said I think the lavender best for tonight, don't you? Help ease your mind. Help sleep claim you."

"How . . ." Words failed me.

This was absurd.

Hanna was here before me now.

Hanna was—

Hanna Whitten has been dead and gone these last twelve years.

No!

She was opening doors, carrying trays. Touching me with tangible heft.

She was not a ghost.

"Did . . . did you happen to overhear the argument?" I asked instead.

She shook her head, squeezing out a generous handful of the oil. After pouring a pitcher of water through my hair, she set to work, scrubbing my scalp and combing through the long locks.

Lavender shimmered in the air between us. Her fingers were an insistent pressure on my head.

"Hanna?" I looked up at her and grabbed her wrist, trying to still her movements.

My fingers passed straight through her arm.

She looked down in surprise. Her following sigh was stained with disappointment. "They finally told you."

"Told me what?" I asked, sick. I needed to hear her say it.

"Told you . . ." She trailed off, turning toward the door as if weighing out a possible retreat.

I tried again to grab her and as my hand inhabited the same space as her wrist, a cold charge crept up my arm, like hoarfrost consuming a field. It wasn't a simple chill, a flurry of shivers due to the water, due to my nakedness. It was an utter absence of warmth, an absence of anything resembling life.

Death.

Gasping, I pushed myself away, fleeing from her until I struck the back wall of the tub. There was nowhere for me to go, but still I sought to escape, crawling up against the slippery side, willing myself to disappear into its mosaic patterns. Water splashed everywhere, flying from the bathtub and soaking the tiled floor. The spray went through Hanna and she flickered again, absolutely dry.

Despite the horror of the moment, Hanna smiled wistfully, the curve of her cheeks rounding further. The soft light of the gas lamps played across her skin, highlighting the fine lines around her eyes.

This wasn't right.

There was no special glow around her, no floating aura casting an otherworldly tint. She looked as she always did.

Like she always had.

"You've never aged, have you?" I asked, sinking back into the tub, quivering and spent. My voice sounded so small, so far away from here and now where *Hanna Whitten was but wasn't because she was gone, dead and gone these last twelve years.* "All my life, you've looked exactly as you do now."

Her smile weakened, listing bittersweet. "A small blessing, I suppose." She touched her soft white hair.

"No." My mind refused it. It was not possible. It was not—

"Yes," she murmured sadly, as if it pained her to refute me.

I drew my knees to my chest, suddenly anxious to be laid so bare before her, before this . . . spirit? Specter. *Thing.*

She sat back on her heels as if sensing my need for space. A little sigh escaped her. "I don't suppose . . . perhaps we could just forget all about this?" She held up one flickering hand, staring at it with regretful contemplation.

"Hanna. You're dead," I whispered.

"I am," she admitted.

"How do you . . . How am I to . . ." The look on her face made me want to cry. "How did it happen?" The words tumbled free without me thinking through them, but they were the right ones. The ones that would help us both.

She rubbed the side of her neck. "The night of the fire . . . that awful, awful, terrible night . . ."

"You were caught in it?" I asked, struggling to remember what had happened. Sometimes Cook would let me and the children help her when she made holiday sweets. It felt like that now, wrestling against a length of taffy, sticky and straining.

Hanna shook her head. "No. Not that night, but . . . but just after. I heard . . . I heard a terrible thing. A shocking thing. It was too big for me to handle. Too horrific for my heart to take. But when it came time to go . . . after, you know . . . I couldn't bring myself to leave this place. I couldn't leave you, or your sisters. You all looked so small against the snow, small and soot-stained and I just . . . couldn't go."

She let out a deep breath—*Why was she breathing? Surely she didn't need to*—and stood up. She traced her fingertips along the edge of the sink.

"I told myself it was better to remain here, to watch over you all, even if you didn't know I was there. It was a comfort to me. More comforting than an afterlife full of unknowns. I could feel the Brine beckoning me. I knew I was meant to go there, to join the Salt, to go to my husband, to go find my . . . son. I felt so torn. But then . . . you wandered over to me as Highmoor burned to the ground. You wandered over and grabbed my hand. You grabbed hold of me and did not let go. And so . . . I stayed."

I uncurled a little, jostling the water around me into swaying waves as I brought my hands up, flexing them experimentally. They did not look different from other hands. They did not seem capable of touching a departed soul and bending it to my will and yet . . .

Hanna watched me carefully from her perch.

"Is it my fault you're still here?"

"Oh no, darling," she said in a warm rush. "Not at all. I had the choice. I chose to stay."

My eyes filled with a sudden swell of unshed tears. How different would my life be if she hadn't? Without her gentle affection, her practical advice, her warm shoulder to cry on . . .

"Thank you—" I broke off before the tears could fall. It sounded too short, too small a phrase to impart my gratitude, but it was all I could manage.

She bobbed her head and I hoped she understood everything those two words meant.

"Why didn't you ever tell me?" I shivered against the chill of the water but made no motion to leave it.

"You left for Hesperus as soon as the funerals were over," she began, her voice growing distant and dreamy. "I remember how your little frame shook at mine . . . but when you returned, it was as though nothing had happened! You didn't remember my death, you didn't remember any of them, and I . . . it had been so many months since anyone had seen me, had talked to me . . ." Her eyes grew bright with tears and—*ghosts shouldn't be able to cry*—she wiped them aside with the back of her hand. "It was selfish, I suppose. No. It *was* selfish. . . . But when you burst into your new rooms for the first time, when you raced up—ignoring your sisters' worried glances—and hugged me, I was too selfish to say anything to change your view. I know it was wrong. I knew it then too. Every day I tried to hide away, watch over you from the shadows, let your sisters' wards push me back, be unseen, but you saw me. You always saw me, Verity."

Tears tracked down my face, salting the water with sorrow. I'd always thought ghosts to be eerie creatures of malice and retribution, haunting the living with their incessant demand to be remembered, to have their wrongs avenged.

But this was Hanna.

She was not a malevolent entity, hell-bent on harming us because we lived and she did not.

She was love. So much love.

It infused everything she'd done, every choice she'd made, every act she'd committed.

"I know you probably want to stay in there and stew on this," she started cautiously, "but that cold water isn't going to do you any good and I can see your fingers are wrinkled from here. Can we continue this talk in your room?"

I ran my thumbs over the pads of my fingers and nodded.

Hanna scrambled into motion again, helping me stand and wrapping the soft linen sheet around my quivering frame.

How is she doing this? How is she doing any of this?

She ushered me down the darkened corridor, briskly rubbing life back into my arms as I kept a watchful eye out for any glimpse of movement. It wasn't just Ligeia and Rosalie I needed to worry about. Six of my sisters had died in this house. My mother. My father. Twenty generations of Thaumases before me. Who knew how many of them roamed the passageways, wanting acknowledgment now that I knew how to see them. How to look.

Thankfully, the hall remained empty.

"Nightgown, tea, and then we'll do something about those tangles, all right?" Hanna muttered, and I honestly wasn't sure if she was talking to me or herself.

"How do you . . . How are you doing that?" I asked as she manhandled me into my nightdress.

"When you want something badly enough, you make it happen," she said, fastening up the row of buttons with surprising dexterity. "Besides, what else am I meant to be doing? I didn't laze about in life and I certainly wasn't going to start in death."

"But ghosts shouldn't . . . *You* shouldn't be able to do that," I amended, watching her pour a cup of tea. When I took it from her, I made sure our fingers brushed. I could feel them again, whole and tangible.

She paused, leveling her dark eyes upon me. "Miss Verity, only hours ago, you didn't know spirits existed. Perhaps it would be wise not to presume you understand anything more than that." Hanna squeezed my shoulder, drawing me to the chaise. "I overheard everyone in the kitchen speculating about the squabble between you and Camille . . . before all this. Do you want to talk about it?"

I set my teacup down.

My fight with Camille, only an hour before, felt like an eternity ago. So much had happened since then. So much had changed.

Only . . .

Had it really?

Looking Hanna over, I knew deep in my bones that Camille was right. I'd always been able to see ghosts; I'd just not known how to properly perceive them.

Well . . . now you'll know to look.

The thought arose unbidden from the recesses of my mind, from that deep shadowy place I assumed all of my forgotten memories were stored, if only I knew how to get to them.

The voice sounded remarkably like me, only . . . less. Smaller. Younger.

Who had I been talking to?

Camille, probably. Or Annaleigh?

I pushed the thought away. It didn't matter now. Both of them had lied to me for years and they would have continued to, covering up an entire facet of my being with ease. But they'd been caught.

Annaleigh's betrayal stung even more than Camille's.

"I told her about the duchess's offer. She doesn't want me to go. She said that I'll get caught talking to . . ." I trailed off, uncertain of how I ought to address it. It seemed indelicate to say *ghost* in front of her.

"Spirits," Hanna supplied.

"Well . . . yes." I brightened as all my swirling thoughts merged together, forming a perfect, crystalline idea. "Hanna—this is perfect! You can come with me, to Bloem! You'll know when I'm around other spirits. You can keep me from embarrassing myself—from embarrassing Camille!"

"Oh, Miss Verity," she interrupted, gently shaking her head. "I'm afraid that's impossible."

"What do you mean?"

"I wouldn't be able to help you with that. With . . . seeing any others."

I blinked.

"It's always been just you and me."

"You can't see other spirits? Not even Rosalie? Or Ligeia?"

Her expression darkened. "You've seen them?"

"Tonight. It's what started . . . all of this."

"I never knew if they were here or not. I'd always hoped they weren't, that they'd found some measure of peace . . ." She licked her lips. "It's like ships at sea. Two boats might be on the same ocean, but it doesn't mean we'll ever bump into one another."

I pictured Hanna out on a sailboat, tossed about by swells and surges, trapped alone forever.

Not alone, though. Not entirely.

"Well, then it'll be just you and me in Bloem. Two girls on a wild adventure." I kept my words light, dazzling. This could still work. This could still be . . .

Her lips rose but it didn't look like any smile I'd ever seen from her before. She didn't need to say it aloud. It was written all over her face.

"You can't leave Highmoor, can you?" I guessed, disappointment crashing through me.

"I can leave the house," she corrected. "Walk the island, even wade out a little onto the shoreline—remember when I'd take you swimming?—but that's as far as I can go."

"What happens if you try to go farther?"

She dropped her hold on me and crossed to the vanity. "It's not comfortable to experience and even less pleasant to talk about."

"I'm sorry." I glanced down at my empty hands.

She kept her back to me and stared at the table for a long moment. When she tried to pick up my hairbrush, it remained staunchly within its silver tray.

"I don't think it's a good idea for you to go to Bloem, Verity." Her voice was so soft, I had to strain to hear all the words. "Whenever I think of you leaving . . . the most awful dread washes over me."

I sank back against the curve of the chaise. "Dread?"

She nodded and tried for the hairbrush again. A sigh of frustration escaped her. "It doesn't feel right. I fear that something will happen to you."

"Happen to me?"

"Stop parroting everything I say. I'd explain it better if I could."

On her third attempt, the brush clattered to the floor. I hadn't seen her hand move toward it. It simply zipped through the air, seemingly of its own accord, and for the briefest moment, I pitied Camille and anyone else who'd ever had to witness the result of

Hanna's movements without seeing the cause behind them. It would be terrifying.

"It will only be for a few weeks—a month at the most."

She shook her head. "It could be for far longer than you think."

"Meaning what?" I snapped. Having everyone around me speak in careful half-truths and vague admonishments was exhausting.

Hanna turned to face me. "Don't go, Verity, please. Another opportunity will present itself. Just don't go to that house. To Chauntilalie."

"Why?" I pressed. "What's wrong with it?"

Her pale eyebrows drew together. "I don't know."

"Is it the people within it?"

"I don't know," she repeated.

I pushed down a growl of irritation. "Then tell me something you do!"

"I don't . . ." Her voice cracked, breaking as her throat thickened with tears. "I don't want you to go there."

Her words echoed in the air, ringing like the clang of a bell, and I straightened as I heard what she'd really meant.

"It's not that you don't want me to go there," I said slowly, spelling it out for her and for me. "You don't want me to go. Anywhere. At all." I stalked away from the chaise, disgusted. "You're just like Camille."

She glanced past me, her eyes growing unfocused. "I don't know how to explain it."

"Try."

I knew my words were hurtful, my tone too strong. I was taking all of the frustrations that had been festering with Camille and lashing out at Hanna. It wasn't fair. It wasn't right. But I was powerless to stop it.

I didn't know how to end the conversation, how to stop this fight. I seemed doomed to repeat it with everyone I encountered here. I wouldn't be surprised in the least to find Artie tapping at my door tomorrow morning, begging me to stay, suffocating and smothering me with a sense of duty and his persistent, unflagging love.

I turned to my window, overlooking the darkened gardens. The topiaries were cut like jellyfish this year, a ridiculous choice—something so free and fluid had no business being stiltedly trimmed into stagnant poses—but Marina and Elodie had pleaded. The low moon limned over their rigid surfaces, casting long shadows across the lawn.

I knew every inch of that garden. Its curving pathways, its fountains and benches. They were all as familiar to me as family. I could walk through it blindfolded and not catch my sleeve on a single barbed bush.

Everywhere I turned on this island was known. Known and drawn over and over so many times I felt as though I was going mad, repeating the same lines again. How many sketchbooks could I fill with the cliffs at slightly different times of day, capturing the same angles, just moving the shadows about?

I needed something strange and new.

I let out a long bone-weary sigh. "I think I'd like to go to bed now."

Behind me, I felt Hanna's appraisal, pausing to study me before turning down my bedsheets. I walked on wooden legs to the side of the bed, allowing her to tuck me in and press a good-night kiss to my forehead.

I pictured the same movements, the same gestures being played out every night for the rest of my life. I would grow older, my dark hair turning silver, my face filled with more and more deep lines, but Hanna would still be there, exactly as she was now, pulling up my sheets, offering a quick burst of affection.

"I hope you sleep well, Miss Verity," she wished from the middle of the doorframe—*Where did ghosts go to sleep? Did they sleep?*—before lowering the gas lamps. "Everything will look better in the morning."

A crushing wall of fear threatened to crumble before me, burying me with its tons of bricks. I nodded, my throat too thick to answer, and she slipped into the hallway, carefully shutting the door behind her.

I lay in bed, listening to Highmoor's familiar creaks and groans, counting to one hundred to make sure she'd really gone and left me alone. Then I threw off my quilt and went to find the large leather valise kept in my wardrobe.

I wasn't going to do it. I wasn't going to grow old and die here, letting my life wither away on the vine.

I would go to Bloem. I would get to the mainland.

Tonight.

I didn't care if I had to row myself all the way to the coast. I couldn't spend another moment in this house, held back not only by my sister but also by the past itself.

I was getting out.

Now.

7

THE CARRIAGE RUMBLED DOWN THE WINDING ROAD, rambling through a line of steady trees.

Everywhere I looked, trees.

Tall, spindly bullies, with jagged branches elbowing for more than their share of sunlight. Plush firs, squat ferns. Ivy and brambles. It was a verdant haze of botanical splendor and I felt somewhat sick encountering its depths. Did mainlanders experience this when first encountering Salann?

The light was different here too. The sun shone brightly on our islands, reflecting off the endless waves with an unchecked brashness. Here, the world seemed washed in lilac and mauve, periwinkle and jade. The air shimmered soft like a dream, like a perpetual twilight. How had Mercy described it?

I took out her letter, pulling it free from the little sketchbook I'd kept at my side since docking on the mainland. I'd reread it so often on my journey that it was nearly in tatters now.

Wistful, she'd written.

Yes. That described this new world perfectly.

"We'll be approaching the Menagerie soon now," the coachman

called out to me, rapping his knuckles on the roof of the carriage. "Just around the bend."

I pressed my cheek to the window, wanting to see the exact moment the forest gave way to civilization. I'd heard so many stories of this fabled province, had spent the past week daydreaming of its splendors.

The first glimpse did not disappoint.

The statues formed a wall that encircled the city like a wedding band. Cool gray quartz and white marble were carved into enormous fantastical creatures, all tangled together in an impenetrable ring of protection. Peacocks the size of dragons lit the wall's summit, showering their bejeweled plumage down to the emerald grass. Swans and nightingales vied for space between chiseled roses and stony peonies. Dahlias burst into full blooms taller than me. Intricate snowbells climbed and entwined around heavily antlered deer and winged horses alike. A unicorn bowed its horned head low, forming the massive archway we now passed under.

My fingers itched to draw it all but I'd spent my last charcoal pencil that morning, wearing it down to a tiny, useless stub.

I pushed open the half pane of glass, leaning as far out the window as I dared, wanting to drink in every detail.

"Is this your first time in Bloem, miss?" the driver asked, his voice colored with amusement.

"It is."

He chuckled. "Then I shall be sure to take the long way."

Riding into the heart of Bloem was like entering another world.

Alabaster white buildings, mottled with delicate friezes and plaques of rose gold, lined wide cobblestoned streets. Most of the shops had closed for the day, their wares lit through windows by globed gas lamps. They cast the stone streets with a strange lavender hue.

Every storefront boasted boxes of well-kept flowers. Their blooms ranged from pinks so soft they seemed to whisper, to magentas, deep and dark as a forbidden tryst. Ropes of greenery, studded with swirls of ranunculus and carnations, formed bowers spanning between the shops.

Their scents mingled together, creating a perfume persistent and exhilarating. My spirits felt buoyed after only a taste. I couldn't imagine what it would be like to walk down the promenade, bathed in such heady bliss. The People of the Petals must always be smiling.

I studied their faces with interest as we rolled along, these people who revered beauty and art and love above all else.

They did look happy, from what I could tell.

The women wore impossibly chic veiled hats with brims so wide I couldn't see how they'd make it through a standard doorway. Their sleeves were puffed like dueling hot-air balloons, their waists cinched tight, and their skirts so tailored that walking seemed an almost unimaginable task. Many of them were assisted by men bedecked in beautifully cut brocaded suits and jewel-topped walking sticks.

I ran trembling fingers over my own traveling clothes, smoothing out a skirt of practical blue gabardine and a blouse I'd always thought pretty, edged in lace and artful tucks. But compared to these embellished beauties, I felt like a drab little field wren, staring down an ostentation of peacocks.

A small burr bit at my insides, working its way to the pit of my stomach. I was out of my depths in this glittering and cosmopolitan land. I didn't know their ways, didn't understand their customs. I would certainly stick out here, for all the wrong reasons, making a fool of myself even before I could chance across some unseen spirit.

Maybe Camille had been right. . . .

Seven days ago, I'd left Highmoor in the dark hours before dawn, taking a skiff and rowing my way to Selkirk. From there I'd paid a fisherman for passage across the channel, landing in the little town of Olamange. I'd hired a coach to take me to Bloem. Only a week had passed since I'd left, but it seemed like years.

I allowed myself to wonder what Camille was doing, how she'd reacted when she found my note. I didn't think she'd come after me—that would cause even more of a scene—but would she accept my return once the commission was finished? Would I even want to go back?

I picked at my nail beds, darkened with the charcoal dust from my earlier sketches.

These weren't the refined hands of a lady.

They didn't look like the hands of someone who was sister to a duchess.

But they were, I reflected, studying their long fingers and trimmed nails. For now at least.

And they were the hands of someone talented enough to paint the next Duke of Bloem.

I stole a quick glance back at the elegant crowds. I may not be as sophisticated as they were, but I could do something that none of them could. I was the one Duchess Laurent had chosen.

I took a deep, steadying breath. I may not look the part, but I belonged here just as much as anyone else.

"This is the main road that cuts through the city," the driver explained, interrupting my worries. "It runs past all of the best shops, the hotel, the salons."

Whizzing through the theater district, we caught sounds of orchestras warming up, of gossip and laughter, corks of champagne popping on outdoor terraces. The merriment was palpable, trails of shimmering cirrus clouds painting an already decadent sunset sky.

The road ahead diverged, moving away from the city, through fields of lavender, under towering arches of azalea trees. Everything here was in bloom, bursting with riots of color and life. Even the brightest spring day on Salten could not compare to this idyllic dreamscape.

"Here we are," the coachman announced, slowing the horses as we approached a gated wall.

It was made of metal, elaborate curlicues winking in the dying light. Each post dripped with trellises of shining flowers, silver and rose gold. They appeared to be hung on twisting loops around the stakes, shifting slightly in the dancing breeze. It sounded like music, peals of chimes ringing along the edge of the property.

The driver hopped down from his seat, jostling the carriage with his sudden departure, and I waited as he spoke with a groundsman on the other side of the fence.

The groundsman finally opened the gate, beckoning us through and pointing toward a fork in the road. We took the right, plodding down a colonnade of the same streetlamps I'd noticed in the shopping district. They burned more softly here, giving just enough of their purple glow to light the path but not the surrounding grounds.

We made our way around a curve in the road and the manor came into view.

It was . . . perfect.

Just two stories high, the house sprawled across the thick lawn, wings unfurling to the right and left, its white bricks overgrown with ivy. A sweeping drive curved up to the main entrance, a grand portico draped in lush blooms of wisteria. More purple gas lamps flanked the drive, illuminating the house with their curious hue.

There was a figure out front, waiting beneath one of the lights, just as I'd imagined he would be. Seated in a tall wicker wheeled chair, I was certain the young man must be Alexander Laurent.

We came to a stop and the driver opened my door. I took the coachman's hand as I exited the carriage, my legs stiff after the long and bumpy ride.

"Miss Thaumas?" the young man guessed, pushing himself forward for a closer inspection. His skin was a warm, golden brown, his face all elongated angles. One dark, wayward curl dipped across his forehead, brushing thick eyebrows. Light eyes, the color of a summer sea, studied me with interest.

I let out a silent sigh of relief.

He'd be a dream to paint.

I could already envision the outlines of the portrait to come, the highlights running across the broad expanse of his shoulders, the shadows beneath his sharp cheekbones. His face was meant to be captured on canvas, saved just as it was now, forever young and handsome and full of limitless potential.

"Verity, please." I stepped toward him, offering out a hand, ready to shake his. "And you must be—"

"Alex," he said, pressing a gallant kiss to the tops of my fingers. With a deft flourish, he turned my hand over and brought my palm to his lips.

I'd heard the customs of the People of the Petals were quite different from the practical and prosaic greetings in Salann, but it still sent a thrill down my spine, watching this beautiful boy touch my smudged skin. His fingers, strong and calloused, lingered on the underside of my wrist and I wondered if he could sense the pattering of my heart.

"Well," he said, releasing his hold as two footmen came out to help the driver with my belongings. "Miss Thaumas. Verity. Welcome to Chauntilalie."

8

"DARLING," A VOICE CALLED FROM INSIDE THE MANOR. It was pitched a resplendent alto, each syllable given the perfect amount of weight and emphasis. "What are you doing out there? It's growing so dark. . . ."

A woman ventured out from the entryway, swathed in raspberry crepe. The gown was all angles, folded and tailored to her trim frame as if she were a nymph emerging from a delicate flower, neither entirely woman nor plant.

I'd never seen anyone look so artfully put together. She was older than Camille, probably in her midforties. Her skin was darker than Alexander's, a rich chestnut. Her hair was tightly curled and swept into a loose chignon, showing off the elegant length of her neck. Streaks of gold swirled in her burnished curls. Her back and shoulders were as straight as a ruler but she moved with polished grace, a bird with air in her bones.

"Oh!" she exclaimed, her heart-shaped face brightening as she spotted me. "Verity! You're here," she said, breezing to me in a cloud of jasmine. Her laughter sounded like music. "Forgive me, Miss Thaumas. I've heard so much about you from Mercy that I feel as though we're already quite good friends."

"Lady Laurent," I guessed. Mercy's friend. My new patron. I crossed one ankle behind the other and dipped into a short curtsy.

She waved my reverence away with a sweep of one hand, delicate chains of gold winking on her wrist. "There's no need to stand on formality for my sake," she assured me. "Please, call me Dauphine." She glanced toward the carriage. "We received your letter a few days ago but weren't sure exactly when to expect you. Then a package arrived yesterday, addressed to you, and I knew you must already be on your way here."

"A package?" I asked, my mouth drying. Camille must have sent her swiftest clipper for it to have arrived before me.

"Mmm." Dauphine nodded. "From your sister, I believe. No doubt you'll want to let her know of your safe arrival. Take her things to the north wing, please," she said, raising her voice for the footmen. "I think those rooms will suit our guest beautifully."

I rubbed at the charcoal staining my fingers, all my confidence draining from me in the face of her serene style. I'd never felt so distinctly rumpled before. "I'm so sorry if my arrival is an imposition. I—"

"Nonsense. We were so pleased you accepted our offer. Weren't we, Alexander?" She ruffled the hairs at the back of his neck and he nodded, his smile lopsided and charming. "I was just coming to find my son, then dress for dinner."

My eyes swept over her, surprised such a sculptured masterpiece was considered afternoon wear.

"You've not eaten yet, I hope?" Her eyebrows rose as she waited for my response, her lips puckered into a perfect question mark. Her eyes were just like Alexander's—a brilliant sea green, ringed in amber. They remained pinned on me, unwavering in their interest and terrifying in their intensity.

"No. No, not yet."

A smile broke across her face, like a bank of clouds shifting to reveal the sun. "Wonderful. Join us, won't you? James will need to know to set another place—Alexander, would you pass along the message, please?"

"Miss Thaumas must be exhausted from her travels. You're not really going to make her suffer through a long, formal dinner, are you, Mother? Perhaps we could bring her up something, once she's had a moment to unpack and refresh herself."

"Suffer?" Her laughter was buoyant as a scarf caught in a brisk breeze. "I should hope my dinners don't cause you pain."

"Only when you serve seven courses of quail," he said with a quick smile. It might have been a trick of the purple gas lights, but I could have sworn he winked at me.

My lips rose, instantly warmed by his charm.

Yes, this would be a magnificent portrait.

"You'll let James know?" Dauphine pressed insistently.

Alexander shrugged at me as if saying he'd tried. "It would be my delight. I'll see you soon, Miss Thaumas," he promised, angling his chair back and heading toward the door. He wheeled himself up the ramp and disappeared into the shadowed depths of the house.

Dauphine turned toward me. "Alex is right. You must be so tired from all your travels." Though she ran a swift look of appraisal over my gabardine, her eyes remained kind.

"It *was* a rather long journey," I admitted. "But I loved every moment of it. I've never been this far into Arcannia's mainland before."

Her eyebrows arched. "That surprises me. Though Mercy mentioned how keen your eldest sister is at keeping to Highmoor. Such a lovely old estate."

"You've been to Salann?" I asked, following her as she gestured toward the front entry. She slowed her pace, matching our strides like a shadow.

"Many years ago. We were on our honeymoon progress. Your mother was pregnant at the time. With the triplets, I think it was?" She nodded to herself. "I'd never seen so much water before. Neither had Gerard—my husband. The poor dear, he didn't fare well on the trip over . . . or back."

"The waves can be brutal if you're not accustomed to— Oh my!" My mouth fell open as we crossed the threshold and stepped into the foyer.

Everything was so . . . light.

Light and green and so very dazzling. The entryway soared up the entire height of the manor, with a set of dueling staircases winding up to a balcony bedecked in bowers of verdure. Higher above was a massive skylight—its panes of windows set like a starburst. Giant fronds danced outside of it—a garden must have been planted on the roof. During peak daylight, I could see they would cast a filtered glow to the room, tingeing the white stone walls a verdant hue.

At present, the room was lit by a sparkling chandelier of twisted metal vines heavy laden with brilliantly cut crystal flowers. Massive potted palms loomed tall and vases of fresh flowers graced every available surface.

The floor was patterned in tiles of cool gray marble with a large family crest inset into the center of the room. Made of tiny chips of rose-gold glass, the mosaic shimmered in the late day's light. Farther down one of the offshooting corridors, I could hear the sound of trickling water, no doubt produced by a fountain.

"This is . . . spectacular."

Dauphine glanced about the room as if to assure herself that nothing was out of place. "I'm so glad you like it. When I first came to Chauntilalie, before Gerard was courting me, it was painted a terribly dreary shade of olive—almost the entire manor was—and I knew that should I ever chance to become mistress, I'd redo everything. A home should be welcoming and airy—a sanctuary, a reprieve from all of the world's harshness, don't you think?"

I forgot to nod, still entranced by the spangled skylight. It would look magnificent on a dark, moonless night. The constellations would reflect and refract through the faceted panes into a dizzying sea of light.

"This way," she said, gently nudging my elbow toward the staircase on the left. "All of the living quarters are on the second floor."

"Even Alexander's?" I asked before cringing, fearing my question sounded unfiltered and indelicate.

If Dauphine thought so, her face didn't reveal it. "Of course. I'll show you the lift system later on. You should learn how to operate it—just in case. It's one of my husband's prized projects—powered by steam."

"How curious."

"It's completely state of the art, one of the first of its kind. After Alexander's accident . . ." She paused, adjusting an arrangement of flowers on the first landing. After picking out an offending stem, she turned it about between her fingers. "We want to ensure that he's always able to get about the manor, that he never feels as though he's at a disadvantage. The whole estate has been adapted to suit his needs. The elevator, of course, and ramps in and out of the house. The walkways in the gardens have been carefully leveled so his wheels won't catch on any unevenness in the ground. There's even a lift at the docks to assist him should he want to go boating."

"That's wonderful."

"He has a valet who helps him in and out of the chair and with all his personal needs. Frederick. You'll meet him soon. He's . . . he's quite hard to miss." Dauphine stabbed the flower back into the vase. "The family's suites are in the south wing. Your rooms are this way."

She led me up the second set of stairs, then down a long hall with a polished dark floor. Tall arched windows lined one side, showing a pretty view of the front of the property.

Between each window, a tree grew, sculpted of white marble, with branches stretching up to form a structural arch. Leaves splayed and spread across the hallway's rounded ceiling, creating a unique spandrel. I didn't know much about trees, but I could tell each arch was different. Some leaves were softly curved and delicate; others spanned larger than my hands, jagged and sharp angled.

On the other side of the corridor was a series of doors framed by intricate carvings of tangled vines and greenery. Rose-gold sconces dotted the walls between, but candles, not gas lamps, burned merrily against the approaching night.

"Here we are," Dauphine announced, stopping at the last door.

"Wisteria," I noted, running my fingers over the bas relief

sweeping along the frame. Ropes of the flowers trailed down the wall, as if hiding an entrance to a secret garden.

"Very good. This is my favorite suite in the manor," she admitted, pushing the door open. "Go on and see."

The footmen had beat us there. My belongings waited in the middle of the sitting room, a small, sad pile at odds against the rest of the chamber's opulence. I spotted a wooden box left upon a writing desk and could practically feel Camille's wrath seeping from it. I glanced away, as if refusing to acknowledge it might make it disappear.

The windows were open wide. Gauzy curtains danced in the night breeze, parted back to reveal a terraced balcony already drizzled with moonlight.

The walls were the perfect shade of green—a tint or two darker and the room would have looked like a sepulcher, gloomy and bereft of life. This color reminded me of stepping into the solarium at Highmoor, velvety and vibrant. I could practically smell the chlorophyll.

A wide set of double doors led to the sleeping quarters—a vast canopied bed dominated one wall. The furniture was flocked in shades of dark pinks, darker greens, and muted purples. The walls were a moody shade of charcoal, plumy as ink. Vases of peonies—each the size of my fist and on the verge of bursting into frilly perfection—were placed throughout the room with an artistic eye. I couldn't imagine a more captivating palette.

"There's a bathroom through there," Dauphine said, pointing to another set of doors. "Armoires for your clothing. The writing desk should be fully stocked with paper and inks, but if anything is missing, you need only to ring that bell."

Beside the bed was a long tasseled cord snaking down from the creamy, lace-patterned ceiling. Small tables flanked either side of the bed. A series of deep pink candles rested on them. They were perfumed, though I couldn't place the scent, and filled the air with a heavy aroma.

"I see why this is your favorite." I spun in a circle, dizzy with delight that—for a time—all this would be mine.

She beamed. "Sometimes I come in at night and just wander through the rooms, admiring everything. It was the first design I put together myself and . . . it's such a lovely sense of accomplishment, isn't it? Creating something from nothing. Something I can look at and say 'Yes that's mine. I made that.'" Dauphine's eyes flitted from thing to thing, pleasure coloring her cheeks. Her gaze fell on me. "I imagine that must be what it feels like with your paintings."

I nodded.

"I wouldn't do that while you're here, of course," she added, and the tinkle of her laugh hung too brightly in the dark floral room. "Sneaking into your sitting room while you slept, just to stare at crown moldings."

I glanced up at them, marveling at how lifelike the petals appeared. "They *are* awfully admirable," I allowed, and the air around us changed as we both seemed to realize we didn't know much about one another, not even enough to save the moment with the banter of mindless small talk.

"Well," Dauphine began. "Dinner is served at eight. I'll send one of the footmen up to show you the way to the hall." She looked toward the fireplace mantel, squinting to see the numbers on the little brass clock. "Will forty minutes be enough time for you to freshen up?"

I almost wished she had agreed with Alexander's suggestion. A quiet night spent in such sumptuousness sounded perfect to me but I was here to work. I nodded hastily, seeking her approval.

"I'll make sure someone unpacks your things while we eat."

"Thank you. That would be very kind."

She smiled. At the door to the hallway, Dauphine paused. "It really is wonderful to have you with us, Verity."

I waited a full minute before moving, crossing to the main door and shutting it tight. Flipping open the lid to my steamer trunk, I pawed through every gown I'd brought with me. My best dress, a jade silk that always made me think of the summer waves of Salann, would have to do, even in its rumpled state.

Salann.

Camille.

The box.

I laid the dress out across the smoke-colored duvet to breathe and wandered into the sitting room to look at the crate.

But instead of Camille's meticulous copperplate, it was Annaleigh's swoopy handwriting marked across the slats, making me pause. I'd have to find something to break it open with. There was probably an ornate letter opener buried somewhere in the desk cubbies I could use as a lever but there wasn't time to look for it now.

I trailed my fingertips over the velvet chaise, wondering what Camille was doing at that exact moment. Had she found the note I'd hastily scrawled for her? Would my impassioned words change anything?

Unlikely.

However childishly, I found myself hoping they would. That they'd somehow eased the sting of my flight and soothed her rage.

I closed my eyes, wanting to sink into the plush comfort of the room. The bed looked unspeakably inviting as the past week caught up with me all in a single crashing moment. I wanted to sleep. I wanted to rest.

I did not want to go downstairs in a wrinkled dress and formally present myself to Gerard Laurent, the twenty-eighth Duke of Bloem.

The clock on the mantel mocked me with its steady beat, counting down the seconds until my appearance would be required.

With a sigh, I trudged back to my trunks and ransacked through them, looking for the kit of toiletries I'd thrown in.

I could do this. I could make myself presentable—no, exceptionable—and go downstairs, ready to dazzle and charm and be exactly who the Laurents thought me, a skilled and worldly portraitist set on capturing their son's likeness. I would be seen as a credit to my family. Camille would regret her words and see that she could and should have trusted me all along.

But to do that, to do any of that, I'd first need to clean every trace of charcoal stain from my fingers.

Dear Verity,

I hope this letter finds you well and settling into your new quarters in Bloem. I was surprised to hear of your impromptu adventure.

As was Camille...

She was so surprised she came all the way out to Hesperus, just to tell me.

In fact... she told me everything. All that was discussed the night of your departure...

I don't want to put words to paper that could jeopardize... anything... but know how terribly sorry I am that you found out all of the things you did, the way you did. I always wanted to tell you—you know how much I hate keeping secrets—but you also know how Camille is. Better than most, I suppose.

You can imagine her state of mind when she found out you'd left. I promise I'll try to smooth things over. I'm sure all of this is nothing more than a little spat between sisters. Ones who do both love each other dearly, whatever they may be feeling now...

Regardless of how it began, I am excited for your first real trip to the mainland. I hope you enjoy your new surroundings and fill up books of new sketches and ideas. I'm sure Duke Laurent's son's portrait will be wonderful. You've always had an eye for seeing the truths of your subjects and capturing their light.

In case you get homesick, I'm sending along a crate of candles for you. I know how fond of them you are. I wasn't sure if you'd be able to find anything like them in Bloem, so I'm making sure there's enough for the whole of your stay... Keep them burning always and try not to miss us too much...

All my love,
Annaleigh

9

THE FOOTMAN WAS LATE.

I swished back and forth before the fireplace, throwing sharp glances at the little clock. It was nearly eight now, when Dauphine said the family sat down for dinner, and he was nowhere in sight.

Anxiety thrummed in my veins, setting my heartbeat off-kilter. I was never late to anything and I certainly didn't want Lord Laurent thinking poorly of me on our first meeting. Dauphine may want to pretend we were good friends but I was certain Lord Laurent would only ever see himself as my patron.

I'd already imagined him as a hazy figure with sharp eyes peering down a commanding hooked nose, judging me, judging my work. His word had the power to make or break my career. I knew—I hoped—my skills as an artist would stand up to even the most rigorous taste . . . but if I offended him as a *person* . . .

With an exasperated sigh, I changed the direction of my pacing, daring to peek into the hallway.

Nothing.

It loomed long and silent without a trace of life within it.

It wasn't *that* big of a manor, I reasoned, fingers drumming against the doorframe. It should be easy enough to find the dining room. . . .

The ticking of the clock spurred me into action.

I fled my rooms, the door shutting behind me with an echoing click.

Perhaps I'd run into the footman on my way down the stairs.

Perhaps I'd run into Dauphine, coming from her wing. She'd spot me and understand at once. We'd go down together, arm in arm, and I wouldn't have to wander the main floor alone.

So caught up in my daydream, I wasn't entirely aware of where I was heading, just going down the hall until I reached the staircase.

Only . . .

I paused, turning back to look the way I'd come.

This wasn't right, was it?

It looked like the same hall, dark wood, light walls, so many carvings, but . . . there was something different about it. Something wrong.

I turned again.

It was too long.

While I'd not taken a precise count of every door we'd passed on my initial trip, it felt as though they'd now somehow multiplied. Doubled. Tripled, even, in number.

"This can't be right," I murmured, turning tail and wandering back toward where I believed my room to be. Had there been a split in the hall someplace? A turn I'd not noticed before but had accidentally taken?

There was not.

I found my room, the trails of wisteria slithering down the wall, and touched one of the blossoms, an unformed question heavy in my mouth. On either side of the door were a pair of old-fashioned candlestick sconces, strange to see in a house run with gas. The tapers—identical to the dark pink ones I'd found in my bedchamber—flickered unhelpfully at me.

"This is ridiculous," I decided with a shake of my head. "I'm going to be late."

Back down the hall again, counting every door I passed, every pair of candles. Three, five, nine, too many, far too many . . .

I stepped toward one of the windows, peering out into the darkened night, trying in vain to see around the glare of the candlelight reflected in the pane. For a moment, my equilibrium felt off and I swayed against the wall, holding on to the curtain.

Uncertainty stilled my limbs, weighing my feet down and rendering them rooted.

"There you are!" a voice exclaimed, buoyant with relief.

An older man, white and tall and trim with sharp angles, raced up to me. He'd been blond once, but wide swathes of silver now framed his temples, slicked back with pomade. His suit was a rich cream, cut from a fine bolt of wool, and, inside my slippers, my toes curled. If that's what the Laurents' servants wore, I was sure to look like a shabby little no one in my simple silk dress.

"You weren't in your room." He held out his arm, as if he were a gentleman, ready to escort me out on an afternoon promenade. I'd never seen staff behave so casually with a guest before, then chastised myself. To him, we were the same—both paid employees of the estate.

Still disorientated by the ever-lengthening corridor, I glanced back to my room. It was at the end of the hall. The footman couldn't have been there. He would have had to pass me to reach it.

And I'd seen no one.

Just me.

The candle closest to us sputtered over a bubble in its pink wax and a terrible thought bloomed in my mind. Slowly, like a fragile marionette pulled on a string, I reached out to lay my hand upon his arm.

I fully expected it to pass straight through him, like a stone in water.

But the sleeve of his jacket was warm and solid. I could feel the rich cloth, the solid heft of his arm beneath it.

He was real.

But then . . . how had he gotten here?

A smile burst across the man's face, as if reading my thoughts. He looked positively jovial.

"I've come from the study now. Just there, you see," he said, pointing to a door a room down from where we stood. "I'm sorry if I alarmed you."

I waved aside his concern.

"Are you all right?" he asked, peering at me curiously.

"I . . . I feel as though I've turned myself completely around in this hallway."

"Turned round?" he echoed, looking back and forth at the straight path.

"It sounds so foolish, doesn't it? But . . . when I left my room, I could have sworn . . ." I trailed off, unable to explain it clearly.

"New settings," he allowed.

"That must be it," I said. "We ought to be going now, though. I'd hate to make a bad first impression."

His dark slate eyes twinkled. "Of course, of course. Well . . . you can't be accused of tardiness if the master of the house isn't there yet himself, now, can you?"

"Is Lord Laurent also running late?" I asked, throwing a quick look over my shoulder toward the study the footman claimed to have come from. He must have been assisting the duke with some matter.

"Lord Laurent is never late," he intoned with theatrical solemnity. "And if it ever appears he is, it's only the clocks in the manor running too fast."

I smiled up at him. "That's very good to know."

"So you're the painter?" he asked conversationally. "From Salann?"

I nodded.

"The whole house has been in an absolute tizzy anticipating your arrival. I know Alexander is quite excited to begin working with you."

"I'm eager to begin as well. The house is so lovely. . . . It will be hard selecting the right spot for the portrait."

"In the library, I should think. That boy has always been fond of his books."

"Have you been with the Laurents long?" I asked. His informal familiarity with the family made me think of Hanna and a sudden bolt of homesickness panged through me.

"Oh . . . for a good long while," he said, smiling again.

We'd just reached the stairs, brightly lit by gas lamps, not glowering pink candles, and I took one parting glance back at the hallway. It seemed as short as the first time I'd seen it. Five doors, maybe six, only.

"Gerard! There you are," Dauphine exclaimed, her lustrous face looking up at us. I was pleased to see she had on an evening gown similar in silhouette to mine, but in a rich shade of plum. "Oh, and you've already found Miss Thaumas. How wonderful."

"Gerard?" I asked, looking back at him, catching all the details about him I'd not noticed. The expensive silk of his cravat. Alexander's long and brooding nose, smack in the middle of his face. The heavy signet ring he wore with effortless air, as though he'd been born with it. In retrospect, he had.

He pushed that hand through the thick waves of his hair, giving me an impish look of chagrin.

"L-Lord Laurent," I stammered, correcting myself.

Before I could dip into a curtsy, he grabbed my wrist, pulling me upright. "There'll be none of that here," he insisted, releasing me with another smile.

Though I knew he meant it as a friendly gesture, my wrist stung at his unexpected force. I rubbed at it, feeling foolish. "I'm so sorry, sir. Lady Laurent—Dauphine," I amended as he wagged his finger at me, "said a footman would be coming to retrieve me. I assumed that you were him. I hope I didn't offend you."

I wanted to sink into my mortification and vanish. What must he think of me, growing disoriented by hallways grown too long? Shame burned through my veins.

With a broad gesture, he bid me start down the stairs, joining Dauphine in the foyer. Above us, the skylight was a deep midnight blue, speckled with little pinpoints of sparkles. I stared up at them, trying to find familiar points. They were hard to make out through the chandelier's splendor.

"My joke was a success," Gerard announced, leaning forward to press a warm kiss on his wife's cheek.

"You pretended to be a footman?" Dauphine guessed, her features drawing together with concern. She gave him a light tap on his shoulder. "I told you not to do that. What will she think of us, treating guests in such a manner?"

Gerard only laughed again. "Where's Alexander? I'm famished!"

He wandered deeper into the house without waiting for a response.

Dauphine slid her arm around mine, guiding me into a new hallway. Mirrors lined either side, reflecting twin vases overflowing with clusters of pink and green hydrangeas. "I'm so sorry for Gerard's behavior. He can be a bit of a prankster . . . and I should have thought to warn you about his punctuality." We passed by a tall grandfather clock and I saw it was already a quarter after eight. "The whole manor has learned to work around his unpredictability. He gets terribly focused on work and only really ever looks up when his belly starts to rumble." She let out a soft laugh. "Sometimes not even then."

"What sort of work does he do?" I asked, thinking of all Camille was in charge of—the manor, the shipyards, listening to disputes between fishermen, keeping the king apprised of any strange ships on the horizon. What problems faced lords on the mainland?

"Oh, he's a—"

"Good evening, ladies," a voice said, farther down the hall.

A second later, Alexander appeared, pushing himself out of the shadows. "You both look lovely."

He had changed for dinner as well. His suit was an immaculate navy, setting his lighter eyes aglow, and he'd tied his mustard-colored silk cravat into the most spectacular series of knots.

"Miss Thaumas, I wondered if I might have the honor of escorting you to the dining hall?"

Dauphine eased her arm from mine. "Go on. Gerard and I will be in after you."

I looked down at Alexander. "I'd be delighted. Thank you, Mr. Laurent."

We set off, side by side. He pushed his chair slowly, matching his speed to my pace. "It's Alexander," he said. "Alex, even."

"Then you must call me Verity."

"Verity," he drew out slowly, warm and rich as a mug of steaming coffee. "Do you really stand so formally upon things in Salann? I've heard the People of the Salt can be quite a cold society."

My mouth fell open, surprised by his assertion. "Is that what people say?"

His eyes sparkled and I had the distinct impression he was teasing me, just as his father had.

I decided to adopt their breezy, blasé attitudes, trying it on as though it were a stylish new cape. "You'd be cold, too, if you had to live through our winters."

He laughed and I liked the sound of it. So easy. Unfiltered.

"You've never been to the islands?" I guessed.

"I've never been much of anywhere," he admitted. "Here at Chauntilalie, I'm able to roam about quite freely, but the rest of the world isn't really designed for people like me." He rapped on the chair's armrest. "Or the things we carry with us."

"I'm so sorry," I started, unsure of what exactly ought to be said and very certain I didn't know how to say it.

"Don't be," he said, giving the wheels another push. "Just think: if I was off gallivanting about the kingdom right now, I wouldn't be here, talking with you."

"Perhaps we might have met someplace else," I said.

He shook his head. "I doubt it. You never leave your islands, and as you've already admitted, they're far too cold for me."

I couldn't hide my smile if I'd wanted to. I'd never spoken to someone with such light banter. My heart pattered merrily and I found myself wanting to match his brilliance.

"Are you always so witty?"

"And charming," he said quickly. "Don't forget charming."

Alexander paused at a wide set of doors, already opened, and gestured for me to go through ahead of him.

A long table stretched out in the center of the hall. It could easily have held fifty guests but was set for five. A series of tall windows ran along one wall. Their curtains, long swags of rosy velvet, were left open, showing a moonlit balcony full of artfully arranged potted plants.

Dozens of candles lined the lacquered table in shades of pinks and greens, creating a more intimate space in the room's vast void. Above us hung three chandeliers, unlit yet glittering like ice.

A footman stepped forward to pull out a chair for me. Alexander rolled up to the spot at my right. Gerard took his place at the head of the table, to my left. Dauphine sat across the table from her son, leaving the seat in front of me open.

A strange hum filled the air, a sound of grinding gears and mechanisms set in motion. It sounded as if the whole house was groaning under sudden duress.

"The lift," Alexander explained softly.

"Mother must be on her way," Gerard said.

I jumped at the loud *thunk* that seemed to punctuate his words.

In an identical sweep, he and Dauphine rose from their seats as a figure entered the room. Alex gave me a short nod, indicating I should stand as well. A pink warmth spread over my cheeks as I followed after.

She was small and gray, swathed in a dour little dress of black beaded damask, hunched over a bamboo cane. Its glass topper caught the candlelight, momentarily dazzling me as she picked her way across the room. Gerard motioned to leave the table to assist her, but she waved him off with a grumpy gesture.

"Stay where you are, stay where you are."

Thin white curls were twisted and carefully pinned into a pouf on the top of her head, but some parts of her pink scalp still peeked through. As frail as she appeared, her face was remarkably smooth, her gray eyes sharp and alert, aided by a small pair of silver spectacles that perched low on her button nose.

We waited for her to take her seat before relaxing again.

"Mother, I'd like to introduce you to Miss Verity Thaumas. She'll be staying with us for the next few weeks. She's come to paint Alexander's portrait." She made a *harumph* noise, acknowledging him, but her eyes remained on the table before her. Gerard turned to me. "Miss Thaumas, this is my mother, Madame Marguerite Laurent."

I remembered what Alexander had said about Salann's stiff formalities and tried smiling warmly at the older woman. "Marguerite, it's such a pleasure to meet you."

Slowly, her eyes drifted to mine. "I'm sorry," she said, and her voice sounded as creaky as an old wooden rocking chair. "I don't believe we've met before."

"We haven't," I clarified, wondering if her mind wandered with age. One of my aunts suffered from a similar malady. My cousins were forever having to remind her of where and when in life she was. Sometimes even who they were. My heart softened at her plight. "I just arrived at Chauntilalie this evening."

The line of her lips tightened. "Then why on earth would you choose to address me as though we are acquaintances?" Her eyes squinted at me with obvious disdain.

"I . . . I'm so sorry, terribly sorry, Lady—Madame Laurent. I—"

"If I wanted to address the help, I would have hired you on myself, but as I have not . . ." She puffed herself as high as her constricting bodice would allow and looked away.

"Mother, Verity Thaumas is more than just—"

She frowned. "Thaumas, did you say, Gerard? She's one of those Thaumas girls?"

He nodded, shooting me a look of apology. "Ehhh, yes, Mother. Her oldest sister is the Duchess in Sal—"

"I know where they're from, boy," she snapped. Marguerite peered across the table with sudden interest. "Thaumas . . . I remember hearing about you. You and yours," she corrected herself, wetting her lips with a quick dart of her tongue. "Yes . . . So, Gerard. You've brought one of those cursed girls into my house."

10

"CURSED?" DAUPHINE ECHOED, THE COLOR DRAINING from her face. It left her stained lips bright as a bloody slash.

The old woman nodded sagely, triumph flashing in her gimlet eyes. "Yes, yes. Don't tell me you've never heard of them. The Thaumas Dozen. The Thaumas Curse."

I cleared my throat, struggling to find my voice. "That's not true."

"You're telling me none of your sisters are dead?" Marguerite asked, leveling her gaze upon me. It burned like a branding iron. "Your father? *Two* mothers?"

"It was . . . Those were accidents." I turned to Dauphine, terrified she'd believe her and throw me from the house before I could taint any of them. "Terrible accidents. But truly, there is no—"

"The soup course," announced the valet before opening a side door.

A flurry of servers hurried in, carrying silver domed dishes for each of us. With choreographed precision, they removed the lids at the exact same moment, releasing a waft of steam.

The bowls were made of a mint-colored glass, shot through with clouds of orchid swirls. I blinked at the soup, laden with creamy white flowers.

"Arugula blossom soup," Gerard explained. "It's one of Raphael's specialties."

Marguerite's eyes narrowed, the matter unforgotten. "But about the girl—"

"Mother," he said roughly, silencing her.

"Raphael is our cook," Dauphine filled in, smoothing out the napkin in her lap over and over. "He's an absolute culinary genius." She'd arranged her face into a careful mask, as if wanting to sweep her mother-in-law's assertions—and possibly the lady herself—under the rug.

"Go on and try it," Gerard said.

"But I—" I wanted to finish the conversation, wanted to assure my patrons that they'd not invited some terribly unlucky charm into their house, but I stilled as Alexander let out a short cough.

When I glanced his way, he gave a discreet shake of his head, as though beseeching me to let the matter die away.

"I've . . . I've never tried a soup with blossoms before," I finished feebly.

"It's one of my favorites," Alexander said, offering a perfectly lopsided grin. He scooped up a bite with theatrical gusto. I was unspeakably gladdened by his small kindness.

"What are these?" I asked, picking up the soup spoon from the lineup of golden flatware flanking the bowl. Bold clusters of pointed flowers bloomed across the handle, circling around the fiery Laurent sigil.

"*Euphorbia marginata*," Gerard said. "Snow-on-the-mountain. In our house, each duke chooses one flower to represent the family, to symbolize all our hopes and goals."

"What a beautiful tradition. We just keep the same octopus, generation after generation. You wouldn't believe the amount of tentacles dripping throughout Highmoor." I could feel myself rambling, nerves taking control of my mouth and making me sound foolish. I quickly dipped the spoon into the broth. If I was eating, I couldn't be talking. "Oh," I murmured. I'd expected it to taste terribly sweet and floral, like catching a mouthful of spritzed perfume, but the soup was surprisingly savory, spicy and thick, with notes of pepper. "This is delicious."

Gerard swallowed, then patted his napkin at the corner of his thin lips. "Do you know what *Euphorbias* signify?"

"I didn't know flowers meant much of anything beyond beauty," I admitted, trying a second bite.

Gerard let out a loud, boisterous laugh and even Dauphine tittered, as though my ignorance had been a well-timed joke. Marguerite continued to eye me with disdain, pushing the wilted blossoms about the bowl without ever tasting them.

Alexander shifted in his chair, leaning in close over the arm, giving the illusion of a private conversation. "There's an entire language to flowers."

"A language?" I repeated, instantly intrigued.

"If you knew their meanings, we could have an entire conversation between us without ever having to say a word. Like"—he pointed toward the bouquet at the center of the table—"the bright white flowers near the top? Those are called *starworts*. They're meant to welcome a stranger."

Dauphine nodded. "I had one of the gardeners add them in once I knew you'd be joining us tonight."

Her thoughtfulness touched me. "And those purple flowers?"

"Those are heliotropes," Gerard explained. "I picked them myself this morning, for Dauphine." He gave her a wink.

"They're meant to show devotion," Alexander said. He sat back in his chair, studying me with thoughtful eyes. "If I were to pick out a flower for you tonight, I think I would choose . . . a gardenia."

"Oh, Alexander," Dauphine murmured, her voice happy and light.

"Good boy," Gerard said approvingly.

Marguerite swiped her napkin under her nose with a sniff.

"What . . . what does that mean?" I glanced about the table.

The corner of Alexander's lips rose with merriment. "You'll have to look it up and see."

The warmth in his tone sent a strange flutter through my chest. It felt almost as if . . . Was he flirting with me? It felt like he could be, but so openly? In front of his family? Perhaps there were more differences between the People of the Petals and the People of the Salt than I would have guessed.

"I . . ." I didn't know the proper way to respond, acutely aware of the many sets of eyes upon me. "I certainly will. I'd love to learn more." An idea struck me. "It would be a lovely addition to your portrait. Have you picked out what your ducal flower will be?"

In a flash, his eyes darted from me to his father and back to his lap. "Alyssum, I think."

I brightened, remembering them on the grounds of Highmoor,

ringed around the tall alders bordering the gardens. "The little white and pink flowers? I love those. They always smell so sweet in the summer months."

The table fell still and I wondered if I'd guessed the wrong flower.

"What . . . what do they signify?"

Dauphine studied her soup, refusing to look up.

After a beat, Alexander cleared his throat. "'A worth beyond beauty.'"

"A wholly ridiculous choice for a Laurent," Gerard muttered, casting his spoon into the soup with a clatter.

"Well, that's the thing about a duke's legacy, isn't it, Father?" Alexander said carefully. "He gets to choose his own."

The tips of Gerard's ears turned a dark red as he threw back a long swig of wine, souring the room with the uncomfortable weight of his sudden anger.

"What does *Euphorbia* mean?" I whispered to Alex as I ran my finger over the cursed soup spoon. I wish I'd never even mentioned those little spangled flowers.

He patted the corner of his mouth with his napkin, hiding his response. "Tenacity."

"Next course," Gerard barked out for the footmen.

The soup was cleared away before any of us could finish it.

༄

"You're going the wrong way."

Dinner was blessedly over—Pontus, how many courses could one family pack away?—and I'd scurried from it as quickly as

I could, with promises to join Dauphine for breakfast before I began my work in the morning.

When I turned to see who spoke, Alexander was right at my heels. "That hall leads out to the back of the house."

I studied the corridor before me. It seemed to open up into a tall, starlit room.

"That's the foyer . . . isn't it?"

"Not at all," Alexander laughed.

"I was sure it was—"

"It's all the plants," he said, wheeling past me. "They give off a false sense of familiarity. You thought you left by the same door we entered in, didn't you?"

I nodded, certain I had.

He shook his head. "You went out its mate. Both have ferns next to them. It's an easy mistake. Come on, I'll show you."

"Its mate?" I echoed.

"The house has always had a rather . . . unusual layout, but after my accident, Father added on the back wing. See?"

We entered a room identical to the foyer I'd thought I'd been heading toward, but instead of the graceful dueling staircases, a metal column rose up to the second story.

"The back of the house is a mirror image to the front, only more accessible for me. When the sun is out, it's easier to feel which side you're on but in the dark, with you so new here . . . The lift," Alexander explained, catching my stare. "Want to try it?"

"I . . ." Though it was covered in beautiful filigreed ironwork, it gave me pause. It looked like the cage of some horrible beast. "I've never been in one before. What does it do?"

"Well, as the name suggests, it lifts off the ground, taking me with it. Sometimes it lifts me this way, sometimes that." He pantomimed wild swings to either end of the room.

I blanched, my stomach queasy at the thought. "It does?"

His eyes crinkled into little half-moons. "Of course not. It's on a track. See?" He pointed to the well-oiled line of metal bolted to the wall. "It's perfectly safe. I use it every day." He pushed himself up a ramp and foisted back the accordion-style doors. "Ladies first."

I stepped past him, entering the small space. "Will there be room enough for us both?"

He rolled in, his knees bumping against the swell of my skirt. "Just barely." An unexpected trace of pink colored his cheeks and I was surprised how endearing I found it. "Can you pull the door closed? It won't start until that latch is in place."

That, at least, was a bit of comfort.

He pulled a lever toward him and a giant mechanical hum rose up around us.

"It's just the steam," he assured me. "We pull the lever to activate the steam, then that button to start it up."

"Where does it come from?"

"The lake. Pipes bring in the water to be heated beneath the house. Sometimes it feels as though the whole manor is groaning."

I imagined the house crying out in torment and swallowed deeply.

"Are you scared? Really?"

I shook my head, wanting to be brave. I kept my eyes trained on the floor of the cage. That looked reassuringly solid and unmovable. Maybe if I could trick myself into thinking we weren't—

He hit the button and with a whirring clank, we were suddenly in motion, rising from the ground, ascending the wall like a spider determinedly scaling its web. I finally dared to look up and stared out the wide windows framing the wall in front of us with wonder. It would make for a spectacular view in daylight.

"What is that?" I pointed to a stately glass-paned building, lit up against the night.

"Father's greenhouse," Alexander said as we reached the second floor. The abrupt end of motion jarred me off-balance and he reached out to steady me, his fingers warm around mine.

"It looks as big as Chauntilalie."

It loomed just as high and sprawled past the window's view. The glass was fogged over with humidity, making it impossible to see inside. It glowed opaque and green against the dark night.

"It nearly is." He released his hold on my hand, turning a dial and pulling on the lever once more. "The door?"

I pushed it open, waited for him to exit, then followed after. On the landing were three hallways leading to different parts of the house. None of them looked familiar.

"Verity," Alexander said, drawing my attention back to him. "This is very important—you have to always remember to shut the door behind you and flip the latch. Grandmère uses the lift as well, and if someone forgets the latch, we're stuck until someone comes along to help."

I studiously watched him pull the latch to its shut position.

"Try it," he insisted, and nodded when I'd properly repeated the movements. "Good." He looked up at me. "You must be tired after such a long day of travel. Well . . . long *days*," he corrected himself. "Will you be able to find your room from here?"

I looked toward the junction again, remembering that I was at the back of the house, and pointed to the hall to the right.

Sharp dimples appeared as he grinned and pointed toward the middle. He pushed off, rolling down the corridor. "Come on, follow me."

"Oh, no, you needn't—" The thought of him escorting me to my chambers felt oddly intimate, especially given I didn't know what his proposed gardenia meant.

"I'm not going to let you wander about the house all night, lost in a sea of identical hallways. What kind of host would that make me?"

"Technically, you're not my host at all," I said, scurrying after him. The wheelchair was so much faster than me. "Your mother wrote, asking me to come. She's the host . . . ess."

He laughed. "You people from Salann do get hung up on the most peculiar details. Take the right there," he said, stopping at another turn and gesturing down a hall.

"Verity, Alexander? Is that you?" Dauphine called out, suddenly before us at the end of the hall. When we joined her, she was poised on the landing of the foyer's staircases. The chandelier's gas orbs had been lowered and the entryway below us was a wash of gray and lavender shadows.

"Alexander, I'll take Miss Thaumas to her rooms. She looks as though she might fall asleep right here and now."

"We were just on our way—"

"I'll take it from here," she said, her voice and smile pleasant yet inflexible.

"Of course," Alexander said, giving us a little bow. "Good night, Mother, Verity. I hope you both have pleasant dreams."

We murmured similar platitudes and he turned himself around, rolling away down a hall I'd not noticed before.

Dauphine watched after him until he turned a corner and was out of sight. "He's a dear boy," she said, placing a hand on my back, prompting me into motion. "Always so kind, considerate. I do hope your portrait can capture that."

"I will try my very best."

"Of course you will. I apologize for the . . . unpleasantness at dinner. Gerard and Alexander . . . they remind me of those woolly rams, high up in the mountains, butting heads, knocking into one another. They've always been so dissimilar, the two of them. Alexander has so many ideas on things he wants for the future of the estate, for the duchy, for the Laurent name. . . . It's hard for Gerard to see all the ways they differ."

I startled as she stopped walking. Somehow, we'd already reached the doorway decorated with the wisteria reliefs. The candles flickered and danced, as if offering out a welcome.

"Well, here we are."

"Thank you, Dauphine. You've been so kind and gracious."

She smiled. "We're happy to have you here. I like to take my breakfast in the Begonia Room—it has the loveliest stained-glass windows, facing east. We can discuss the portrait more then."

I nodded, reddening as I stifled a sudden yawn. Every moment of the past week seemed to crash over me all at once, leaving me spent.

"That sounds wonderful."

"Good night, then," she said, squeezing my arm before leaving.

"Good night," I called after her.

When I stepped into the parlor, the scent of the burning pink candles overwhelmed me, coating my tongue with their sickly sweet perfume.

I opened the crate from Annaleigh and quietly replaced all the candles with her salted sage ones. Truthfully, they weren't much better, but at least it made the room smell a little more familiar, a little more like home.

A maid must have returned during my absence. My suitcases had been stored away, out of sight. When I checked the armoire, all of my clothing hung in a neat row, pressed fresh and free of wrinkles.

I spied my nightdress and pulled it out, having every intention of shimmying free of my evening gown. But when I sat on the edge of the bed to remove my stockings, my tired mind took over. I sank back into the decadent pile of pillows, limbs heavy, closed my eyes, and knew no more.

~~Dear Sister,~~

~~My dearest Camille,~~
   ~~I wanted to write you to~~

~~To her grand majesty, the all mighty Duchess of Salann.~~

Camille—

I know that you're unlikely to ever read this letter so I suppose it doesn't matter how I begin it. I can already picture you tearing the paper to bits by now.
   But.
   I wanted to let you know I've arrived in Bloem and that my journey went well. I never would have guessed Arcannia was so vast. Even with all its space and scope, I still can feel your eyes following my every move. It's as though I've never truly left Highmoor.
   I wanted to apologize for how I left things—running away as I did. I just didn't know how else to do it. I couldn't bear to stay another night under that roof, not now. Now that I know ... everything I do. I understand your concerns and I promise I will do everything I can to keep from bringing shame to our family.
   I'm not sure why I'm even writing any of this out. I don't have the courage to ever send it and will probably stick it in the back of my writing desk here, forgotten until my commission is at an end and I must pack all my belongings once more.
   But it's nice talking to you, like this. I can almost picture you listening to me and understanding everything I wish I could say.
   I wonder where I will go from here.
   I hope it's back to you, back to Highmoor.
   One day.
   Just not yet—

                                                            Your sister,
                                                            Verity

11

THE CHARCOAL SCRATCHED AT THE PAPER, A STARK line of black curving the wrong way. I smudged at it with the side of my thumb, attempting to correct its angle. Alexander's eyes tracked my every movement.

Sunlight streamed through the windows behind him, casting golden highlights over his raven hair and giving him a look of holy appointment. Even the palm fronds flanking either side leaned toward him in a graceful curve of reverence, completing the illusion.

Dauphine had whisked us here after breakfast, promising me the best light in the whole of the manor. She'd called it the East Solarium, leaving me to wonder just how many of them Chauntilalie could boast of.

The light *was* perfect, but with so much of it pouring through the glass-paned walls, it was overly warm and the air was heavy enough to dampen my skin. I could feel the starch in my ruffled collar begin to wilt.

"How much am I allowed to move?" Alexander asked from the corner of his mouth. He'd been taking shallow breaths since we began our session nearly an hour ago, his chest barely rising and falling.

"As much as you like."

He remained frozen in place. "It won't ruin anything you're doing?"

"These are only preliminary sketches." I traced the contour of his cheekbones. "I'm just getting acquainted with your face." I froze myself, hearing how intimate my comment sounded, and wondering if he had too.

He broke out of his position, shifting to lean his weight on the wheelchair's arm. "And how is it?" He smirked, on the verge of a grin. "My face?"

I hid behind the sanctuary of the sketchbook. "Perfectly adequate."

"Perfectly adequate?" he repeated. "Oh, Miss Thaumas, you wound me."

"Your nose is much too long," I teased, putting on an authoritative air. "When I finally title the painting, I'll call it *Alexander*—What's your full name?"

"Alexander Etienne Cornelius Leopold Laurent," he intoned with mock solemnity.

"Truly? That's even longer than your nose." He grinned and I glanced around the easel, meeting his gaze. "You'll make a fine portrait. Generations of future Laurents will look upon it and say 'This man had too many names, but look at how striking he was and what an exactly proportionate nose he possessed.'"

"Mother will be glad of that." A minute of silence passed. "This is all right? Us talking? I don't want to be a distraction, but it does pass the time more pleasantly."

My fingers zipped across the page, shading in lines of hair, working on the quirk of his brow. "It's fine. I actually prefer it when I'm drawing someone new. The more I know about you, the more I can show in the paint."

"Tell me about Salann," he said, leaning back and fidgeting with the buttons on his brushed velvet jacket. He'd chosen a silk cravat the same shade of green as his eyes, making them glow in the early morning light.

"Talking about myself won't help me learn more of you." I flipped the drawing pad over, starting a new sketch. This time, my strokes felt sure and right. My lines flowed over the page with confidence.

He scratched at the back of his neck. "Yes, but it can be difficult to open up to a stranger. I don't know anything about you."

"Fair enough." I picked up a pencil with a harder lead, drawing quick, sharp lines to suggest his chair. "You answer a question and then I will."

He nodded.

I paused, trying to perfect the angle of the wicker back. It was taller than he was, with a tufted pillow at his head. "If you weren't here with me right now, sitting for this portrait, what would you be doing?"

Alexander's laugh was loose and easy. "Probably sitting somewhere else. I tend to do quite a bit of— Stop," he ordered.

My mouth was caught open on the cusp of an apology. "What?"

"You're about to say you're sorry. Don't. Please." He sighed. "People get so squeamish about the chair, about me being in the chair. They shouldn't. *You* shouldn't," he said with emphasis. "I've been in it most of my life. I don't really remember a time when I wasn't. It's part of who I am but it's not the only thing that defines me. It's not uncomfortable for me to talk about, to joke about."

I set down my pencil, meeting his gaze. "I . . . I heard it was an accident."

"It was."

"Can I ask . . . how it happened?"

"The stairs in the foyer. They're quite steep for a small boy. I was racing down for breakfast one morning—the day of my fourth birthday—and fell."

"And that caused . . ." I trailed off, uncertain of what exactly I meant to articulate.

"Paralysis in both legs. I can't feel or move anything from here down." He gestured toward his thighs.

"Can you—"

"Uh-uh-uh," Alexander interrupted, shaking his head. "We're meant to go back and forth with questions. You've asked two in a row." He settled back against his headrest, studying me. "Why does my grandmother think you're cursed?"

My mouth soured and I wished he'd chosen any other thing to ask me. "I . . . I suppose because of all of my sisters. They . . . died."

"How many?"

"Six."

He whistled through his teeth. "That does seem . . . excessively unlucky."

All I could do was nod. I picked up the pencil once more, rolling it between my fingers.

"But you have others, don't you? Other sisters?"

"Five."

"Such a large family." His eyes drifted from mine, soft and thoughtful. "I've always wondered what it would be like to have grown up with someone else my age in the house."

"Not all of us are close. My oldest sister, Camille, is fourteen years older than me."

He let out a quiet *hmm*. "I wanted a brother. When I was much smaller, I begged and pleaded for Mother to go to the shops and pick one out for me—as though that was how they were created." His smile turned wistful. "It's an awfully big estate to be at by yourself."

It did seem a waste, having a house so sprawling remain mostly empty. The hallways and corridors should have been alive with the sound of pattering footsteps, of shouts and laughter. I turned over another page but couldn't bring myself to start a new sketch.

"Did they ever try for other children?" I asked, the invasive question falling from me before I could think better of it.

Alex shook his head. "Father wanted to . . . but it wasn't . . . Mother couldn't . . ." He cleared his throat. "I gather she had a difficult time, pregnant with me."

"It certainly can be hard on women. My mother died after having me," I admitted slowly, then let out an approximation of a laugh. "Perhaps I *am* cursed."

Alex frowned. "I don't believe in all that. The gods . . . they made us, they made all of this." He gestured in a swooping circle, indicating a larger space than just the solarium. "What good comes from cursing your own creations?"

"Amusement?" I guessed.

He shook his head again. "They care about us too much. Far

too much at times. Did you know Mother—" He stopped short but his eyes sparkled.

"What?"

"She'd probably die of mortification if I told you, but . . ." He lowered his voice. "She's actually a descendant of Arina."

My eyebrows rose. "Truly?"

Annaleigh's husband, Cassius, was half immortal himself—the son of the night goddess, Versia—but it wasn't something he liked discussing much. Many people were wary of anyone with that touch of divinity, of what powers they might possess. Most were wholly average, without a trace of anything special marking them, but there were enough stories of others, others with such extraordinary endowments, that a stigma was formed.

Alex bit his lip, nervous he'd said too much. "Her mother . . . it was suggested she might have had an affair with one of Arina's sons but tried to pass off Dauphine as her husband's."

"Did it work?"

His dimples winked. "The rumors still persist. . . . What do you think?"

We shared a smile and I started in on another rendering.

"She left, you know," he mentioned carefully. "Grandmère. This morning."

"Left?" I echoed in alarm. "Why?"

Alex's eyes slipped away from mine like oil against water. "To get away from 'that cursed Thaumas girl.'"

My cheeks heated, shocked my presence had such an impact on the older woman. I chewed on the inside of my cheek, hesitating over my next words. "Perhaps if she feels so strongly . . . I'm sure your mother could find another painter. . . . I could . . . I could leave today if . . ."

I stopped short.

Leave and go where?

Not back to Highmoor.

Not back to Camille.

I wouldn't put it past her to have an array of ships outside Salten's harbor, ready to send my little skiff all the way back to the mainland to make her point, and her anger, known.

"Oh, no," Alex said quickly. "Certainly no. Grandmère has a flair for the dramatic. I'm sure she's trying to punish Mother for . . ." He shrugged. "Something, undoubtedly."

"But to leave the house . . ."

"She's not wandering the streets of Bloem, I promise you," he said with a wry smile. "We have several other smaller estates throughout the country. A little lakeside cottage in Forestia. An apartment in the capital. Marchioly House, of course."

"Marchioly House." I said the name slowly, tasting it.

He nodded. "Marchioly is our winter house, though Mother and Father haven't used it in years. Not since . . ." He glanced down at his legs meaningfully. "My grandfather had it built shortly after he became duke. He couldn't bear to see Chauntilalie in the winter, with all the plants dead or sleeping till spring. It doesn't seem to bother Father as much, not with his greenhouse."

My stomach felt as though I was precariously balanced on a tightrope. One wrong move could have me topple off and fall to my demise. "So . . . she's at Marchioly House, you think?"

He shook his head. "Far too long a trip for Grandmère. She probably went to the capital. Visiting old friends at court, trying out new restaurants. You know."

I sat back, unsure if it was worth finishing the sketch I'd started.

"Don't let it trouble you for a moment. Mother wants you here. I . . . I want you here." Alex offered out a soft smile of reassurance.

My lips rose, feeling too tight and thin. I returned to the sketch, tracing out lines across the page with half-hearted effort.

"Reading," Alex said suddenly, breaking the uneasy silence that had settled over us. "You asked what I'd be doing right now if you weren't here. I . . . I like to read. By the lake if the weather is nice. Or, there's a little room on the second floor with big windows overlooking the gardens. If it's a stormy day, I take my book there. I like to see the lightning dance in the sky, feel the thunder shake the glass."

"Reading."

I could picture the scene in my head easily, see the towering stack of books beside him, hear the turning pages, smell the ozone and ink. It fit him well. He looked comfortable, happy.

Alex nodded fervently, the previous conversation forgotten. "So much of the world outside these walls was simply not built for me, for this chair, for . . . all of it. . . . But with books, I can go anywhere, readily and unencumbered. I can stroll down the streets of Arcannus, solve a murder in Pelage, even see what your little islands are like."

As he spoke, a spark of passion lit his face and I hurried to sketch what that looked like, merging it with my vision. "Where's your favorite spot by the lake?" I asked, feeling inspired.

Alexander tilted his head in thoughtful deliberation. "There's a grove of trees—"

"Stop!" I pushed my easel to the side as I stood. "Don't tell me. Show me."

"Oh my . . . ," I murmured, looking up.

Alex's favorite trees towered above us, bending their thin branches down in a shower of bright pink blossoms and tiny green leaves. Sunlight filtered through them, creating a dazzling effect of dappled shadows and bursts of blinding white. Beyond the grove, an enormous lake spread before us. Its gray waters ran deep and little whitecaps skirted across the surface.

"It's a weeping redbud," Alexander explained, patting a papery white trunk as though they were old friends. "These are some of the only specimens in the whole of Arcannia."

"Did the others . . . die?" I reached out to touch the flowers dancing around us. Their centers were a lovely shade of red, like little hearts tucked away within the showy blooms.

"No, Father only created so many."

"He grew them?"

"Grafted," he corrected. "That's what he does. He's a botanist. He experiments with strains of flowers, crossbreeding and creating hybrids, but when he was younger, he loved working with trees. He made these five and even sent one to King Alderon. I've heard it's still blooming somewhere on the palace grounds."

"They're incredible." A breeze blew past, setting the branches into motion and filling the air with a light floral sweetness. "I can see why this is your favorite spot."

"I like to watch the water," he said, turning his attention to the lake. "It's so mercurial—yesterday it looked nearly turquoise and was almost as still as a pond, without a hint of waves. Then today . . ." He gestured toward the choppiness. "Well, you would know all about that."

I spread out the quilt Alexander had found us, positioning it directly beneath the tallest of the trees. He pushed down two levers against the wheels of his chair to keep them from moving as his valet, Frederick, stepped forward to help assist him from the chair.

Dauphine had not been joking. The man was the tallest I'd ever seen, a veritable giant and so very strong. He scooped Alexander up, as though he were no more than a child, before setting him onto the blanket. Frederick fussed over his legs for a moment, arranging Alex into a comfortable position, and a second servant was there with pillows for him to recline on.

"Thank you, Frederick, Johann," Alexander said, nodding to them as they retreated. "They'll stay nearby, in case they're needed," he explained, glancing back at me. "So what are we doing out here exactly?"

"This portrait is meant to be a representation of you—of you in this moment of your life. So many portraitists get bogged down in the trappings of it—the velvet swags, the globe and the library, the swords and the symbols. They're all meant to bolster that feeling of importance in the subject, to make them seem larger than life, grander than their audience. But when you look back on yours, years and years from now, I want you to be able to recognize yourself. I want you to look at it and say, 'There's that young man who liked to read at the lake and look up at the weeping redbuds. What fun we used to have together.'"

Alexander studied me and, as the waves lapped upon the shore and the curtains of blossoms swayed around us, I wondered if I'd said too much, if he thought my speech insufferable and pretentious, the aspirations of a novice painter who had no business capturing the image of a future duke.

"That's . . . I've never heard anyone so eloquently express such sentiments. I feel . . . I feel exactly the same way. There are so many here in Bloem who put on that show of importance—like you said—valuing the appearance of something over its content. They're more concerned about how they're perceived than who they truly are. The People of the Salt may be hung up on prosaic formalities but the People of the Petals are so wrapped in artifice we can't look deeper than surface level on anything. That—*that*—is why I shall add the alyssum to my crest, Father be damned."

"A worth beyond beauty," I said, his words from last night echoing in my mind. "I'd guessed your differences were over more than just a little flower."

He nodded. "We have *so* many differences, Father and I. So many warring opinions. I don't think we, as a people, were always like this, craving the new, the flawless. We need to go back to the older ways, the simpler times." His jaw hardened. "Father obviously thinks not."

"What will others think?"

Alex shrugged. "Does it matter?"

"Perhaps not, but you *do* worship a goddess of love and beauty. I imagine Arina's postulants would have quite a bit to say on the matter. I can't even guess what our High Mariner would do if Camille suddenly declared a moratorium on going out to sea."

His eyebrows drew together in a thick, dark line. "You misunderstand me. I don't want to ban what Arina represents—that would be impossible. Beauty exists everywhere in the world. Love resides in all of us. That's the point. I only . . . I only want to deepen that. Show that there can be—that there *should* be—substance in it all. Of course a bride on her wedding day is beautiful, but that radiance doesn't diminish in old age, when she's too tired to keep up with whatever ridiculous fashions the shops and salons put out. I know Arina smiles upon an old couple walking down the road together, hand in hand, firm in their commitment to one another. There is love in caring for the sick, the weak, the ugly. A wilting flower holds just as much splendor as one on the cusp of opening. People are so quick to idolize the fresh and the new. They fetishize it." He rubbed at his forehead, his eyes bright with fervor. "Why should we celebrate one without the other?"

"We shouldn't," I said, my hand furious at work as I raced to put this moment on paper. I wanted to capture the exact tilt of his head, the passion and conviction coloring his face, the fire in his eyes.

This. This was what Alexander's portrait would look like.

12

WE STAYED BY THE LAKE UNTIL LONG AFTERNOON shadows crept across the grounds.

Dauphine sent trays laden with fresh bread and cold roasted meats, cheeses and fruit for an impromptu picnic. Later, a cart appeared with a full tea service and towers of little cakes that looked like tiny works of art.

I filled nearly half my book with bits and pieces of Alexander. There were dozens of studies on his hands, the curve of his smile, his eyes. The drawings became more detailed as I grew familiar with his shapes and lines. Some of the renderings seemed to come right off the page, perfect copies of him.

Sometimes we talked; sometimes we were silent. He'd tucked a book into the side of his wicker chair and after lunch, he read it aloud, making me laugh as he created funny voices for the characters, performing with dramatic flair. I couldn't imagine a more perfect afternoon.

"I suppose we ought to go in, shouldn't we?" he mused as a chorus of spring peepers began a twilight song. "We'll need to dress for dinner—Arina help us all if someone should see me wearing the same clothes I've had on all afternoon."

I pressed my lips together, trying to hide the threatening smile. It did sound rather preposterous when he put it that way.

He let out a long breath, watching the water. "This has been the most marvelous day. I hate to see it end."

"It has been beautiful," I agreed, scooping my charcoal pencils into their tin and brushing aside the curled shavings dusting my lap. My hands, black with smudges, hummed with a tired but satisfied ache. "And aren't we lucky we get to do it again tomorrow?"

"It won't be the same. The water will be different. So will you. The blossoms will be a day older. So will I . . . I don't believe you're cursed, for what it's worth," he admitted softly, finally shifting his gaze from the lake to me. "I just . . . I wanted you to know that. And I'm sorry that Grandmère brought up such a painful time in your life."

"It's all right—" I started, but he quickly cut me off.

"It's not," he insisted. "And I shall speak to her about it when she returns. You have my word on that."

I smiled. I hadn't known him for long, but I'd already noticed how earnestly Alexander craved for the right things to be done. His moral compass was fixed with unwavering focus. I'd never met someone so good, so kind.

His intense reassurance made my chest warm and I looked away before a blush could fully bloom over me.

"What's that?" I asked, just now noticing a dark shape far out in the middle of the lake. The sinking sun played off its lines, making it sparkle. It was a statue of some sort. I squinted, trying to see it better. It almost looked like . . .

"Arina's burning heart," Alexander explained. "Part of the Laurents' old shrine."

"A statue? In the middle of a lake? How is it supported? The water looks so deep."

"There's a little island of sorts there. I'll take you out to it one day."

I liked the way he said that, with such a casual assumption that we'd have so many future *one days* together.

After a beat, he waved his hand, gesturing for Frederick and Johann to come over. Alexander winced as Frederick helped him from the ground and settled him back into the chair. "Thank you."

"Shall I take those up to your room, Miss Thaumas?" Johann asked, scooping my pencils up from the quilt.

"Oh, thank you, please," I said, also relinquishing my hold on the book.

Alex pushed himself along a path toward the manor, straining to get the momentum to go up the embankment.

"May I?" I offered.

"Oh, you needn't—"

"I know," I said, cutting him off. "But I can and I want to." I took hold of the bars at the back of the chair. It moved easier than I expected but still required a focused effort to keep him on the boarded walkway.

"Well, thank you." His face was rosy from the sudden exertion. "I must rely on Frederick for so many things—he helps me in and out of the chair and with other . . . personal tasks . . . but I try to make it a point to move about the grounds on my own."

"You enjoy being self-sufficient."

He nodded. "Take the right at the fork."

I steered the chair as he said, shifting my weight on one handle to keep the change in direction smooth. As we settled onto more level ground, he reached behind his shoulder and patted my hand.

"You're a terribly kind person, Miss Thaumas."

His fingers lingered over mine and the warmth sent a small thrill through me. "All day long it's been 'Miss Thaumas this' and 'Miss Thaumas that.' I thought you were going to call me Verity?"

His head bobbed. "That was last night. It's easier to feel bold and cavalier in darkness. Easier to play the role of a charming boy meeting a pretty girl for the first time. Daylight comes and strips away such audacity. It makes you wonder if you were too forward, too brash." He dared to glance back at me, his eyes uncertain.

I felt poised on a precipice, standing on unfamiliar ground. Though there were many young men who worked at Highmoor, Camille had made it clear she wouldn't welcome casual friendliness between them and myself. As sister to a duchess, I'd been told I was meant for grander matches but—with a decided lack of possible suitors on the islands—I had to assume all of *that* would happen later on in my life.

Was that happening now?

I'd enjoyed my day with Alexander, immensely. He was smart and funny and even an afternoon spent drawing out his every feature had not made me appreciate his appearance any less.

But I was new to this.

I was new to feeling like this.

Were these stirrings due to the marvel of a new situation or the persuasiveness of Alex's charms?

Because he *was* charming; there was no doubt there. I could imagine him working his way about a ballroom, half a dozen young ladies following his every movement, stars dancing in their besotted eyes. I pictured his gaze falling upon me, choosing me.

"I think . . ." I stopped, my voice failing. "I think that you shouldn't worry about that. About any of that. And I think you should call me Verity."

Acting with an uncharacteristic boldness, I twisted my hand beneath his, so our palms pressed against one another. His thumb traced the soft skin of my wrist and my breath caught in my throat, delighted with the intimate sensation.

This doesn't mean anything, I told myself. *Anything at all.*

Though it was true both our fathers were dukes, I was the last and least of my sisters. A girl like me would never end up with a boy like him.

But still. It gave me a thrill to test what a bit of harmless flirtation could feel like.

"Verity," he agreed. He grinned, squeezing my hand. "Alex. And Verity."

"Alex!" A voice rang out before I could respond. "Is that you?" Gerard Laurent came around a tall manicured hedge and I pulled my hand free, tucking it behind the wheelchair as though we'd been caught doing something terrible. "Oh, and Verity, excellent! It's finally happening. You must come and see, both of you. Come, come!" He disappeared behind another set of bushes.

Alex glanced up at me, a bright smile still on his lips. "Ladies first . . . Verity."

"What are they?" I asked, puzzled.

We were inside the enormous greenhouse I'd spotted last night, standing before a long worktable. The glass panes were angled at their edges, sending rainbow refractions of light across the plants within. The air was warm and wet and smelled *green*. I could practically taste the chlorophyll on my tongue, fresh and bright.

On the table were dozens of pots and spilled dirt, clumps of dried moss and vials of colorful liquid. Rows of brass instruments were laid out with ordered care. It would make an intriguing still-life composition, but Gerard's attention rested solely on the three potted plants at the center.

They were a strange tangled mess of spiraled vines and dark purple buds, clenched as tightly as fists.

"Father's been tinkering with these flowers for nearly a year," Alex explained.

"And they've not bloomed once," Gerard said, missing his son's veiled reproach. "The buds just wither away, dried little husks of disappointment and failure. But here, look here," Gerard said, fiddling with the center pot's position.

One of the buds looked looser than the others, bigger and softer, as if it were a dreamer, stretching out in sleep, moments before rising to greet the new day. Its edges were as frilled as a confetti streamer, speckled with dazzling shades of Byzantium and claret.

"I've never seen anything like it," I murmured, leaning in for a closer look.

Slowly, spectacularly, it unfurled, a lady twirling her skirts across a ballroom. The iridescent petals had a soft texture, like the peach fuzz of a baby's cheek, with extravagantly thick layers gathered together. When it fully opened, a bright red stamen jutted proudly from the bloom.

"Congratulations, Father," Alex said dutifully.

"Oh," Gerard whispered, his voice thick and reverent. "It's more wondrous than I could have ever imagined." He brought his right hand toward the flower and for one awful moment, I feared he was going to pluck it, but instead, he swooped his fingers in wide circles, wafting the fragrance to us.

It was a curious scent, as deep as pine resin but with an overlaying complexity that felt familiar, though I couldn't place from where.

"So you . . . you created this from other flowers?" I asked, feeling adrift in a sea of unfamiliar concepts.

Gerard nodded. "This is the result of endless cross-pollination and grafting. It started with a pretty little aster I'd always been fond of and a nyxmist plant."

I could feel Alex's unspoken judgment radiating from him and could almost see him thinking that it had been better when the two plants were on their own, separate creations, as the gods intended.

I reached up and tucked a strand of hair behind my ear, trying to keep Gerard from sensing his son's mood. Regardless of how Alex felt, this was a big moment for his father, something he'd worked hard on. "I've never heard of nyxmist before." I wanted to reach out and stroke the velvety leaves, so dark they almost appeared black, but held myself in check.

"It's a rare flower, found only in the Cardanian Mountains and nearly impossible to grow outside their acrid landscape. But

I finally perfected the right blend of fertilizer to add to our soil." He tapped at one of the glass vials. "Sulfur, ash, and tea leaves."

"Really?" I squinted at the murky liquid. "However did you come up with it?"

"Trial and error, my dear Verity, trial and error."

I counted the pots before us. "And you'll only make three?"

"In this trial, yes. Three. Always three. One is too small a sample. Anything it produces could be a fluke. Two isn't enough either. Both could fail and you're back where you started. But with three, you can observe where the problems are. Where things went wrong." He nodded earnestly. "Always three."

"We were just on our way to dinner," Alex said, pushing his chair from the worktable.

"Of course, of course. Dinner . . ." He drifted off, his attention focused entirely on the plant. "Not tonight, I think. There's simply too much to do. I need to take measurements and start sketching . . ."

My interest stirred. "Sketching?"

Gerard looked up, blinking at me in surprise. "Yes, of course. I must document everything. . . . Perhaps you might be interested in helping me? Dauphine says your skills with a paintbrush are quite commendable."

"Father, she's been working all day. I'm sure she—"

"I'd love to," I said, overriding Alex's protestation.

His eyebrows rose with surprise.

"This is a once-in-a-lifetime sort of flower," I said, offering him a smile of reassurance. "I couldn't miss that over something as trivial as dinner. Besides . . . now *I* don't have to dress."

An amused grin flashed over Alex's face. "Touché."

"Excellent." Gerard patted my back with a hearty swipe. "I have a working field guide here. . . ." He reached beneath the table and pulled out a massive ledger. "And there are watercolors stored in that bin over there." He pulled open a drawer and removed tiny rulers and nibbed pens from its cluttered depths. "Alexander—go and tell your mother not to expect us . . . but have her send down some plates, will you? And maybe a bottle of champagne—yes! This calls for a celebration, wouldn't you say?"

"Mother, dinner, and champagne," Alex recited. "Anything else? Verity?"

The way he drew out my name's syllables brought a wash of warmth over my cheeks and I was very grateful for Gerard's single-minded focus on his instruments.

I shook my head and he began pushing his chair away, backing along the tiled path of the greenhouse in reverse, so that he could hold my gaze all the way to the ramp leading into the manor. Just before he rolled out, he winked, then was gone.

13

"EXQUISITE, JUST EXQUISITE," GERARD MURMURED, leaning over my shoulder to study my work.

Another two flowers had begun to bloom and I was determined to catch exactly how the strange petals looked at each step of their unfurling.

The tins of watercolors lay scattered across the tabletop like bits of the puzzles Marina and Elodie loved to while away their afternoons with. I flicked a damp brush through a well of juniper green, then dragged it across the page, following the looped stalks of the plant. A splash of red followed, hinting at the shadowy pot beneath.

Gerard crossed around to the other side of the work area, taking a long swallow from his coupe of champagne. He'd emptied most of the bottle already and his gait teetered unevenly.

"You know," he began thoughtfully, "I thought Dauphine's idea to bring in a painter from Salann was mad when she proposed it. Anyone worth their salt"—he paused to chortle at his own pun—"would be from here. From Bloem. They would have gone through our conservatories, found a patron, and would live in some little bohemian garret above their gallery." Gerard raised the glass toward me with a solemn salute. "I was wrong and I shall certainly tell my wife so."

His mention of Salann fell uneasily over me. It was simple enough to push aside creeping thoughts of my sister as I worked on the sketches of Alexander, but here, in the dark, my worries multiplied, gathering up behind my sternum and squeezing at my lungs.

He was happy with my work now, but what if Camille should write to him, tell him all of the awful things she thought of me?

Surely she wouldn't dare.

As she'd said, a hint of madness would taint everyone, herself included.

Still, I scratched at the side of my thumbnail with anxious repetition.

Perhaps I ought to write her a letter—a real one—and actually send it instead of hiding it away in the depths of my steamer trunk.

Gerard sensed none of my troubles. He tapped an earlier drawing I'd finished, focus always drawn to his work. "You're a wonder, Verity. Truly. I wish you'd documented all of my studies. My chambers are full of these ledgers but nothing in them looks as real as what you've done here. I almost . . ." He shook his head, chuckling at thoughts I was not privy to.

"What?"

The corners of his mouth rose, caught. "I'd always hoped Alexander and I would have moments such as these—sleeves rolled up, side by side, working toward a common goal." His half-smile died away. "But he's shown no interest in any of this. Tonight gave me a little taste of those daydreams."

I paused, freezing the paintbrush just above the paper,

wondering how to best approach such an obviously delicate situation. "Why do you think that is?"

Gerard traced his finger over the edge of one of the leaves. "He thinks my work frivolous. Blasphemous even."

"Blasphemous?"

His eyes rolled up to the top of the greenhouse. "Alexander reminds me so much of my father at times. Very devout. Very strict in his beliefs." He shook his head and downed the last of his champagne. "I hate to see him following Father's path. That man was unbearably stubborn."

"Stubbornness isn't always a bad thing," I murmured cautiously. I had the distinct feeling both men were trying to pull me toward their side of the argument and I didn't want to let either of them down. "Alex said it took you a year to grow these flowers, trying again and again."

Gerard nodded.

"A less stubborn man wouldn't have bothered." I added in a soft shadow beneath the pot and the rendering was complete.

"Perfect," he agreed, letting the matter drop as he refilled our glasses with the dregs of the bottle. "To you . . . and to Alexander's portrait. If it's anything like these watercolors, I'll have to find a better position for it in the Great Hall."

"To you," I said, my face flushing with pleasure under his praise. I raised my glass toward him. "And your achievement here today. You've created a true marvel."

His chest puffed with pride and our glasses chimed happily as we clinked them together. The dancing bubbles tickled my throat on their way down, making me feel warm and a little fuzzy around the edges.

"Alexander showed me your red bud trees. They're beautiful."

He smiled, pleased. "Those were a tricky lot."

"How do you decide what plants to graft together? I wouldn't have the slightest idea on how to go about any of this."

Gerard took a great swallow, mulling over my question. "I look around the world and try to imagine the best version of everything I see. Like . . . that line of strawberries growing there?" He pointed. "The climate of the greenhouse helps them to grow year-round, but the winter ones never seemed to taste as sweet. One day I went for a ramble in the forest after a big snowstorm and discovered a cluster of pink berries, growing in the dead of winter. They were delicious. I dug up a plant and brought it back here to study. There was quite a lot of trial and error, but now our berries are perfect all year round."

"What a thrill that must be," I mused. "Creating something so useful out of nothing."

"I imagine it must be like when you finish a painting. You started with a blank canvas and then—behold! Art! It does rather make one feel a bit like a god, doesn't it?"

I tried to mask my face into a look of indifference. I'd never met anyone who spoke so casually about the gods and it gave me an uneasy feeling in the pit of my stomach. "I suppose it does. A little. Maybe."

He raised his glass again. "To achieving godhood!"

His boisterous irreverence drew a smile to my lips but I was not daring enough to repeat it myself. When I clinked my glass against his, the last of his champagne sloshed out, and I could feel our evening wind to a close.

"What will you call this one?" I asked, drawing my attention back to the flower for one last glimpse.

He set the coupe down, leveling an unsteady eye toward it. "*Callistephus constancensia.*"

"Beautiful."

He nodded. "It's only right. She's helped so much with this."

"Dauphine?" I guessed, wondering why she hadn't joined us, especially knowing how long Gerard had worked on the blossoms. Dinner must have been over by now. There were no clocks to confirm it but it felt close to midnight.

"Constance," he corrected without explanation. "I suppose it's getting rather late . . . and you've already had a full day's work." Gerard glanced up through the condensation-slick windows above us. "A full moon tonight." He chewed on the corner of his lip, mulling over something. "Would you be interested in seeing one last spectacle before you retire?"

Curiosity pushed aside any weariness I'd felt. "A spectacle?"

He nodded once more. "I promise you there's absolutely nothing like this at Highmoor. Come on. Follow me."

Out in the garden of Chauntilalie, dozens of eyes glowed at us, blinking realistically as the flowers swayed in the soft evening breeze.

"Black wraiths," Gerard said, pointing toward the patch in case I'd somehow missed them. "They bloom at night, only under the strongest moonbeams."

Squinting, I could just make out their shape, swooping petals that looked drawn by a childish hand. They were so dark blue, they blended into the night, leaving their white ringed center on full and horrible display.

"We used to have an old horned owl that lived somewhere near here. A giant beast, wingspan longer than my arms. It was incredible to see but the brute kept destroying my flowerbeds. He'd scoop up great clumps of earth in his talons every time he dove after an unsuspecting vole and rip out the marigolds I'd spent seasons cultivating. I planted these along his favorite haunts and he's never bothered us again."

"They're terrifying," I said, stooping down to get a better glimpse. "I would never have guessed them flowers. They look more like—"

"Demons," Gerard filled in. "I got the seeds from a traveler who claimed they'd been secreted out of the Sanctum. Can you imagine what sort of things grow in the land of the gods?"

I shook my head even as I glanced about the garden, morphing the darkened shapes into more fantastical forms, things that grew too big, too fast, too *everything* for our world.

"What wonders I could create . . . what dazzling marvels . . ."

"Do you really think you could transform the gods' gardens into something better?" I wanted to keep my voice as light and witty as Gerard's but his easy impertinence left me with a dark, squirming sense of discontent.

"My dear Verity, I don't think," he said with an impish wink. "I know."

"Don't you ever worry Seland might overhear all this and decide to come after you?" I pictured the god of earth stomping about through Gerard's gardens, plucking him into the air as a farmer would harvest carrots. "He made the flowers and trees a certain way for a reason."

"Yes, but they were *his* reasons. He made our world for himself but then retreated into another. He's not been seen in a millennia, even on his holiest of feast days. He left all this a particular way but I dare to imagine it better. I am like a god watching over this estate, crafting and creating it for my needs. My desires." He ran his fingers through his hair, mussing the pomade's hold, as he surveyed his domain. His lips curled, pleased with what he saw, and I tried not to shiver. "But come, come. Dauphine will have my head if I keep you out too late. There's a shortcut this way. . . ."

He led me to a little path on the back end of the garden.

"We cut across here and . . ." He glanced back, sensing I wasn't beside him. His gaze followed mine. "Oh, yes, of course."

A cluster of tombstones had stopped me in my tracks. They'd been nestled under the sweeping branches of a willow tree, like chicks tucked under their mother's wings. The quartz headers sparkled in the moonlight, glowing an otherworldly white.

The spacing was wrong, too close together, too close to the house. "Are those . . . pets?"

He sucked in his lower lip. "Those are . . . well . . . those are my children."

My heart stopped, flooding with embarrassment. I'd clearly misunderstood Alex's conversation earlier. Dauphine must have tried for more children, so many times. I took a step toward him, fumbling to repair any damage my mistake had caused. "I'm so sorry for . . . so many losses," I murmured, counting the small stones, nine in total.

He shook his head as if the sight no longer bothered him. "They weren't . . . They just weren't meant to be."

Together, we stared at the little markers and my heart ached for him. I'd never met anyone so determined on fixing and improving the world around him, but some things were beyond even Gerard Laurent's grasp.

"It's growing late," he murmured after an appropriate moment of silence. "We really should be going."

"Thank you for showing me the wraiths," I said once we were back inside, in the now-too-bright gaslights. I blinked hard against their glare, swirls of color spotting my vision. "And the Calli . . . Calla . . . the Constance."

He stiffened, glancing about as if worried we might be overheard. "I don't . . . upon further reflection, I'm not sure that's entirely the right name for them. I shall have to ponder that a bit more. This way," he said, and pressed a bit of floral molding along the hallway's wainscoting.

A section of the wall swung open, revealing a narrow staircase.

"A secret passage!" I exclaimed.

Gerard shook his head. "That makes it sound far more mysterious than it is. When my ancestors built Chauntilalie, they didn't want to see any traces of the staff needed to manage such a large estate. All of the servants' staircases were hidden away, to not disrupt the beauty of the house."

"Oh." My voice was colored with disappointment. Such a prosaic explanation.

"Careful on the treads. They're quite a steep," he said, ducking in first. "I've greatly appreciated your assistance," he mentioned over his shoulder as we twisted up the spiral staircase. His words echoed against the stone walls. "It will be quite useful to have so many images for reference later. It was quite enjoyable working with you. I hope that one day . . . perhaps Alexander will find a bride with your talent and mind."

I didn't know what else to do but nod and hope my agreement wasn't taken as vanity.

"I imagine your dance card to be quite full," he mused, reaching the top of the stairs. He pushed open the door, revealing the hallway just outside my suite of rooms. "If you don't mind my metaphor."

"Oh . . . no," I stammered. "There've been no . . . partners."

His eyebrows rose with surprise. "How curious. Well. I'm confident some young man will come along and see you for the catch you are." He nodded. "Yes. Yes, I'm sure of it."

With a gallant flourish, he opened the door to my rooms and gestured me in.

"I enjoyed our evening as well," I said, ready to say good night. My room had already been prepared for the evening. The bedding was turned down and a bank of low flames burned within the fireplace.

"Yes, I—" Gerard stopped, a peculiar expression on his face. Without waiting to be invited in, he stepped past me, his eyes darting about the parlor. He took a deep breath. "What a strange scent."

I sniffed, catching the notes of Annaleigh's candles. Whoever had readied the rooms had left a trio of them burning on my nightstand.

"The candles," I explained, pointing. "My sister shipped a crate of them here, from Salann. So I wouldn't be homesick."

"Most thoughtful," he murmured. "Sage and"—he smelled

the air again—"salt, if I'm not mistaken." He frowned. "What a curious combination."

"Annaleigh has always been partial to it."

"Probably an old island superstition."

"Superstition?" I echoed.

He nodded, seemingly unaware of my confusion. "Salt. Sage. Together they're said to ward off unwelcome spirits. Ghosts," he clarified, and my heart stuttered painfully within my chest.

"Oh," I said, managing a weak smile. Why were his eyes lingering upon me? I could feel their weight boring in deep. "I've never heard that before."

In my mind, I saw every crate of candles Annaleigh had ever given me, on birthdays, blessing days, thoughtful gifts offered out "just because."

Just because.

Just because.

Just because she knew what I saw.

But did Gerard?

He turned from the bedroom, crossing back to the door with an easy stroll, giving nothing away. He didn't seem to sense my alarm, nor offer out any telltale sign of misgiving. "It's quite late; I ought to let you rest. Thank you again for all your work today."

"Of course." I trailed after him, scrutinizing his every movement.

His smile was bland and he seemed a bit weary himself. "Pleasant dreams, then, Verity."

14

WHEN I WOKE, IT WAS DARK. ANNALEIGH'S TAPERS had long since sputtered out and were now pools of hardened wax, spilling from the candleholders and ruining the nightstand.

I flicked my nails under the residue, freeing flakes of salt and sage.

It was a wonder I'd not burned the manor down.

I peered groggily across the bedroom, feeling a tug of something amiss.

I strained my ears, listening for an echo of something, *anything* loud enough to have woken me. There must have been a noise that jarred my conscious mind to action, sinking its merciless claws into my slumber. The two glasses of champagne in the greenhouse, paired with Gerard's surprising revelation about my sister's candles, had left my head feeling off-kilter and achy and all I wanted in the world was a glass of water and to go back to sleep.

With a soft groan, I pushed myself from the warm nest of pillows and sat up, peering blearily for the water basin.

A shrill cry sliced the silence, setting my teeth on edge.

I flung off layers of bedclothes and stumbled for the switch of the gaslights, which hissed as their flames lit the room. For a moment, I couldn't see around their blinding glare, could only hear the noise ring out again, piercing clean through me.

Was that . . . weeping?

I made my way through the sitting room. The air felt colder in here, draftier. Retreating back to the bedroom, I grabbed my robe. Just as I finished fastening it, my fingers fumbling against the silken belt, another volley of noise rose up.

I covered my ears but could still hear it, could still *feel* it, vibrating off my bones, rattling the curves of my ribs and making the length of my sternum ache.

Not weeping.

Screaming.

As it died away, I dared to peek into the hall. I'd expected to hear shouts from servants calling for help, pounding footsteps and moans of torment, anything to explain away such anguish, but all was still. All was silent.

Again, the shriek.

It sounded like it was behind me now and I turned.

The gardens.

The greenhouse.

It was coming from outside.

I peered out the window, searching the darkened yard.

The cries lowered in tone, turning harsh and ugly, as if ripped from someone's gut. Was it an animal, some unfortunate, cornered prey?

The full moon rained soft light over the garden, limning the edges of trees, catching outlines of statues, setting the quartz walkways to sparkle.

Then I saw it.

A large shape scurried out from under a canopy of trees.

It was a woman, tall, with long skirts trailing behind her. Caught by the moon, they glowed a strange and eerie blue.

I squinted. Was that Dauphine?

What was she doing out in the garden so late? Had she, too, heard the sounds and went to investigate?

I fumbled at the window, wanting to throw open the sash and ask if she was all right, ask if she needed help, but there was no opening. The panes were soldered shut. I rapped my knuckles on the glass instead, wanting to let her know she wasn't alone, wanting to somehow guide her to safety.

She startled at the sound of my knocking and turned to face me. With a sharp twist, her neck wrenched at a terrible angle, an impossible angle. It looked as though it had snapped from her body. Then she opened her mouth and screamed again.

In my alarmed haste to back away from the window, I tripped over a tufted footstool, falling against the wooden floorboards and striking the side of a curio cabinet.

My cry of pain echoed in the chamber.

I sat up, wincing as I rubbed at the back of my head. I could already feel a bump forming, throbbing and tender and rising off my scalp like a goose egg. The room swayed unevenly around me as I crawled to the window.

When I looked outside, I realized I was seeing double.

Two women now stood in the garden, their white dresses gleaming, their attention trained on the manor.

On me.

Two women stared up.

I blinked, trying to regain my vision.

One woman screamed.

Then the other.

One strolled away, deeper into the garden.

The other stayed behind.

I wasn't seeing double.

I ducked down, cowering in the gauzy curtains, childishly convinced that if I couldn't see them, then they certainly couldn't see me, and if they couldn't see me, then I must be safe.

What were they? Their screams, their bellows, those weren't the sounds a human throat was capable of. They were too high, too loud, too . . . wicked.

A shiver ran over me even as I broke into a sweat. I felt clammy and sick as I remembered the strange pace at which Rosalie and Ligeia had moved through the halls of Highmoor, the way their whispers were heard directly behind my ears, even as I watched them walk away from me.

I dared to peek down into the gardens once more.

The woman had moved.

She now sat on the bough of a tree, ten feet off the ground, her skirts falling over the branches like a satin waterfall. Her mouth opened, stretched too wide, too gaping, and again *that sound*.

"That's not possible," I murmured.

How had she climbed a tree so quickly? How was she making—

She shrieked again.

—those cries?

I leaned against the wall, keeping my back to the window, to the woman, to that awful noise, and covered my ears.

A ghost, a small voice within my head whispered. *You're seeing a ghost.*

"That's not possible," I repeated, resolution tightening my voice. "The candles," I murmured, grasping the thought with the desperation of a drowning man searching for a life preserver. "The candles are supposed to keep them away. Light another a candle."

The same candles you saw Hanna light hundreds of times? the voice asked unhelpfully. *Hanna Whitten who has been dead and gone these last twelve years? Those candles?*

Another scream echoed through the night.

Why didn't anyone else hear it?

Unbidden memories of my last conversation with Camille welled up in my mind, like a festering blister swelled to the point of bursting.

Do you know how strange you look, speaking to them, carrying on entire conversations overheard as one-sided? You look mad, Verity, as though you've entirely lost your mind.

As the screams echoed around me, I sniffed, pushing back tears.

The halls had been still when I'd checked.

No one else in the manor heard any of this.

If they were ghosts, if ghosts were real, others would have seen them. Others would have heard them.

But no one else did. No one else had.

It was all me.

It was all in my mind.

Camille was right.

I was mad.

Dear Camille,

As I write this, huddled on the floor of my sitting room, just before dawn, a dead woman is outside my window, screaming her death knell, and I now know that everything you said to me was true.

There is something deeply, painfully wrong with me. I feel as though a part of myself—some terribly important vital part—is broken. And I don't know if it's possible to ever fix it.

I wanted to show you I was strong and capable. I wanted to be like you—master of my own fate and destiny—but I can't see a way forward now, knowing what I know.

Please send help. I know I've angered you but I'm still your sister and I'm asking for your mercy. I'll do whatever penance you insist upon. Just hurry. Yourself. Please.

Your sister,
Verity

15

A KNOCK ON MY DOOR RUSTLED ME FROM SLEEP. Beams of light fell over my face and I scrunched my eyes against the painful rays.

"Miss Thaumas? Breakfast," a muffled voice announced from the other side.

Breakfast?

Morning.

It was morning.

I untwisted my tangled limbs, wincing as my spine popped and joints protested. Somehow, I'd managed to drift off, curled within the curtains, hiding from the dreadful creatures I'd conjured up last night. Scattered sheets of paper—half-begun, half-finished drafts of letters to Camille—littered the floor around me.

"Coming," I called out to the footman. My throat felt rusted over, as if I'd spent the whole night screaming.

Had I?

No.

Surely someone would have heard *that* and checked on me.

After stumbling toward the door, I opened it a few inches wide, squinting out into the hall.

It was Alex. His face fell as he took in my rumpled state. "Oh, Verity, are you all right? You look unwell."

"I . . ." I frowned, confusion muddling my speech. "I'm sorry, I thought . . . I thought you were . . ." Realizing my robe was open, I hurriedly pulled it around my frame, but not before he caught sight of my nightgown. In my fitful sleep, the neck ties had come undone, revealing bare collarbones.

His face instantly flushed. "Oh, yes—it had been meant as a joke. Not a very good one," he admitted. "I'm so sorry. It's past nine. I assumed . . ."

Alex glanced down the hall as if desperately wishing someone would come along to rescue him.

I pulled the top of the robe against my throat, every inch of me burning with mortification. "No, *I'm* sorry. I didn't sleep well last night and I'm afraid I'm not prepared for company just yet."

"Why don't I have breakfast brought here for you?" he suggested, his eyes carefully avoiding me. "I should have known Father would have kept you working too late and . . . I . . . I'll just go see about someone bringing up a tray. Yes." He backed his chair down the hall before coming to a sudden halt. "Coffee? Do you take coffee? Or tea?"

I angled my body around the half-shut door so only my head peeked out. "Either is fine. Well . . . coffee," I decided. After such a night, I'd need every bit of help I could gather. "Black, please. Thank you."

Alex nodded and raced away, his wheels flying.

"I truly am sorry," I said again, perched on one of the chairs in the sitting room as I smoothed my hands over the skirt of my best tea dress. I'd picked it out hoping the clusters of blue embroidered flowers would lift my spirits and the white lawn fabric would give the appearance of color in my cheeks. It also boasted the highest neckline I could find, fastening down my nape with three pearl buttons.

Alex had had the decency to wait half an hour before returning. A footman had followed close behind, bringing a tray of coffee, toast, a beautifully poached egg, and a small bowl of colorful fruit.

"The apology is all mine. When you didn't come down this morning, I thought . . ." His cheeks reddened again. "I wasn't sure if it was something I'd said yesterday or . . . I'm sorry to hear you had an unpleasant night."

A sharp bark of laughter burst from me at his unintended understatement. "It was . . ." I paused, remembering how I'd scrawled out my defeat to Camille before crying myself to sleep. Even in my dreams the ghastly women continued to scream at me. "It was *awful*. But it didn't have anything to do with you," I added in a hurried rush.

It hurt to meet Alex's gaze, knowing something was so terribly wrong with me. When he found out—and I was certain it was *when* and not *if*—any budding friendship between us would be over.

I wondered how he would react. Would he pull away instantly, thanking his lucky stars to have escaped such an unlucky acquaintance? Or worst of all, would his eyes turn cloudy with pity, worrying over the girl gone mad? The thought burned.

"I didn't sleep well either," he confessed after taking a sip of his own coffee. "Those damn birds kept half the house up last night."

"Birds?" I echoed, confident I'd heard him wrong.

"They were screeching like banshees. You must have heard them."

"I heard . . . I heard something last night, but it couldn't possibly have been birds."

He nodded. "Mother's peacocks. They're horrible things. You can hear them for miles."

I blinked at him.

Alex let out a chuckle of disbelief as realization dawned over him. "Oh, Verity. I can't imagine how terrifying that must have been for you, not knowing what it was."

I leaned forward, needing to hear him say it out loud again. "You . . . you heard it too?"

"They usually roost quietly in the trees, but there's something about a full moon. . . . They wail all night long. I'm so sorry no one thought to warn you."

"But I saw . . . I mean, I thought I saw . . ." I stopped short before I mentioned women in white dresses roaming the grounds. "You said they roost in trees?"

༄

"They're white!" I exclaimed as we entered the side garden.

In front of us, two peacocks strutted across the lawn, dragging trains of dotted feathers behind them, six feet long.

"Mother insists upon it," Alexander said.

"Albino peacocks," I murmured in wonder.

Yes. In the dark, under a full moon, I could have easily mistaken them for women. They were enormously tall, coming well past my waist. And their feathers . . . they trailed the birds as easily as a silk dress would.

"Not albinos," he corrected. "They're actually blue peafowl but a mutation drains their color away. See their eyes? Blue, not red. Our entire ostentation is made up of the leucistic whites. Though occasionally, a chick grows up and sprouts traces of blue or green mottled throughout their plumage. It's called a pied."

"What happens then?" I asked, glancing about the garden, hoping to catch a glimpse of such an unusual bird.

"We eat them," Alex said, his voice deadpan.

I waited for him to laugh at the joke.

He didn't.

I swallowed. "So . . . the noises last night . . . it was them?"

He nodded and as if on cue, one of the males tilted back his head and released a guttural shriek. Instantly, the hairs on my arms rose.

I let out a short laugh of relief. "You have no idea how good it is to hear that!"

"Is it?" Alexander asked, covering his ears.

"I'd pictured so many horrible things last night. I'd thought . . ." I hesitated, then pushed forward, ready to admit my fears. "I thought I was going mad."

"If listening to that for half the night doesn't drive you mad, nothing will," he assured me as the other peacock responded to the first. He charged, shaking his body as the long train rose up into an impressive fan. Strange cream-colored eyes dotted the tips of each feather, staring with an unsettling blindness.

I watched the peacocks square off against one another, already mentally balling up my letter to Camille.

"It's a beautiful morning," Alex said, glancing up at the trail of cirrus clouds breaking up an otherwise perfect blue sky. "Should we take the long way back around the house before starting our session?"

"Please," I agreed, following after him.

We rounded a corner, coming to the far side of the house. Another garden greeted us, full of pink and yellow blooms. Bees and hummingbirds danced in the early sunlight.

"What is that?" I asked, squinting past the low hedges bordering the area.

Alex peered in the direction I was staring. "Oh. That." He angled his chair and took off down the path that would lead us closer to the strange shapes.

In the field past the garden, great mounds of earth rose up, softly rounded and covered in wild grasses. Some were long, spanning several yards, while others were broken into series of segments. There was no discernable pattern that I could see, but it was obvious that the mounds were meant to be something, a project half started before becoming abandoned and forgotten.

"That's one of Father's ideas that never quite took root." Alex didn't seem to notice the pun.

"What was it meant to be?"

"Roses. Father wanted to create a garden maze, made up entirely of roses. The mounds are supposed to help anchor the walls. Or something," he said with a little shrug.

"That would be beautiful," I said, picturing how Gerard must have envisioned it would become.

"He never could seem to make it work. The soil is never the right balance. Too much sun, not enough shade." Alex shook his head. "It's the one thing he's never been able to grow properly, but every so often, a new mound will show up and he'll start talking about trying to make the maze work again."

I approached the mound closest to us, circling all the way around its mass. "They look oddly ominous, don't they? Not flat enough to be a swell in the meadow, but not tall enough to be a proper hill."

Alex began backing his chair down the path, expedition over. "My bedroom window faces this garden," he said, pointing up toward the manor. "They gave me such nightmares as a child."

I gave the mounds one final glance before trailing after him. "Nightmares?"

"Oh yes," he laughed. "I often would stay up far too late, reading ghoulish tales by candlelight, long after Mother had tucked me into bed. My imagination was always running away from me."

"What would you dream about?"

"I thought the mounds were full of bones," he said, a wicked grin crossing his face. "I imagined them sprouting up out of the black earth and growing like the roses Father so badly wanted." He raised his hands, twining his fingers together in a twisted knot.

"What an unsettling idea," I murmured. Goose bumps rose across my arms despite the morning's warmth.

"I was full of them as a boy," he agreed, breaking the tangle apart before continuing to push himself toward the house.

A giant white form glided down from out of the trees and landed before us. The peacock rose to his full height, cocked his head, and let out a lingering cry.

∽

"Leucistic," I tried again from behind my easel, sketching out the base for a practice painting. After being chased from the gardens by the unhappy peacock, we'd moved to a small library on the second floor to begin our session.

"Leucistic," Alexander repeated, drawing out the middle syllable.

"Leucissssssstic."

"Better."

"Such a strange thing." I set my pencil aside and pulled free one of my wooden palettes.

"The word?" he asked, stretching his arms out before him and flexing his wrists.

"The concept. White birds that are meant to be blue . . . or are they blue birds that turned white?"

"Either, I suppose."

I squeezed a series of paints in the center of the palette. Together they'd create the right shade of warmth for Alex's skin.

"Why white? Aren't the blues meant to be dazzling?"

"Mother had a leucistic as a girl. It was her favorite pet. When she became mistress over Chauntilalie, she thought they'd better fit the manor's aesthetic. Father agreed. They've spent years refining the group. Only the birds with the mutation are allowed to grow to reproductive maturity."

I started blending the colors together. "So they've weeded out an entire line of . . . of genetic material," I stammered, the words and concepts feeling foreign on my tongue, "just for decoration?"

Alex's face shifted, showing everything he thought of the practice in one distasteful grimace. "Indeed. Can you see now why I'm so keen to add the alyssum to my crest?"

"I can."

And I did. If I was ever forced to choose sides in the matter, I knew I'd agree with Alex. The thought of so many beautifully mottled birds being slaughtered, just to preserve the look of the Laurents' grounds, was abhorrent. I pushed the bloody vision from me.

"I think I'm ready to begin. I'm starting with your face, so once I've got you in the proper position, it would help if you could stay as still as you can."

"No talking?"

"A little talking is okay, but I will need you to hold the pose as faithfully as you can." I rummaged through a kit, searching for the right brush. "This isn't meant to be torturous for you. If you feel as though you need to"—out of habit, I almost said "get up" but stopped myself short—"shift about, get a drink, do anything, we can take a break. I always try to be mindful that there's a living, breathing person behind my canvas, but if I get caught up in the moment and need reminding . . . remind me."

He smiled. "I promise to. How should we begin?"

Frederick had taken Alex out of the wheelchair and sat him on a tufted sofa of olive green velvet.

"What feels most natural to you?" I asked, approaching him with a studious eye.

He stretched about, trying different poses: resting the side of his face in the cup of his hand, sitting on the sofa's edge with his posture formal and ramrod straight, leaning into the cushions as one arm reclined along the back. Nothing looked quite right.

"We can try that last pose," I said uncertainly, not exactly pleased with it, but it was a start in any case. I'd undoubtedly end up painting this canvas over with a coat of gesso, covering up my practice anyhow.

"Can you tilt your head just a touch to the right? Your right," I amended as he went the wrong way. "And back? Too far . . ." My hands danced restlessly. "May I try adjusting you?" I asked.

"Please do. I feel a bit ridiculous," he admitted, his forehead tilting far from the center of his body.

"You look it too," I teased.

Just before I placed my fingertips upon his face, I paused. I'd painted dozens of portraits before, filling the halls of Highmoor with my sisters and nieces, little Artie and William. I'd talked maids and butlers into sitting for me in their free moments, painted fishermen unaware as they sat on the docks, waiting for a bite on their lines.

But I'd never painted someone as singularly attractive as Alex. Someone close to my age. Someone I found myself ever drawn to. Touching him, carefully drawing my fingers across his skin to move him into just the right position . . .

It was such an intimate thing to do.

When I finally seized hold of my courage and cupped his cheeks, correcting the tilt of his head, he took in a sharp breath.

"Your hands are cold."

"Sorry."

I rubbed them together before continuing on. His skin was softer than I'd expected, freshly shaven, without a hint of stubble. I pressed my fingertips to his jaw, turning his head slightly to the right. I hated when portraits were done completely head-on. Angles were so much more interesting, engaging. They invited the audience to linger, wondering over what secrets the subject kept.

"Like this."

I touched his chin, my thumb just shy of his lips, gently adjusting. As I cupped his face, he laid his hand over mine, leaning his cheek into the curve of my fingers and sending the most delicious shivers down my spine.

"You smell like what I imagine the sea does," he murmured.

"My lotion," I said, thinking of the little container I'd brought from Highmoor. We made it from long strands of kelp harvested on the beaches of Salten. I pulled away, self-conscious. "Is it too strong?"

Slowly, he took my hand in his and pressed his nose against my wrist, breathing in deep. "Not at all. It's very subtle. Very soft. Very Verity."

"Oh."

It was the only word I could think of as my throat constricted and my insides squirmed, suddenly filled with an unknown want.

No.

It was more than that, I reasoned, shimmers of warmth radiating through me.

More than a want.

There was an ache, a need.

A yearning.

I'd never felt anything like this before. It hit me straight on, like a boulder crashing off a rock ledge. I didn't even know I was capable of such feelings. There'd never been anyone at Highmoor—boy or girl—who had inspired such a heated reaction within me.

His lips were close, so close, and I suddenly had the overwhelming desire to lean down and press mine against them. I imagined them whispering over each other, exploring each line, his parting as I gently nipped at the full curve—

Before I could act on such wild thoughts, I straightened and backed away. "The paints are going to dry out. . . ."

I sat back down on my stool, fanning my heated cheek, hidden behind the wall of canvas.

"How's this?" he asked, and I dared to hazard a peek around the easel. He'd fallen back into the exact pose I'd first set him into.

"You're perfect." The words flew from my mouth before I could stop them. "It. *It.* It's perfect," I amended, but his smile deepened into a wicked grin.

"Then let's get started, shall we?"

Dear Annaleigh,

Thank you so much for your letter and crate of candles. I've been burning them nearly every day. I wanted to let you know that I am safe and well. The commission I was brought here for is progressing nicely and ... I ... I think the heir of Chauntilalie may be interested in starting a courtship with me ...

    You'll note the ellipses ending that statement. I'm not certain if I'm meant to use an exclamation or a question mark. I honestly don't know much of anything I'm meant to do in the matter.

    I'm terribly flattered and I think I too might be developing feelings for him—he's terribly smart and funny and very, very handsome.

    But ...

    (Those ellipses again.)

    I've never had attention upon me like this before. It's a strange, heady thing, suspecting someone might be attracted to you. Can one be in love with being in love? I could see this emotion clouding many judgments.

    I wish you were here. I wish we could sneak away to my room and speak openly on this. I miss your guidance and wisdom. I miss my sister.

    I take it your talk with Camille didn't go well? Though entirely painful, I did write a letter letting her know I'd arrived safely but have heard nothing back. I want to pretend it's simply a delay due to distance but your letter arrived so quickly. Some rifts can't be mended, I suppose.

    Write soon. I still have a few more weeks until the painting will be done. Give little Cecilia a kiss for me.

                                             All my love,
                                             Verity

16

LATER THAT AFTERNOON, I WAS BACK IN MY CHAMbers, at the little writing desk. A well of ink, pen, and envelope lay before me. I finished off Annaleigh's address with a flourish of jade-green ink.

"Verity?"

Dauphine peered in from the hall, waiting for permission to enter. She was dressed in complex pleats of cerulean brocade today. A comb of brilliantly hued peacock eyes held back her sweep of hair and I briefly wondered if they'd come from one of the slaughtered pieds.

"Come in," I greeted her, rising from the chair. "I was just writing to my sister to let her know I've arrived safely." I stuffed the letter into the envelope lest Dauphine spot any of my musings toward her son.

"I can take that for you," she offered, sliding the envelope across the desk toward her.

"Oh, I haven't sealed it yet," I began, but she spoke over me with an easy smile.

"It's no trouble. I'll have Bastian do that before he takes the rest of the correspondence into town."

Before I could protest, my letter was tucked away into the depths of her skirts.

"We missed you last night. And this morning," she added, her brow twisting with concern. "Alexander told me about the peacocks scaring you. I'm so terribly sorry I forgot to mention them. I hope your night wasn't too awful?"

I knew she expected me to assuage her guilt. "No harm done."

"And . . . I thought it might be fun for us to go into town tomorrow? You've been working so hard, with the portrait and all of Gerard's silly flowers, surely a break is in order. I thought we might have lunch, visit some of the shops? We could leave after breakfast."

"That sounds . . ." I paused, searching for the right word. It was certainly unexpected. I'd only just arrived and had assumed Dauphine would want me to complete my commission as soon as possible.

"Oh, please say yes," she continued on as if she'd not heard my hesitation. "I'm cooped up here with all of these men and . . . Marguerite." She gave me a knowing, wicked smile. "It would be wonderful to spend some time with you."

After a moment, I nodded. "I would enjoy that, Dauphine. Thank you."

She smiled, brightening the air around her. "Oh, thrilling! I'll let the coachmen know. How *is* the portrait coming along?"

"Very well, I think. I started a first attempt this morning, just to get a feel for the pose. We still need to find the right location."

Dauphine nodded. "Alexander told me how much he's enjoyed being in your company."

I thought of his fingers closed around my wrist and my cheeks heated. "He makes for a wonderful subject."

She twisted the set of rings on her left hand, their jewels sparkling even in the late afternoon light. "He's such a dear boy. I'm glad he has someone new to talk with. I'm afraid he doesn't get much company here. Especially from young ladies, such as yourself."

"No?" I mused. "I would have thought—"

Dauphine shook her head and her earrings—giant emerald orbs—bobbed back and forth. "Alexander is quite particular about who he allows into his life. He had a very solitary childhood. After the accident, I was so scared of what else might happen to him, I did everything I could to keep him safe. Perhaps I was a bit overzealous."

"I understand how that feels, being so isolated while growing up."

"Of course you do," she exclaimed. "Highmoor is the only estate on your island, isn't it?"

"Our closest neighbors are a three-hour boat ride away. In good weather," I added.

Her forehead creased with concern. "I'm sure both of you have much in common, then. You're sure to be close companions in no time."

"I . . . I hope so."

Dauphine smiled. "I do too."

༄

"That shade of blue is all wrong for you," the shop assistant said, removing a swatch of fabric from under my face.

"But I've always liked—"

"No, no. It's too at odds with your skin tone. See?"

She held up the satin again, pointing toward a mirror edged in golden swans and showers of gilt petals. Her expression curdled with horror.

"I think it looks nice."

The young woman shook her head and whisked the fabric away as though she thought I might try to wrestle it from her.

Dauphine offered me a smile of commiseration. Dress sketches littered the tufted chaise around her.

"Is it always so stressful here?" I whispered, lest the shop assistant overhear me.

"Only when you dare to have the wrong opinion," she murmured, tittering with amusement. "That blue *did* wash you out."

"This isn't necessary," I said, stepping down from the dais. "I don't need a new dress. Certainly nothing as fancy as all these." I took a seat at the other end of the chaise, flipping through the cast-off designs.

They were all ridiculously over the top—skirts poofed and bolstered by dozens of yards of trim, shoulders so accentuated by sharp angles that the wearer would look more reptilian than woman, bodices drowning in paillettes and paste jewels.

"Every woman is always in need of a new dress," Dauphine insisted. "This is my favorite salon in Bloem and I want you to have a little piece of it when you go home." She sighed as if the thought pained her. "Where will you go to next, after the portrait is done?"

I hadn't fully contemplated life past the Laurents' commission. I wasn't sure Camille would welcome me back to

Highmoor with open arms and even less sure I wanted to return there myself.

But there was nowhere else to go. Mercy lived in a sprawling set of rooms at the palace but her residence was only by the favor of the king. It wasn't as if the apartment was hers to lend out to wayward family members in their time of need. Honor was in the same situation as a live-in governess, and there had hardly been enough room for Annaleigh and Cassius in their cottage on Hesperus even before their colicky baby arrived.

Mentally, I counted up the scant number of my remaining florettes tucked into one of my valises back at Chauntilalie.

"We'll certainly miss you," she added when it became clear that I had no answer for her.

"I will miss you as well."

"I wonder if . . ." She paused thoughtfully, then shook her head as if chastising herself.

"What?"

"A mother's silly daydream, nothing more."

I recalled Camille's initial response to Dauphine's letter, assuming she wanted Mercy to come stay with them, to arrange a match between Alex and my sister.

I would have thought a young man as attractive and as charming as Alex would have had a list of eligible girls lined up for the chance to hang off his arm but Dauphine had said how particular he was, how isolated he kept himself.

Perhaps Camille had been right.

Perhaps the Laurents *were* in search of a wife for their son.

I wasn't opposed to an arranged match. Marriages—especially between noble families—were almost always the result of the parents' careful planning. Just because I no longer had mine didn't mean my future couldn't be just as deliberately arranged. . . .

"You look very deep in thought, my dear," Dauphine said, interrupting the battle raging in my mind and heart. "Is everything all right?"

I pushed my tongue against the sharp point of my incisor, feeling the importance of the moment before me. I could say nothing, let her dress me up in an ostentatious gown that would only ever be sent back to Highmoor to sit in an armoire and undoubtedly never see the light of day. Camille certainly wouldn't let me out of her sight again upon my return.

If I returned . . .

And if I didn't, what then? I had a bit—a very little bit—of my own money, and what the Laurents would pay me upon completion of Alexander's portrait. It could get me by for a while . . . but where? To what end? What was it that I really wanted?

I wanted to paint.

I wanted adventures.

I *did* want someone to share that with.

Eventually.

And Alex was kind. He was smart. He treated me with affection and respect. He listened and made me laugh. He'd become a duke. I could become a duchess. The same as Camille. There was no doubt in my mind that a life with him could be full and happy.

I pressed my lips together, turning through the pages of gowns, ready to cast the die. "I only . . . It just struck me how terribly much I shall miss all this. I know I've only been here a few days, but I've already fallen in love with Bloem. It will be difficult to leave it."

I glanced over to see how well my performance affected her but the shop assistant returned just then, carrying with her an armful of tulle in lavender, peach, and gold. Dauphine shifted her attention back to the sketches, murmuring thoughtfully about the waistline on one of the dresses.

But as she did, I caught the corner of her mouth curling into a small, secret smile.

17

"THESE ARE FOR YOU," GERARD SAID, ENTERING THE study without warning and dropping a pile of books beside the small table at the left of my easel.

"*Secrets Kept,*" I murmured, tilting my head to read their spines. "*Lessons in the Hidden World of Botanical Language. The Art of Arrangement.*"

He nodded approvingly. "Dauphine mentioned you'd selected this for the location of Alexander's portrait." He gestured about the room. "I thought it might be nice to have a bouquet painted into the foreground someplace. I may not be able to pick out his legacy but I certainly can remind him of everything that has come before."

"I see. Are there any flowers in particular you were thinking about?"

"Here," he said, thrusting a list into my hands.

I read through the list, nodding even though I had no idea what message they were meant to convey. I glanced at the stack of books. I'd have a busy morning ahead of me. "I don't know what some of these are . . . what most of them are, actually. Would it be possible to see examples of them in the greenhouse?"

"We have all of them but the *Fragaria vesca*. I suppose you can cross that one off the list. It won't be ready for another few weeks," he said, and swooped forward to steal my pencil right out of my hand to slash off the name himself.

"Father." Alexander paused on the lip of the threshold, eyes narrowed, before rolling into the study. "I didn't expect to see you here today. Are you going to watch Verity's session? Make sure it's up to standard?"

"Hmmm." He looked around the room, noting all the changes we'd done—reconfiguring the position of the writing desk so it could be included while keeping Alexander in the best light, arranging a stack of meaningful books in the background, along with a small statute of Arina's burning heart and a framed rendering of Chauntilalie hung on the wall.

Alexander positioned himself at the center of it all, exactly where we'd decided he'd go at the end of our last session.

"You're not staying in the chair, are you?" Gerard asked, leaning over beside me to see the composition as I did. He crossed away to fuss with the angle of the statue.

Alex looked unconcerned. "Where else would I be?"

Gerard unfastened the clasp of a window drape, shifting the folds of fabric into a more attractive angle, despite my rough outline of it already sketched across the canvas. "There're dozens of other chairs to choose from. Surely you don't want that old wicker thing immortalized forever."

"Surely *you* don't."

"Well. No," Gerard admitted, finally turning to his son. He picked at a bit of lint on Alex's shoulder, truly unable to help himself. "You . . . You're so much more than that chair, Alexander. Why include it?"

"It's part of who I am, Father. Painting in some stuffy fauteuil won't change that. And they're terribly uncomfortable."

"But do you really want generations of Laurents to remember you as . . ." Gerard stopped abruptly.

"As a cripple?" Alexander asked challengingly. "An invalid? A gimp?"

His father's eyebrows drew together, as if he were in pain. I noticed his fingers ball into fists. "As . . . as less than perfect."

A long, uneasy moment passed between them.

"If perfection is what you're after, perhaps you ought to have Verity repaint that great ugly nose from yours."

I sucked in a deep breath. Gerard stared down at his son in disbelief and I braced myself against the impending explosion.

But instead, he laughed.

Swells of laughter so great, he had to hold a hand over his stomach to keep from doubling over.

"Perhaps I might, perhaps I might." Gerard wiped at the corner of his eye and slapped Alexander across the back with an approving smack. "I suppose I ought to let you get on with all this." He gestured toward the canvas.

"Would you like to stay?" I offered, surprising them both but wanting to capitalize on the unexpected and happy moment. "I'm sketching out the foundation today and then we'll start painting tomorrow."

Gerard waved my offer aside. "No, no, I've work of my own that needs attending."

"The Constances?" I asked. It had been a week since I'd seen the purple flowers. I'd been busy getting everything set up for Alexander's portrait and Gerard's tinkering often kept him secreted away, missing meals and working long into the nights, the greenhouse glowing like a beacon even as I blew out my candles at bedtime.

His eyes darted toward Alex, then away again just as quickly. "No, no. Other things. Other flowers. But you must see them. More have bloomed, about this big now . . ." He held up his hand, fisted. "Look over my list and the books and then come find me. I'm always in one of the greenhouses." Gerard nodded absentmindedly and then took his leave, his footsteps echoing down the hall long after his departure.

"He named those purple flowers after a woman?" Alexander asked once it was clear Gerard was far from the study and couldn't overhear.

"At first. *Callistephus constancensia*," I said, trying to remember the exact phrase Gerard had bestowed upon the little blooms. "But then he said he might decide on something else."

He let out a tiff of disapproval. "That man."

"She'd helped with them, he said. Who is she? An assistant? A gardener?"

Alex let out a sigh. "I suppose you'll notice sooner or later. Father . . ." He looked toward the ceiling, trying to conjure up the best phrasing. "Father is a man of . . . insatiable appetites."

His eyes drifted down, leveling me with the certainty that Alex wasn't referencing Gerard's proclivities for long, drawn-out dinners.

"Oh," I murmured, coloring instantly.

"I didn't always understand that growing up. Didn't understand who all the women were. I'd see them for a spell and then they'd be gone. . . . He moves through them quickly, always wanting something new."

"Poor Dauphine." My heart ached for her. "Do you think she knows?"

Alex's face was grim. "I think Mother buries herself deeply in her own pursuits—socializing and shopping—to avoid thinking on it too long. But I'm sure it stings. I know it does," he added. "So, this Constance," he mused, then shrugged. "I've no idea *who* she is but I've no doubt I know exactly *what* kind of help she was giving him."

I squirmed, uncertain of what to say.

"He mentioned a list," Alex said, abruptly changing the conversation as he pushed himself over to the writing desk to reposition the statue. "What list?"

I rose to fix the drapes and offered him the slip of paper.

"Oh, Father."

"What is it? What do they mean?"

He crumpled the list before tossing it into a refuse basket. "Only that a leopard can certainly never change its spots. He wants to add in a bouquet?" he guessed, spotting the books on my worktable. I nodded and he picked them up. "Don't bother. This isn't his painting."

"Wait—" I said, grabbing at the stack. "I actually would like to look through those. The meaning in the flowers . . . I'd like to learn more."

Alex relented, releasing his hold on them. "As you wish."

I opened the first one, skimming through the pages, captivated by the botanical renderings and the lists of possible meanings each flower could impart. "Perhaps I'll make you a bouquet later today. I could put in . . ." I flipped to a new page, trying to spot something appropriate. Something that would bring back his smile. "A rose."

The skin around his eyes crinkled as he laughed. "So unimaginative!"

"It's my first time ever trying to speak in flower!" I exclaimed, feigning indignity.

"Well, you'll need to take care with your colors. What will you pick?"

I scanned the surprisingly long entry. "Blush, I think." I read further. "A thornless blush rose." I glanced up, hoping I'd selected right. It was meant to represent an early affection, earnestly held out with the hopes of reciprocation.

He considered this as he moved back to his position, ready for our session to begin. "I would be honored to receive that from you."

I picked up my pencil and looked around the easel. "Would you send anything back?"

Alexander's face broke into a perfect grin and I went to work, quickly capturing it on the canvas.

"Oh, Verity, you'll have to wait and see."

18

"WHAT ARE WE DOING ALL THE WAY OUT HERE?" I asked as we ventured past the gardens, following a planked walkway into Chauntilalie's nearby forest.

Forest was perhaps too strong a word. The greenery was obviously well cared for—the brambles and vines that would normally creep and crawl with abandon along a woodland floor were manicured back, keeping the path passable for Alex's chair. But the trees looked rough and wild, giving the illusion that we were setting off on a reckless adventure.

We took most of our lunches outdoors. Alexander liked showing off the hidden treasures of the vast estate and the picnics were a welcome diversion after our long morning sessions.

"You saw the Menagerie Wall as you came into the city?" Alex asked, the wheels of his chair rattling brightly along the boardwalk. I nodded. "Most people don't know this, but there were a handful of statues made for the wall that were never used. They were deemed too terrifying. It's said even the sculptors' own children cried when they saw their parents working on them. My great-great-grandfather had them brought to Chauntilalie."

"A reasonable course of action," I laughed. "And you're bringing me out to these horrific beasts for a picnic?"

"Would you rather join Mother at her society luncheon today? I'm sure we have time to turn around." He winked up at me. "You might want to ready yourself," he continued as the walkway curved round a bend. "They're designed to be a bit of a surprise and the first one is rather shocking."

Even with his warning, I was caught unprepared.

The statue was affixed to the side of a monstrous willow tree. My eyes couldn't help but sweep upward, expecting to gaze in wonder at the soaring canopy of dangling branches.

Instead, they spotted a monster crawling headfirst down the trunk. Its neck snapped backward at an impossible angle as it studied the garden's inhabitants. An extra-wide mouth was drawn back into a sneer and hooked fangs curled from its upper and lower jaws.

"Why would anyone make something like that?" I asked, trying to cover my gasp.

"When the Menagerie Wall was first built, Bloem was seen as a small region of very little consequence. The People of the Petals were a bit of a joke—espousing love and beauty in a time when there was so much strife in the land. The Menagerie was built to show that art could have importance, that beauty could be powerful." He pushed himself past the willow. "Up here is one of my favorites."

"What is it?" I asked as the lumbering giant came into view.

It wasn't quite a bear, it wasn't exactly a frog, but it was enormous enough to hide the rest of the garden from immediate view. Bulging eyes bugged out of a square muzzle. Its wide, stocky legs ended on webbed feet.

"I named him Brutus," Alex said with a smile. "When I was a boy, I'd bring out stacks of stories and read aloud to him. Mother would send tea."

I couldn't help but smile, picturing him propped between the monster's forelegs, clinking his cup against the beast's strange toes. "He certainly seems a better companion than that first thing we saw. Hello, Brutus," I called up to the statue. His quartz eyes seemed to wink back at me.

"You should have brought your sketchbook."

"Indeed. Where should we set up?" I had the wicker basket looped over one arm. Raphael had laden it heavy with sandwiches of thickly sliced ham and salted butter, a sealed carafe of pink lemonade, and all the cups, plates, and flatware we could possibly need.

"Keep going," Alex said, pointing to the walkway. "Behold, the Garden of Giants."

Once we were around Brutus, I could see how big the area was. In the middle of the garden was a verdigris-choked pond. The boardwalk crossed over the dark green waters, dotted with benches to sit and stare at the creatures peeking out from under trees and behind bushes. There were a mishmash of beasts both fantastic and horrible.

"Will this do?" Alex asked, pausing next to one of the benches. A stony, misshapen head poked out from the waves, insect-like save for the very human-looking fingers grasping the lip of the boardwalk.

I hid my shudder and nodded, setting to work on unpacking the basket.

"What a beautiful afternoon," Alex murmured appreciatively, tipping his face to the sun as a pair of black swans swam by, eyeing us with haughty disdain.

I scanned the garden, spotting a dragon onshore so covered in moss and lichens, it nearly blended into the landscape. A curved vine broke through a beast's eye socket, creating a verdant iris. "It's strangely perfect," I admitted. "I'd love to sketch it all."

He smiled, clearly pleased with his selection, before sinking his teeth into his sandwich.

"Maybe I could run back to the house after lunch," I went on, musing. "The portrait is going well. We could afford to take an afternoon off."

Alex shook his head. "Your afternoon has already been claimed. Mother mentioned a note was delivered this morning. Your dress is ready for a fitting." He leaned back in his chair, studying me with pupils dark and wide. "I look forward to seeing it on you."

A delicious flush crept over me, tingling the hollow of my throat and spreading up my neck where it bloomed across my cheeks, hot and thrilling. I'd never been looked at like that before and it was exhilarating. "The dress? Oh, it's far too formal for everyday wear."

"Wear it to the party." He popped a sugar-dusted blackberry into his mouth.

"Party?"

"Surely you've heard Mother going on and on about it. Next week."

I frowned. "She mentioned a small dinner . . ."

He grinned. "Nothing is ever small with Dauphine Laurent. At least twenty families have been invited."

Surprise washed over me. "So many."

"She's keen on introducing you to all her friends and take credit for discovering your talents." He pressed his lips together, carefully weighing out his next words. "I was rather hoping it could be a chance to show you off as well. To show *us* off."

"Us?" I echoed, delighted by this turn in the conversation.

We spent our sessions together talking through a wide variety of topics—everything from art and his beloved books, to funny stories of distant relations and all the changes he wanted to make for Bloem in the future. Alexander had an easy, charming wit, but while I knew he enjoyed my company—and his parents both seemed quick to pair us together—he'd never exactly spelled out his intentions.

And because *he* didn't say anything, I felt *I* couldn't say anything. So we each said nothing but talked about everything, learning the way the other thought, their cadences and rhythms. We made little jokes, sure to dissolve us into giggles.

It was a far cry from how I'd watched Camille's courtship with William play out, sneaking peeks of them as they sat on opposing chairs in the Gold Room, murmuring from behind silver-lined teacups about the weather or prices at the fish market.

We had no formal pretenses or stilted checking off of moments—compliments paid, batting of eyes accomplished. It was just . . . us.

"Us," he repeated uncertainly. "That is . . . if you'd like there to be . . . an us?"

He licked his lips and I wanted to reach out and squeeze him. He looked unspeakably uncomfortable, as though finally putting a definition to our relationship left him vulnerable and worried.

"I . . . I've grown quite fond of you, Verity. I hope you know that."

I nodded, fearing any words from me would break the moment.

"I never allowed myself to imagine ever being in this position . . . meeting someone as lovely and wonderful as you are, so talented and smart, and such a good fit . . ."

He reached out and placed the palm of his hand over my cheek, brushing his thumb across its soft curve. I offered a smile to encourage him on.

"I'd always assumed, because of this"—he tapped his free hand against the wheelchair's arm—"that I wouldn't ever marry." A burst of red broke over his face, staining his cheeks and neck, and he pulled back, his hand swiping through the air as he tried to sort out his words. "Not that I'm saying we'll be married. I just . . . I only . . ." He scrunched his eyes closed. "What I'm trying to say is . . . I should very much like to court you, Verity Thaumas, if I may." The words poured from him in a heated rush as if he couldn't get them out fast enough. After a moment, he dared to peek at me from one eye. "You . . . you're laughing at me!"

I couldn't contain my smile. "You sound so nervous right now."

"I am," he admitted.

"I'm sorry," I said, covering his hand with an encouraging caress. "You needn't be . . . you know that, don't you?"

"It's a difficult subject to speak on and it's why I've not brought it up till now . . . I like you, Verity. More than like . . . I . . . I care for you. Deeply." He raked his fingers through his dark waves. "You're the first thing I think of when I open my eyes and the only thing I spend my nights dreaming of. But I know that a life with me . . . with this chair . . . may not be something that would appeal to you."

My heart swelled with hurt as I imagined all the dark and lonely thoughts racing through his mind. Carefully, I scooted down the bench, drawing closer to him. "It's never bothered me before," I promised. "And I can't believe it ever would."

"You don't know that," he protested. "You—"

"I know I want—that I've *always* wanted—to do this," I insisted, and surprised us both by leaning forward and pressing my lips to his.

It was our first kiss, *my* first kiss, and it was . . .

It's only a first kiss, I reminded myself, feeling oddly detached from the moment.

I registered that he tasted of lemonade and berries and the sweet afternoon sunlight. My fingertips slid along his face, tracing the lines I'd drawn dozens of times but never truly understood till now.

I analyzed each action, every movement, every sensation, his scent, his taste, and was left with a troubling hollowness in my chest. Wasn't I supposed to be feeling something? Wasn't I supposed to be caught in a wave of ecstasy, swooning and breathless and . . . something? Anything.

Was this . . .

Was this all there was to a kiss?

That couldn't be right.

Poets didn't write sonnets about this.

Songs were not sung over feelings like this.

This felt . . . perfunctory.

I pulled away, trying to figure out what I'd done wrong. What we'd done wrong.

Was it the angle? The pressure?

Alex smiled but I found I couldn't read it, couldn't guess at the thoughts running through his mind.

Was he as confused as I felt?

I was certain I desired him—I thought of him often and in increasingly intimate ways—but had I been wrong? Or were the physical aspects of love impossible to live up to the wild fantasies of an overactive imagination? Though wholly inexperienced myself, I was no prude. I'd skimmed through my sisters' tattered romance novels. I'd been to the opera. I knew what a gloriously thrilling moment a kiss was meant to be.

I waited for those sensations to take over and claim me, swelling my heart till it felt it would burst and shower the world with the splendor of new love.

Nothing.

∽

With a disgruntled sigh, I stabbed one last pin in my hair and turned, studying my reflection in the mirror before me. I looked peevish and sour and forced a smile, seeing if it would help.

It didn't.

Dauphine and I had returned from my fitting with just enough time to dress for dinner and, though I felt horribly rushed, I wanted to make sure I looked especially nice for Alexander.

Our first kiss worried me.

I'd expected fireworks and shooting stars, effervescent bubbles and delight.

Not . . .

That.

I'd spent the entire trip into town only half listening to Dauphine while I compiled a mental list of things I'd once been bad at but, with practice, had improved upon.

Drawing.

Sailing.

Embroidery.

My penmanship.

Surely I would one day be able to add kissing to this list.

There were reasons, plenty of reasons, for it not to have gone right. It was a decidedly awkward act—pressing your face to another's with the expectation of it being miraculously pleasant.

With time, it was certain to become more agreeable.

I hoped.

What worried me most was Alex's read on the matter.

If he'd felt the kiss to be lackluster as well, would he account for how new to this I was? Had he considered that I could be an apt pupil and would seek to improve? What if he wrote me off before giving me another chance?

As I pinched my cheeks, drawing spots of color into them,

there was a short tap on the sitting room door and I felt as though I might become ill. Our next conversation could determine the rest of my life. Would I remain at Chauntilalie or be tossed out, never to be kissed again?

"Coming," I called out, certain it was Alexander. Just before turning the glass doorknob, I took a deep, steadying breath.

But when I opened the door, there was no one in the hall.

Puzzled, I stepped out, nearly crushing a small parcel left on the threshold.

A bouquet!

I swooped down to pick up the little nosegay, admiring the clusters of snowy white and pink spectacled blooms. A small card was tucked into the ribbon tying the flowers together.

Sometimes words are not needed. (Rock-roses and gardenias), it read in Alex's bold, jagged print.

Smiling, I brought them into my bedroom, to add to one of the large vases on my nightstand, before turning to Gerard's stack of books.

I looked up the gardenia first, remembering Alex had mentioned them the night I'd first arrived at the manor.

"*'Gardenia jasminoides,'*" I read aloud. It had several possible meanings. "'You are so lovely,'" it began. "'I too am happy, joy, a most tender love.'"

I pressed my nose to the creamy blooms, breathing in their sweet scent before flipping to the rock-rose.

The book offered only one definition.

"*'Cistaceae,'*" I said, and traced its phrase, a smile growing deep in my heart. "'Of this I am most certain.'"

Certain.

He was certain.

I felt all of the anxieties that had spent the afternoon building within me drop away, like racing water falling over the edge of a cliff.

He was certain.

Our courtship would continue. There was still hope for a secure future.

With Alex.

He was certain.

A tiny dark thought pushed its way into my mind but I batted it from me before it could take root.

He is certain, but are you?

~~Dear Mercy,~~

~~There's simply so much I need to catch you up upon.~~

~~Dearest Mercy,~~

~~Thank you, thank you, thank you the world over, darling sister of mine! I've been at Chauntilalie for nearly three weeks now and imagine I might remain here for quite a longer while yet.~~

~~Alexander Laurent has asked to court me and I've said yes.~~

~~Dear Sister,~~

~~Thank you so much for recommending me to Lady Laurent. I've begun work on Alexander's portrait and~~

~~Mercy,~~

~~I so wish you were here. There's so much I need to tell you and... I just really wish you were here.~~

Camille—

Why is it that no matter what I do, everything always comes back to you?

19

THE CLOCK ON THE DESK OF THE STUDY TICKED softly, announcing the passing seconds with a mocking persistence. I fiddled with the order of paints laid upon the side table, then lined up the brushes, nudging them about until they ran perfectly parallel to each other.

I studied the portrait before me. Alexander's form popped from the white canvas, half finished. His body, shown from the chest up, was nearly done. I'd need to add in little strokes of highlights over his fingers and the folds of fabric gathered across his sleeves, but was pleased with its current state.

Still, the clock ticked.

With a forceful exhale, I stood and paced the room, fluffing out the curtains to create a different effect, plumping pillows on the short settee, all the while listening to the incessant ticks go by.

Where was Alex?

It wasn't like him to be late.

Usually, he joined Dauphine and me at the end of breakfast and we headed to the second floor for our first session together. But I'd eaten alone this morning after Dauphine sent word of a migraine. The footman who had delivered the message had offered Dauphine's condolences in an unworried tone, saying the duchess was often prone to the headaches.

First Dauphine, now Alexander.

More ticks.

At a quarter past the hour, spun into agitation by all my pacing, I left the study, making my way deeper into the south wing. I had a vague approximation of where Alex's bedroom was and when I heard a sudden moan, echoing in a familiar baritone, I knew I was heading in the right direction.

The door was ajar.

"Alex?" I asked, stepping inside the parlor.

Thrashing sounds came from the bedroom beyond, cries of pain and torment. A voice I recognized as Frederick's ordered for a valise to be brought in.

That door swung open.

"Miss Thaumas, what are you doing here?" Johann asked, eyes wide with surprise.

I'd never seen him look so unkempt. His jacket had been removed and shirtsleeves rolled up. His vest was left undone and hung askew, as if something—or someone—had been tugging on it. His blond locks, usually so carefully pomaded back, fell into his eyes and he breathed through an open mouth.

"Alexander and I were supposed to have a session this morning but he never arrived. I thought I'd come check on him." In the room beyond, Alex's voice rose into a howl that pierced my chest. "What happened?"

"Pains in his legs," Johann explained, his eyes darting about the room. "He gets this way sometimes."

"I thought he couldn't feel anything—"

"Where's that damn valise?" Frederick shouted over a fresh volley of Alex's struggles.

"Make it stop, please, Arina, make it stop," he wept.

Johann dove forward, snatching the black bag from beneath a side table. "Master Laurent won't be able to see you today."

"Is that Verity?" Alex called out, panicked. "No. No. I don't want her to see—" His words broke off, dropping into a groan. "Don't let her see . . . see me . . ."

Heavy footsteps approached the parlor. Frederick peered through the gap, face splotched and eyes dark. "You have to go," he stated firmly.

I didn't want to disobey but I couldn't just leave either. "If I could just see him for a moment, please? Wish him w—"

"No," Frederick insisted. "Go."

The door clicked shut with decisive resolution.

For a moment, I lingered in the parlor, listening to the horrible noises as my gaze drifted about the room. This was Alexander's private retreat from the rest of Chauntilalie, a space wholly his own.

It smelled of him, like paper and ink, spiced tea and green clippings.

Piles of books stacked high on every surface. Some had bits of paper or ribbons poking from their tops, indicating where he left off in his reading. Others laid facedown, their spines splayed over the arm of a chair, the edge of a table. On his writing desk was one of the renderings I'd first drawn of him, from our afternoon under the redbuds. I traced my finger over his penciled form, wishing there was something I could do to help him now.

A great and terrible cry ripped through the air, raising the hairs of my arm. The silence that followed was even more dreadful. Then came his whispers.

"Thank you, thank you," he murmured over and over, his voice broken and beatific. "Thank you."

I turned and fled the room.

༄

Gerard was in the main greenhouse, bent over a table. Rows of tiny terra-cotta pots lined the workspace and he spooned a sample of rich, black soil into each of them with care.

I was so relieved to see one of the Laurents in their usual state, I nearly hugged him.

"Verity," he greeted, looking up from his work at the sound of my approach. He checked his pocket watch, a little rose-gold bauble hanging from a sparkling chain at his waist. It sprung open, revealing the clock face on one side and a small portrait of a much younger Dauphine on the other. "I thought you'd be with Alexander."

"He's . . . he's not well," I murmured, unsure of how to explain what I'd caught glimpses of upstairs, of the things I'd heard. "You might want to check on him."

His eyes darkened and flickered over to the looming shadow of Chauntilalie. "One of his fits?"

"I didn't see it . . . but he sounded in so much pain."

He nodded gravely. "It happens from time to time. Was Frederick with him?"

"And Johann."

His face relaxed. "Good."

I waited for him to stir into action but he turned back to the pots before him. "Aren't you going to see him?"

He shook his head. "He's in fine hands. I'm sure they've already administered his medicine—he won't be particularly coherent for hours now."

"What . . . what was happening?"

"Muscle spasms. He's been prone to them ever since the accident. His limbs seize up, curdling like spoiled milk." He brought up his hand, fingers loose, then clenched it into a tight fist. "It's obviously quite painful."

"And the medicine?" I asked, remembering the black valise.

He brightened, looking proud. "One of my own concoctions, actually. A mixture of chamomile to help soothe, cherries to fight inflammation, and willow bark. There're other things incorporated too, of course."

"Of course," I echoed, feeling uneasy at his pleasant tone, as though we were sharing afternoon tea and Alex wasn't upstairs, writhing in pain. Or rendered unconscious. I couldn't decide which was worse.

"And every bit of it was grown right here," he added, waving his arm across the greenhouse.

"I didn't realize the plants were used for anything more than decoration," I admitted, glancing about his worktable. "Or perfumes. Alexander makes them sound so—"

"Frivolous," he guessed, a quick look of displeasure flashing over his face.

I couldn't pretend otherwise.

Gerard sighed. "That boy only sees what he wants to. . . . My work is so much more than pretty petals and scents. Look at these plants, Verity. They're beautiful, certainly, but the work I do here is important. It has meaning. These plants contain medicine, have healing properties. They can ease Alexander's spasms, take the ache from his limbs. They heal burns, cure sickness, banish scars. These plants—things my son holds in such low esteem—hold the powers of life and death."

"Death?" I glanced up toward where I assumed Alex's window was.

"See the section over there?"

I followed the point of his fingertip and saw a plot isolated, carefully kept from the rest of the greenhouse. It was bordered by a tall gate made of wrought-iron filigree. Grimacing metal skulls leered down from the top points of the fencing. They were such an unexpected sight in this world of green, growing things, my breath caught sharply in my throat. "What is that?"

"Complete ruination," Gerard said, awestruck. He picked up a pair of work gloves and offered them to me. Once I'd put them on, he removed another pair from a flap on his vest and suited up. "Come with me, only don't touch or smell anything."

"Smell?" I asked, but he was too busy at the latch to respond.

The gate let out a shriek of scraping metal as he opened it.

"You ought to have that oiled," I commented, unsure if I wanted to step over.

"I've kept it that way for years," he said with a smile. "I'm the only one who has the key to the greenhouse, but I usually leave it unlocked while working—in case Dauphine or Alexander need me. If anyone else should sneak in, while I'm in the middle of something, to try and ferry out any of these plants . . ."

He whipped the gate back and forth. "It's like an alarm system, you see?"

I felt sick. What kind of plants needed these security measures?

"Come, come." We wandered down the central path. "What do you see?"

I turned in a circle, looking at the caged plants with a critical eye. The tension in my chest dissipated, like fog burning off under a morning sun. "Everything looks so . . . normal."

He chuckled. "That's the great misconception of plants. People believe themselves so superior to the rest of the living world—we're civilized, we ride in fancy carriages and create lasting pieces of art and fall in love. We must be so far above all of the dirt and weeds and *this*." He pointed to a short tree with an ugly, thick trunk. The leaves were dark green points and a few orange orbs hung from the branches. "*Strychnos nux-vomica*. If you were to breathe in the ground seeds of those fruits, convulsions would overtake you within minutes. Before the hour was out, you'd be dead."

He pulled me down another path, stopping before a patch of green shoots topped with lovely little purple bells.

"We have these on the grounds of Highmoor," I said, bending down to examine the spotted tubular blossoms. I looked up in alarm. "Should we get rid of them?"

Gerard chuckled. "Foxglove doesn't often kill, but it can wreak havoc on your digestive system and heart if an antidote isn't supplied."

I glanced warily at the dainty blooms. Now that I knew the secrets they held, they suddenly seemed strange and suspicious.

"Would you like to see my prized jewel?"

"I . . . I suppose?" I swallowed back a growing lump of fear.

He helped me to my feet and brought us to the center of the poison garden. Gerard held out his hand to a shrub nearly as tall me, as if at court, presenting a grand dame. "I give you *Atropa belladonna*."

Small, bruised-looking flowers nestled between its leaves, and scatterings of dark berries glistened seductively in the morning light.

"One of the most dangerous plants in all the known world," he said, staring in rapt wonder. "She's the only specimen I've ever been able to grow to maturity. The seeds are nearly impossible to germinate. But look at her. Isn't she magnificent? So lovely, so deadly. Even ingesting a few berries will—"

"Stop," I interrupted. "I don't want to know."

He tilted his head, as if unable to fathom my aversion. "I only thought—"

I turned away from the plant, itching to free myself from this garden of death. The greenery—which had seemed so benign, so lovely, only moments before—now leaned toward us with malicious intent, as if plotting our demise with eager glee.

I fled past plants with pale, starry-shaped leaves and spiky blossoms as red as blisters, trees dangling trails of flowers so yellow they looked like vomit, a thick hedge that smelled strangely of almonds, tickling my nose with terrible persistence. My vision swam before me, spinning too light, too bright, and I felt my knees give way. My head struck the lavender-chipped tiles and the world went black.

20

EVERYTHING CAME SCREAMING BACK IN A RIOT OF colors that burned too bright, leaving trails of glowing comets dancing across my corneas.

"Verity? Verity!" Gerard said, leaning over to shake me. Points of light shot out from his face; his eyes burned like sizzling embers. He looked radiant. He looked like a god.

My head throbbed, every beat of my heart pulsing too strong, sending erratic reverberations echoing through my limbs.

A sudden swing of movement seemed to suggest I'd sat up, but when I stared ahead, all I saw were panes of the greenhouse windows. They twirled like a prismatic kaleidoscope, iridescently hued and bursting with wonder.

"Verity," a voice called out, teasing and flippant.

I turned to see my sisters, my six dead sisters, there in the greenhouse.

Ava's skin still erupted in plague pustules. Octavia's limbs splayed out in angles so wrong I felt as though I might grow sick. Elizabeth's wrists dripped bathwater and blood onto the ground below, wetting the dry earth like a warm summer rain.

"You're not here," I muttered, and my tongue felt too thick and sluggish, a sausage casing stuffed too full and on the verge of splitting. "You're not here because you're dead."

"Verity," the voice said again.

Gerard.

I think.

I blinked, struggling to keep my eyes on my sisters. They wanted to turn, wanted to roll back, back into my head, back into the welcoming embrace of oblivion, back into the bleak, black nothing.

"Verity . . ."

My eyes snapped open. Snapped toward the voice.

Only it wasn't Gerard who'd been speaking.

Her skin was pale and ashen. Long streaks of black hair showered down her shoulders, wafting in a breeze that I absolutely knew wasn't in the greenhouse. She smiled, revealing sharpened gray teeth, and her eyes . . .

I whimpered, pushing myself backward, trying to get away from them but they pinned me in place, a butterfly staked through its middle to a mounting board. Deep pools of black stared down at me, mesmerizing and hypnotic. There was no white, no iris. Just oily, writhing black.

"Verity . . . ," she said, drawing my name out like we were playing a game, caught in the middle of a dance. She blinked and the black—the awful, horrible black—came rolling down her cheeks, staining her face with streaks of malevolence.

"What an odd expression on your face," she mused, tilting her head with playfulness that read as strained and strange and utterly wrong. "It's as though you're surprised to see me."

"I . . . I . . ." My head felt heavy, listing to one side as I struggled to speak.

"You look like a fish out of water, dear heart. Though"—she paused, looking around the greenhouse—"I suppose you rather are."

"Who . . . who are you?"

The black eyes flashed, their luster as cold as snakeskin. "Don't you remember? We're old friends, you and I."

"We're not." I fought to push myself up, even as white, threadlike roots inexplicably grew out of my arms, splitting open my skin, burrowing deep into the soil, and securing me in place. Vines from nearby trees crept in to wrap themselves around my ankles, spiraling up my legs, digging into my flesh as I squirmed from their groping grasp. Creeping green things burst from my chest, blooming into nightmarish flowers that snapped and bit at me. "I don't know you."

"Of course you do. I know you . . . I know them . . . ," she said, glancing back to my sisters.

Eulalie, her head hanging low against her chest, collarbones shattered, vertebrae crushed, raised her hand and offered us both a little wave. "Verity," she said, sounding sadder than I could ever remember hearing her.

My mind struggled against the thought, bucking like a horse gone mad.

I *couldn't* remember hearing her.

Not Eulalie.

Could I?

"Verity," the black-eyed woman crooned. "I need you to listen to me, girl. I need you to hear me well."

I blinked and she was gone, off me and across the greenhouse, in the trees, hanging down from branches miles away.

"Can you hear me?" she mouthed, and I *did* hear her, her voice directly in my ear, in my mind, thrumming through my bloodstream, squirming and sick.

Weakly, I nodded.

"Good," she said, and in an instant, she was back, her weight pressing me farther into the earth. "You need to leave this place." She leaned forward, digging her pointed elbows into my neck and cutting off my breath. "Do you understand me? Leave Chauntilalie."

Dark stars spun over my eyes and I felt as though I were gasping for air even though my mouth was heavy and full.

"Do you hear me, Verity?" the wraith asked, but I couldn't respond.

Peat and loam coated my mouth. I was suffocating on soil.

"Verity?" Her face was so close to mine, too close. Her eyes swam large, growing bigger and bigger until all I saw was the endless stretch of their inky depths.

"Verity!"

A swift hand came out of the terrifying void and slapped me hard across the cheek.

I sat up, gasping, wincing at a world gone too bright.

Gerard sat beside me on a wicker lounging chair. We were outdoors, in the garden. I could feel the fresh air against my face. The woman—the monster—was nowhere to be seen. My sisters were gone, leaving only an echo of Eulalie's forlorn voice in my mind.

"Oh thank Arina," Gerard praised, out of breath as though he'd just sprinted a marathon.

Someone out of sight pressed a glass into my hands and Gerard helped me tip it back, letting the cold water flow down my throat, bringing back a rush of clarity.

"What . . . what happened?"

"The laurel hedge," he stated, as if it explained it all. "I'd pruned it this morning. I didn't even think—" He stopped, berating himself with a string of curses beneath his breath. "It was so foolish of me."

"I don't . . . I don't understand."

"The sap of a laurel tree contains a powerful poison. . . . When you prune the branches, you must take great care not to breathe in the fumes. . . . I'd had the doors open to air everything out. I certainly didn't think it would linger so long, or that you'd be so affected. I've been working in the greenhouse all morning without seeing a thing."

"Seeing." I licked my lips. "What is it I'm meant to have seen?"

Gerard's shoulders rose. "People have reported seeing hallucinations, having nightmarish comas they couldn't wake from. Sometimes their throats seize up—they suffocate on their own blistered tongues." He blinked down at me. "I can never apologize enough for this. I can't believe I was so careless."

"So . . . it was like a dream?" I asked, a wave of relief washing over me.

Only a dream.

Not me.

Not my mind.

Not truly.

Gerard frowned. "It's hard to say. Some people believe it's more than that. That it's an experience, doors opening up to other worlds.

A portal to realms beyond ours. I've read many accounts from survivors saying they saw all sorts of unimaginable wonders. Some even claim to have spoken with the gods." Gerard leaned forward. "Is that who you saw?"

"Who I saw . . . ," I repeated.

The woman with her weeping eyes.

She'd not been human, that much was abundantly clear.

Could she have been a god?

I opened my mouth, forming the answer.

I wanted to tell him. I wanted to tell him everything.

The ghosts.

This god.

But what would Gerard think of me?

Surely a girl with the capacity for such terrible thoughts—Eulalie's drooping clavicle swayed in my memory—such terrible visions, was not the right choice for his son.

Camille's words haunted me.

No one is going to want a mad little fiancée, for a mad little wife, issuing out mad little children. You'd be ruined forever.

But it wasn't my fault.

I wasn't mad.

It was the laurel.

Wasn't it?

"There was no laurel on the night you saw those women," a little voice deep in my head taunted.

Those were peacocks.

"Hanna wasn't. Hanna Whitten who has been dead and gone these last twelve years," it reminded.

Stop it.

Stop it right now.

"It's not dreams and it's not the laurel," the voice insisted, sounding uncannily like the weeping woman. *"It's only ever been you."*

I took a great swallow of water, choking back the scream fighting to break out.

Gerard could never know. Any of it. I couldn't risk my relationship with Alex, my place at Chauntilalie, the very security of my future over this.

I couldn't.

"I can't remember," I lied, then took another gulp of water.

"There must be something," he insisted, a strange light growing in his eyes. "It seemed to affect you so strongly. You can tell me, Verity. Even if it's just a fragment of memory." His hand fell over mine, covering it with the appearance of concern.

I shook my head. "There's nothing. Truly."

"You called out several times."

I shrugged helplessly.

"You spoke to someone. You seemed afraid of them." He squeezed my fingers, his grip unusually tight.

"I wasn't . . . I can't remember." I felt pinned in place, unable to break free of his grasp or from his fervent gaze. "Gerard, you're hurting me," I gasped.

Instantly, he released his hold. "I'm . . . I'm so sorry, Verity. I'm not sure what came over me." He pushed back a lock of hair. "Perhaps I breathed in too much of the laurel myself. . . ." He reached out as if to smooth away any lingering pain in my hand but then froze, thinking the better of it. "I'm deeply sorry."

"It's all right," I said, trying to hide away the quiver I felt. "It's been a strange day for everyone."

He nodded gratefully. "Indeed. Indeed."

"I should like to return to my rooms now," I said, struggling to stand up from the chaise.

"Of course, yes. I'll escort you there," he offered, jumping to his feet and lending out an arm.

"No," I said hastily. "I . . . I know you've so much work that needs tending to. And . . . you'll want to air out the greenhouse more, of course."

Gerard looked chagrined. "Of course. Of course, yes. I will make sure to do that."

I took an unsteady step from him. Then another. "Good. Thank you." I was two steps up the terrace before he stopped me.

"Verity."

The sound of my name on his lips, an exact echo of how Eulalie had spoken it, made me wince.

How had I remembered Eulalie's voice?

I turned.

"If you do remember anything, you'll let me know, won't you?"

A flurry of trembles fluttered through me and despite the heat of the day, I suddenly felt painfully cold. "Of course," I lied.

Gerard smiled and turned back toward the greenhouse.

21

MY ROOMS WERE BLESSEDLY FREE OF SERVANTS when I returned, feeling as though I were shaking apart from the inside.

"Water," I muttered, coaching myself through the rising panic welling within me. My throat felt dry all the way down to my stomach. With trembling hands, I poured a tall glass from my bedside pitcher and chugged it back fast, not stopping until it was empty. "More."

I imagined the water running down my throat and pushing the last of the laurel nightmare from me, cleaning away any remaining traces of that wicked woman.

Still, it wasn't enough.

I stared at the empty pitcher and was about to pull the plush chain dangling at the side of the bed when something Hanna once told me stirred in my mind.

Whenever something's troubling you, you always turn to the water.

I nodded at the sage wisdom of her phantom voice.

I just needed more water.

Ropes of gilt flowers wound themselves round the rose-gold faucet. The water rushed into the sunken tub. Rows of glass bottles lined the bathroom's vanity, filled with salts, flakes, oils, and dried flowers. I opened them without thought, pouring messy and extravagant amounts into the tub. They bloomed across the water in a beguiling purple hue, shimmering with iridescent luster, and perfuming the air.

I didn't care about any of it, the colors, the redolent scents. I just wanted to get into the water.

I struggled out of my blouse and skirt. They clung to me in the steamy air and I nearly tore my chemise to be free of it. I felt slowly strangled, the snug embrace of my corset reminding me too uncomfortably of the vines creeping over my skin. My fingers shook as I undid the final set of hooks and eyes and tossed the garment to the floor.

I all but fell into the dazzling water.

The tub was exceptionally deep and long and I dove beneath the surface, completely submerging myself for as long as my lungs could stand.

When I finally bobbed back up, the water rose past my chest, coming up to my chin. I turned one of the handles with a flick of my toes and the faucet's steady stream slowed to a trickle before petering out. I inhaled deeply, basking in my wet surroundings and finally feeling as though I could draw in a proper breath.

The water was warm and comforting, surrounding me in an embrace that felt of home. I stretched out, lying on my back, and stared up at the painted ceiling. Leaves, blossoms, and birds edged its surface, thick at the sides, then tapering off as they approached the small, vined chandelier in the center of the room.

My body swayed back and forth, tossed on the momentum of the little ripples pacing about. I'd obviously cleaned myself since coming to Chauntilalie but this was the first time I'd truly stopped to appreciate the wonders of the room, of the tub.

The water was unusually slippery, flowing over my limbs with sensuous caresses and I glanced at the half-empty bottles of oils, feeling guilty I'd blindly used up so much of them in my haste.

I'd replace them later.

For now, all I wanted was to close my eyes and let the water soothe my frayed nerves. I could already feel the tension in my head disappearing, breaking away from me as calved glaciers fell into the sea, melting smaller and smaller until they were nothing more than water themselves.

When I finally emerged from the bath, the pads of my fingers and toes were wrinkled as prunes but I felt like myself once more.

Being in the water had given me a chance to think, unencumbered, to put together all of the swirling fears that had plagued me since that fateful night at Highmoor, when I'd first seen Rosalie and Ligeia roaming the halls.

Camille believed I saw ghosts and after having listened to Hanna, having seen her flicker, and feel my hand pass through her, I believed she was right.

Ghosts were real. I could see them.

But that did not make me mad.

What happened to me in the poison garden . . . that was less certain and felt impossible to clearly explain.

My sisters—my long-dead sisters—had been there.

If they were ghosts, and I knew ghosts were real, what did that make the weeping woman?

Real, certainly, but a ghost?

Not necessarily.

Gerard's theory, that the toxins in the laurel plant were powerful enough to open up a portal in the mind, a thin spot between worlds where wonders grand and dreadful could be experienced, seemed plausible. And if I was already the sort of person prone to seeing otherworldly figures . . .

Had I seen a god? Or was there a more rational explanation?

Was it a hallucination? A poisoning of my mind? A mind full of locked away memories, memories long forgotten that could be turned into something strange and monstrous?

Or . . .

Could it be even easier to explain away?

None of the things had happened to me. Not ghosts, not gods, because it was all in my head. Something within me was broken and twisted and wrong.

Was I mad?

I didn't feel like I was.

And wasn't the fact that I was even entertaining this line of thought, carefully rationed out and logically presented, evidence that I was not?

Camille had put that poisonous thought within me, instilling me with fear and doubt, a sharp burr intended to forever poke at me, ruining any chance I might have at a normal life away from her and Highmoor.

With sudden resolve, I threw on my robe and crossed to the

little writing desk where another unfinished letter to Camille still waited. I seized the paper and began to rip it in two pieces, then four, then eight, methodically destroying the last of my guilt in leaving as I had. I had no need to apologize. I'd done nothing wrong.

When the paper was nothing but bits of confetti, too mangled to ever repair, I tossed it into the waste bin and sat back in the chair, only now noticing the late hour.

Twilight had washed over the world, painting the sky a rosy lavender. A scattering of stars twinkled brightly and an enormous crescent moon hung just above the tree line, looking wistful and dreamy.

I took a deep breath, grounding myself in the moment. This was where I wanted to be. Not back at Highmoor, forever under my sister's thumb, always wanting things beyond my reach.

I wanted to be here. To stay here. With Alex.

As if bidden by my thoughts, a soft knock rapped on the door.

"Come in," I called out from the chair, and brightened when I saw him.

"Stay there, stay there," Alex said as I struggled to stand. He rolled over to me instead, cupping his hands on my cheeks with concern as he assessed me. "I'm so sorry I didn't come sooner. I only just woke and heard what happened. Are you all right?"

His hands felt warm on my forehead as he checked my temperature and I pulled them away, tangling our fingers together. "Are *you* all right?"

He seemed slightly off-color and there were circles under his eyes dark enough to look like bruises. He was dressed in his pajamas, a plush emerald robe tied about him, and his hair was rumpled from sleep. I could picture exactly what he must have looked like as a little boy.

Alex nodded. "The pains are gone now. Father's tinctures always help to ease them away but I'm so sorry you heard all—"

"Stop," I interrupted. "You don't need to apologize for that, for any of that. I was so concerned for you."

"Then I'm sorry for *that*," he insisted. "I feel terrible. I should have told you about the fits, but I haven't had one in so long, I'd hoped that they were somehow over. I hate that I worried you."

"Did something happen to trigger it?" Our afternoon picnics, our adventures about the estate. Was he pushing himself too much for my sake?

"I don't think so. They usually come and go without rhyme or reason. This one was . . . particularly bad, but it's over now."

The pads of my thumbs traced the bumps of his knuckles. "You shouldn't be out of bed. You should be resting."

His grip tightened, as if afraid I was about to send him away. "I had to come see you. When Father said what happened, I could hardly see straight." His voice cracked. "I raced over as fast as I could. I just kept imagining the worst and . . . I can't believe he could have done something so dangerous. So stupid." He pushed the back of his hand over his eyes. "That garden needs to be destroyed."

"Alex—"

"It does," he insisted. "What if you'd touched a different plant? What if I had lost you? Verity. I . . . I couldn't . . ." He pressed his forehead to mine as his words failed, pulling me into a close embrace around the chair.

I closed my eyes, leaning into his arms. In them I felt safe.

It was impossible to think of ghosts or wraiths. It was only Alex. Only us.

"Your hair," he murmured, his fingers slipping over the dark tangles.

"It's still wet, I'm sorry," I said, pulling away, certain the long strands had soaked him.

But he was smiling. "I've never seen it down before. It's so long. So beautiful." He cleared his throat as if embarrassed by his admission. "*You* are so beautiful."

He traced his fingers down my cheeks and I was suddenly, acutely aware that neither of us wore anything but nightclothes. Alex's eyes flickered over the tassels of our robes, tangled together. His dark green and gold, mine a light jade.

"What a pair we make," he murmured.

Breathing felt too heavy an act. Speaking, impossible. I nodded.

"Tell me the truth—are you all right?"

"I am now," I promised.

"I've heard the most horrible stories of people who—"

"Alex," I said, trying to cut him off.

"I'm sorry, I just . . . I had this awful image in my mind that when I came in, you wouldn't be here, that you'd be . . ." He swallowed back the thought. "And I . . . I'm not ready to live in a world without you, Verity."

"I'm here. I'm better. I'm not going anywhere."

His hands framed my face, cupping my cheeks and directing my gaze to him. "I love you," he said clearly, breaking through my assurances. "I'm trying to tell you I love you."

My breath caught, stilling me.

Alex's eyes were impossibly large, earnest and vulnerable, as he waited for my response. I could feel the weight of his anticipation, his hope, pressing against me with tangible heft. I did not want to let him down. "You love me?"

"It's probably too soon to say it—much too soon, I'm sure—but the feelings are there. They're true and they're real, and, Verity, I love you."

"I—"

He stopped me with a swift finger to my lips. "You don't have to say it just because I did. I know . . . I know we've only known each other for a few weeks, a month, at the most, but I've loved every moment of our time together, talking and laughing—you've no idea how much I love to see you laugh. When we're apart, I count down the minutes, the seconds till I get to see you again. Sometimes I feel as though I've lost my mind, but I know I haven't. I just . . ."

"Oh, Alex." Even in my confusion, a smile broke across my face. I felt like a flower, turning its face to bask in the sun's warmth.

I didn't love him, not yet, not in the way he described, with fervor and zest, but I appreciated him. I enjoyed his company, respected his thoughts, worried over his welfare.

That was love, wasn't it? Of a sort?

"I care about you too." The words were out of my mouth and I meant them.

The foundation was there. The rest would come later.

I was sure of it.

He froze, his relief palpable. "You do?"

I nodded, determined. "I do."

Alex's breath came out in a rush. "Really?"

"Really."

With a whoop of joy, he leaned forward, catching my mouth in his.

Instantly I froze, surprised by the sudden change from conversation to intimacy. His lips moved over mine, gentle but persistent. How did he know how to do this? I didn't dare reciprocate, terrified any movement would be wrong.

His fingers curved at the back of my neck and I marveled at how confidently he touched me. Wasn't he concerned I might think him too forward? Didn't he worry I might not find his caresses appealing?

Alex murmured noises of appreciation, drawing me farther into my tailspin of thoughts. Shouldn't he sense I wasn't with him in this moment, as present and eager to explore him as he seemed to me? We shared everything with one another, all of our thoughts and dreams. Now we should be together in this physical space and I couldn't help but feel left behind.

His breath deepened with obvious enjoyment.

He was enjoying these kisses.

Why wasn't I? What was wrong with me?

Let me get this right, I thought, finally daring to let my fingertips rest on his shoulders. *Pontus, please, let me do this right.*

After a moment's lingering, Alex broke away, smiling and giddy. "Would you want to meet me down by the lake tomorrow? There's something I'd love to show you."

I wanted to. I wanted to be the kind of girl who was ready to be fallen in love with. We'd been all over the estate together, without even a hint of a chaperone. So why did the thought of being alone with him suddenly fill me with dread?

There was sure to be more of this there. More kissing. More moments where I was bound to get it wrong and ruin everything.

"Tomorrow is the big soiree," I reminded him. Couldn't he hear my heart clunking out of rhythm? My face felt impossibly hot—he had to see my reddened cheeks. Did they look flushed with pleasure or like the embarrassed stain of a girl who felt in over her head?

"I know."

"Won't your mother need help with . . . things?" On the few occasions Camille had hosted any sort of event at Highmoor, the entire manor was thrown into chaos. At our breakfasts together, Dauphine had talked of nothing but the party. So many details to plan, so many specifics to work through.

"Not with all the extra footmen she's bringing in."

"But—"

"You're going to love it, I know you will. You should bring your sketchbook."

Curiosity stirred within me, strong enough to cut through the anxieties pattering through my veins.

"You really think we won't be missed?"

"Wear the gown too," he instructed. "The one Mother has been going on and on about."

"You want me to draw . . . in a ball gown?" I asked dubiously.

"You're the one who likes to draw. . . . I just want to see you in the gown." He flashed me a grin and I knew I couldn't say no.

"Tomorrow," I promised.

Alex's fingers twined through mine and he brought his lips to my palm, mirroring the gesture he made on our first meeting and sparking a little flutter of affection in my chest. I didn't mind kisses like that, soft and one-sided and with no pressure to return them.

"I should let you get some rest. I can't imagine how tired you must be." He pressed a final kiss to my forehead. His mouth was warm and tender and I ached to experience that same easy affection he so effortlessly gave away.

"Have a good night's sleep," I murmured, tentatively running my hand down his arm. It seemed overly formal and stilted but Alex smiled at me all the same.

"How could I not?" he replied, easing his chair through the room. At the threshold, he turned around to wink at me. "I'll be dreaming of you."

22

THE ROOM WAS TOO HOT.

Bedsheets knotted around my legs, as twisted and tangled as the vines of ivy growing up over Chauntilalie. I flipped my pillow over again, desperate for the cooling relief of its underside but found no comfort.

When the first peacock called out, shrieking in the humid night, I sat up with a groan.

It would be impossible to fall back asleep with those birds at it again.

On the bedside table were two candlesticks—one with Annaleigh's offering, the other with the Chauntilalie blend of pink wax. I fiddled with the little glass cloche beside them, fumbling to free a wooden match, as I pondered which of the candles to light.

Gerard's revelation that my sister's gift was meant to act as a ward against ghosts should have felt as a surprise, but the more I thought on it, I found it was not. It was a typical Annaleigh thing to do—protecting, always protecting, even when she couldn't be present herself.

As much as I wanted to dismiss the idea as an island superstition, the candles must work. I'd seen no evidence of spirits since arriving at Chauntilalie.

But you saw Hanna, that awful little voice in my head reminded me. *You saw Hanna Whitten who has been dead and gone these last twelve years light them herself. Hundreds of times. How effective could they truly be?*

But how many other ghosts had they kept me from seeing?

Highmoor, for all its grand renovations, was an old manor, centuries ancient. My sisters and parents were hardly the first Thaumases to perish within its walls.

"And I only ever saw Hanna," I told the voice, feeling foolish for speaking aloud. "Hanna, who said she fought to stay with us. To stay with *me*."

"And the triplets," it threw back. *"You saw them too."*

That detail *had* been bothering me, a tiny gnat flittering around in the back of my mind that I tried to swat aside and forget but kept returning with annoying persistence.

The night I'd watched Rosalie and Ligeia traipse through the halls, the night I learned that ghosts were real, that I had some sort of gift—

—curse—

—what had been different? Why had I seen them then and not before?

Had I been holding a candle?

Camille had tried to offer me one. I'd said no. Had she pressed it into my hand anyway? It seemed like she would have.

I can't imagine that she'd have taken no for an answer.

I just couldn't remember.

The match snapped to life with a decisive flick of my wrist and I lit Annaleigh's candle.

Better to be abundantly cautious. I could not take any chances here. Not in this house. Not with this family. Not when my future was so uncertain.

After slipping on my robe, I padded out to the parlor, looking for something to do. From a small side table, Gerard's stack of books seemed to glare up at me. I wanted to read them, truly I did, but there never seemed to be enough time.

The little clock on the mantel chimed twice and I scooped up the first book, heedless of the title, and began thumbing through the pages.

"*'Withania somnifera,'*" I read aloud, stumbling over the unfamiliar term. "Winter cherry."

The accompanying illustration showed green sprigs of leaves boasting a series of orange fruit, each covered in a wrinkled husk, like a paper lantern.

There was only a single definition for it. "Deception."

There was a small skull drawn after the definition, indicating it was a poisonous plant, and I briefly wondered if the winter cherries grew within Gerard's deadly garden.

A sudden chill lowered over me and I slammed the book shut.

I didn't want to think about what lay behind that macabre gate.

I didn't want to sit still any longer, reading pages and pages of information I could never hope to retain.

I wanted to be up.

Moving.

Exploring.

"*Dancing,*" the voice suggested.

Another shrill cry rang out, sounding as if the hateful bird had roosted right outside on the terrace.

I was out in the corridor, as far from the peacocks as I could get, before I even realized I'd made up my mind to leave the chaise.

I wandered aimlessly for a time, strolling down halls I never had cause to visit during the day. I looked for the hidden spiral staircase Gerard had shown me, staring hard at the section of wall I knew it to be behind, until I noticed a frescoed leaf that was a slightly different hue than the rest of its companions, as if it had been touched by countless fingertips. I pressed it, pleased when the door swung open, revealing the steps.

I'd never seen the manor so dark before. Weak moonlight cast strange highlights over the painted walls and hung tapestries. It really was a beautiful manor, so different from the imposing austerity of Highmoor.

Every bit of architecture, from the sweeping beams acting as the skeleton bracing up the rest of the house down to the tiny screws used to keep the door hinges in place, were works of art. I stopped before a bas-relief, taking in every detail.

It was a field of wildflowers, carved into the wall with such depth that individual buds could be seen from all sides, perfect replicas of coneflowers and poppies and a dozen other blooms I couldn't identify. I walked the relief slowly, trying to guess how long it must have taken the artist to create this one section of wall.

Off to the side, nearly hidden away in the gilded border, was a series of little bells with a wrinkled texture, almost like . . .

Almost like paper lanterns.

"*Withania somnifera,*" I exclaimed to the empty hall, delighted I'd remembered the entry I'd just read. "You don't look so dangerous when you're made out of marble," I said, running my finger over their creased surface.

A little ways down the corridor came a soft click and sigh, like a door opening, and I froze, certain an early rising footman was about to stumble across me.

I glanced over my shoulder, ready to conjure up an excuse about why I was up so late, and stopped.

It *had* been a door that opened.

A very hidden door.

Its edges were jagged and misshapen, cut along the bits of wildflowers to conceal its presence. The door had been there all along, right in front of me.

Another secret passage!

I glanced back to the seemingly innocuous winter cherries and laughed. "Deception, indeed."

The passage that lay past the door was dark, a gaping maw seemingly ready to swallow me whole. Feeling as though I were trespassing, I stuck my taper inside, trying to make out where this unexpected entry led. There was no staircase that I could see, only a narrow corridor, lined in thin lengths of wooden slats.

"Where do you go?" I asked, daring to peek inside. The hall ran longer than the light of my candle could illuminate, and after a moment's pause, I stepped inside.

Immediately, the door swung shut, blending in so well with the inner wall, I was at a loss to guess how to open it. I traced over every inch of the space, waiting for the door to swing out once more.

It remained shut.

I was trapped.

"Stuck," I said, trying to push down the wave of panic building within my chest. "You just need to see where this passage leads and then you can get out on the other end."

I traveled slowly, not wanting to miss anything that might open another door. After several dozen yards, the hall came to a fork.

"This must run the whole length of the house," I murmured, trying to visualize exactly where I was within the manor.

I chose the left turn.

It was wider, but far more crowded.

Three bookcases, towering from floor to ceiling, lined one side of the passageway. Each shelf was filled with old volumes and stacks of papers crammed in tight. I raised my candle, scanning the spines, but most of their aged ink had been rubbed away. Curiosity got the better of me and I set the candle down, grabbing the first book I saw.

I flipped through it and immediately understood why these books were kept hidden away from the open shelves of Chauntilalie's library.

I turned another page, then another, blushing madly.

It was a book of illustrations, depicting acts of intimacy among an orgy of scantily clad people. Page after page showed flushed breasts and open mouths, terrifying erect phalluses, eyes rolled back in ecstasy.

Men fondled women as others gazed on, their eyes heavy-lidded with desire. Women kissed women, running their fingers down curves of exposed flesh, slipping inside each other with a dexterity that made me squirm. Men reached out, stroking other men's . . .

I flipped the book on its side, trying to understand what exactly was happening in the drawing and snapped the book closed once I had. My heart raced with a strange, illicit thrill. I pushed the book back into its place on the shelf, feeling a hot stain spread across my chest.

Though I'd never so much as held anyone's hand before coming to Chauntilalie, I had a vague understanding of what transpired behind closed doors. But I'd never dreamed it could be so . . . inventive.

I glanced at the multitudes of books with an uneasy hunger. I could barely make it through kissing Alexander without freezing in panic, unsure of myself and what I was meant to be doing. The people in the drawings not only seemed to understand what to do, but they also *relished* it, making the wanton acts seem exciting. Something to be enjoyed. Desirable.

Perhaps . . .

I pushed the wicked thought away, even as my hand reached for another volume.

It couldn't hurt to look again.

It might even help.

What were books for if not instruction?

This book was different from the other, a journal, filled with Gerard's familiar, cramped scrawl.

I ran my fingers over his tiny printing.

The book was filled with words I didn't know and I wondered if he was writing in a code. Every so often there were little drawings made in the margins. Plants, I guessed, though they were unlike anything I'd ever seen before. One drawing spanned an entire two pages—a triangular base, with a pair of orblike blooms sprouting from either side of its top. There was a strange musculature to it, reminding me of an anatomy book I'd once seen in Annaleigh's collection on Hesperus.

I put it back with a shudder and withdrew another.

Another journal, but this one I could read.

Mostly.

It was a list of names.

A list of women's names.

A very long list of women's names, I realized, flipping through the pages.

Here and there were dates, spanning over a decade, with more words I didn't understand jotted beside the women's names. Some had brackets beneath them, listing others' names, always in sets of three.

I flashed back to one of the illustrations in the other book, a group of people all engaged in pleasuring each other, together. Was that . . . was that what I was looking at? Alex had said his father was a man of insatiable appetites. Had he documented every one of his intimate encounters, not only recording those involved but also making a coded list of what had been performed? There were so many names within the book. . . .

Poor Dauphine.

I pushed the book back onto the shelf and picked up my candle once more.

My stomach felt queasy as I imagined Gerard with so many others, re-creating the pictures I'd just seen. I wanted to get out of this hidden hallway, wanted to get as far from the books and the dark ideas within them as I could. I stumbled down the path, taking a right, then a left, before ending at a stone staircase.

Peering up into the void, I could make out the faint shine of metal hinges.

A door!

It opened easily, spilling me out into the hallway not far from my suite of rooms.

I closed it softly, marveling at how perfectly the edges of the door were concealed in a pattern of wallpaper, then heard approaching footsteps and the soft hum of someone singing off-key to themselves.

Gerard! The last person in the world I wanted to see.

My room was too far to duck into so I lunged for the door nearest me, cursing under my breath as the handle rattled uselessly. It was locked.

Before I could turn tail, Gerard rounded the corner. Finding me in the hallway, he stopped short, squinting in the dim light.

"Verity?"

"I . . ." I tried the door again, knowing it would not help me but still hoping for a way to escape. "I was just looking for . . ." I trailed off, every excuse sounding impossibly wrong in my mind.

"That's my study," he said, remaining in place, watching me carefully.

"Is it?" My hand fell from the cut-glass knob.

The space between us felt as wide as a canyon but my feet still itched to get farther away.

"It is."

"I wasn't going to . . ." I wasn't sure what I was about to deny doing and stopped. "It's locked."

He fussed with his cravat for a moment before pulling free a silver key, dangling from a chain round his neck. "It's one of the only doors in the manor kept that way," he said. "As a duke, there are many sensitive papers that need to be kept under lock and key."

It was a simple explanation. "Of course."

"Your sister undoubtedly does the same with hers."

I nodded.

He slid the key back under his shirt. "Is there anything I can help you with?"

I took a step backward, unwanted memories of the illustrations flashing in my mind. "No. Thank you. I . . . I should be getting back to my room. Back to sleep," I clarified, finally acknowledging the lateness of the hour. I offered out a quick smile before turning toward my rooms.

"Bad dreams?" he asked, calling after me and forcing me to look back.

"Hmm?"

"You're up late. Did you have bad dreams? I shouldn't wonder after everything that happened today."

"No," I said swiftly, stopping him before he could press again about what I'd seen in the poison garden. "I . . . I was up late, reading the books you loaned me and . . . there were phrases I didn't know," I said, grabbing onto the excuse as it came to me. "About the flowers. Botanical terms. I thought I'd go to the library."

"The library," he repeated in a tone so even I couldn't tell whether or not he believed me.

I nodded, falling into the story. "For a dictionary. I wanted to be able to ask you questions about the books later without sounding foolish."

Gerard smiled, looking pleased. "You didn't find it?"

I cocked my head, not following.

"The dictionary."

I glanced down at my hands, only holding the candlestick. Quick as a wink, he removed the key once more, unlocking the study door before I could stop him. He ducked inside and returned with a thick tome.

"This should be able to help with whatever you're looking for," he said, offering it out to me.

I cradled the oversized book to my chest. "Thank you. This will be most helpful."

Gerard nodded, remaining on the threshold of the study.

"What are you doing up so late?" I asked, edging back toward my rooms. "Or early? It feels early, doesn't it?" I licked my lips, trying not to prattle as more images from his hidden cache of books returned to me.

"Late, I think," he said. "I just left the greenhouse. There's a bit of correspondence I need to get out at first light."

"I'll let you get to that, then," I said, grateful for the conversation coming to an end. "Thank you for the dictionary."

"Of course. Good night, Verity."

"Good night, Gerard," I echoed as he began to edge the study door shut.

I was nearly to my room before he called out. "Don't read too late into the night. Dauphine's soiree is tomorrow. I'm sure you'll want to look your absolute best for all of the excitement."

"Of course," I said, turning back to glance at him.

He was standing in the middle of the hallway now, watching me with an unreadable expression.

I closed my door with a quick swish, turning the locking mechanism slowly, so he wouldn't hear the click.

23

THE MORNING DAWNED IN SHADES OF SCARLET AND crimson. The sky looked like a bolt of bloody satin unfurled and every bit of my island upbringing cringed, feeling the storm that was bound to set in later.

From the parlor terrace, I watched the flurry of activity in the garden as footmen hung strings of lanterns and set out series of candles across railings and parapets.

Poor Dauphine.

So much effort, doomed to be washed away.

There was a rustling noise from inside the room behind me, and I turned.

A young woman, blond with dark eyes and only a few years older than myself, was in the middle of the sitting room, creeping toward the mannequin form Dauphine had sent up earlier. My gown had arrived late yesterday, and she'd already had it steamed and fluffed to perfection.

It was an enormous confection of lavender, blush, and champagne tulle. The skirt was gathered and as puffed as a meringue, but remarkably lightweight, as though a cloud had floated down to earth, deciding to adorn me. The bodice was wickedly sheer, cleverly embroidered with flowers in beads and metallic thread to cover my breasts. Echoes of the same flowers were embroidered into every other layer of the skirt, so that when I walked, there was an impression of blossoms in the misty swell, but they'd disappear before you were certain of what your eyes saw.

She reached out to touch the silk tulle with unchecked hunger, but then seemed to think better of it and her hand was left raised, poised and frozen midair.

She was the first maid I'd seen at Chauntilalie. It had been strange to notice the overwhelming presence of so many footmen and valets but given Gerard's extramarital proclivities, it gave me a deep sense of amusement, imagining Dauphine's clever workaround.

Which made this girl—so young and quite pretty—an unlikely presence.

I froze, glancing to the candlestick I'd used last night, its taper now nothing more than a melted stump.

Was this maid truly here or did she belong to another Chauntilalie household, one long gone and forgotten?

Her hair was plaited into a simple, timeless braid but her dress—a smock of blue linen—was peculiar in style and very poorly fitted. The waist seemed to be cut higher in the front than at the back and seemed far too large on her.

"Good morning," I called out, curious to see if the would-be ghost would acknowledge me.

The young woman startled, as if she'd been unaware of my presence on the terrace. She dipped her head in greeting to cover her surprise.

"Good morning."

So she *could* see me.

"Did . . . did Dauphine send you up to help me dress?" I watched her carefully, waiting for the moment when she'd briefly flicker, giving away her state.

"It looks quite complicated," she observed, circling the mannequin to understand the gown's intricacies without answering my question.

A row of eighteen buttons hung as if by magic across the delicate netting of the back, like couture vertebrae. One wrong snag by me and the entire bodice would be ruined.

"I suppose so," I murmured, keeping a steady eye upon her. I was certain there would be some otherworldly tell about her, but she moved easily about the room, a solid shape, occupying exactly the right amount of space.

Doubt tickled my throat.

"You won't be able to wear a corset."

I shook my head, feeling a blush rise over my chest. "Is that . . . is that a common practice in Bloem? To leave oneself . . . so exposed?"

She shrugged, eyes fixed on the long, sheer sleeves. "There's nothing exactly common about fashion, is there? The moment something becomes everyday, it's already stale and forgotten for the next new thing."

I took a step closer to her. "But will people . . . Do you think they'll think me . . . too loose?" Feigning concern, I reached out to touch her shoulder, nearly laughing in relief as I felt the tangible heft of her body.

I'd been quick to jump to conclusions.

This maid was as real as I was.

My mind, exhausted after the night of fitful sleep, was playing tricks on me.

The young woman finally met my gaze, her lips twisted in a smirk. "You'll be the most modestly dressed one there."

My eyebrows rose with surprise.

"I suppose I can help you," she said.

"Oh, thank you," I said, ignoring the peculiarity of her phrasing as I stepped into the center of the sitting room, away from the furniture. I'd already pinned my hair up in a crown of braids and flowers and wore my garters and stockings beneath my robe. "I don't think we've ever been introduced," I said, feeling self-conscious as she stripped the robe away, leaving me completely exposed.

With an expert flick of her fingers, the maid unfastened the row of buttons and eased the dress up and over the mannequin's frame. Wordlessly, she hoisted it over my head, helping me through the long sleeves and making sure everything settled where it should. I felt her begin to work on the buttons and then she stepped to the front of me, studying everything with a critical gaze.

"I'm Verity," I added.

"I know." She blinked at me, her dark brown eyes flat. "Will you need help with your shoes?"

I glanced toward my bedroom where a new pair of slippers waited, butter-soft leather, flecked with champagne and gold shimmers. I'd seen them in a store window, and though Dauphine claimed a young lady ought to live in heels, I'd been inexplicably drawn to them.

Wordlessly, I shook my head.

"Are you sure . . ." Her voice trailed off and I sensed she was questioning something greater than the shoes. "Are you sure you want all this?"

I shifted from foot to foot in the gown, acutely aware of the enormous footprint it took up. "Honestly . . . no. Dauphine picked out this style. It's a bit too much for my taste."

She narrowed her eyes, looking at me as if I were incredibly stupid. "Not the dress. This. All this." She waved her hand about the room. "All them."

"The Laurents?"

She nodded.

"You ought to be careful," she said, swiftly cutting me off before I could respond. "You . . . you seem like a good person. You shouldn't let them hurt you."

"Hurt me?" My mouth dropped open. "Alex would never—"

"Not him," she hissed. Her head darted toward the door as the sound of approaching footsteps rang out. "I think we're all done here. Enjoy your party."

Before I could protest, she bustled out of the room and disappeared down the hall.

༄

"Oh my dear, you look like a dream but it's far too early to be dressed," Dauphine said, looking up from her desk as I walked into her private parlor.

"Alex wanted to show me something before the party tonight. . . . He asked if I'd wear this."

Her eyes flashed with understanding. "Oh, how wonderful! Then I won't keep you long. . . . I only wanted to give you an itinerary for the day . . . but it seems you've already checked off most of your list. Turn for me?"

I spun around slowly for her inspection, the layers of tulle fluttering.

"That shade of purple is perfect with your coloring," she murmured. "You look positively ethereal. If the Sisters of the Ardor saw you, they'd snatch you up to serve Arina for the rest of your days." She let out a soft sigh. "Alexander will be utterly smitten."

I glanced down at the skirts, feeling a coil of nerves unspool in my belly. His affection was not whose I worried for most. "You think so?"

"I know it." She stood up and took my hands, beaming at me. "I hope you know how happy you make him. Before you came to us . . . he was always so shrouded away in his own thoughts, his own world. I knew he was lonely but I wasn't sure how to help him, what to do. . . . You've brought him out, made him shine. I can't thank you enough for what you've done for him."

"I care for him immensely," I promised, telling myself that as much as her.

Dauphine nodded. "Anyone with eyes can see it. You both flow so well together. It's lovely to watch. When Gerard and I were courting . . . it was a different time, I suppose." She offered out a small smile, and deep in my sparkling slippers, my toes curled. "There are a thousand different ways for a couple to love one another, and here in Bloem, each of them is as important and valid as the other."

My mouth ran dry as she danced around the subject. "Do you

think . . . Is he planning . . ." I faltered, the thought too giant to wield. "Do you know where Alex is taking me today?"

She shrugged, though it seemed clear she had an idea of it. "Wherever it is, don't be gone too long. We'll have much to celebrate tonight."

༄

Alex was going to propose.

Today.

I was absolutely certain of it.

I hurried down the halls of Chauntilalie, the massive volume of skirts flying behind me like a boat's wake. Footmen jumped out of the way but my mind was too fixed on Dauphine's words to take notice of their horrified, confused faces.

We'll have much to celebrate, she'd said.

What else was I to assume that meant?

A proposal.

Of marriage.

To Alex.

A flutter of nerves drove me into an alcove, safely tucked away from the hustle and bustle of the party preparation. A quiet place where I could be alone with my thoughts. Alone with my terror.

"Marriage," I gasped, hands trembling.

It shouldn't have been a shock; any fool could see the trajectory of our paths. We'd begun our courtship. He'd declared his love. Dauphine had all but winked as I left her.

I pressed my forehead to the windowpane, letting its cool surface soothe my fevered thoughts.

"It's Alex," I reminded myself. "He's a good man. He's going to become a *great* man." My breath steadied and I felt a sliver of calm wedge itself under my ribs, easing its way through the rest of me. "This is what you wanted."

I nodded.

Alex's wife.

I stilled, meditating on the phrase, imagining what my life would look like, forever entangled with his. I pictured his face grown old, wrinkles and silver hair claiming the planes and shapes I'd grown to know so well. I saw his hand, thicker now and spotted with age, take mine, holding it with a soft fondness as we sat on a garden bench, his nose in a book, a sketchpad across my lap. Alyssums bloomed all around us.

My heart stretched, warm and bright.

This was more than a daydream.

It felt like a vision.

A prophecy.

An omen of good luck.

We would have a happy life together.

Full of peace and certainty, I opened my eyes and immediately jumped.

Alex was on the other side of the window, watching me with intense eyes. Before I could call out a greeting, he turned and walked away.

My mouth fell open as wild confusion pounded at my chest.

I blinked, wondering if I'd somehow misunderstood what I'd seen.

Alex, walking.

Unconvinced, I raced down the hall and hurried out the nearest door to the garden.

Rounding a tall hedge, I ran straight into him and wanted to laugh.

He wasn't Alex.

Judging by his clothes, he was a worker Dauphine had undoubtedly brought in as extra help. His dark hair and build bore a striking resemblance to Alex's, but nothing more.

"I'm so sorry," I said, stepping out of his way. He carried a tray of tea candles. "I thought . . . I thought for a moment you were someone else."

He offered a small smile and stepped around me, leaving me alone in the corner of the garden.

Overhead, the sky had rounded into a deep blue with traces of clouds at the horizon. Alex was surely waiting for me at the lake by now. I ran my hands over the gown, making sure everything was just so before finding the proper path, going toward my future with a steadfast and ready heart.

24

ALEX WAS ALREADY SEATED IN A ROWBOAT AS I APproached the dock.

It was a special boat, I noted. His feet had been slipped into covered holsters to help keep him in place as he manned the oars and a wooden back was built into the planked seat. Frederick had undoubtedly assisted him into it but was now nowhere to be seen.

Alex didn't notice my approach at first, his gaze fixed on the water. He too was already dressed in formal wear. A set of tails dangled down from the rustic seat and his cravat was folded into the most complicated series of knots I'd ever seen.

My slippers crunched over the gravel and he turned.

For a moment, he didn't say anything, didn't even move. He just stared. Quietly. Reverently.

Then, the most beautiful smile broke over his face.

"Oh, Verity. You're even lovelier than I could have ever imagined."

"You like it?" I asked, giving a playful twirl so he could see the whole effect.

"I love it. I . . ." He pressed his lips together and his eyes roved over me hungrily, as if etching the moment into his memory forever. "I am dazzled. Truly."

Heat crept into my face, pleased he was so taken aback. "What . . . what are you doing down there?" I asked, nodding toward the rowboat.

"Join me," he said, his grin widening.

I glanced at the dock. The wood was weathered gray and boasted several long, jagged splinters.

I hesitated. "I don't think all this skirt will fit."

"It'll be fine. There's a ladder right here. I'll help you," he said, offering out one hand. He held on to a post with the other to keep the boat from swaying.

I turned back toward Chauntilalie, praying Dauphine wasn't watching, then gathered up the layers of tulle and silk, bunching them about my knees as if they were nothing more than gabardine, before descending the ladder.

"Thank you," I said, and lowered myself to the second bench. I was no stranger to getting in and out of boats, but the giant, delicate gown hindered my usual movements, making me feel as ungainly as a gosling, legs too long, feet too wide. I fluffed out the skirts, keeping them far from the edges of the water. "No damage done, I think."

For a moment, we simply stared, appreciating all the efforts we'd put in for each other. Alex had taken great care with his dark locks, pomading them into lustrous waves, and his face was freshly shaven and dewy.

"You look very handsome," I confided shyly, my voice pitched lower and hushed.

"I'm glad you think so," he said, pleased. "And you . . . Words fail me." He took my hand, pressing a kiss across the knuckles. "Even Arina herself has never looked as becoming."

"Where are we going?"

His dimples winked. "You'll see."

With a strong push, he shoved us from the dock and took the oars, rowing us into deeper waters.

Little breezes skittered over the lake, bringing with them the scent of algae and water lilies. A fish jumped from a nearby wave, a quick splash of silver, before disappearing again.

"The manor looks so lovely from here," I murmured, squinting across the lake to marvel at the picturesque views of Chauntilalie.

"I told you to bring a sketchbook," he teased.

I glanced down at my bespoke finery. "And where exactly would I have stored it?"

"Oh . . . you know," he said, releasing one of the oars to gesture toward the skirt. "That thing is absolutely enormous. There must be a pocket somewhere."

Our laughter mingled in the bright morning light.

"It seems a shame," I murmured, pointing to the bustling activity across the lawn. Footmen now hung scalloped floral bowers and ribboned pennants.

"What do you mean?"

"The sky was so red this morning. Can't you feel the storm coming?" Toward the west, a pile of dark blue clouds gathered, massing together.

"Bad weather would never dare to thwart any plans of Dauphine Laurent," Alex said, but I did notice he gave the clouds a second glance, chewing his lip thoughtfully.

"I hadn't realized the lake was so vast," I said, filling the silence as he rowed. "Is it fed by a spring? It doesn't look as though any streams run into it."

"You've a sharp eye. It's actually stagnant, man-made. There used to be a lake farther up along the northern ridge of the estate but my great-grandfather had it diverted . . . after some adjustments to the landscape here."

"He moved an entire lake?" It was incomprehensible to me. "Why?"

Again, he smiled. "You'll see . . . Look!" he exclaimed, pointing behind me.

Arina's statue, the giant hand pointing into the fiery heart, rose out of the water like a breaching whale. It was made of pale gray stone, with veins of gold snaking through it, giving the flames a realistic flicker.

"The shrine," I said in wonder. The statue loomed over us but yards away, I saw a small slip of land, resting so low to the water, I'd not noticed it before. "It's an island!"

Marble bouquets of flowers stood watch at each corner of the platform. Their stony ribbons trailed down and across the border, creating a whimsical railing.

"This is the shrine?" I asked as I squinted at the little slab. Frederick stood at the dock, already waiting for us. This had been an expertly planned operation.

Alex drew the rowboat along the back side of the island, throwing a line of rope to Frederick, who tied it off before holding out his hand to help pull me from the dinghy.

I wandered about the platform as Frederick helped Alexander from the boat. Large circles of green glass were curiously pressed into the pale tiles. There were ten altogether, dotting the island like confetti, and I wondered what importance they had for the People of the Petals.

I leaned out over one of the ribbon railings as far as I dared. Through the dark green water, I spotted the faint curved lines of the structure that held Arina's burning heart in place.

"How deep is the lake?"

"Quite. Are you wanting to go for a swim?" Alex asked, smiling mischievously. He was standing upright, leaning heavily against Frederick, no wheelchair in sight. I'd never given thought to how tall he would be without the chair, but he loomed over me, even propped at such an awkward angle.

"If you throw me in, your mother will never forgive you."

"I wouldn't dare!"

"I was only wondering why the statue was built so far off the island? Surely it would have been easier to use this as a base?"

"Come, I want to show you something."

With impressive effort, Frederick picked him up and ferried Alex over to where a staircase spiraled down into an area beneath the island.

"What is that?" I asked. It was too dark to make anything out.

Alex laughed. "So many questions! I promise, I will show you everything. Unfortunately, this is one of the few places at Chauntilalie without a lift or ramp, though Father does keep a chair here for me. And thankfully, we have Frederick."

He went first, carrying Alex down the narrow, metal steps. After a last look around the platform, I followed after them. Reaching the bottom, I was amazed to see a large secret room open up. Skylights were used to brighten the space—the same ten large circles I'd noticed earlier.

"How ingenious!" I murmured, looking up through the windows.

Potted palms were placed about with care, trying to camouflage bulky support columns. In the center of the room was a gaming table. Four tufted wingback chairs nestled around it, ready for an evening of cards. Paintings of horse hunts and moody florals hung framed on a gallery wall. In the far corner was a mahogany bar, stocked with dozens of glass bottles and decanters. Cigar smoke lingered in the air, giving the room a decidedly masculine feel.

"Where are we?"

Alex, now back in a chair, rolled over, joining me. It was more compact than the wicker chair he normally used.

"One of Father's little hideaways. In the warm months, after dinner parties, he entertains guests here."

I pictured a party of men, playing cards and drinking brandy as curls of smoke and boisterous laughter filled the air. The unusual singularity of the room was enough to make up for the faint whiff of mildew and the damp chill of the air.

Frederick cleared his throat, as if reminding us of his presence.

"Yes, of course. That will be all, thank you, Frederick," Alex murmured. "We'll see you soon."

The manservant turned back up the staircase, disappearing to the top side.

"Where is he going?"

"He's taking the boat back. I mentioned the storm while on the roof. We'll take a different way home."

"A different way?" I repeated. We were underground, on an

island, in the middle of a lake. What other way home could there be?

"I'll show you," he said, and wheeled around to a doorway at the back of the room.

It was shaped like a tall teardrop and led down a tunnel molded in the same shape. I caught a glimmer of light at its end but the rest of the passageway was dark with shadows.

"Go on," Alex prompted.

I hesitated. How far underwater were we? The tunnel didn't appear to be too long, but it definitely headed away from the island, taking us deeper into the lake.

"Are we allowed to be down here?" I stalled and my voice bounced back and forth against the white stucco walls. "Is it safe?"

Alexander practically danced with excitement in his chair. "Go on, go on!"

The tunnel was too narrow for us to roam down side by side. I wished Alexander would have taken the lead, but he gently urged me to the front. I moved cautiously, fearful of catching my ankle on an unseen dip in the cement floor. My eyes quickly adjusted to the dark, making whatever lit the end of the tunnel unspeakably bright.

When we reached the end, I stopped so abruptly, Alex bumped into me. With a laugh, he nudged me forward.

"Oh my," I gasped, turning in a slow circle to take everything in.

We were impossibly underwater, in the center of a great glass dome entirely submerged beneath the lake. Hundreds of curved windowpanes rose from the floor to the ceiling's crest, nearly two stories above us. Thick plaster and metal bands held them together, with a little rosette centered at each joining. Sunlight filtered through the water and into the dome, casting an algae-tinted glow. Raised flowerbeds lined the round walls, with an incredible assortment of blooms and greenery. A thick wool rug rested in the middle of the floor, patterned in florals of midnight blue and ivory.

"What is this place?" I whispered, not wanting to break the magic of the moment. I'd never seen anything more enchanting in my entire life.

"Great-Grandfather used it as a music room and dance hall. He actually had an entire grand piano brought in, piece by piece, and assembled here, for parties."

"Where is it now?" I couldn't imagine a more surreal location for a concert. My fingers itched to capture the idea on paper, with grand lords and ladies dancing against the hazy verdigris windows.

"It sounds like a wonderful idea until you realize how humid it gets in here. The piano was forever out of tune and its innards started warping. It had to be taken apart and removed. Grandpère used it for his prayers—he was the one to add the Burning Heart statue. Father found the climate perfect for some of his more particular specimens." He pointed to the boxes. "I promise, none of them are dangerous."

"I've never seen anything so wondrous," I murmured, tracing my fingertips along one of the windows. The glass was inches thick, distorting the view.

A dark form flashed out of the murky depths and struck the window. I let out a startled cry of surprise, jumping back.

"Oh, don't be alarmed," Alex said, immediately at my side. "The lake is stocked with fish. The carp can be rather aggressive."

"They can see us in here?"

He nodded, drawing close. "Of course. Look."

He took my hand and pressed it back to the glass, holding it in place. Moments later, the carp returned and another appeared. They jostled against each other, each trying to be the one closest to my fingers. Their great mouths bobbed open, scraping their lips against the window, tails wriggling furiously.

They were enormously fat. I hoped it was merely an illusion of the thick glass, but their pectoral fins seemed larger than even Alex's hands, also now spread out on the windows, drawing more of the beasts to him.

"They used to terrify me as a boy," he admitted. "Now . . . I find them fascinating."

I stepped away, letting my eyes trail up to the center of the dome. The light was brighter there and I could make out the caps of waves at the waterline. Smaller fish swam by, chased by what appeared to be a duck.

"I've never seen webbed feet from this angle," I giggled.

"The heart is up there," Alex explained, following my gaze. "The dome holds it up. When Father is down here with the gas lamps on at night, you can see the glow of it around the statue, as if Arina is truly here at the shrine, shining her light everywhere."

"It's amazing, Alex." I smiled as the wonder of the room sent thrills through me. "What will you do with it?"

He looked surprised. "Me?"

I nodded.

"I . . . I'm not certain. I suppose it will have to be something elaborate and grand. It's such an extraordinary place. . . . It seems destined for extraordinary things." He swallowed and his eyebrows furrowed together as he shifted about in his seat. "Well. It's not mine. Not yet. But I think I know what I'd like my first extraordinary act here to be."

Alex blew out a deep, shaky breath and removed a small velvet box from the inner pocket of his tuxedo jacket.

I froze.

This was it.

It was really happening.

Here, in the most magical and romantic spot I could have ever dreamed of.

"Verity . . . I don't know how things like this are done between the People of the Salt, but here in Bloem, when you know you've found your love, you act on it. Life is unpredictable, so you need to seize hold of what you love and cherish every moment together."

He reached up and cupped my cheek, stroking its curve.

"I've found my love. I've found you and I want to celebrate that, here: in a spot that is both waves and blossoms. It's you and me. I couldn't imagine a better place to ask this of you . . . Verity Adelaide Thaumas, will you let me love you for the rest of my life?"

My breath hitched at his unusual phrasing, catching in the hollow of my throat and stopping any hope I might have had in answering him. After a moment, I nodded.

He took my hands in his, clasping them in the gentlest of holds. "Will you let me cherish you, adore you, respect you, and honor you most earnestly?"

I nodded again, tears pricking at my eyes.

"Will you let my life twine with yours, two threads making up one cord, fine on our own, but so much better together?"

I pressed my lips into a tight line, fighting their trembles. I'd never heard a more perfect ode to what a marriage ought to be.

"And will you promise, from this day onward, to be my dearest, my other half, my . . . *wife*?"

Tears streamed down my cheeks. "I will."

I expected him to open the box and reveal the engagement ring, but he remained still, just holding my hands, my gaze, my heart.

Eventually, he smiled, leaning forward to whisper, "You're supposed to ask the same of me."

"I am?" I asked with alarm, a little bubble of laughter rising up. "In Salann it's such a simple, prosaic affair."

Alex looked horrified. "Prosaic? How can a proposal be prosaic?"

I shifted my weight to one side, my hands still entwined with his. "Usually the man gets down on one knee and says something perfunctory about how beautiful the woman is or how happy she makes him, and then he pulls out a ring and asks if she'll marry him."

His hands flew from mine. "Should I have gotten down on one knee? I . . . I could try."

"No! No, yours was perfect. Everything, all of it, was perfect."

The corner of his eyes crinkled as he smiled. "It's not over yet."

"There's more?"

He opened the box and held out the ring, dazzling me with the amount of diamonds clustered around the band. It was like a garden in full bloom, a night sky filled with stars.

"This was my great-grandmother's ring but it's been in the Laurent family for many, many generations."

"It's beautiful," I murmured. The gold band was polished to a lustrous shine and the center diamond seemed to wink at me.

"It suits you."

Alex took my hand and started to slip the sparkling ring on my finger.

I pulled my hand back. "Wait, you said I was supposed to ask you the questions too."

He shook his head. "We don't have to follow that. You're not from Bloem and you don't—"

Inspired, I pushed aside the fullness of my skirts and knelt down on one knee, putting us face to face. I took his hands as he had mine, shaky with the overwhelmingly gigantic moment. "Alexander Etienne Cornelius Leopold Laurent . . . you have too many names but you also have all of my heart. Will you let me spend the rest of my life loving you?"

His smile was pure joy. "I will."

"Will you let me adore you, revere you, respect you, and make you laugh?" I asked, unable to remember the exact words he'd used.

His grip tightened around my hands, lacing our fingers together. I could feel the ring pressed heavily between them. "Every day, always."

"Will you entangle your life with mine as my friend, my darling, my husband?"

Alex beamed. "Nothing would make me happier. Now . . . may I put on the ring?"

I nodded and he slid it over my finger. He held up my hand, tilting back and forth to catch the diamonds in the light.

"Thank you," he murmured, his voice thick. "This really is one of the happiest moments of my life. I'm in absolute awe of you, Verity." His fingers brushed along my face, trailing over my lips. "I suppose we ought to seal everything with a kiss, don't you?"

I took a breath, praying that here and now, in the wondrous moment, I would get it right. "Is that what engaged people in Bloem are meant to do?"

"Oh yes." He grinned, leaning in for his mouth to find mine.

∽

It wasn't . . . awful.

He'd pulled me up, bringing me in to sit on his lap, perched on his legs, between the wheels of the chair. It was a bit awkward at first, and I'd worried I was hurting him, but then his lips were on mine and I had an entirely new set of things to worry over.

"Alex," I murmured as he nibbled at the corner of my mouth. I momentarily entertained the idea of doing the same but stopped short, fearing I'd somehow draw blood. "Alex, we should be getting back."

"We ought to stay here," he countered, his voice dreamy and distant, lacing his fingers through mine.

My hands felt so different now, with the weight of Alex's ring. More important, more grown up. These were no longer the hands of a girl, but a young woman, loved and cherished. I held on to that feeling, that sense of security and comfort.

"The party," I reminded him.

He groaned and kissed me deeper, his tongue finding mine. I spent the moment trying to visualize exactly what each mouth was doing. The more I thought about it, the more confusing it seemed. His breaths grew drawn and ragged and I did feel a little pleased that whatever I was doing satisfied him so thoroughly.

"Won't Frederick be back soon?"

"He already took the boat."

"So, how do we get back?" I wondered, cupping my hands over his face, holding him still so our eyes met, the kisses at a blessed end.

"We take the stairs." His voice sounded strange and strained and he seemed completely out of breath. Had a handful of kisses truly put him in such a state? Why couldn't I stop overthinking the moment and join him?

"What stairs?"

"The ones down there," he murmured, pointing to a second tunnel on the opposite end of the room.

"Another tunnel?"

"Mmmm," he said, snaking his arms around my waist, trying to draw me back.

But I was already pushing myself from his lap, brushing out my skirts as he protested.

"Where does it go?"

Alex's face was adorably flushed, pink and rosy, and he ran his fingers through his hair, attempting to straighten the muss I'd created. "Great-Grandfather knew there needed to be two exit points, just in case something were to happen in here. That tunnel heads back to shore. There's a little gatehouse just around the corner from the dock. We've walked past it before. There's another spiral staircase and then we'll be back at Chauntilalie."

"And Frederick will be there, waiting for us?"

He took my hand in his, trying to draw me back. "But I don't think he'd mind waiting a few minutes more...."

"It's tempting," I said, with no intention of giving in and returning to his lap.

"Is it?" Alex's voice was low and husky as he wheeled closer. "How tempting?"

"Very...," I said, easing back away. "But there's the dinner and your parents will want to know all about this before then, I'm sure."

"They already know," Alex admitted. "I had to ask Father to retrieve the ring from the family vault and of course Mother wanted to hear everything. They're going to be so, so pleased."

"But they don't know that I said yes," I pointed out. "Let's go tell them the good news."

With a great sigh of resignation, he agreed.

We made our way down the tunnel. It was far longer than the first, and much darker. The air felt charged and I was terribly aware of the amount of water surrounding us now, pressing in, heavy and horrifying.

I trailed my left hand along the side of the wall for balance. Even in the dim lighting, I could make out the giant cluster of diamonds upon it.

Alex reached the exit first. More circular skylights illuminated a winding staircase rounding up to a landing above us. The light they offered was faint and I realized that bank of dark clouds must have finally arrived at the estate while we were tucked away, hidden in our own little world beneath the waves.

"Frederick?" Alex called up uncertainly.

There was no response.

"Why don't I go up and find him?" I offered, climbing the stairs. They were slick with green growth and the handrails were covered with spongy moss. This side felt abandoned, clearly not used as often as the more impressive and surprising lake entrance.

When I got to the door at the top, I tried the handle. It rattled in its casing but did not budge.

I tried again, wondering if the rusted metal needed a little extra force.

There was no give, no turning.

We were locked in.

25

LOCKED.

We were locked in.

In a ballroom.

Under a lake.

A bubble of laughter rose up my throat, colored in disbelief.

I rapped on the door but it was heavy metal and my strikes were absorbed with dull thuds.

"Verity?" Alex's voice echoed up the circular room, sounding uncertain.

"I'm still here," I called back, and tried striking the door again.

No response.

I peeked down the staircase. Alex was looking up at me with hopeful eyes.

"It's locked."

"Locked?" he echoed. "But Frederick should have been here by now. Perhaps he's still back on the island, waiting for us with the boat."

"Perhaps," I murmured, hoping with all my might it was true.

A strange current charged the air. The storm was approaching fast. I made my way back down the stairs. On the last step, my foot slipped out from beneath me, sliding on a slick patch of lichens. Alex grabbed at my elbow, steadying me.

"Are you all right?"

I nodded.

"Why don't you take the lead this time?" Alex suggested. "You'll have a better view of the light ahead."

Gratefully, I stepped into the dark tunnel. We reached the glass dome and kept going.

The smoking room was dark and as I made my way up the spiral stairs, feeling Alex's eyes on me like a weight, I could already tell we were too late. The storm was here.

"Frederick?" I called out, stepping onto the platform.

It was empty. The boat was gone.

Overhead the sky had turned dark as the rain clouds we'd spotted earlier rolled in, ready to open up. I squinted against the rising winds, hoping to see a stray footman outdoors, who I could shout to for help. But the party preparations had been put on hold. Everyone seemed to have scurried indoors to wait out the storm.

I considered jumping in and swimming to shore. I could alert the staff about the locked door and we'd free Alex. But that would take so much time and my dress would be utterly ruined.

"I could leave the dress here," I muttered to myself, weighing out options. Bending over the railing, I dipped my fingers into the water and winced. It was still cold from its spring thaw but I'd swam in worse before, off Salten. Losing the full skirts would make it easier to freely kick and I'd certainly need all the speed I could get. Those giant carp had seemed likely to attack anything that moved.

The wind picked up, snapping stray hairs across my face like little whips. A bolt of lightning shot out from a dark cloud, hitting a tree on the shoreline. The force of the following thunder exploded through my chest and I shook my head. The last place I'd want to be during a lightning storm was on the open water. It would be a death sentence.

Another glittering branch danced overhead, hopping from cloud to cloud, searching for an outlet. It was absolute madness to remain out here. I scurried back to the stairs as the sky opened up, raining torrents down upon me. I was soaked through in an instant.

I hurried down the stairs, clinging to the wooden handrail. It was much darker in the smoking room now. The skylights glowed faintly overhead but it wasn't enough to lift the gloom. Rain pounded down on them, a painfully loud cacophony.

"No Frederick, no boat," I told Alex, rubbing my arms against the flurry of shivers racing down them. "Are there lights in here?"

Several hurricane lamps were positioned throughout the room, but we couldn't find any matches. With so much rain coming down the open stairwell, a growing puddle inched its way into the room, heading for a drain.

"You said the dome glows at night, didn't you?" I shouted, trying to be heard over the chaos. Another crack of thunder rumbled, shaking the bottles of liquor at the bar.

Alex held his hands over his ears. "What?"

"Gas lights. In the dome?"

He nodded and turned back for the tunnel, wheels racing. At

the entrance to the dome, he found a little brass plate and flipped its toggle.

Several lamps came to life, brightening the green murkiness. With a cry of relief, I sank down on a bench tucked between Gerard's flowerbeds. Water dripped from my hair, setting my teeth to chatter.

A sharp thud from the glass made me jump away.

The water around the dome came to life in a frenzy as dozens of carp pressed themselves to the windows, drawn to the light and wild from the storm. They bashed against each other, mouths gaped open.

Their bodies were disgusting, strangely muscled and too great in size. They looked like something from a fevered dream come to life.

"Do you think they can break through?"

Alex studied the windows as more fish hurled themselves at the dome, churning the water into a brown murk, mouths puckered and tails swishing with madness. "No . . . the framework was engineered to hold up against the constant pressure and weight of the water. The carp don't stand a chance against that, no matter how hard they try." One hit higher up on the dome and it sounded like cannon fire. Alex winced and gestured toward me. "Why don't you come over here, though, just to be safe? I don't . . . I don't think they can see us in the center of the room."

"They see the light," I said, nodding toward the glass orbs. "It's drawing them in."

He glanced up at the room's zenith, dubiously studying the amount of light coming through the water. "Should we . . . should we turn them off?"

There was another crack against the glass and I nodded.

Alex flipped the switch, plunging the dome into blackness.

For a moment, it was too dark to see but my eyes adjusted. Dim green light cast strange filters over us, barely limning our edges.

"You're shivering," Alex noticed, rolling in close. He took off his jacket and handed it to me.

"Thank you," I murmured, slipping it on. It was still warm from his body heat and smelled of him.

"Can you help me from the chair? It seems we're going to be here for a while. . . . We might as well be comfortable." He flipped the latches that would hold the wheels in place, then talked me through how best to help him out. Once Alex was on the floor, I pushed the chair away, letting him stretch long, and then shyly sat beside him. My skirts, once so boisterous and full, now looked like a sad tulip, pummeled by a rainstorm, limp and listing.

We watched the shadowy bodies of the carp wriggle and squirm, fighting for things they could no longer see. Eventually, they lost interest and swam off to other parts of the lake, looking for things to scare. I wanted to cheer as the last of the beasts left us and the dome's silence was restored.

"I'm so terribly sorry, Verity," Alex said quietly.

I turned to him. He was staring down at his hands, his face drawn with remorse.

"What's wrong?"

"Everything. I wanted to give us this amazing moment, show you how surprising and wonderful life with me could be, and now we're sitting at the bottom of a lake, waiting out a thunderstorm, and I've ruined your dress. I've ruined the day. I . . ." He muttered something too low to hear.

I leaned in. "What did you say?"

A sigh escaped him. "I ruin everything."

"Alex . . . that's not true."

He laughed. It was bitter and barbed and held no trace of amusement. "My entire life . . . the line of the Laurent family, the ducal seat, it's all in jeopardy, just because I fell down a set of stairs as a child."

"That wasn't your fault. Things happen. Accidents happen."

"Tell that to my father."

My mouth fell open, aghast. "Gerard has said he blames you for that?"

"Never to my face but I've heard him in his study at night, when he thinks everyone has gone to bed. Crying. Screaming. Bemoaning the waste of it all."

"Alex, that's awful. I . . . I'm sorry you heard that, but you must know it's not true. You're going to become a wonderful duke. You've so many ideas, so many big, good ideas for change. For improvements."

"I could be the greatest leader this province has ever seen but none of it will matter if I can't carry out the one task every duke is meant to perform."

"What task?"

He paused for such a long moment, I wondered if he hadn't heard me. Then, another sigh. "Heirs."

"Oh." A second later, the full implication of his statement bloomed over me, a drop of ink in a pool of water, spreading its tint, changing everything around it. *"Oh."*

We sat together in the dark, heads full but lips still.

I certainly understood *where* heirs came from. I'd helped Camille through all her pregnancies and had to assist in Annaleigh's delivery just last year when she went into labor early during one of my visits to Hesperus.

"Do you . . . do you know if . . ." Words utterly failed me, turning me into a stammering, rosy mess.

"It's not as though I've ever had cause to try," he admitted. "I . . . I think everything works as it should, but . . ." He exhaled sharply. "This is absurd. You're the one person in the world I ought to be able to speak with about this without feeling embarrassed or ashamed but I—" A small sob cut off his words. "I'm so scared I've failed you already."

"Alex."

I covered his hands with mine, trying to offer him some little bit of soothing comfort, but he jerked them away, crossing his arms over his chest.

"You've not failed me. You've not failed your family. We . . . we'll find out soon enough if . . ."

"If," he agreed sadly.

I sighed myself. "We'll make it work, however it goes."

"But I don't want you to have to make it work. I don't want you to deal with disappointment. I want, *I so badly want,* to be the man who can give you everything. Who can give you the world. But I can't. And this"—he gestured broadly across the darkened dome—"this just shows it. I can't even propose to you without mucking it up."

I glanced about the dome. The water at the base, churned up brown and murky by the carp, had begun to settle back into a dark green. The verdigris tint lightened the farther up along the glass windows, and I as studied the top of the dome, where the water was only a few inches deep, I caught sight of something I'd never expected to see.

"Alex, look at that," I said, pointing.

He tilted his head, craning his neck uncomfortably.

"No, like this." I helped him lie down on the thick wool carpet to peer up at the zenith. I joined him, nestling my body against his long, rigid frame.

"What are we supposed to be looking at?"

"Up there. Up where the water is the brightest. Do you see that? The little sparkles?"

His eyebrows furrowed. "The raindrops?"

I nodded. "I've spent my entire life by the water. I know how to swim in it, how to sail on it, how to read the weather by it. It has dictated every part of my life—how I traveled, what I ate. I *feel* the changing of the tides in my blood. I thought I'd seen every possible version of water—waves and ice, storms and steam—Salann has it all. But I have never, *never*," I repeated with emphasis, "seen the rain fall like this."

He made a soft noise of consideration, studying the inverse drops with fresh eyes.

"And I never would have either, had it not been for you." I kissed his cheek, then settled against him, resting my head on his chest so we could watch the raindrops hitting the lake. "Thank you. This . . . this is a wonder."

I felt him open his mouth to say something but then he changed his mind with a shake of his head. He pressed his lips to the crown of my hair, his kiss impossibly tender and sweet. "You," he murmured and kissed me again. "You are my wonder."

The entire lake lit up as a bolt of lightning danced across the sky, high above our little hideaway.

"I know what I want to do with this room, when the time comes," Alex said, wrapping his arm around my back, drawing me closer.

I shifted to look up at him. "What's that?"

"I want to put a giant bed right here, in the middle of the room, and fill it with the softest pillows and blankets, and every time there's a rainstorm, you and I can come down here and watch it, just the two of us."

"And all the carp," I reasoned.

"Of course."

I leaned up to kiss him. "That. That, Alexander Laurent, sounds nothing short of extraordinary."

26

"AND THEN ALEXANDER'S ATTENDANT BURST through the door and found the two of them, soaked to the bone and chilled to near death, huddling for warmth in Gerard's conservatory! Can you believe such a harrowing ordeal? Poor brave Verity had faced down the storm, trying to save them both, but what was she to do?" Dauphine took another sip of her wine and shook her head. "But now, look. Look at my stunning and radiant daughter-to-be. I couldn't be more proud of either of them."

All the guests turned to stare openly at us. Alex and I had been positioned at the center of the banquet table, Alex at my left so he was able to pick up my hand and show off the diamond ring whenever anyone asked. And so many had asked.

"To our brilliantly minded and beautifully brilliant Verity," Gerard exclaimed, foisting his wineglass in the air with boisterous zeal. "And my brilliantly lucky son, Alexander. May their union be nothing short of . . . brilliant," he laughed.

I raised my glass, accepting everyone's well-wishes and feigning a smile toward Gerard. I could not, I would not forget what

Alex had said about his father. But this was not the night to question him.

"How on earth did the door manage to lock?" an older woman asked, turning her attention to us, her copper skin shining with a beautiful luster in the candlelight. She was Binita Peaseblossom, a marchioness from a neighboring estate.

Alex cleared his throat. "Well, it—"

"That was the strangest thing of all!" Dauphine interrupted, the spots of color on her cheeks as high as her spirits. "There *is* no lock on that door! Not a real one at least. Gerard has a false front plate, to ward off the curious, but he keeps it open—"

"As a safety precaution, for events such as these. A secret one at that, my love," he said, and though his words were friendly, his tone pinched with irritation.

"Oh, my dear, we're among friends. Yes?" she asked the table brightly.

Everyone nodded, raising their glasses again.

"If there was no lock, how were they locked in?" Binita persisted.

"It had been tampered with! An iron rod was shoved through the handles."

The room broke into murmurs of surprise.

"I can't imagine who . . ." Dauphine's sentence trailed away as an army of footmen arrived, bringing in the next course.

Once the last of the servants exited the hall, Dauphine let out a sigh. "It's such a mystery. Boggles the mind."

Several seats down, Marguerite sniffed as if in disagreement.

If I'd had to wager who had been behind the door tampering, I would have laid bets on her.

The Laurent matriarch had returned to Chauntilalie sometime that morning, pulled away from whatever summer cottage she'd been hiding away in for the last few weeks.

Once rescued, Alex had brought the family together to tell them the news and Marguerite had cried. Not tears of happiness, as Dauphine had burst into, but actual tears. Her sobs were so severe Gerard had to escort her off to her room, giving us smiles of encouragement over his shoulder as he left.

"What an odd incident. You must have been terrified," an older viscount commiserated, turning the group's attention back to us once more.

"I had Alexander with me," I said, feeling as though I were performing in a play. "I wasn't afraid of anything."

He brought my hand up to his lips and the Laurents' guests cheered.

It was exhausting being this animated for so long.

Only hours before, Frederick had discovered us. He'd begged for Alex's forgiveness, swearing he'd seen him earlier in the house and had assumed we'd somehow made our way back to the estate on our own. It wasn't until Dauphine went looking for us that anyone realized something was amiss.

After we'd announced the engagement, Dauphine had whisked me back to my room, fretting over the state of my dress.

"I certainly appreciate a grand gesture," she'd muttered as she'd worked me free of the buttons. "But now, oh dear. Oh dear, oh dear, oh dear."

She'd had the dress carried away for a steaming and it had returned a little less boisterous, a little more subdued, but it would work.

"We'll have to have more gowns made up for you," Dauphine had promised before leaving me to fix my hair.

At the end of the table, a man cleared his throat, drawing me back to the present. Even seated, he towered above most of the other guests, and the rich sheen of his green velvet suit complemented his dark skin and quick smile. "Speaking of strange goings-on, I've been meaning to ask you, Gerard, how is Marchioly House? Have you had a chance to see the damage yet?"

"Lord Udoh has an estate in the north, near our winter house," Alex explained, leaning in.

"Damage?" Binita echoed, eyebrows arched with worry. "Has something happened?"

Dauphine began to shake her head, but before she could disagree, Gerard nodded.

"A bit of bad luck is all. Part of the manor caught fire in a storm last week. Lightning can be so treacherous in the mountains, you know."

"Oh my," the marchioness said, clutching at her necklaces, fingers hooked in a protective gesture. "Was anyone injured?"

Gerard dabbed his napkin at the corner of his lips. "Blessedly no. We haven't kept a staff there in ages. Work keeps me so preoccupied, it's difficult to make time to visit."

Lord Udoh leaned forward to catch the duke's eye. "Are you certain on that?"

Gerard tilted his head as if he didn't understand.

"I've heard all sorts of stories of Marchioly House from the village. Strange noises. Screams in the night. Bloodcurdling cries."

Several of the guests murmured with surprise.

Lord Udoh continued. "When we heard word of the fire, I

sent my valet out to investigate. He said the door to the front of the house was open and a set of blackened footprints tracked across the threshold. Someone must have been there."

Gerard cleared his throat. "I'm told villagers came out when they saw the flames. To help put out the fire, you know." His fingers danced restlessly. "The footprints undoubtedly belonged to them."

Lord Udoh's eyes narrowed and the air between the men shifted as if their masks of joviality had grown too weighty to hold up. "But that wouldn't account for the curious noises, would it? They've been going on for years."

Gerard opened his mouth but Dauphine cut him off with a quick clap of her hands. "Is everyone done with their oysters? I can't wait for you to try the sorbet. Raphael has been experimenting with new blends all week. You simply must let me know what you think!"

Her tone was bright enough to push aside the tensions brewing between Gerard and the earl, and the rest of the dinner guests fell into easy conversations once more.

"What was that all about?" I whispered to Alex, watching Lord Udoh turn his attention toward his plate. The serving staff had returned and begun scooping up the dishes.

Alex shook his head, seemingly unconcerned. "He and Father have butted heads for years. Lord Udoh dabbles in beekeeping. He's been after Father to allow him to keep a hive here at Chauntilalie. He believes that with all the unique flowers Father has created, the honey produced could be extraordinary."

"That sounds like a wonderful idea."

"I agree. But Father . . . he worries about what the bees might do to his curated pollinations. 'Introducing a hive into such a controlled environment would be utter chaos. Utter chaos!'" His impersonation of Gerard was remarkably accurate.

"So the cries in the night . . . ?"

Alex laughed. "Nothing more than Lord Udoh trying to stir the pot in front of all of Father's friends, I'm certain. Or," he reflected thoughtfully, his mouth warming into a grin. "Mother's peacocks have taken to wandering!"

Covered trays were set in front of us and the guests burst into applause as the silver domes were removed, revealing a sorbet coupe, piled high with exotic fruit. All of it had come from Gerard's orchards and he puffed with pride as everyone exclaimed with delight.

The conversation shifted as easily as the courses and Dauphine fell into an animated story about something that had happened at a charity luncheon she'd attended recently.

In no time at all, the sorbet was gone and the army of footmen returned, whisking the plates away with practiced poise.

"Thank you," I said, acknowledging the server at my left. He had a shock of red hair and his pale, freckled cheeks stained just as bright before he scurried off, joining the line of footmen leaving the room.

I studied each of the men before they left, curious to see if the footman I'd taken for Alex earlier was present. Frederick must have made the same mistake, spotting the server and assuming him to be his charge.

But he wasn't among the young men working the hall now.

"Shall we?" Alex asked, drawing my attention after our plates were cleared.

"Shall we what?"

"Mother just announced brandies in the library." He studied me thoughtfully. "Where were you just now?"

"I was still thinking about that door."

"I wouldn't worry on it. I spoke with Frederick after everything had settled down. A branch fell during the storm, barring the exit. We couldn't have gotten out no matter how hard we tried, but no one intentionally locked us in."

"But Dauphine said that a rod—"

He made a face, amused. "Mother would never let the truth get in the way of a good story, particularly at a party she was hosting."

That certainly felt true. "And your doppelgänger?"

He shrugged. "There are so many extra people here at the house today. . . . It could have been any of them."

It made perfect sense and I was glad to have someone else come to the same conclusion. "I actually thought I saw you earlier as well," I confided. "Through the windows, in the garden."

"Really?" Alex tilted his head, amused. "Was he as handsome as me?"

I squinted as if trying to remember the other man's face. "About the same, I think. But he was much more modest."

He chuckled as we made our way to the library. "Then perhaps you ought to marry him instead."

27

THE SCREAMS WOKE ME.

My eyes flashed open and I sat up with a start, listening to the quiet stirrings of my dark room.

I was utterly spent and annoyed at having been woken.

The dinner party had lasted for far too long. Brandies in the library had led to some of the bolder guests requesting to see the now-infamous underwater room. Tipsy and full of giggles, they made their way out into the dark gardens, to search for the gatehouse. Tired footmen raced ahead to light the lanterns but even still, the marchioness took a tumble, twisting an ankle in her headlong haste to be the first to find the door. Alex had wisely remained behind, claiming the room would be too crowded for his chair. I had hoped I might stay as well, but Gerard had clasped an insistent hand around my shoulders, exhorting me to tell the tale once more.

I'd returned to my chambers in the wee hours of the morning, my body exhausted and my head spinning. A case of champagne had been brought out from behind the bar and the guests delighted in popping bottle after bottle, toasting the engagement, the underwater room, and the carp that had inevitably swarmed the glass windows when the lights flipped on.

Another cry echoed through the night and I collapsed back into the bedclothes.

"Those blasted peacocks," I muttered, and rolled over, bringing a pillow up over my ears to muffle their screeching.

Sleep quickly claimed its hold but it settled over me as a light blanket, easily snatched away, and when another scream rang out, I pushed the pillows back with a mumbled curse.

Surely there ought to be something that could be done about the birds. Covered cages or a roosting house. Something. Anything.

I poured a glass of water and sipped it slowly, willing myself to drift off once more.

When the next scream came, it wasn't from within the gardens.

It sounded as if it was coming from inside the house, just down the hall.

I frowned, setting the water aside.

Had one of the birds broken into the house?

With a groan, I stood and found my robe. Pulling it on against the chill, I wandered into the hallway, wondering if anyone else realized one of Dauphine's beloved pets had infiltrated the manor.

Another cry, this time higher and smaller. It ended in a breathy rattle, choked and gasping.

Was that . . . Was it a child?

I backtracked into the parlor and lit a candle, frowning as I noticed it was pink. I brandished the little light around the room, trying to find one of Annaleigh's. It seemed a footman had come through and replaced all the salt and sage stubs with fresh pink ones.

Another scream rang out, awful and lingering, and the hairs at the back of my neck stood on end.

That wasn't a peacock.

It sounded like a person. One in great distress.

I could almost hear words within it, calling out for mercy.

It set me into action. I'd look for Annaleigh's candles later. Someone needed my help.

The open wick danced as I wandered into the hallway once more, causing leering shadows to sway around me. They swooped about the corridor like nightmarish bats, ethereal and fantastic, my imagination soaring to horrible heights.

The air filled now with a groan, a moan, a tearing asunder of a soul, and I nearly dropped the candle to cover my ears.

What was that?

Who was that?

My breath caught, remembering Alex's agonies. Had another fit overcome him?

I pushed aside my fears and made my way to the far wing, ready to help however I could.

But when I turned at Alex's hallway, everything was still. I could hear the ticking of a tall grandfather clock a few doors down. Its steady beats tapped out an even, metronomic rhythm. I counted the passing seconds, waiting for another cry that did not come.

After three minutes of silence, I wandered back toward my wing. My insides felt jumbled and unsettled. Sleep was unlikely to return, even in my stupor, so when I reached the foyer, cast in shadows, I took the stairs.

I'd find the kitchen and see if I could rustle up a cup of tea.

Dauphine enjoyed making blends from all of the herbs and leaves within the gardens. She was always offering out new creations at our shared breakfasts. Surely there was something to steady my nerves and set my mind toward rest once more.

In the kitchen, I filled a kettle and found a container of matches. Within moments, the stove was lit, the water heating.

Tins of tea lined a small shelf along one wall and I tilted my head, making my way through their scratchy handwritten labels. Just as I reached for the chamomile, the gaslights in the room flared, startling me.

I turned, expecting to see a valet or footman, or perhaps even the cook, rising early to begin work on the day's bread, but it was Gerard who stepped down into the galley.

"Verity!" he exclaimed, jumping back so far in surprise he nearly slipped down the shallow steps. "I didn't expect to find you up at this hour."

"I heard . . . noises. It sounded as though someone was screaming."

"Damn peacocks," he muttered, wiping his hands across his work apron. "Nothing but nuisances."

The apron was covered with bright stains.

Bright bloody red stains.

The memory of that final, awful cry echoed in my mind and I took an unconscious step away from him.

His eyes followed my horrified gaze and he froze. Frantically, I glanced about the kitchen, formulating a plan of escape. There was only one way in or out and he was standing right in front of it. My eyes fell on the block of knives between us and my throat dried up. Could I truly use a weapon against someone? Could I even get to them before he did?

But Gerard offered out a smile of chagrin. "I was working with a new strain of beets in the greenhouse, mashing them for compost. They create such a mess."

I teetered on the ball of my foot, wanting to be ready to sprint for the knives if needed. "After the dinner party? So late?" My voice quavered, giving away my uncertainty.

He didn't seem to notice. "No rest for the wicked, as they say."

"You look like a farmer on butchering day," I pointed out, catching note of all the dirt encrusted into the beds of his fingernails with a sense of relief.

Gerard let out a sharp laugh. "You thought this was blood? No wonder you've gone so white. Oh, Verity, you look as though you've seen a ghost!"

"Well," I said, feeling foolish as the spike of adrenaline left me. Of course it was beet juice. "What would you think? All those screams and then you come in here looking like that."

"It's true, it's true!" he tittered. "I suppose I'd holler for help. Thank you for having a more collected mind than me. The last thing the staff needs after all that fuss yesterday is shouting in the night. Murderers on the loose. A madman at Chauntilalie."

My cheeks colored as he laughed again.

"Oh me." He wiped away a tear of mirth from the corner of his eye, leaving behind a swish of red. "I was just coming down to have a bit of a snack before I turned in. Dauphine's party menus are always portioned out so meanly. Would you care to join me?"

He turned to the sink, washing his hands. Black dirt and beet juice—yes, I was certain it was that now—dripped into the porcelain basin and swirled away down the drain.

I shook my head. "I was only making some tea." As if on cue, the kettle behind me began to whistle.

"Something to help you sleep?"

I held up the chamomile.

In two bounds, he was across the kitchen, snatching it from me. He rummaged through the other tins, searching.

I tried not to recoil from his scent. There was an acrid bite of soil and damp moldering things, a thick, meaty funk of sweat, and beneath that all, something even worse, a foulness that burned my nostrils and made my stomach churn.

"This . . . this is just the thing," he said, holding up a hexagonal tin. "Have you ever tried a blooming tea?"

"I've never even heard of it before," I admitted, wishing there was a discreet way to cover my nose.

He pulled out a translucent glass teapot and dropped a great ball of twigs and leaves into it. It hit the glass bottom with a rasp, skittering across the curved center, like an insect. Reaching in front of me, Gerard retrieved the steaming kettle and poured the hot water over the curious object.

"Now," he said, setting the kettle back in place and turning off the burners. "Watch carefully."

I peered down. The dark bulb appeared to be shifting, responding to the water around it. A leaf unfurled from the body of the pod, then another and another, and suddenly the entire thing bloomed, turning into a gorgeous flower. Its petals stretched out, twirling in the water like a little spinning top.

"Oh my," I murmured. The flower steeped, turning the water into a bright aqua-colored tea. "It's beautiful."

Gerard nodded, watching on. "And far more effective than that drivel Dauphine makes. You'll have the best night's sleep of your life with this, even if those peacocks continue their caterwauling."

I smiled at that. "It's curious you don't hear them in this part of the house. They were so loud earlier, I'd have guessed half the manor would have been up."

He cocked his head, listening, as he pulled down a cup and saucer from a shelf. "Perhaps the silly things finally tired themselves out."

"Hopefully."

He arranged a tray with the teapot, cup and saucer, a spoon, and a little jar of honey. "It may taste bitter at first."

"Thank you." I reached out to take it from him but he kept the tray on the counter, held firmly in place with his hands.

"Verity . . . I . . . I didn't get the chance to truly speak with you in all of the excitement earlier, but I'm very pleased you'll be joining our family. Alexander is quite . . . quite special and I've always known that whoever he chose to welcome into his heart would be as well." He licked his lips. "I think he made an excellent choice."

"Thank you, Lord Laurent. Gerard," I amended.

"Father," he offered. "Though, perhaps . . . that might be . . ." He sounded flustered. "Marriage can be a difficult undertaking, even in the best of circumstances, and I'm glad you have a working understanding of what our lives here are like. As a daughter of a duke—sister to a duchess—you understand that . . . families like ours have specific duties, obligations. . . . I assume you were given lessons as a girl . . . ?"

I thought back to my school days, listening to our governess drone on and on about taxes and tenants, storerooms and stewardship. I nodded.

"Good. Good. Excellent. Then you know how things are passed along from parents to children, within estates such as ours."

I felt my face instantly redden and prayed to Pontus that he was talking about landholdings and not genetics. Camille's words burned as hotly in my mind now as the night she'd hissed them at me.

No one is going to want a mad little fiancée, for a mad little wife, issuing out mad little children.

As much as it pained me to admit it, she was right. No one would.

Becoming engaged to Alex was a step toward securing my future but it still could so easily be snatched out from under me with one wrong word, one careless moment.

I'd been so close to telling Gerard the terrible things I'd seen in the poison garden. I did not doubt that if I had, Alex's ring would not be sparkling upon my finger now.

I needed to be more vigilant. I needed to make sure Annaleigh's candles were kept burning.

"Of course," I murmured when it became clear he was waiting for an audible response.

"What sorts of things do you think you'll pass on to yours?"

I froze, my heart thudding painfully in my chest and shooting its pulse to the end of my fingertips. They throbbed with the pressure.

He knew.

He knew something.

But how?

"You mean my dowry?" I asked, finding my voice. "I . . . I don't know all the particulars of it. Camille does, of course."

"Of course." Gerard paused, as if struggling for the right words to continue. "You'll become a fine duchess one day." He opened his mouth, as if to say more, but I slid the tray away from him.

"I'm glad to hear you say how special Alexander is," I started, fighting the urge to flee. "Perhaps you ought to tell him so more often. I think it would mean a great deal to him, hearing you say that."

He blinked at me and I did my best not to look away first. "Perhaps you're right."

"I know I am . . . I think my tea is getting cold."

"Oh, yes. Yes, of course." He ran his fingers through his silver waves. Beet juice had made its way into his hairline, splattered in a fine mist of droplets. "I hope you have pleasant dreams, Verity, and that sleep finds you fast."

I wished him a good night and took the tray upstairs, making sure to keep my footsteps regulated and unhurried, unbothered. I was not a girl running from a situation grown perilous. Everything was fine.

The tea was bitter, even sweetened with the largest dollop of honey I could stomach, but I did not hear the peacocks again.

28

I WOKE THE NEXT DAY CONFUSED, MY BED DAMP AND sour. The sun came through the windows at a strange angle, far too high in the sky, and it wasn't until I glanced at the mantel clock that I realized I'd slept past noon.

There was a tapping at my door, persistent and small.

"Come . . . come in," I said, my voice strange and raspy. It was horribly dry, as if I'd spent the entire night with my mouth open, slack and gaping. Whatever flower had been in Gerard's tea, it had certainly done the trick.

Dauphine entered, carrying a giant ledger, and with a pair of footmen following her. One pushed a cart laden with silver domes and flatware. I prayed it contained a kettle full of coffee. The other footman held an intimidatingly tall stack of books.

Dauphine directed them to set everything in the sitting room and they were off.

"Just as I guessed," she said, peeking into the bedroom with a knowing smile. I pulled the bedsheets up to my chin. "I wanted to let you sleep in longer, but there simply is so much to do, I fear we'll never accomplish it all. Are you ready to start?"

"Start?"

"Wedding preparations, of course!"

"Oh." I pushed back strands of wild hair, feeling slightly queasy. Last night Dauphine had drank even more champagne than me. How did she look so radiantly fresh? "Shouldn't Alex be here for that as well?"

"My, someone is bleary when she wakes up," she said with a smile, bustling about the room, pushing open curtains and tying their sashes back. "We really will need to find you an attendant now, I suppose."

"Oh, that's not necessary. I can just—"

"Of course it is," Dauphine said, turning to study me. "You're a part of this family now, Verity. We want for you to feel at home, and to *be* at home. You're not simply a guest here anymore. Chauntilalie is your home too. We'll see that you get all you need."

I considered this carefully. "In that case . . . do you think it would be possible to switch out the candles used in my room?"

"Candles?" she echoed, blinking curiously about the suite.

I gestured to the crate of Annaleigh's sage and salt tapers. "My sister sent me these. They remind me of Highmoor. I'd prefer if they were kept in my rooms. The staff keeps refreshing my candlesticks with these pink ones. They're terribly pretty—but there's such a distinct scent, even when they're not lit."

She picked up the taper I'd used the night before and gave it an experimental whiff. "I'm not even sure where these came from," she admitted, wincing at the smell. "I'll see that they're all removed. In fact," she said, jotting down the note, "I'll make sure that's the first thing your new valet does."

"Bringing in another servant seems so wasteful. I could just borrow yours, as I need her."

"Her? I don't know who you mean."

"Your maid. I never caught her name."

She blinked at me curiously.

"She's blond . . . with very dark eyes?"

"I don't have a maid. . . . Bastian is my valet. His hands are far more nimble than any scullery maid's." Her grin deepened, as if remembering exactly how dexterous those fingers were, and then she laughed. "My dresses always have the most impossibly tiny buttons."

"Oh," I said, remembering the short man who trailed after her with the books. "Of course. She must have been a housemaid, then."

Dauphine gave me a peculiar stare. "There are no maids at Chauntilalie, Verity. I . . . I like to keep a firm control over"—she bit her lip—"the household expenses. It's far too extravagant, having so many girls underfoot."

"But . . ." I swallowed hard as I realized exactly who the young woman had been.

She wasn't a maid; she was one of Gerard's new conquests.

A mistress.

Kept right underneath Dauphine's nose.

I opened my mouth, ready to tell her, but there was something in her eyes. She knew. She knew or she suspected and was already bracing herself for the pain to come. I couldn't stand to be the one to bring it down upon her.

So I rubbed my forehead, feigning confusion. "Did I say a maid? I meant a footman. How silly of me." I offered out a remorseful grin. "I'm afraid last night's champagne has completely muddled my mind."

Dauphine paused before smiling, a beat late. "The fault is all mine. I shouldn't have burst in on you with all of this, just as you're waking. Why don't I let you get ready for the day and then we can begin our work? There's coffee and a light breakfast. I think that will do you a world of good. Will one hour be enough?"

I nodded.

"Out on the terrace, then, away from all this candle smoke."

༄

"You didn't say she was joining us," Marguerite grumbled as I stepped onto the terrace an hour later. I'd dressed in my best afternoon gown, pale blush linen with ladders of crocheted lace set into the bodice. It looked like the thing a bride-to-be ought to wear as she planned her wedding. I'd felt confident and assured as I walked through the halls of Chauntilalie. But three seconds of Marguerite's grousing already had me feeling wilted.

"We're looking through wedding details," Dauphine said, the corners of her painted lips tight. "Where else would she be?"

"You didn't say that either." Marguerite sipped at her tea, its surface dotted with tiny lilac petals, appraising me with a cool eye before turning away, making her stance completely known.

"Now, then," Dauphine said, setting aside her own cup of tea and picking up a pen. The table before us was a mess of paper and ink, color swatches and a calendar. "Will all your sisters serve as attendants?"

"The cursed girls? *They'll* be coming here?" Marguerite rubbed at her temple. "This truly is too much to bear."

"Mother," Dauphine hissed.

"Attendants, for the wedding," I repeated, trying to ignore the older woman. "I'm sure my sisters will be here, though I'll have to ask them. They still haven't heard about any of this, obviously."

I'd have to write them all and explain my news. I was sure Honor and Mercy would be delighted for me. Annaleigh too, probably. Pontus knows if I'd ever be able to locate Lenore to tell her. And Camille . . .

Part of me believed she would be happy. After all, I was marrying into a duchy; it would be a great honor for our family, help solidify her alliances on the mainland. But even still . . .

She'd not wanted me to leave in the first place. Telling her that I was to remain here forever might not go over well. Would she try to stop it? A sliver of worry flickered within me. I could absolutely imagine her writing to Gerard, making up an excuse why the wedding should not take place.

"Perhaps your older nieces could serve as flower girls."

"That's sweet of you to include them both. It would have been difficult to choose just one."

"Oh my dear, you'll have far more than just them! The flower ring is one of the most important parts of the ceremony—other than the vows, of course. You'll need at least eight for the traditional blossoms. Alexander will probably want alyssums as well . . . ," she murmured, jotting the note down. "So nine . . . Are there any flowers particularly meaningful to you?"

"I . . . I'm not sure. I don't even know what a flower ring is."

Marguerite let out a noise of strangled surprise. "You dragged me back for this? Why on earth are you allowing Alexander to marry this incompetent girl?"

Dauphine took a sip of her tea, stifling a sigh. I wasn't sure if it had meant to be directed at her mother-in-law or me. "I should have guessed the People of the Salt would have considerably different traditions than us. The flower ring begins the ceremony. Once your guests are seated, the little girls come out. Each girl represents one flower, one symbol. Myrtle for sacred love, ranunculus for future joy, and so on and so on. The girls cast their petals in a ring around the ceremony site to bind the couple in beauty and love. It's said that Arina herself used the traditional eight on her own wedding day to Vaipany."

"What a lovely idea," I murmured as I imagined it playing out. "Rock-roses, I think. Alex used them in a bouquet for me once."

She nodded approvingly. "'Of this I am most certain.' A perfect choice." She wrote it down with a flourish. "Next . . . your trousseau. I'd imagine you'll want to send for your things from home but . . . if I may speak frankly with you, Verity, your fashions lack a certain . . . style that's common for women in Bloem."

Marguerite cackled and I flushed the color of my day dress.

"I would like to help you select a new wardrobe. Your own clothing can be incorporated into it, of course, but there will be so many events over the next few weeks that will require . . . a touch more."

"More what?" I asked, glancing at each of the women's gowns.

"More everything," Marguerite said.

Dauphine's eyebrows furrowed in concern. "Oh, I don't mean to upset you, Verity, dear. I only want to make sure we're putting your best foot forward, yes? This is a different world than you're accustomed to."

"I know that. And I wouldn't want to do anything to cause embarrassment for Alexander or any of you."

"And you never could," Dauphine insisted.

Marguerite sniffed in disagreement.

I nodded and she pulled out the calendar.

"Now, the wedding will fall on . . . hmm . . . the eighteenth, so that won't give us much time."

"The eighteenth of . . ."

"Next month."

"Next month?" I gasped. "We're not getting married next month . . . are we?"

Dauphine blinked at my disbelief.

"Shouldn't we . . . shouldn't we find Alex? I'd hate for him to think we planned the whole event without his input."

"He already knows all of this, I'm certain. You've seen how devout he is and there are only a handful of dates sacred enough for a wedding. The eighteenth is the next one. If we don't choose that, you wouldn't be able to be married until"—she flipped through half a dozen pages, scouring the squares—"late fall."

"That wouldn't be so bad, though, would it? It would give us time to plan everything . . . send out invitations, make sure people will be able to attend."

Dauphine looked horrified. "Why wouldn't they attend?"

"Just . . . with it coming up so soon, I'm sure people have already committed to other—"

Marguerite's hand fell upon the tabletop, jostling the cups and saucers with a clatter. "What on earth could be more important than a wedding? The joining of two souls. If you don't comprehend the magnitude of what you're getting yourself into, girl, then you ought to give my grandson back his ring and be gone from us." She held out her hand, as if expecting me to acquiesce then and there.

"Mother!" a new voice rang out. Our heads snapped toward the house where Gerard stood, paused on the terrace threshold, listening to every hateful word Marguerite uttered. "I'm sorry to interrupt your tea, ladies, but Mother and I need to speak. Now."

"But—"

"Now," he repeated firmly, and came forward to pull her chair out from the table. It almost seemed like a gesture of polite deference, but I saw the tips of his fingers curved around the chair's back, white-hot in his anger.

I wanted to speak up, wanted to say something to assure everyone that Alex had made the right choice, that I would be the right match for him—for the family—but I couldn't. I didn't have the words, wasn't sure of the proper way to approach it.

With a brisk nod to Dauphine, then me, Gerard left, escorting Marguerite from the table with a firm grip around her elbow. We listened to their retreating footsteps in silence.

"So . . . ," Dauphine began after a long moment. Her smile looked too forced. "The eighteenth. We'll need dresses for the engagement party, the blessing ceremony . . ." Dauphine ran a finger over the weeks, reading her notes. "There's the Peaseblossoms' anniversary celebration. And the opening of the new botanical gardens—you're going to love the lily pond, it's magnificent. . . ."

"And the wedding, of course," I joked, trying to lighten the air between us. She didn't laugh. "I'll have to return to Salann, at least twice, I suppose." I already dreaded the thought.

"For what?"

"For the wedding gown. There's a designer on Astrea who has been making all of the Thaumas women's dresses for decades. Mrs. Drexel. She made both my sisters' wedding gowns—and my mother's."

Dauphine shook her head. "As you say, there's no time for all of that. Besides, a Salann designer wouldn't know all of the proper stitches that go into a wedding gown."

I smiled, certain she was teasing me. "Mrs. Drexel's gowns are legendary on the islands. Even Arina is said to shop there.... I'm confident her design will be spectacular."

"I'm sure they're very lovely, but there are specific knots and stitching that make up a Bloem wedding gown. Little slips of paper, with prayers and petals, are sewn into the boning. Roots in the hem to anchor the new couple. Every knot, every gather, is a symbol of two souls joining together. They may seem like silly customs to an outsider, but they mean a great deal to us. To him," she added with emphasis.

"I . . ." I bit my lip hard, summoning the courage to continue. "I don't want to be seen as an outsider and I don't want to let Alex down."

Dauphine softened. "I know this must be a lot to take in right now. But look over these designs," she said, and removed a pile of renderings from underneath a ledger. "Aren't they magnificent?"

In each sketch, the bride looked exactly like me.

A strange laugh tickled its way free from my throat. "Alex only proposed yesterday . . . where did all these come from?"

Now Dauphine smiled. "Oh, Verity, it's amazing the things you can accomplish if you don't spend the whole morning lazing about in bed." She took a sip of her tea, her lips leaving a perfect coral crescent on the rim of her cup, and started another list.

Dear Mercy,

I'm sorry it's been an age since I've written. Things here have been happening so quickly I scarcely know where to begin. I wish I was sitting in front of you, telling you this in person but ... I am engaged! To Alexander Laurent! Because of all the traditions the People of the Petals have for weddings, we'll be marrying in less than a month, on their next sacred date. I'm sending this missive by the Laurents' fastest messenger to personally ask you to be one of my bridal attendants. I promise you can have your pick of gowns and the prettiest bouquet. Write soon!

All my love,
Verity

Dear Annaleigh,

Alexander's courtship was swift—we are engaged to be married, and I want you to be one of my attendants, if you're willing. The wedding is set for next month—the Laurents have so many wildly different traditions than we do—but I hope you and Cassius and little Cecelia will be able to make it out. I know things are ... strained with Camille, but it is my most sincere wish that she's able to set aside her grievances with me and come here, ready to celebrate. I want things to return to how they were before. I want all my sisters back. Do you think you might try to reach out to her again? She's answered none of my letters but surely she will now—with such happy news? Also ... would you mind bringing another crate or two of the salted sage candles with you? They've been most helpful in keeping the ... homesickness at bay.

All my love,
Verity

Camille—

I'm not even sure why I'm writing this to you. I know you won't read it, but... you're my sister and I love you and I miss you and I wish you were here to tell this to in person... Alexander Laurent has proposed and I've accepted. We will be married next month—formal invitations will be sent out quite soon, I'm sure—but I wanted you to hear it from me first. I know you didn't approve of me coming here and I can't begin to guess at how you'll respond to this news... but I hope you're happy.

I am.

I hate this rift between us. I hate that I've been here so long and haven't heard one word from you. I know you're angry but please, please put those feelings aside. For the wedding day. Just one day. For me. Your littlest sister. Who loves you.

All my heart,
Verity

29

"YOU SEEM QUIET TODAY," ALEX OBSERVED, KEEPING his frame so still that even his lips barely moved. "Is everything all right?"

I flicked my paintbrush through a dab of gray paint on the palette. "Just tired, I suppose."

"You sound it," he said. "Another bad night?"

"I don't understand how you sleep through those peacocks," I admitted, running the brush over the canvas with a careful hand. They were trembling a little today. Weeks of sleepless nights were taking a toll on me. I'd indulged in an extra cup of coffee at breakfast and now felt like a coil wound too tight, about to snap. "You really don't hear them?"

The peacocks' cries lingered in my ears, even long after the screaming stopped. I'd be up for hours after waking, too rattled and unable to drift off until I stole down to the kitchen to make myself a pot of Gerard's blooming tea. It was the only thing that could soothe me enough to slip back to sleep.

"Occasionally, but not as you describe. They must prefer the northern end of the gardens for some reason. I'll talk to one of the groundskeepers about it. Perhaps they can try creating a roost for them somewhere farther from the house."

"That would be wonderful. Last night, they sounded so close I actually went into the hall, brandishing a poker from the fireplace."

Those cries were the worst, high-pitched and throaty. It reminded me of when the twins had been born and all of Highmoor was kept awake with their wails.

"Oh, Verity," Alex murmured, looking concerned. He ruined it a moment later by bursting into a snort of laughter.

"You find my predicament amusing?" I asked, peeking around the canvas. "You do know I'm more than capable of adding a series of warts across your face, don't you? Your portrait will be resoundingly mocked by generations of future Laurents."

He held up a hand, trying to stop, but doubled over again anyway. "I just pictured you, running out in the hall—obviously looking quite alluring in your nightdress," he added quickly, "with the poker thrown outward, ready for harm." Alex pantomimed slaying one of the beasts before glancing up at me. His eyes danced with happiness and despite my irritation over the birds, I found myself smiling back before I resumed painting.

The portrait was nearing completion. I only needed to add in the highlights and shadows that would make the work seem more realistic, and finish up a couple of details in the background before I started his face. I liked to save the face for last.

In truth, I didn't want the sessions to end.

My moments with Alex were the best parts of my day.

Dauphine had every one of my waking moments planned and

accounted for. She always had a reason for us to go to town, pushing the portrait sessions to the often forgotten back burner. She seemed to take delight in overriding any suggestions or ideas I might have for the wedding. Or my clothing. Or my very appearance.

Earlier that morning, she'd declared we had an appointment at a perfumery to pick out my new signature scent, something to befit a future duchess.

"I don't really wear perfume," I'd said, looking up from my third cup of coffee.

She had nodded, as if more than aware.

Gerard spent nearly all of his hours in the greenhouse, delaying dinners and causing bright spots of anger across Dauphine's cheeks, except for when he popped up at the most inconvenient times, ready to test my knowledge of the noble houses of Arcannia and peppering the conversation with veiled hints and increasingly unsubtle statements alluding to the long line of progeny I was meant to issue forth.

Stacks of books grew in my sitting room, filled with things he expected me to become well versed in. They teetered on my writing desk as tall as towers. I meant to read them, I really did, but by the end of the day, after portrait sessions and dress fittings, food tastings and luncheons with Dauphine's friends, I often collapsed into bed, utterly spent.

And then . . . the peacocks.

It was as if I were trapped in a whirlpool, circling and spinning around, drawn in tighter, unable to swim out of its hold. Moments with Alex made me feel like myself. Our time together was still and sweet and . . . us. There were no ulterior motives, no barbed comments. I could breathe freely.

"The Peaseblossoms' anniversary banquet is later this week," he mentioned, his mind wandering.

I recalled the older couple from Dauphine's dinner. It felt like an age had passed since then, though it had only been three weeks. "How many years have they been together?"

"Fifty-five."

I raised my eyebrows, impressed.

"That will be us one day," he predicted confidently. "Fifty-five years from now, I'll look over to you in the middle of our party and say, 'Remember that spring you painted my portrait? What a foolish young man I was then. I'd thought you'd never look lovelier, but, look at you now . . . magnificent.'"

"And I'll lean in and squawk at you to repeat everything you said because I couldn't hear it the first time."

Alex beamed. "I've no doubt our love will be stronger then than it is today, even if our hearing is not."

My smile froze, then faltered.

"What are you thinking about?" Alex asked, astute as ever.

I pushed a bit of paint about the palette, buying myself a moment. I hadn't yet told Alex about my encounter with Gerard's mistress on the day of our engagement. I knew I needed to—I kept far too many other secrets from him to let another add up—but I wasn't sure how to go about it. It wasn't something that found a natural outlet into everyday conversation.

"Verity?" he prompted, rolling forward. He reached out for my hand but stopped short of touching me. "Did I say something wrong?"

"Of course not."

"Sometimes I worry that—" He stopped short.

"What?"

"Nothing." He looked away.

I tipped my head, trying to catch his gaze.

He pressed his lips together. "I'm so new at all this. I fear . . . I worry that I might come on too strong, too zealous."

"Oh, Alex, no," I started, then registered what he'd admitted. "You get nervous?"

He nodded and my heart swelled, touched by the vulnerability of his admission.

"I do too." I set the palette and paintbrush aside. "I worry . . . all of the time."

Alex's eyebrows furrowed together. "About what?"

"That I'm going to do something to mess this up . . . to mess *us* up. I don't know what I'm doing—ever really—but especially with you. I don't want to do the wrong thing and end up with you . . . unsatisfied."

"Oh, Verity," he murmured, his hand falling on mine. "That's not possible. Never."

"You say that, but . . ." I trailed off, thinking of Dauphine, of the hurt that had been in her eyes.

"I am *nothing* like my father," he said, guessing at the words I didn't say. "I swear to you, here and now, you are it. You are everything. No one else in the world could ever steal me from you." He cupped his hands over my cheeks. "I will never do anything to hurt you." He pressed his lips to my forehead, sealing his promise with a kiss. "I will never stray." Another kiss. "I would never want to."

My insides squirmed, wondering if he would make such declarations if he fully knew me, if he fully knew what things crept into my vision, what things resided within my mind.

"I . . . I have a bit of a surprise for you," he admitted.

"You do?"

He nodded and took my hands once more. "Come to the settee for a moment."

"Oh." I glanced at the paints, wondering if I ought to cover them.

"It won't be long, but you might as well be comfortable," he said, catching my worry. He drew me over to the tufted couch, letting me settle in before positioning his chair beside me. "I've been thinking about after the wedding."

"After?" I echoed. Dauphine had me so focused on every detail for the day itself, I hadn't given much thought to what came after.

"Most couples go away for a trip, a tour of the continent or to a little retreat, while their home is being readied for its new mistress."

"Oh, of course." Camille had been gone for nearly a month after marrying William. Mercy, Honor, and I had remained at Highmoor, looked after by our governess and Hanna. *Only not*, I reflected, my chest tightening as it always did when I thought of her.

Alex licked his lips. "But as far as homes go . . . we're in a bit of a unique situation . . . because of me. There are several houses we could choose to start out in . . . until the day comes for us to move back to Chauntilalie."

He said it with such certainty, and I wondered what that must feel like, to have so much of your life planned away and assured. Camille hadn't grown up knowing she would become duchess. She'd been born fifth of twelve. Most of her childhood must have been like mine, wondering over what was in store for her, wondering where and how she would make her place in the world.

But Alex has always known. He was the heir. He would become the duke.

He chewed on the inside of his cheek. "Though . . . Father has said we'd be more than welcome to stay here, at Chauntilalie, for as long as we like. . . ."

I swallowed, wanting to protest but unsure of how Alex would react. It sounded harsh and ungrateful but I had looked forward to a future without Dauphine planning every moment of my existence, one where I wouldn't need to fear run-ins with Marguerite and her scowls. One without Gerard ferreting out my secrets like a bloodhound on the hunt.

"But I told him no," he continued on, a look of worry crossing his face.

"You did?"

"I want us to have the chance to be us . . . away from them . . . away from everything, for a time."

I reached out to cup his cheek, rubbing my thumb softly over his skin. It felt like the right thing to do and I was surprised at how naturally it happened, without the slightest bit of overthinking. "I'm so glad."

"You are?"

I smiled. "Very, very glad."

Alex breathed out a sigh of relief. "I was so nervous you'd say you wanted to stay at Chauntilalie. It's a lovely old house and I can't wait to grow old here with you, but . . ."

"But first we need a home, for just us."

"I agree. Just us." His eyes were warm, his pupils dark and

dilated. "Verity? Might I . . . Would it be all right if I . . . Could I hold you?"

"Hold me?" I echoed, uncertain of what he was suggesting.

He nodded, his eyes hopeful and earnest.

"How?"

Carefully, he brought his chair forward before reaching out to scoop me into his lap. I laughed, too surprised to feel uncomfortable with our closeness. He folded my skirts out of the way of the wheels. For a moment, his hand rested on my upper thigh, perched as lightly as a question. Then he embraced me, pulling my side flush against his chest. I could hear his heart beat and breathed in his scent, a combination of his soap and aftershave, something green and wholly Alexander.

"We'll need a studio," he mused thoughtfully. "In our house. A room with bright, big windows overlooking some water. I don't want you ever to be far away from the waves."

"Our house," I repeated, a smile playing fondly on my lips. "And there will be a library for you. Low bookshelves lining all the walls. You'll be able to reach them all."

"I like that idea." His voice was low and dreamy and he wrapped his arms around me, holding me close.

I liked this. I loved us.

It felt as though we were wrapped up in a sunbeam, warmed by thoughts of a future together. I was comfortable and happy and didn't feel pressured to do anything but this.

I snuggled closer to Alex, pressing an experimental kiss to his cheek.

I didn't stop to overthink it.

I wanted.

And I did.

And it felt . . . nice.

Easy.

Right.

Finally.

"This is perfect," I whispered.

All of the vexations and slights I'd felt since the engagement slid away. It didn't matter that his mother thought I was unsophisticated and lacking in style. It didn't matter his grandmother thought me cursed.

Alex was the only one who mattered. The only one I trusted wholly and implicitly.

We'd be the ones writing our story.

Us, on our own.

Together.

"This is us," he promised, kissing my forehead with a tenderness so sweet I ached for another. "For the rest of our lives."

Later that night, the peacocks woke me once again.

A giant full moon hung low in the sky, casting an otherworldly blue glow over my bedchambers.

"Go downstairs, get the tea," I muttered, pulling myself out from under the coverlet with a sigh.

I was too exhausted to search for my slippers, and the cold floorboards chilled my bare feet as I padded downstairs. The route had become so familiar to me, I didn't bother with a candle. I now knew the path by heart.

All the lights in the manor were off, but moonlight poured in through the open windows, illuminating the rooms and hallways. The air was redolent and sweet with Gerard's night-blooming jasmine fragrant on the breeze.

My conversation with Alexander was still fresh on my mind and as I wandered the long corridors, I tried imagining myself as mistress of all this wonder. What painting would I one day hang there? Would I keep those damask drapes? How would we leave our mark on this manor?

However we did it, I knew it would be done together. Generations of Laurents would speak of us in reverent, awed tones. Our love story would be the stuff of legends.

Movement drew my attention farther down the hall.

Up ahead, someone stood in the center of the arched corridor, studying a portrait on the wall.

The figure was too masculine to be Dauphine, too tall to be Gerard.

A footman, then, up far too late, just like me.

I let out a short cough, to alert him of my presence, and he turned, startled. A moonbeam cut across his face and I gasped.

There, standing unassisted, without support of any kind, was Alex.

We stared at each other for a long moment. Disbelief silenced me.

He brought one finger up to his lips, a gesture beseeching for my silence. Then he smiled, the curve of his so familiar lips now twisted and strange, and turned and walked away.

30

I STARED AT THE SPOT HE'D STOOD—

Alex.

Standing.

—blinking as if it would somehow bring him back, but of course it didn't.

So I went after him.

I wasn't familiar with this section of Chauntilalie, and as soon as I stepped into the new corridor—the walls painted in murals of wildflower fields—I knew it. Carpeted runners spanned the length of the hall, deadening my footsteps. After a month of hearing my progress in the house marked by echoes around me, it felt strange to suddenly hear nothing.

I stopped, trying to hear movement in the rooms off the hallway, but there was none.

Then, a strange silvery crunch, like glass breaking. It rang out sharply, coming from somewhere down the hallway.

Several doors were ajar and I cautiously peeked into each. A grand piano rested in one, a hulking black structure in the middle of an otherwise empty room. The next contained stacks of crates and barrels—storage for the manor.

The third room's door was half closed and I pushed it open fully, then jumped.

It was another storeroom, but its contents were not dry goods or salted meats. It was artwork.

Statues.

Life-sized and filling the room like an army, each covered in a pale protective drop cloth.

Alex had gone in there, I was certain of it. There was a difference here, the heavier feeling of another presence, another person. The air moved about to let a second body occupy its space.

"Alex?" I called out, my voice sounding too high.

What was he doing in here?

So late at night.

Standing.

Walking.

I sighed. "I know you're in here."

Somewhere deeper in the room, obscured by the sea of sheets, something stirred.

I took a step in, breathing in the scent of long-forgotten items and dust. "Alex, I know it's you. Just come out. Come out and explain—"

Behind me, another sound, like someone had cleared their throat.

I studied the pair of statues on either side of the door suspiciously.

Was he hiding behind one of them?

Without warning, I whipped off the sheet, revealing a trio of winged angels, flying in a cluster of limbs and beatific smiles.

The second statue was a pair of cranes, their necks bent down at strange angles to study a small brass frog between their feet.

A soft sigh came from farther in the room.

"Alex, this isn't funny." My voice wasn't as assured as I wished it was. A quaver of uncertainty reverberated my tone.

I sounded scared.

Standing on the threshold, I tried to rationalize this situation, this bizarre and bewildering predicament.

I'd seen Alex.

Walking.

But he couldn't. I'd witnessed his struggles getting in and out of the chair, his reliance on Frederick. He couldn't fake that.

Could he?

That was madness.

So it wasn't Alex.

Then who?

I glanced about the storeroom, fear stealing its way across my heart like the icy creep of hoarfrost over a winter field.

There was that servant, the night of Dauphine's dinner party. I'd seen him. Frederick had seen him. We'd both thought him Alex.

He was here again. Right now. Back at Chauntilalie and roaming the halls in the middle of the night and I'd cornered him.

A light hiss, like someone letting out a breath held for too long. The hairs on my arms rose. It sounded closer now. Didn't it?

I bit the inside of my cheek. I had to act. I had to do something.

The young man in the hallway had been quite tall. On my own, I'd be nearly powerless against such a formidable opponent.

I needed help.

But if I went to find it, I'd risk losing him, letting him slip away.

I could scream—my voice joining the peacocks' cries. The cries that still filled the air, unnoticed and unchecked.

No.

I'd have to do this myself.

"You're still here," a voice behind me muttered, and I did scream then, crying out in alarm and the sudden terrible notion that this doppelgänger had somehow worked his way out of the room before circling back to harm me.

But it was the young woman who had dressed me the morning of Alex's proposal.

The young woman who was not a maid.

My eyes narrowed.

This was the girl Gerard had named his flowers after.

The girl who had filled Alex's heart with scorn.

Gerard's mistress.

"Why are you still here?" she asked.

"There's someone in there," I whispered, dragging her into the situation whether she wanted to come or not. "Constance."

Her eyes widened. "You know my name?"

I ignored her surprise. "You need to help me. There's an intruder in the house. I think it's someone who was here the day of the dinner party, come back to . . . I don't know . . . steal . . . *something*." It sounded right, a wayward man using temporary jobs to scope out new locations for his heists.

"And you think he's in there?" she murmured slowly. Her eyes flickered over the statues. "I don't see anyone."

"He's hiding. Under the drops."

"That seems rather far-fetched, don't you think?"

"I saw him," I insisted. "Go in and see for yourself."

Constance's face twisted. "I don't . . . I wish I could."

"Go," I ordered, all but pushing her into the room.

With a muttered sigh, Constance reached for the light switch. The room remained dark. "See?" she said, turning back to me. "I can't—"

"Look," I pointed.

Sparkles of glass lay on the ground, all around her. The globes covering the gas lamps had been shattered. It was a wonder she'd not cut herself.

"Do you believe me now?" I hissed.

Constance swept her gaze over the room, now worried, and nodded.

"Open the drapes," she mouthed.

On silent tiptoes, I made my way to the other side of the room and, after a moment of struggling within the folds of heavy curtains, pulled on a set of cords and flooded the space with moonlight.

The canvas drops glowed an eerie blue and I watched them for any telltale trace of movement.

The room was still.

I looked at the girl, at Gerard's mistress, and shrugged.

Constance raised one pointer finger to her lips, a chilling echo of the gesture the young man had made just minutes before. Then she pointed to one of the statues and motioned to rip the sheet off. She glanced meaningfully at the statue by me.

I nodded.

Raising my hand, I counted us down.

Three.

My stomach churned, feeling sick.

Two.

My palms were sweaty as I picked up the edge of the cover.

One.

I whipped my drop cloth away, revealing a marbled statue of more cherubs. Undeterred, I removed more cloths, sending dust soaring into the air, burning our eyes. Smaller pieces tipped over in our haste to uncover everything, falling to the floor and creating a terrible cacophony. Over and over we ripped off sheets, making our way toward the center of the room until . . .

Only a single statue remained.

It was tall, taller than me, and I could so easily envision someone hiding beneath the fabric. I squinted, almost certain I could see the folds rise and fall. Someone was there, breathing.

I was the one closest to it.

The mistress nodded at me, her eyes wide with fear.

I licked my lips, then pulled. The canvas cover sailed away, revealing a dark figure.

Constance screeched and I shouted and the figure remained silent.

And still.

Arina's eyes, blank and bronzed, regarded us with an expression of mirth, as if she found our predicament amusing.

"He's not . . . he's not here," I murmured, looking through the mess we'd made. He must have been there, hiding beneath the fallen covers or toppled metal urns. "Where is he?"

Constance scoured the room, her sharp eyes missing nothing.

"You're sure you saw someone?" I nodded. "In here?" she persisted.

"I . . . I thought I had." My voice sounded childish and small.

She waited to speak for such a long moment that I was left wondering if she believed me at all.

"But you . . ."

I sensed she was struggling with something inside herself, weighing her options, deciding her next action.

"You see many things, don't you?"

A chill ran over me. It was obvious that Gerard suspected me capable of . . . something, though I prayed he didn't understand the full scope of my abilities. And he'd told her this. Was that what they spoke of while they . . . I shook my head against the unwanted images.

She sighed. "Come with me, Verity."

∽

"Tell me everything," Constance ordered once we were in the kitchen, the gas lamps glowing brightly.

I sat down on a stool along the island, tucking my feet up on its highest rung, wishing I could curl into myself and forget the humiliating shame of this night. All of my secrets—seeing spirits, that terrible little voice in my head—were about to be yanked out.

By this girl.

Gerard's mistress.

She'd tell him everything I said and that would be that.

My engagement would be broken.

I'd never see Alex again.

I'd be lucky if I wasn't cast off to an asylum.

Perhaps Camille would visit, lording her sanity and unquestionable rightness over me.

Constance reached out as if to put her hand over mine, drawing me from my spiral of thoughts. But she stopped just short of touching me, indecision written across her features. "Verity . . . you can tell me anything. I'll believe you. You don't have to hold all this on your own." An intense fervor brightened her eyes. "I won't tell a soul."

"You wouldn't tell Gerard?" I asked cautiously, feeling like an animal approaching a trap, sensing the danger but willing to ignore it for the allure of the promised bait.

She bit back a laugh. "I assure you, he'll never hear a thing from me."

My question fell out before I could think through its appropriateness. "Did something happen between you?"

Her head dipped, cheeks red, though I couldn't tell if it was shame or anger that caused them to burn. "Yes. You could say that."

"I . . ." I didn't know what to say.

I hated that this girl had hurt Dauphine, that her presence in the house was a jagged burr, tearing a marriage apart with its festering thorns. When she was a mere concept, a name listed in some little notebook, one girl out of dozens, it had been so easy to despise her, to dismiss her. She was just a mistress.

But the pained expression etched across her face made my heart ache.

It wasn't her I hated, or all the women who had come before her.

It was Gerard.

He had brought these girls here, these *mistresses*, and when he was done with them, finished wringing out whatever novel pleasure it was he'd found within them, he moved on to the next. I wondered how many girls had left Chauntilalie with those hollow eyes, those burning cheeks.

Constance balled her hands into fists. "None of that matters right now. I need to know about tonight. What happened? What did you see?"

Slowly, in half starts, I told her everything. Hearing the peacocks, spotting Alex in the hall, seeing him walk away. I told her about the servant I'd seen the morning of Dauphine's party, the one who looked so much like Alexander. How Frederick had seen him too. When I was done, I felt wrung out, impossibly exhausted.

She pressed her lips together, mulling over my tale. "You said you were going to get tea?"

I nodded wearily.

"A cup of chamomile will do you a world of good," Constance reasoned, glancing toward the rack of tins lining the wall above the sink.

"Not chamomile," I protested. "The blooming tea. In the purple hexagon."

With obvious reluctance, she reached on tiptoe to grab it. The tin fell through her fingers and clattered onto the countertop. Constance turned toward me, shaking her head slowly, fearfully. "Oh, Verity. I'm certain this isn't what you want."

"Of course it is." I slid off the stool and busied myself, preparing the kettle of water, lighting the stove. "It's the only thing that helps me sleep."

I picked up the tin and removed one of the tightly packed blossoms. Her face wrinkled with disgust and she swatted her hand out, casting the flower into the fire. Constance looked as stunned by her sudden action as I was.

The scent of the burning tea leaves filled the room. It was a familiar scent but I couldn't place exactly where I'd smelled it before.

Unease flickered through my insides. "What is it?"

"They're poppy flowers. Poppies," she repeated with emphasis, as if that was enough to make me understand.

"What . . . what does that mean? I don't know anything about . . ." I stopped short, my words dying away as I remembered the sectioned off area of the greenhouse. "Are they poisonous?"

Her eyebrows furrowed. "Not exactly. But . . . the pods of the flowers can create a terribly powerful drug. They can cause you to fall into deep sleeps, almost like an unconscious swoon. Some people don't wake for days. Some . . . don't wake at all."

I recalled my mornings after drinking the tea: waking in the same position I'd fallen asleep in, hot and disoriented, my limbs aching from not shifting at all in sleep. I'd blamed the peacocks for causing such exhaustion, but what if . . .

"Why . . . why would anyone drink that?"

"It's said that these states, these trances, help to open minds. The tea can thin the veil between worlds. It lets you see beyond the here and now."

"What do you mean? What worlds?" I flashed back to the memory of the woman with the black tears. Of my terribly, terribly dead sisters. Gerard had said something similar after my encounter with the laurel tree in the poison garden. "The afterlife? People see the afterlife?"

She offered me a weak smile. "Or . . . the Sanctum. Some use this to speak to the gods. . . . It also can make you see things," Constance added meaningfully. "Things here, that others can't."

"Things like . . . like Alexander walking through corridors," I guessed.

She nodded.

A hallucination.

The boy I'd seen had been nothing but a hallucination.

It had felt so real.

"How long do its effects last? I've been drinking it for weeks. Would it . . . would it still be in me tonight?" I squirmed, imagining the toxic tea slithering through my bloodstream, a jeweled snake with poison dripping from its fangs.

Constance peered at the canister as if the answer might be printed upon its metal sides. I noticed she would not touch it. "I don't know. I think it depends on how much you drink, on the potency of the brew."

"Why would Gerard give me this?"

Her gaze listed away, carefully avoiding me. "Maybe he wanted to see what you would see . . ."

There was a mistake, a misunderstanding somewhere. Perhaps someone else had put the poppies in and Gerard hadn't realized it. Perhaps *I* had grabbed the wrong tin. Gerard was capable of many things but he would never willingly hurt me.

Would he?

A scream sliced through the air, sharp in pitch, pounding my head and scraping my eardrums raw. I flinched.

Constance turned to the whistling kettle. So quick was she to silence it, she forgot to grab a cloth. I cried out a warning as her fingers wrapped around the hot handle.

"Let me," I said, hastily pushing her back as I wrapped a towel round the metal. I moved the whistling pot to the back burner. Its cry died away. I cringed before looking toward Constance, fearing the worst.

But she seemed fine.

She stood at attention, watching me with wide eyes.

Her hands remained loose at her sides.

"You should run cold water over that," I said, gesturing.

She remained still.

Had she gone into shock?

"Constance?" I prompted.

When I stepped forward, gently tugging her toward the sink, I saw her fingers were unharmed. I flipped her hands over, certain I'd somehow missed seeing the burns, but there was nothing, just pink, unmarred skin.

"Could you let go of me, please?" Her request was strained, taut.

"What?" I ran my fingers over hers, unable to understand what I was seeing.

"It's harder to do this when you're touching me."

A strange dread prickled at the back of my neck. I could feel it work its way lower, skittering down my vertebrae like a long-legged spider, testing a strand of silk.

"Do what?" Each word fell from my lips like stone boulders and I was struck by the dreamy sensation that we were moving too slowly, caught in a moment of time gone wrong.

"Touch things," she admitted. "Move things. Be here."

My hand, clutched so tightly around hers, was suddenly empty.

She'd disappeared, flickering from sight like a candle blown out by a draft.

My mouth fell open as I looked around, acknowledging I was the only one in the kitchen.

"Constance?" I asked, my voice carrying small and stupidly through the empty space.

She was gone.

"Constance?" I repeated, and I could hear a note of hysteria rising up, threatening to break me.

There was no response.

Of course there wasn't.

Constance, Gerard's Constance, was gone.

Gone, as if she'd never been there at all.

Gone, like the ghost she was.

31

A GHOST.

Constance.

Constance was a ghost.

"How?" I asked aloud, feeling foolish. The room was empty. No one was going to answer. Least of all . . .

Constance.

Who was. . . .

I shook my head.

This wasn't right. This couldn't be.

I'd worried she was a ghost the day I'd first seen her, standing in the parlor, drawn to that enormous confection of a dress. I'd thought she was a spirit until . . .

I'd grabbed her hand.

Or she'd grabbed mine.

Something.

There'd been something that day. Something that had assuaged my fears and convinced me she was real.

But I'd touched her tonight too. I'd seen her pick up the tin of poppy tea. I'd watched her pull down the canvas covers in the storage room.

Hadn't I?

I rubbed at my forehead, trying to remember.

I hadn't touched her. Not in the hallway. Once I'd realized she was Gerard's mistress, my stomach had churned with disgust, holding me from her. But the tea . . .

The tea had fallen through her hands.

I remembered its metallic clank as it struck the counter.

And in the storage room, I'd been so preoccupied with pulling down as many drop cloths as quickly as I could. It had been a moment of such flurried, singular focus. I couldn't deny it was possible I'd torn them all away myself. . . .

I covered my mouth, stifling back the cry that wanted to rip free. My ribs ached from the strain of holding such pressure in.

Constance had been alive and well the day of my engagement.

But now she was a ghost.

Once alive. Now dead.

What had happened to her?

A sudden scream filled the air.

It wasn't the teakettle. It wasn't me. And the peacocks had fallen silent.

I trembled as the cries echoed off the tiled walls. The keening pitched flat, saturating the night with a pained anguish impossible to ignore. I didn't want to see what caused such a sound. But I also couldn't do nothing.

Holding my breath, I tiptoed from the kitchen, unsure of what horror I was about to stumble upon.

The corridor was empty.

Until it wasn't.

Far down the hall, I caught sight of Constance. There was a wink of blue linen as she flickered in and out of sight, like the sun playing peekaboo on a cloudy day. There for a moment and gone the next, only to reappear farther away.

She was going somewhere, deeper into the house.

"Constance?" I murmured.

She didn't turn, didn't acknowledge that she'd heard me at all.

"Constance!" I hissed.

Still no response. She carried on, traveling down the hall with unknown purpose, disappearing every few seconds, only to flare back into sight.

I wanted to call after her, to cry and shout and scream, but Chauntilalie's silence stopped me short. I wouldn't learn anything if I woke up everyone in the manor. So I kept my mouth shut and followed after her.

Constance came to a fork in the hall, then took the left.

I hurried to catch up before I lost sight of her completely.

As I got closer, I became aware she was talking, her voice low and furtive, as if she didn't want anyone to overhear her. I strained to make out her words.

"You must do something for them. They—" Her voice cut off as she disappeared again.

She came back farther away. "You said you could help me. You said you could help them." Her words rose in pitch, growing tremulous and tinged with agitation.

"Constance?"

This time she paused and turned, looking down the hall, worry evident. But our eyes didn't meet. It was as though she didn't see me at all, as if it was suddenly I, not her, who was the ghost.

"I thought I heard something," she murmured, her brown eyes scanning the darkened space. They fell briefly on me but flitted away again without acknowledgment. "I think someone's following us." She blinked out again, leaving me alone.

All around me, shadows seemed to press in, darker than before, cloaking me in their heavy murk. The silence stretched out like a line of silk ribbon, fibers pulling apart and fraying the tighter I held on. When Constance finally reappeared—this time coming up from behind me, turning the corner as she had just a moment before—I nearly shrieked aloud.

"You must do something for them. You said you could help me. You said you could help them."

I frowned. Hadn't she just said that?

"I thought I heard something." Her eyes swept up and down the corridor, the expression on her face identical to before. "I think someone's following us."

Again, she disappeared, only to reappear once more, coming up from behind me. I watched her repeat this procession again. And again. And a third time. My head darted back and forth as if watching Camille's twins playing a game of badminton on Highmoor's lawn.

Constance seemed to be retracing the steps she'd carried out in life, over and over, as if caught in a swift current, unable to break free. As she started the loop once more, I stepped in front of her, trying to alter her route, but she walked straight through me. The hairs on my arms rose as goose bumps broke out all over my body.

It wasn't a chill that made me shiver.

This was wrong.

She felt wrong, an entity thrown into the wrong time and place.

I wanted to help her but I was powerless to stop the cycle from playing out again and again.

"What happened next?" I whispered, rubbing my hands over my arms. I didn't feel right. It was as though her wrongness had somehow imprinted itself upon me. "What are you trying to show me, Constance?"

"You said you could help me." She flickered. "You said you could help them."

Again, the pause. Again her words. "I thought I heard something." But this time Constance faded out, dropping the last line.

I glanced back toward the kitchen, ready for the sequence to start again.

But then she reappeared in the middle of the corridor, farther along it than she'd ever reached before. She had paused beside a bas-relief, anger marring her face.

"No. No. You said you could fix them," she protested. "That's not good enough!" I watched her hands rise, striking out at an unseen companion. Her shoulder jerked as though they'd hit back and her eyes grew round and fearful.

Constance's form flickered with greater frequency now, nearly translucent even in her strongest moments, and I wondered if she was tiring. I'd never noticed Hanna struggle so—it certainly would have helped tip me off to her secret sooner if she had—but she'd also been dead for far longer than Constance.

"You must come and see—" She swiped at the stone mural,

her hands disappearing into a cluster of flowers, and walked through the wall, leaving me behind.

I studied the artwork before me, certain there was a secret passage concealed behind it.

I brightened when I spotted the spiky leaves of an oleander plant.

Oleanders meant distrust, warning that you couldn't always believe what your eyes told you.

With a smile, I pushed the little plaster blooms, and a hidden panel swung open.

The tunnel beyond was as black as a tomb.

I glanced back hopefully down the hall, praying for a candlestick or lantern, anything to help light my way. But there was nothing and as I hesitated, I could hear Constance's voice echoing off the brick walls, growing fainter. I'd have to go in blind.

The door clicked shut behind me and I waved my hands about, trying to situate myself within the darkened space. The walls on either side of me were close and rough. In front, there was nothing but a void perforated with dusty cobwebs.

"You can't keep doing this."

Constance's voice rang out as shrill as a siren. I followed after it.

The floor was uneven, riddled with unexpected dips that sent me stumbling into the walls. My hips ached, already sore with the promise of bruises to come, but I pressed on.

"She'll never go along with it."

Gradually, the passage sloped upward at such an angle I knew we were no longer on the first floor of the manor. But it didn't feel as if we were on the second either.

"I'm going to tell her," Constance warned, sounding closer now, though I still couldn't see her. "I'm going to tell her tonight."

I reached out, hoping to grab hold of her.

"You won't get away with it," she promised. "She's going to find out everything."

"Find out what?" I asked before crashing into something suddenly in front of me. Dazzling stars burst across my vision and my head spun.

"Stay away from me," Constance hissed. "Get back."

For a moment, I thought she had struck me, but then I felt a new brick wall. The passage must have come to a split. To my left I saw a faint glow of candlelight, limning the surface of the tunnel a dull gray. Constance was between the light and me, her wavering silhouette filling up the tight space.

"Stop it."

She raised her hands in a defensive posture, backing away from me.

"Put those down," she ordered. "You won't hurt me. You can't. They won't live without me."

Constance fell back with pained surprise, struggling against the unseen assailant. She clutched at her chest, a spot of red blooming across her bodice. She was struck again, her cries low and guttural.

"No. No, please. I didn't mean it. I won't . . . I promise—"

Her boots scuffled against the floor, thrashing and kicking. There was a moment I thought she might be able to escape the attack, but then she floundered, falling over. Her head struck the wall. She clutched at her neck and wet, rattling gasps filled the passage.

"No!" she screamed once, and I recognized the anguish and despair. It was the scream I'd heard in the kitchen.

Then she flickered out, gone.

I stood in frozen horror, unable to look away from the spot she'd just been.

Constance had been murdered, here in this very corridor.

But by who?

She'd indicated she and Gerard had had a falling-out. Had it become physical? He had his faults—many, many faults—but I couldn't picture him taking a life. His hands created, fashioning growth out of nothing but soil and seeds.

It couldn't have been him.

I pictured Dauphine's expression the day after my engagement, when we'd talked about hiring a servant for me, when she'd flatly explained there were no maids in her house. She'd known then that Gerard had brought in another mistress. Had she discovered Constance's whereabouts and gone after the girl?

I cringed, picturing a twisted, jealous glint in Dauphine's eyes.

Yes. I could see all that play out again, with her at the helm.

The tunnel seemed suddenly darker and I could feel the weight of all of the stones and shadows around me. I imagined a deep rumble, the bricks shifting loose as the house shuddered. Everything would come collapsing down on me. I would be swallowed alive, trapped forever in the ruins of Chauntilalie.

I needed to get out of here. I needed to escape this darkness.

I fled down the corridor, chasing after the promise of candlelight.

I crashed through the partially open door, blinking in surprise at the unexpectedly cheerful surroundings.

Where was I?

Feeling ill, I turned about in a slow circle, taking in every detail with dull incomprehension.

It was a playroom.

The walls were painted a rich blue, like the night sky, with foiled stars pressed in deep.

A trio of rocking horses lined one wall, as if at the start of a race. Their painted eyes were wide and their mouths peeled back into grimaces around wooden bits. For a moment, I could almost hear their whinnies.

There were stuffed bears, rattles, and blocks.

Everything was in sets of three.

Clusters of pink candles burned, tall and bright, and filled the nursery with their pungent, familiar odor. A paper mobile hung in front of an ivy-covered window, little stars and moons spinning in slow circles, caught in a draft.

I tried peeking out the window, to give myself a sense of where exactly I was in the house, but the vines made for an effective cover and I couldn't see beyond them.

An open door led to another room. A single candle lit the new space with a soft glow.

"What is this place?" I whispered, stepping over the threshold.

I froze when I realized I was not alone. A series of cribs lined one wall.

There were three of them.

And each crib was occupied by a small, mewing form.

There were babies here.

My head felt strange, as wobbly as a screw loose in a sheath too big. Whatever Constance had done when she'd stepped through me lingered, growing and festering like a gangrenous wound.

I reached out to one of the cribs, trying to steady myself, then peeked into the blanketed depths.

Light golden curls framed a tiny, beatific face. Slate-blue eyes stared drowsily up at me.

I knew those eyes.

Those were Gerard's eyes.

These were Gerard's . . . sons?

Without warning, Constance bustled into the room, whole and unharmed. Her form looked more solid than before.

"What is this place?" I asked her, but she was still caught in the past, unaware of me.

Humming a soft, happy tune, Constance gathered up one of the infants, then crossed over to a rocking chair. Her feet barely skimmed the floor, pushing the chair back and forth on tiptoe, lulling the babe into a quiet trance. With one hand, she unbuttoned the front of her shapeless dress, revealing a milk-swollen breast, riddled with veins strange and green and wrong. The hungry infant went to work, suckling noisily.

"Constance?" I tried again, unable to look away from her dark veins. "What are you doing? What is all this?"

She and the infant flickered, fully disappearing for a second, for two, then three, before returning. I took a step forward, waving my hands, trying to steal her attention, but she only had eyes for the baby.

Gazing up at her in mutual adoration, he placed his tiny hand upon her chest and I gasped.

It wasn't a hand at all, but some sort of stump, malformed

and a horrible shade of verdigris. As I watched, the arm unfurled, like the coiling fiddlehead of a fern, and leaves—actual leaves—opened up. They spread across Constance's skin, a lacy network of vines and tendrils.

I retreated from the macabre tableaux, choking back a cry, and bumped into the first crib. I cringed as the baby within struggled to roll over and look at me. He was young. He was so young and small. The babies couldn't have been more than a month old.

His face was red and tight with an impending howl. Tufts of green fuzz, like feathered moss, poked out from behind his ears. His little fingers were curling tendrils of dark green and purple.

The same shade as the flowers in the greenhouse.

My stomach heaved and the room spun.

"I don't want to be here anymore," I whispered, gulping back a sob.

I hadn't heard Constance get up.

I hadn't felt her approach.

But she was beside me now, her face distorted and beaten. A long slash ripped the bridge of her nose open wide, flaying back her pallid skin till it hung in tatters. A pair of gardening shears protruded from her chest and bursts of red bloomed there, staining the linen bloody. She smelled foul, as dark and dank as a grave.

I didn't have to study the baby in her arms to know it, too, was terribly dead.

"Leave us!" she screamed, flickering in and out of the past, and her voice was awful and rasping. A death rattle, grating across a throat so severed I could see the wink of bones and sinews, muscle striations and cords that were never meant to be glimpsed.

With a cry, I turned and fled from the nursery, leaving behind the splattered, moldering cribs and the horribly dead-yet-not things within them. The babies' little noises of indignation turned into full cries, then shrieks, growing to match their mother's outrage. Their screams reverberated in my head and I was suddenly horribly aware it had not been peacocks waking me every night.

My screams joined theirs as I raced away, flying down the darkened passageway until I crashed through the hidden door and slammed it shut behind me.

32

I WAS WIDE AWAKE WHEN THE SUN PEEKED UP FROM the horizon, casting its golden rays over Chauntilalie and bathing the world with the promise of a beautiful day. I could feel its warmth over my skin as I stared sightlessly out the window, lost in my own mind. The sky turned peach and shimmery as I picked my nails bloody, trying to make sense of everything I'd seen.

A man who was not Alexander walked the halls of the manor, wearing his face.

But he might have been a hallucination.

Constance was dead, murdered by Dauphine.

Maybe.

And those babies . . .

Gerard's babies . . .

A nightingale strutted along the terrace railing, singing out the last notes of a warbling melody, but I couldn't hear it. Not truly.

After fleeing from that cursed nursery, I'd trudged back to my room, sat down, and waited.

Waited for this moment, when the birds were chirping and the sky was brightening.

Alex would be up soon.

Alex would know what to do.

I just had to figure out how to tell him.

"You can do this," I whispered, my voice low and unconvincing. "You just need to tell him . . . everything."

I nodded and visualized myself standing up, leaving the room, and going to find Alex.

I pictured walking through the halls, one foot in front of the other, coaching myself on how to begin. I was certain that the right words would come, as long as I imagined everything perfectly.

"Alex, there's something I need to tell you. . . ."

I see ghosts. I speak to ghosts. They speak to me. But I'm not mad. At least, I don't think so.

"Alex, I'm afraid I have some upsetting news. . . ."

Your father sired some sort of monstrous offspring that look more like plants than babies. And then your mother killed his mistress. Also the babies. Probably.

"Alex, could we . . ."

Run away from this house before all of this darkness rises up and somehow claims us.

I nodded again, but remained motionless and still, rooted to the bed.

"Alex . . ."

༄

"There you are, I've been waiting for over an hour."

Alex's words hit me like a cold wave as I stepped into the little study.

I'd been all over the house searching for him—his bedroom,

the dining room, the terrace. I'd even walked down to the lake, studying the shoreline in case he'd decided on an alfresco breakfast.

I hadn't found a trace of him or Frederick.

"I . . . I've been looking for you. You weren't in your rooms."

He squinted at me. "Of course not. I've been here. Waiting."

His testiness threw me off-balance, causing me to react to it and not my meticulously laid plans. "I'm sorry. I didn't . . . I didn't think we had a session this morning?"

He rubbed at his forehead. "What else would we be doing?"

"Could we talk for a moment?" I asked, sinking my fingernails into the soft flesh of my palm.

He checked his pocket watch. "Now?" I started to nod but he cut me off. "We've already wasted most of the morning. Just get on with it."

I nearly fell onto my stool in my haste to comply. I'd never seen Alex in such a state of irritation before. I uncovered the palette, still wet from the day before, and picked up a paintbrush. "You look as though you might have a headache. Would some coffee help? I could ring for some—"

"I've had coffee!" he snapped. "Hours ago."

"I'm sorry," I said, even though I wasn't sure what I was apologizing for.

Only the thickness of the canvas separated us, but I felt miles from him.

I dipped the paintbrush into a dab of tawny taupe and tried to push back all the words I'd carefully prepared. Trying to tell him anything when he was feeling so poorly was bound to end in disaster. We could work in silence until his mood improved.

Then.

Then, I would tell him everything.

I closed my eyes and took a deep, steadying breath.

I just needed to focus on this, on the work, on Alex.

But when I opened my eyes, ready to begin laying out the sharp line of his cheekbones, I paused in confusion.

There was something off.

The painting didn't line up exactly with Alex today.

"You're slouching a bit to the right," I said, glancing around the canvas, trying to make the images match. "Could you sit up?"

I watched in dismay as the shadows and highlights across his face changed, still not right. Nothing lined up properly with what I'd already painted.

"Can you go back to what you were doing before?" I asked unhelpfully.

He flexed his shoulders but it still wasn't right.

I studied the painted portrait and the boy before me. They looked so similar but still didn't add up.

"Just tilt your head a bit . . . The other way." I watched him try twice before setting down my palette. "Like this." I came around the easel to gently cup his face, angling it back into his pose. I hoped he might lean into my hands, press a kiss to my wrist, and all would go back to normal.

"I know!" he exploded, striking the arm of his chair. "I know what I'm supposed to do!"

His words burst from him like cannon fire, startling me. I'd never once heard him raise his voice before and was floored to have so much frustration aimed directly at me. Retreating, I sat behind the easel, shocked, and hid from his angry eyes. "Why don't we . . . why don't we just call it a day? It's clear nothing is working right. It's fine. It'll be fine."

Though I managed to hold back tears, my voice quavered.

On the other side of the easel, there was silence. Then a sigh. "I . . . I'm sorry, Ver." His wheelchair creaked and from under the canvas, I watched as the wheels pushed forward, only to pause with indecision. "I didn't mean to shout."

"It's all right," I said, even though it felt anything but. "We're both tired."

"Too many late nights, too many parties," he agreed. "Dauphine seems determined to show us off at every event of the season."

I nodded, even though he couldn't see it.

"I *am* sorry," he said again, and he pushed himself over to peek around the edge of the portrait. His face was stricken with contrition. "Please forgive me." And then he leaned in and kissed me.

It was soft at first, tentative and apologetic. I stayed still and motionless, but he let out a soft sigh and kissed me again with renewed vigor. It felt differently from our other kisses. His mouth was insistent, enticing. Intrigued, I tilted my head, offering him a better angle. He murmured his appreciation and his tongue parted my lips.

He'd never kissed me like this before.

I hadn't known kissing *could* be like this.

His hands explored over me, sinking in here, smoothing over there, pulling me closer until I was pressed against his chest. His embrace was powerful, possessive, as if he was trying to leave his mark upon me.

And for the first time ever, I wanted him to.

I closed my eyes. My skin tingled, yearning for more of his touch. It was electrifying, a bolt of lightning striking a tree over and over, sending me into a sweep of sparks and embers.

"Alex?" I wasn't sure if it was meant to be a question or an exaltation.

He grinned and his fingers sank into the thick of my chignon, pulling my head back and baring the length of my throat. His mouth roved hungrily over my skin, drawing out a gasp so feral, I didn't immediately know it had come from me.

I kissed him back, wanting to respond with as much fervency as he was showering upon me, wanting to explore this new and exhilarating side of him. Of me. Of us working together, each spurring the other on to untold, dizzying heights.

So often, I felt like a clipper, held in check by the weighted anchor of others' expectations and demands of me. Alex's kisses snapped that chain apart, freeing my little ship to race off with the wind.

What others wanted no longer mattered, only what I did.

And I wanted him.

I wanted to laugh with delight.

This, *this* was what all the fuss was about.

This was what a kiss could be.

I tugged at his hair, returning his lips to mine, and he groaned. The reverberations echoed down with my racing pulse, festering in my middle like a squirming, aching, wild *thing*. Oh Pontus, how I wanted him.

The kisses grew faster, more frenzied. He tasted of spiced tea and almonds.

I lost the notion of where our hands were, caressing and stroking, raking and tugging. It didn't matter where they were, what they were doing—I only knew I wanted more of it.

He pulled me from the stool and lowered me onto his lap, my back stretched against his chest as he worked his way down the column of my throat, kisses wet and ravenous.

"You smell so good," he murmured, his voice low and dark, his lips against the curve of my ear.

Words failed me utterly. It was too much of an effort to speak. His kisses were like champagne, effervescent bursts of joy that I craved more and more of, even as they muddled my mind, spinning it like falling blossoms.

"I hate that perfume Dauphine bought you. It's so cloying and sweet. It's not you at all." He nipped at my earlobe, then drew it into his mouth, sucking and soothing. "This . . . this is just you. And it's perfect."

His hands grew bold, running over my bodice and even unbuttoning the first few clasps of my blouse. His palm pressed against the bare skin of my chest, searching for its racing heartbeat, and I felt him smile against my cheek when he found it.

"I've wanted to do this for so long, Ver," he whispered, toying with the lace edging of my corset. "You're just as soft as I thought you'd be."

I leaned back against his chest, studying his profile as his fingers slipped lower, bunching aside the fullness of my skirt to race brazenly up my leg.

"Alex, I—" My hand grabbed his, stilling it against my thigh, fingers splayed long, his handprint as hot as a branding iron. "Not . . . not just yet."

His eyes met mine, dark and heavy-lidded. His pupils were wide with desire and I nearly dropped my hold of him, longing to bring his mouth back to mine and sink into the wicked ecstasy of his kisses. What would those fingers feel like if I let them sneak up another inch? And an inch after that?

But my breath caught in my throat as I noticed something strange about his eyes. Strange about the thick line rounding his irises.

They were the wrong color.

A ring of bronze circled the green.

It was impossibly subtle, but I'd spent hours studying Alex's face, memorizing every bit of him, the fullness of his lips, the sharp, proud line of his nose. I knew his eyes better than I did my own, and these were not Alex's eyes.

This was not Alex.

I fell to the ground in my haste to break away from him. To put a good amount of protective space between us. To get away.

The boy who was not Alex watched me hurriedly button my blouse up with an expression of interest, but not alarm.

Amusement, not fear.

He knew I knew.

And then he smiled.

"Who . . . who are you?"

33

"WHAT DO YOU MEAN, VER?"

As he said my name, shortened into an unfamiliar diminution, so many things came together for me. I saw all the details of his face that were almost Alex, but not quite. His eyebrows were slightly thicker, the plane of his cheekbones almost imperceptibly higher.

No wonder I couldn't make the portrait align to this boy.

"You're not Alex."

One corner of his mouth rose, delight coloring him. He crossed one leg over the other, sitting back in the wheelchair with a relaxed stance I'd never seen Alex manage. "Brava," he murmured appreciatively.

"Who are you?"

"Viktor," he said, as if a single name could explain everything. "I honestly didn't think you'd figure it out so quickly. What gave me away?"

"Your eyes. There's a hazel ring around them."

He made a face, *tsk*ing as if it was of no concern. "Julien probably should have been here instead."

"Julien?"

He nodded. "My brother. Dearest Alexander's brother."

I frowned. "Alex doesn't have any brothers."

"Then how do you explain me?"

His ears looked just like Gerard's. "A cousin," I faltered.

"Father has no siblings."

"He's not your father."

Viktor's smile deepened. "As often as I might wish that were true, he most unfortunately is."

"No," I said, shaking my head. "Alex doesn't have a brother."

"You're right," he said, surprising me. "He has two. Triplets."

"Triplets," I echoed, thinking back to the babies I'd seen in the nursery.

There'd been three of them there.

Three of the plants Gerard had named after Constance.

Gerard had said something about sets of three that night in the greenhouse. I strained to remember what it had been.

Three. Always three. One is too small a sample. Anything it produces could be a fluke. Two isn't enough either. Both could fail and you're back where you started. But three, three is the perfect amount.

An uneasy feeling expanded through my gut like a spilled slick of oil spreading out and poisoning everything it touched.

Three plants.

Three babies.

Three sons.

Gerard was experimenting with . . . *something*, that much was clear. But what?

I wanted to howl my frustrations, let them rip free from my throat, foisting them into the world where they could be someone else's problems. If only Constance had shown me more . . .

Realization dawned over me, sudden and swift.

"You're not really here." It slipped out before I could stop it, the idea too big to stay trapped and unspoken. "You're a ghost."

Viktor blinked, as if intrigued by my suggestion. "Am I?"

I nodded, uncertain.

His eyes narrowed. "Is this a common thing for you? Seeing ghosts? Talking with spirits?" He leaned back, studying me with amusement. "Ver, you were just sitting in my lap. Kissing me. *Being* kissed by me . . . You know firsthand how very solid I am." As if to prove his point, he leaned forward and traced his fingers from my cheek, down my neck, lingering at the hollow of my throat, feeling my pulse race. His touch felt unmistakably real.

I sucked in a deep breath, pulling away from his seductive fingers. "So you're alive, then."

He leaned forward, eyes bright with an unchecked fixation. "That doesn't answer my question."

"I only kissed you because I thought you were Alex," I snapped, purposefully avoiding what he really was poking at.

Viktor's smile deepened, turning wicked. "Does Alexander often kiss you that way?"

I folded my arms over my chest, trying hard not to look away.

He laughed. "I thought not. Oh, dear brother. I should have been here to teach you so many things."

"Where *have* you been?" I asked, my words as sharp as scalpels. "Alex doesn't remember you. Gerard and Dauphine have never spoken of you."

With a groan, he pushed himself out of the wheelchair and stood, stretching tall, his joints cracking. "I don't see how he sits in that thing all day long. What a toll is must be on his back."

"It's not exactly as though he has a choice in the matter."

Viktor looked down, contemplating the chair and my words, then shrugged and walked to the window.

Carefully, I lifted myself from the floor, righting my skirts and trying to draw up as much height as I possessed. Even from across the room, I could feel him tower over me. I inched toward the open door.

"Oh, Ver," he said. His gaze was fixed on something outside, making it impossible for him to see any movement I'd made. "Running off to call for help while my back is turned? I have to admit, I'm disappointed."

"Where's Alex?" I tried to keep my voice steady and firm, pushing back the worry and fear.

"In bed, sleeping."

I shook my head. "I looked for him there earlier. His rooms were empty. What did you do to him?"

"Nothing." He sounded hurt, as though my accusation had wounded him.

It didn't matter. "Where is he?"

"Downstairs, in the sickroom. He had one of those fits of his last night. That giant of a manservant took him for treatment. I suspect he's still there, sleeping it off. I meant what I said earlier. Those long nights are taking a toll on him. On us all."

"But you don't—"

"You don't know a damn thing about me, about any of us, little Thaumas girl."

His temper was sudden and swift, a dark cloud bursting open

to unleash its torrent and storm. But when he finally turned to face me, he seemed calm, his anger reined in, held tight in an even tighter fist.

"Since you're already so close, would you mind shutting the door? There's a story that needs to be told and I'd hate for us to be interrupted."

I wanted to call out for help. I wanted to scream and holler and bring the entire staff of Chauntilalie to my aid. But Alex had once said he liked this study best because it was in the most secluded corner of the manor, far from the bedchambers or other places the servants usually trafficked. No one would hear me.

I'd need to run, then.

I reached for the doorknob—a splayed tail of a brass peacock—summoning the burst of energy needed to race out of the room, fling the door closed behind me, and find help. But before I could spring into action, I was forced back into the room as a figure appeared, stepping over the threshold.

For a moment, I thought it was Alex.

Then Viktor.

No.

Julien.

"I thought we'd agreed we were staying out of sight, brother," he said, his voice clipped and clinical. His eyes, a perfect match to Alex's, ran over me with a curious disinterest.

"Julien," I guessed, and he sighed.

"You told her our names?"

"I thought she could help us."

Another sigh.

"Close the door before anyone else stumbles in here," Viktor instructed, leaving the window to make his way toward the seating area, striding through the room with comfortable confidence, a king at home in his palace.

The door swung shut and Julien flipped the lock with a decisive click.

I was trapped.

"Why don't you join me over here, Ver?" Viktor invited, patting a spot on the chaise beside him. "It's a long, curious tale. We might as well all be comfortable."

I had no intention of going anywhere near him, but Julien stepped forward, herding me over to the chairs. I chose an armchair instead, as far from the offered seat as I could get, but stayed standing behind it, using its size as a protective, well-padded barrier.

Julien took the chair opposite me as Viktor sprawled across the chaise, kicking up his feet and tucking his arms behind his head. He looked like a cat stretched in a sunbeam, sleek and wholly satisfied with its place in the universe.

"Where should we begin?" he asked.

"Must we?" Julien questioned.

His clothing was different from his brother's. Viktor wore the jacket and cravat I'd been painting Alex in, but Julien was less formally dressed. His vest remained unbuttoned, his shirtsleeves rolled to the elbow. I could see a shine of wear on the knees of his trousers and noted the cheaper cloth, the patches and darning. This was not someone who had spent his life in the comforts of Chauntilalie.

"I think we must. We've wasted weeks here, looking for answers on our own. She can help us. She's terribly clever."

"Help you?" I echoed, wanting to laugh.

Julien did laugh, a flat, unaffected little clearing of his throat. It sounded disturbing, like the rustling of an insect's wings. "She'll run straight to Papa and tell him everything."

Viktor smiled, unconcerned. "She wouldn't dare. Because *she* knows that *we* know."

"That you know what?" I pressed my fingers into the back of the armchair, clawing at the brocade. My heart was pounding so loudly I was certain they must hear it.

"What you see." Viktor wiggled his fingers. "Ghosts."

"Ghosts?" I tried smiling, as if his words didn't send a bolt of panic down my spine. "I don't . . . I don't know what you mean."

Viktor tilted his head, his eyes little crescent moons of amusement. "Of course you do. You just thought me one, only moments ago."

I shook my head. "Nothing more than a joke."

"She's a terrible liar," Julien observed.

Viktor nodded. "We heard you last night. In the storage room."

"The storage room."

I recalled the noises I'd heard standing in that darkened space, shifting and sighing from the far side of the room one moment, behind me the next. "You both were in the storage room last night."

Their heads bobbed in unison.

"How did you disappear without us seeing you?"

"Secret passage," Viktor started, but Julien held up his hand, stopping him.

"You said 'us,'" he observed, and I inwardly cursed. "But by our account, there were only three people present in that room last night. You," he said, pointing. "And him. And me."

"Yes," I agreed, unconvincingly.

"Then who were you speaking to? We listened to an entire conversation, quite animated I'll grant you, but only ever heard your side of it."

I licked my lips.

Viktor rolled his head back into a throw pillow. "He knows, Ver. We both know. You might as well stop trying to hide it."

I shifted my weight uneasily from foot to foot. "What does he know?"

"Everything," Julien said. "You see ghosts. You're scared of others finding that out. You're scared of us. You're pretending you're not. You're wondering why I think that." He peered at me with Alex's eyes and I wanted to duck behind the chair and cower away from that stare. "You're worrying over the number three. And something about a set of babies . . ."

I froze. "How . . . how do you know that?"

"I hear every thought racing through you right now, Miss Thaumas."

A noise of disbelief barked out of me. "You're a mind reader?"

Julien raised his lips in an approximation of a smile.

The concept was far too large and weighty to absorb. "I don't understand."

Julien glanced at Viktor with disdain. "I thought you said she was so terribly clever?"

"She saw through my ruse, quick as a wink."

He sighed. "That's not saying much."

"Would one of you please explain what's going on?" I demanded. Too many things were happening too fast. I felt bogged down in their collective mire.

Julien turned to me. "I'm special." His tone was flat and expressionless, making the word sound anything but. "Viktor's special. We're both so terribly special."

"You read people's minds?" I repeated, needing to hear him say it.

I knew there were things, many things, about the world that I did not know, did not understand. Things too fantastical to be believed. Mind reading sounded far-fetched but they'd overheard me talking to a ghost. Who was I to say their story was outlandish?

"Yes," Julien said simply, offering no other explanation.

"Both of you?" I asked, carefully avoiding Viktor's gaze. My cheeks flamed as I remembered all the things he might have overheard while I enjoyed his kisses.

Julien let out a short laugh, more a burst of sound than actual amusement. "No. Viktor has other . . . talents."

I dared to look over at him. "What?"

"I . . ." His eyes fell to the floor, looking somber.

Julien sighed with impatience. "Just show her."

"But—"

"We're all laying our cards upon the proverbial table. There's little use in keeping secrets now."

Viktor pursed his lips before gesturing to the writing desk on the far side of the room.

At first, I wasn't sure what I was meant to notice.

Then, a flicker of movement.

The slight dance of a slip of flame.

I turned back to Viktor. "You lit the candle?"

He nodded and a candelabra on the side table ignited as well.

Then the tapers lined in the windows.

Then the gas lamps.

"Stop!" I ordered. The illumination was too great, too bright to trick myself into believing what happened before me was an illusion, some sleight-of-hand mischief designed to impress and enthrall.

Viktor shrugged and, one by one, the flames extinguished, wicked away by hands unseen.

"How?"

Another shrug. "I just . . . concentrate on the feelings inside me and—"

I struggled to find the right words. "No, not *how*—" I paused, all the swirling chaos of my mind stilling down to the only question that really mattered to me. "If you are Alex's brothers, and both of you can do those *things* . . . what about him?"

Viktor shrugged. "Father sent us away before we ever noticed Alexander's . . . gift."

"Sent you away?"

They nodded together.

"To . . . to boarding school?" I guessed, trying to pry the story free.

Julien shook his head. "We were young."

"Too young," Viktor agreed. "Days after our fourth birthday. We didn't understand what was happening. Why we were being sent away. Only that one day, we were a family, happy and whole, and the next . . ."

"Exiled," Julien finished.

The corners of Viktor's eyes crinkled as he laughed. "You make it sound as though we were cast into the forest, raised by feral dogs. We had servants. Tutors. The best Father's money could buy. Julien speaks eight languages," he informed me.

"Nine," Julien corrected flatly.

"But we didn't have . . . this," Viktor continued, waving his hand about the room. "Our home. Our family."

I thought of all the things I'd learned of Gerard and Dauphine last night and wondered if that might have been a blessing.

Julien drummed his fingers on the tops of his knees. "There's an old family estate in the north. We were sent there."

"Marchioly House," I guessed, then froze. "There was an incident there recently. A fire . . ." I glanced uneasily at Viktor.

"It wasn't me," he said sharply. "I swear it."

"It was a storm," Julien admitted. "You know how fierce they can be in spring. Lightning struck the north end of the house. There was some festivity going on in the nearby village. A wedding. Only two of the staff was with us. Brahms—"

"He was a terrible cook," Viktor quipped.

"—and Sheffield," Julien continued, speaking over his brother's interruption.

"Father's watchdog," Viktor said. "Our jailer. He controlled the grounds, the gates. He was the only one who had keys for anything. He made sure no one ever came to Marchioly."

"Or left," Julien added pointedly, his eyes as hollow as his voice. "In his haste to put out the flames that night, Sheffield's keys fell from his pocket. I saw them in the hall as we ran for buckets of water. . . ."

"We used the cover of the storm to escape," Viktor said.

"And you came back here?" I asked, sitting down, drawn into their tale. I could so easily envision the rain lashing at tall windows. I could hear the pops and crackles of embers, could smell the building smoke.

"Where else would we have gone?" Julien asked with a little shrug. "Chauntilalie is the only home—the only real home—we've known."

I imagined the two of them as small boys, wandering around a quiet, lonely estate with only the other for friendly companionship, their faces tight and frightened. It was an impossibly sad tale but one fact poked at me like a thorn, catching on my sleeve and refusing to go unacknowledged.

"I don't understand why Gerard would have sent his sons away in the first place."

Silence settled over the room and I had the distinctly uneasy feeling that the two of them were somehow talking to each other without me overhearing.

"They kept their son. Their *favorite* son," Viktor finally said, his bitterness evident. With a flick of his fingers, every candle in the room sprang to life, flames jumping to dangerous heights.

"Stop it," Julien hissed at him, and after a moment, the flames settled down to manageable, soft glows. He turned to me. "From what I've been able to draw out from the tutors, our . . . talents . . . would have drawn too much attention among the polite company our family kept. Alexander was deemed . . . palatable."

The explanation did have a horrible ring of truth. How would Dauphine possibly explain one of Viktor's outbursts at a society luncheon?

"Which makes me all the more curious . . . you've been around our brother for weeks now," Julien pressed. "Have you noticed anything . . . peculiar about him?"

"Nothing."

He squinted his eyes. "Think about it. Think hard. There must be something."

"I don't . . . I haven't seen anything. Certainly nothing like either of you."

Julien sighed. "There must be something. Otherwise there's no point in you being here." I started to counter but he leveled me silent with his gaze. "You see ghosts, Miss Thaumas. There's little use in pretending otherwise. It's nothing to be ashamed of. These gifts make us more, not less."

"Yours might," I said. "Mine could send me to the madhouse."

Julien shook his head. "Papa would never. It's the single reason you were brought here."

"Dauphine wanted me to paint Alex's portrait," I protested. "*She* picked me."

Viktor tilted his head, peeking around the easel at my work, and made a face. "You're not untalented but do you really think you were the best choice, out of all the artists out there?"

"Yes," I asserted, indignation bubbling within me.

The boys exchanged a glance, furthering my irritation.

"I'm a good painter," I insisted.

Julien tutted his disappointment in me. "There's no point in being insulted. You're decent at best. A decent painter who found herself hastily engaged to a duke's son. Didn't you ever stop to marvel at the timing? At the coincidence? Surely some part of you must wonder at the speed of courtship, at all the haste preparing for the ceremony?"

Viktor smiled sympathetically. "I don't blame you for not. We've watched you for weeks, parading about in new gowns, new perfume, new silk nightdresses." I stiffened as he smirked. "You're a girl far from home. A girl with a dark secret. A girl down to her last florette. It's easy to look the other way when you're being offered the world."

I wanted to protest, but could not.

His words weren't untrue.

Gerard had never asked after a dowry.

Dauphine had insisted they pay for everything.

She claimed it was a joy gifting her soon-to-be daughter-in-law the very best Bloem could lay before us and I went along with it, as silent and compliant as a paper doll.

They were master gardeners, sculpting me around their wants as they saw fit.

And I, too scared to be on my own, too afraid my secrets would spill out, let them.

A chill settled over me like a bank of icy morning fog.

"Alex loves me," I whispered.

He did. That much I knew.

Whatever his parents had done, whatever plans his father had set in motion bringing me here, I was sure that Alex didn't know. Alex had fallen in love with me, truly in love with *me*.

Not my gift.

Your curse.

Just me.

I clung to that thought, holding it deep in my heart, unwilling to doubt its veracity.

Julien looked unimpressed. "I'm certain he thinks so. But everything, from the moment you stepped foot in this cursed house, has been carefully arranged, impeccably tended. Neither you nor

Alexander are anything more than grafted shoots, transplanted roots on Papa's worktable. He tinkers with everything about him. His house. His plants. His family. Weeding out the imperfections, forcing out more desirable traits. It's his raison d'être."

"To what end?"

Julien let out a sigh, as if my incomprehension physically pained him. He raised his pointer finger in the air. "You," he said, then raised the other. "Alexander." He merged them together. "One can only assume your union would issue forth a new, distinct set of progeny."

My mouth went dry as I remembered Constance's children and just how *distinct* they'd been. "That's absurd. And . . . and we don't even know if . . . if Alex . . ." I came to a flustered halt.

Viktor let out a snort of laughter. "With all you've witnessed here, do you really think Gerard Laurent would let a little bit of paralysis stop his plans?"

I bristled. "How could he . . . I can't imagine—"

Julien rolled his eyes. "Don't be so completely naïve, please. It makes you look a fool."

"Then perhaps I'm a fool," I snapped, growing tired of Julien's condescension.

"I don't doubt it," he said, ignoring my venom. "But you're a special one, all the same. Special enough for Papa to think you worthy of his favorite son."

My stomach flexed as I recalled the baby's frond-like arm uncurling last night. Gerard had done something to them, had done something to Constance. There was no other explanation for their appearances. And if he'd done that to his mistress, to a set of bastard offspring he'd never be able to claim, what did he intend to do to me? What plans did he have for the Laurent line?

"What do they look like?" Viktor asked with sudden curiosity, sitting up. "The ghosts?"

I twisted my fingers into a knot, grasping them so close together the tips turned white, then bright red. There was no way of skirting out of his questions this time. They knew too much. "I don't . . . I didn't always know they were ghosts."

Julien tilted his head, intrigued. "What do you mean?"

"They don't look like what you expect them to. . . . There's no rattling chains or spooky mist."

"What *do* they look like?" he pressed.

"Like you or me." I held up one of my hands. "Solid, like this. Though . . . not always." My hand fell back into my lap. "My whole life, I thought I was as normal as anyone else. Then I saw two of my dead sisters and . . . the whole truth came out, all at once."

A flicker of understanding lit Viktor's eyes. "That's why you're here, isn't it? You learned the truth and you ran."

I squirmed against the tall back of the chair, wishing I could sink into its tufted depths. I hated how thoroughly these boys saw me. "My sister . . . the duchess . . . she never wanted anyone to know about my . . . curse."

"Gift," Julien corrected gently. It was the first time he'd ever bothered to soften his words and I glanced up, daring to meet his eyes.

"I couldn't bear to stay at Highmoor, at her home. She would have kept me trapped there forever."

Slowly, as if approaching a wild animal, Viktor eased off the chaise and knelt before me, settling himself so that his elbows leaned on either arm of the chair. He invaded my space, uncomfortably close, and yet I couldn't bring myself to protest. I recalled the way his lips had moved over mine and a flush of treacherous yearning rekindled in my middle.

I glanced to Julien, pushing the thoughts away with haste, but his face remained as impassive as ever.

Viktor leaned in, dipping his head as if suddenly shy. "We're alike, Ver. You and me and Julien. We're all the same. Our families wanted to hide us away, pretending we don't exist, but we do. We burn more fiercely than they could ever imagine. Will you help us?"

"Help you?" I echoed, wanting to back away, to scoot as far from the insistent pressure of his body against mine as I could and clear my head from his maddening scent of autumn leaves and bonfires and danger. But then he glanced up, pinning me in place.

"Please?"

"Help how?"

"We're looking for papers," Julien spoke up.

I shifted from Viktor then, arching my back into the cushion to secure a sense of breathing room. "What kind of papers?"

"Birth certificates, announcements, diary entries. Papa undoubtedly altered all of the important documents but there still might be something that proves who we are. Who I am."

"Gerard's sons," I realized. "You want to prove you're Gerard's sons."

Julien nodded. "And heir to Chauntilalie, of course."

My eyebrows rose. "What?" I glanced to Viktor, trying to make sense of it. "Alex is the heir."

Viktor shook his head. "Our baby brother is most decidedly not. I'm the middle. Julien is the eldest. The firstborn. Father's successor. The future duke."

Julien crossed his ankle over his other leg, adjusting the cuff of his trousers with sharp precision.

"That's why you've come back to Chauntilalie," I guessed, feeling queasy. I'd listened to these boys, truly sympathizing with them. Learning they were only here to snatch away Alex's place felt like a betrayal. To me, to him. "To claim the title. The inheritance. All that?"

Viktor leaned back on his heels, his smile sly and winsome. "It sounds quite romantic when you phrase it like that. Like it should be put into a play. *The Thwarted Heir!*" He swished his hand across the space between us, as if seeing the title played out on a painted sign. "*The Forgotten Prince! Heirs in Exile!*"

"Quiet!" Julien snapped. "Your voice carries more than you know. If someone comes to check on her, we're both done for." He sighed and shifted toward me. "Miss Thaumas, you may rest assured, I have no desire to upset Alexander's position within the family. I only want to be acknowledged as a Laurent myself, to be accorded what should be mine as a son of the duke. You can't make your way through the world without proof of who you are. That's all I want. For Papa to claim me. To claim us," he added, nodding toward Viktor.

"Then . . . what's your plan exactly? You say you've been here for weeks. What are you doing? Where have you even been staying?"

"Here and there," Viktor said. "There's an obscene amount of space in this house that's not in use. The passages help keep us out of sight."

"And what have you been doing all this time?" I stopped short, remembering the morning of Dauphine's dinner party, the day Alex had proposed. "That was you," I said, recalling the servant I'd seen through the window. The one I'd briefly thought was Alex. I turned to Julien. "Or you. You were pretending to be servants, wandering about the house."

"We were just boys when we were sent away," Julien said, neither confirming nor denying. "We wanted to reacquaint ourselves with the manor. With our family."

"And Gerard and Dauphine truly haven't seen you?" It seemed impossible that they had not.

"I refilled Mother's champagne coupe three times that night and she never even blinked," Viktor said, triumph evident in his voice. "The mind only sees what it wants to. And all that woman wanted was a full glass and a good party."

"We've searched every inch of the manor, looking for answers," Julien continued. "All but one place."

Viktor's mirth died away. "Father's study. It's always locked."

"He wears the key around his neck," I confirmed. "He's never without it."

"That's where he's storing the records." Julien nodded. "I'm certain of it."

"We've tried picking the lock," Viktor admitted. "It's impossible. Could . . . could you help us?"

"Get you into the study?" I clarified.

The boys both nodded.

I paused, feeling uneasy with what I was about to suggest. "Couldn't you just approach Gerard—or Dauphine—yourselves? I'm certain once they see you both—"

Disdain and disappointment flashed across Viktor's face. "Oh, Ver, the man has spent our entire lives pretending we don't exist. He'd laugh us all the way back to Marchioly House. And then put iron bars across every door and window. If we even made it there alive . . ."

"Gerard wouldn't—"

"Gerard would," he snapped.

I thought of the garden shears sunk deep in Constance's chest and swallowed back rising bile.

If Gerard wouldn't, Dauphine certainly would.

"He'd do anything to protect himself," Julien said.

Viktor's face turned into a sneer. "To protect his perfect family and his perfect legacy. His perfect son!"

"Alex isn't your enemy," I said.

He scoffed. "He's stolen our birthright, our inheritance, our very identities. I'd say that puts us at odds."

I shook my head. "You said how young you were when you left. . . . He doesn't remember you. He'd never willingly have gone along with such a scheme. He's a good man, I swear that to you."

"We'll see."

"What does that mean?"

"It means . . ." Viktor shrugged, looking suddenly weary. "We're not the villains in this, Verity. We're just two people who've been put into a terrible situation, one that was not our creation, and we're only doing what you're trying to."

"Me? What do you think I'm doing?"

His eyes danced over mine, naked and vulnerable. "Surviving."

Julien nodded. "Will you help us? Please?"

Viktor took my hands in his. The pads of his fingers brushed against my palms, electrifying me. "Do you believe our story?"

Reluctantly, lost in the depths of his eyes, I nodded.

"Do you believe a great wrong was committed? Not only against me, but Julien as well?"

Another nod.

"Then let us right it, Ver. *Please*."

It was the *please* that did it. Such a simple word, stretched and beseeching.

He was right. They were in the same situation I'd run from myself. Secreted away by a family who didn't want our talents shown to the world. Hushed and hidden. I didn't know these boys, I didn't trust them, but I knew what it felt like to be in their shoes.

I licked my lips. "How?"

A smile of relief washed over him, as if I'd promised him the moon. "Give us time. A day or two. Three at the most—if we haven't found a way into the study by then, we'll come forward. Just don't tell anyone we're here till then."

"I can't keep this from Alex. He deserves to know."

Viktor shook his head in alarm. "He can't know. No one can know."

I hesitated.

I'd started the morning ready to tell Alex everything. To give him all my secrets.

But if I told him now, if I told him all this . . . I knew exactly how he'd react. He'd go straight to Gerard, seeking answers, demanding wrongs be righted. He'd steal away any chance to let his brothers handle it the way they wished to.

Because he was a good person.

The best one I knew.

I glanced back and forth between the two boys.

I was already so full of secrets.

I could keep hold of theirs for a little longer.

"A day," I finally said, countering. "I'll give you one day and then I'm telling Alex. All of it. He could help us. He'll have ideas. I know he will."

"One day," Julien said, focusing on the only part of my agreement he cared about.

"One day."

Viktor breathed out a sigh of relief, smiling again. "Thank you." He cupped my feverish cheeks, his long fingers chilling them, and pressed a kiss of gratitude on the top of my head. "Thank you. Thank you. Thank you."

I fought the temptation to pull him closer, to pull him down upon me, and let the wild yearnings spiking through me have their way.

He grinned darkly, as if it was he, not Julien, who could overhear my thoughts; then he paused, listening intently to something I could not. "Jules, we need to go."

"Go?" I echoed.

Julien nodded, standing abruptly, his movements sharp and focused. Viktor slipped out of his jacket—Alex's jacket—and folded it over the back of the wheelchair. "We'll see you soon," he promised, stopping for just a moment to press a kiss to the back of my hand.

My fingertips curled around Viktor's, wanting to keep him here, with me, but in a flash, Julien was across the room, twisting a bit of molding along one of the sconces. A hidden door swung open, revealing another tunnel.

"Viktor," he snapped, drawing his brother's attention.

Viktor left me, racing first to flip the lock on the escutcheon before ducking into the darkness after Julien.

The wall shut with a dull click and they were gone.

Moments later, the door to the study opened and Alex wheeled in, in a different chair, looking flustered.

"Oh, Verity, you're here," he said in a rush. "What a day! I had another bad spell last night and overslept and then couldn't find my chair, of all things. Oh," he said, spotting the wicker chair in the middle of the room. "It's here."

Hidden in the depths of my skirts, I balled my hands into fists, preparing the first lie I'd ever told him. "I . . . borrowed it. I'm so sorry. I heard you weren't feeling well last night so I thought it best to let you rest. I was going to work on the chair details today . . . I didn't think how disconcerting it would be to wake and find it gone."

He waved off my false words with a generosity I did not deserve. "I'm the one who ought to be apologizing. I feel terrible you were here working without me." His hand wrapped around mine, squeezing it with a gentle affection. "I'm so sorry."

"Don't be silly. You weren't well." I studied him, taking in the dark circles beneath his eyes, the weariness that clung to him like a tailored suit. "How are you feeling now?"

Alex shook his head. "I'll be better. There's just been so many late nights, too many celebrations. They're taking a toll on me. On you," he said, reaching out to touch the shadows under my own eyes.

The moment reminded me uncomfortably of Viktor's own words. It seemed impossible they could be brothers and yet . . . so undeniably right. I wondered where the boys were now—if they'd escaped into a deeper region of the house or if they were lingering behind the hidden door, listening. Was Viktor watching my hand wrapped up in his brother's?

I pushed the thought away. It didn't matter if he was.

"You look as tired as I feel. Tell me the peacocks were quiet at least. I spoke to Erikson about having them roost farther from the house."

I opened my mouth, feeling the words about to fall free.

The babies, Constance and her murder, my visions. I wanted to tell him everything.

But if I started with one thread of the story, the whole tale would unravel until everything came out.

His long-lost brothers. Their abilities. Their very existence.

And I'd given my word I'd keep their secret.

For one day.

I could feel Viktor with us, somehow, somewhere. His eyes were at the back of my neck, keenly watching on from a hidden distance, making sure I kept my oath, assuring himself that he and Julien were safe.

"Verity?" Alex prompted, looking worried by my silence.

I offered out a weak smile, my stomach roiling with the lie. "No. No, nothing like that. I slept like the dead."

34

"HOW DO YOU FIND THE FISH THIS EVENING?" DAUphine asked, far down along the opposite end of the formal dining room. I could barely see her around the staggeringly tall vases of flowers.

Earlier today—while I'd been learning the existence of Alexander's brothers—an army of wedding designers had gone through Chauntilalie with their ideas for the best table settings and arrangements. We were meant to be trying everything out this evening, each sitting in front of a completely different set of dishes and cutlery, decorations and goblets.

I was inclined to choose my seat's arrangement. Giant puffs of petal pink pampas grass sprung from vases on either side of my plate, allowing me a false sense of safety. I could hide away in their frothy depths, keeping a careful watch on both Dauphine and Gerard.

"Verity?" Dauphine prompted. I could see from the twitch at the corner of her lips that she wasn't pleased to have had to ask twice.

I glanced down at the untouched salmon on my plate. A thick crust of yellow flowers had been seared to its side.

My stomach was a mess of anxious knots and I'd spent most of dinner pushing courses from one side of the plate to the other. It was exhausting to pretend that this was a normal night, that I'd not found out my future mother-in-law was a murderer, that my father-in-law-to-be was a mad scientist, experimenting on girls and babies as if they were no more than plants in his greenhouse. As if I hadn't learned he might have the same nefarious plan for me. As if I'd not met two brothers Alex never knew existed.

Now I jumped at every unexpected movement from the periphery of my eyes, certain Gerard was coming at me with a pair of manacles and an arsenal of potions and drafts. Looking at Dauphine made my sternum ache. I could almost understand the jealous rage she must have felt when discovering Constance, but how could a mother bear to cast away her own children? I did not honestly believe the gods meted out punishments or blessings based upon behavior but in the deepest, darkest part of my heart, I was glad she'd never had any other babies.

"I was thinking it might be a nice selection for the wedding reception," Dauphine continued. "It's certainly different, but is it right?"

"We don't serve fish at weddings," Marguerite spoke up, indignant.

Her setting was full of ivory and silver, patterned in sharp angles. I'd never seen a more menacing arrangement of vases and cutlery. I studied the sour old woman, wondering what she knew of Julien and Viktor. Had she lived at Chauntilalie then? Was she aware of her two missing grandsons? I couldn't believe it possible. If Gerard had truly sent them away because of their abilities, I'd guess he'd tell as few people as possible. He'd want his sins kept secret.

"Cold-blooded and unfeeling beasts? To celebrate a life of love?" Marguerite carried on and the ruby droplets hanging from her ears bobbled back and forth with surprising force. "We will feast on swan, as we always have." She took a sip of her wine as if the matter was settled.

My insides curdled, imagining a slaughterhouse of the great white birds. The image morphed, turning into the memory of Constance wheeling round at me, exposed sinews and bloodied sheers gleaming.

"I think fish is a fine idea, Mother," Alex disagreed, lost in a sea of green goblets, black flatware, and twisting bamboo. "I'm sure Verity's family would welcome such thoughtful hospitality. It's kind of you for thinking of them."

I plunged my rose-gold fork into the flaky cut. My hands trembled. "Are these fennel flowers?"

Dauphine nodded, pleased I'd recognized them. "They represent endurance. Each course will be a new wish for your marriage."

"How lovely." I took a bite of the fish, determined to save as many swans as I could, even though everything I ate tasted of ash.

Marguerite sniffed and we lapsed into silence. It felt as though everyone's mind was elsewhere this evening. Alex crossed his fork and knife over the empty plate and they rang unusually loud. He looked over to me, a guilty smile on his lips.

"Have you received any of my sisters' responses yet?" I asked when the quiet grew too long.

There had been so many invitations sent out—each made of pressed flowers thin as onionskin paper, dipped rose-gold edging and lined with a row of pearls as a nod to me—that seven footmen had ridden into town, their satchels bursting with the precious stationery.

"I haven't seen the post today. Have you, darling?" Dauphine glanced at Gerard, tilting her head to be seen around a cloud of peonies.

Gerard looked up from his plate. He'd been quiet most of the evening, setting me further on edge. His eyes were glazed over and distant, clearly working through something in his mind and patently ignoring the arrangement of uninspired roses surrounding him. "Yes, yes, I believe I have. Three letters, I think."

Three.

Beneath the table, I ticked off their names on my fingertips.

Annaleigh.

Mercy.

Honor.

It had to be.

I'd known not to expect anything from Lenore, but where was Camille's reply? Would she really not come, just to prove she was still upset with me? The wedding was only a week away. No matter what happened in the days between now and then, at the very least, Annaleigh would soon be here. She'd never disappoint me.

Dauphine's mouth dropped with surprise and anger, a dark cloud hiding the sun on an otherwise brilliant day. "Three! You were supposed to send along any responses, not keep them squirreled away. Bastian and I have lists—so many lists—and if we don't know how many guests are attending, then we can't plan for the—"

"They're in my study," he said, cutting her litany blessedly short. He took a great bite of the salmon, drawing out the silence. "I'll make sure to bring them to you."

My heart thudded out of rhythm in my chest. The study!

"I could go get them," I volunteered, pushing my chair from the table, my flatware clattering loudly. "It would be no trouble at all. I'd just need the key. . . ."

Gerard blinked at me, his expression unreadable.

"We're in the middle of dinner, child," Marguerite gasped, peering up at me with horrified wonder. She glanced to Alex. "Is she always this excitable? Such fuss over a handful of letters."

"Dauphine said how important they were . . ." I looked to her for help.

"Well, they are, of course," she said, her eyes still sharp on Gerard. "But you needn't miss a meal over them."

"Don't concern yourself, Verity," Gerard said, waving me back down. "It isn't worth fussing over."

The servers arrived and changed courses.

"I'm anxious to hear what you think of this one," Dauphine called out.

The silver dome was pulled away to reveal the small body of a quail, set on a bed of wild rice and roasted grapes. I offered Alex a sympathetic smile. Apparently none of our preferences were being taken into account.

"Verity and I were discussing the honeymoon the other day," Alex mentioned, poking at the small bird. "I'd like to take her on a tour of the estates. Find a house that suits us both."

"There's no hurry in all that, of course," Gerard protested. "You're welcome to stay at Chauntilalie as long as you like." He picked at one of the tea roses circling a small candleholder in front of him as if just now noticing the new décor.

I studied him. He was so seemingly absentminded. Was he actually that lost in his work, or was it all a ruse to cover up cold calculations and buried secrets?

So much of Gerard's persona contradicted itself—he brought Dauphine fresh-cut flowers every morning, bestowing them with big, wet kisses, but he'd been with countless women over the years. He often pretended to lose track of time in the greenhouse, but I knew that while he worked, he kept meticulous notes, jotting down a running timeline of every action within his scores of notebooks, his eyes glued to his pocket watch and the plants before him. He showed the world what a thoughtful father he was—rebuilding half of Chauntilalie to accommodate for Alex's chair—all while exiling two other sons to a remote estate, out of sight, out of mind.

What else was he secreting away?

When *was* the last time I'd heard from home?

Camille obviously wasn't going to send anything but I should have received something from Mercy by now. She was terrible at correspondence, only writing when she had a particularly juicy bit of gossip to share, but I would have thought she'd have checked in, at least to see how the commission was going. She'd been the one to set this entire thing in motion after all.

There'd been the one letter from Annaleigh, sent with the candles, promising to try to mend the rift between Camille and I but then there'd been nothing. I'd assumed that was only due to Camille's stubbornness, that Annaleigh had nothing good to report and so chose the most Annaleigh way of breaking bad news—avoidance. Our fight was too big, my bold act too great for Camille to forgive.

But what if there'd been other letters? Other letters left tucked away in Gerard's office? Through neglect or . . .

. . . design?

"Is there any house you had in mind?" Dauphine asked, drawing me back into the conversation at hand. "The cottage at Halcyon Hollow would be just darling for you. Verity, you're sure to fall in love with it. It's right on a lake—you'd never be far from the water."

Inspiration struck me, fast as lightning, and I pounced before Alex could respond. "Actually, I'm most interested in seeing Marchioly House. Alex has made it sound so picturesque. Maybe we should start th—"

"Oh no," Gerard said, interrupting me. "Marchioly House is all wrong for you."

I blinked.

"Terribly wrong," Dauphine agreed quickly.

"But why?" I persisted.

"You're such a young couple, starting out . . . ," Dauphine began.

"It's too big, far too big a house for just the two of you. Perhaps in a few years . . . once you've given us a handful of grandchildren," Gerard added. His smile, on the verge of a smirk, sent a chill of dread down my spine. "Then. Then we can talk about Marchioly."

"I'd still love to visit it, wouldn't you, Alex?" I asked, turning to him, wanting him on my side.

"I . . . I suppose," he murmured.

"Oh, but there was a fire, wasn't there?" I asked, keeping my tone as even as I could, as if I'd just remembered the bad news. "Did anyone ever figure out what happened?"

"No one has been up there in an age," Gerard said, waving off the matter as if it was of no importance.

"A kitchen girl," Dauphine interjected suddenly. "There was a fire in the kitchens."

I glanced between the two of them, my eyes narrowed. The boys had said all the servants were gone, celebrating a wedding.

"We ought to draw up a list of the houses you'll want to review and make sure they're fit for visiting," Gerard said, moving on. "Aired out. Fresh bedding." He waggled his eyebrows at Alex.

"Halcyon Hollow, certainly," Alex said, ignoring his father's overly playful nudge.

He had answered quickly, as if to keep hold of the conversation, steer it in the direction he wanted it to go. But his rapid response created a burr of worry in me, rubbing at the pit of my stomach with painful tenacity. Had he been trying to appease his parents or did he, too, know of the secrets kept at Marchioly House?

Paranoia gripped my insides. I'd always felt safe with Alex. He'd been my one constant at Chauntilalie. But how well did I actually know him?

I needed to talk to Alex—to take him outside of Chauntilalie, where the walls quite literally had ears—and find out what he knew. I needed someone else on my side. Someone who wasn't acting in their own best interest but in mine. In ours.

I prayed to Pontus there was still an *ours*.

"We'll be trying a new sorbet tonight," Dauphine announced

as the servers returned, carrying in coupes of bright red ice. "It's made from pomegranate wine and is supposed to be quite evocative. I thought it would pair well with the cake to come."

Alex pushed a bit of rice over the quail, to cover up the fact he'd tried none of it. He caught me staring and winked, his smile guileless and easy.

My breath caught in my throat.

He was so beautiful. So good and pure and completely not a part of this madness.

Wasn't he?

I just needed to get through dinner and return to my room. I needed to be alone with my thoughts and then—surely then—I'd be able to work out a solution, work out exactly what was going on and who I was meant to trust in it all.

"What is the pomegranate meant to represent?" I asked, pushing the sorbet about with my spoon, trying to tamp down the waves of panic growing within me.

"Why, fertility, of course," Dauphine said, taking a big scoop from her lavender-colored glass. She closed her eyes, savoring the flavor.

Gerard let out a bark of laughter. "Marchioly might be in your future after all!" He raised the sorbet coupe toward us, in a cheeky toast.

༄

"What a night," Alex groaned as we made our way down the corridor. "I am so sorry for my family. I feel as though they've collectively lost their minds."

"They're . . . excited," I allowed, then cringed, remembering the knowing wink Gerard had given me after his little joke.

"They're mad," he persisted. "This wedding has turned the house upside down. I wish . . . I wish we could just race ahead through the next week and have it be over and done with."

He rolled into the lift first and I set to work shutting the gate, flipping the latch. He waited until the steam went to work, its groans filling the air, before continuing.

"This will sound wholly blasphemous, but I don't care a whiff about any of the wedding stuff. At least not the parts Mother is so fixated on. I want us to get Arina's blessing. I want to see you come down the aisle to me. And I want to say our vows. That's it. That's all that matters."

I wanted to believe him. Every bit of me wanted that.

The lift rattled to a stop.

I started the process with the latch and the gate again. Alex rolled free and I closed the door, flipping the lever. The routine had become second nature to me, movements I could do without stopping to ponder them.

Alex pushed his way down the corridor, turning to escort me to my rooms.

The pink candles were back, filling the hallway with their perfumed persistence and making my head spin. We passed the door to Gerard's study and I paused before it, taking in the carved clusters of *Euphorbia marginatas* gracing its front.

"Verity?" Alex called, turning his chair around as he realized I wasn't at his side.

"I was just . . ." I trailed off, unsure. "I was thinking about my sisters' letters. In there." I glanced back to the door again. "Gerard has probably already forgotten about them."

Alex offered a sympathetic smile. "I wouldn't worry on it. Now that Mother knows, I'm sure she won't let him rest until he brings them to her."

A half-formed idea crossed my mind and before I could fully think it through, I plunged headfirst into it. "But what if he doesn't? He can be so forgetful at times."

Alex nodded.

"What . . . what would happen if he was to misplace his keys?"

"To the study?" Alex asked, and I felt a warning bell set off in my chest. He didn't look suspicious, not quite, but there was a touch of bemusement, as though he couldn't understand what I was getting at.

"Or the greenhouses or work sheds," I said hastily. "The silver cabinets or vaults. He could lock everyone out of half of Chauntilalie with one errant mistake."

"I'm certain his valet has a skeleton key for most of those things," he said reassuringly.

"The study too?" I persisted, then cringed, wondering if I'd overplayed my hand.

Alex shrugged. "Probably not there but you know how Father is. Always has three sets of everything."

I stilled, feeling like a lock myself as internal tumblers twisted and turned, falling into the proper combination. Once everything had clicked in place, the answer was revealed. "Sets of three."

He pushed himself farther down the hall, ready to continue on. "You've noticed, haven't you?"

I followed after him. "With the plants, of course."

Alex laughed. "With everything. Always. Three fountain pens, lined up at the ready. Three pocket watches in case the first two fail. Three bouquets for Mother when one would do."

"He has three sets of keys," I murmured, wanting to hear him say it out loud.

"I've not seen them myself but I'm sure he does." He smiled wistfully. "If I knew where he kept them, I'd let you in the study myself."

"You would?"

He nodded. "I know how much your sisters mean to you. You must be missing them dreadfully. If Father hasn't brought their missives by breakfast, I shall herd him up here myself and make certain he does."

I sucked in my lower lip, my heart swelling.

I wanted to tell him. I wanted to tell Alex everything, right here and now and be done with it.

I'd promised Viktor and Julien I'd give them a day and it was nearly midnight. I could confess everything with only a tremor of a guilty conscience.

Alex deserved to know.

Where should I start?

The ghosts?

Constance?

His mother?

His brothers?

"Alex?"

"Hmm?" He yawned loudly as we stopped outside my chamber door, then looked sheepish. "I'm so sorry. It's not the company, I promise."

I stopped short. He looked completely wrung out, drained of all energy.

"I . . ."

I couldn't do it. Not yet. Not tonight. I needed him to be rested, ready to hear everything I had to say with a clear mind, an open mind, and then we could attempt to fix it all. Together.

Tomorrow, I promised myself.

Tomorrow, I would tell Alex everything.

"Let's take the day off from the portrait," I decided. "You're exhausted. Sleep in tomorrow, get some rest."

"That sounds wonderful." He laced his fingers through mine and pulled me close for a soft kiss good night.

Curiously, I kissed him back, moving my lips over his as I had when I'd thought Viktor him. A soft ember flickered to life but before I could explore it, letting it kindle into something larger, Alex pulled away, running his palm over my cheek with a tired smile.

"A late breakfast on the terrace?" he asked, making it clear the night was over.

I pushed back my disappointment and nodded. "I hope you have sweet dreams."

"They'll all be of you," he promised sleepily, then wheeled away. I watched him roll down the hall and disappear around the foyer's turn.

There were two other keys out there, hidden somewhere within Chauntilalie.

I was going to find them.

Tonight.

With a nod of determination, I slipped inside my suite. I'd change into something more practical than this beaded gown, wait till the house had gone to sleep, then start my search.

"Thank Arina," a voice called out in the dark, immediately squashing all of my plans.

Startled, I flipped on the gas lamps and spotted Viktor sprawled across the room's little green settee. Julien perched on the edge of a wide, blush-colored bergère.

"We thought he'd never leave."

35

"WHAT ARE YOU DOING IN HERE?" I MUTTERED, PUSHing the door closed behind me.

Viktor's legs dangled off the end of the velvet sofa, kicking back and forth listlessly. "We've been waiting for ages. Are all meals here so infernally long?"

"Viktor," I prompted.

His head lolled round. "I'm bored, Ver. You've no idea how exhausting it is to spend every waking hour with this one, on one fruitless search after another," he said, gesturing to Julien, who bit back a sigh. "But waiting about your parlor is even worse. Who eats seven courses for family dinner?"

"It was for the wedding," I began, feeling oddly defensive.

He raised his eyebrows with a suggestive look. "And how *are* the wedding preparations going? Have you told your fiancé about your little dalliance with his long-lost frère?"

"There's nothing *to* tell. Unless, you want me to *tell*," I said, layering my words with extra meaning.

"I was only toying with you," Viktor said, sitting up with alarm. "Both now and then."

His cavalier admission stung more than I wanted it to.

Julien tilted his head, adjusting his neck with a crack. "We were thinking, with Alexander gone to an early bed, and Papa doubtlessly in his greenhouse tonight—"

"We should play a game," Viktor said, talking over his brother.

"A game."

The boys nodded and Viktor leapt up from the settee. "Let's see who can find the secret passage to Father's study first."

The knowledge of the other two keys weighed on my mind. I could feel my tongue curving to form the words, to alert these boys of their existence, but I held myself in check. I wasn't ready to trust them with such sensitive information. Not yet.

"You've been searching for days," I said instead. "What makes you think I'll be any help?"

"You see things others don't." Viktor let out a funny laugh. "Many, many things others don't."

I shook my head. "It's been a long day. I—"

Before I could finish my excuse, almost as if Viktor's insinuation had drawn her in, Constance walked into the parlor, straight through the closed door. Her face was whole once more, the blood and gardening shears gone. But she faded in and out of sight, her form translucent and tenuous.

She paused just past the threshold, her eyes fixed on something no longer in front of her, and I was reminded of the day we'd first met. She'd crept into the sitting room for a peek at my engagement dress, just as she had now.

She was caught in another cycle, I realized, living that day over and over once again.

"Constance," I said, trying to halt her progress. I was

halfway across the room before remembering Viktor and Julien were present.

"What are you . . ." Viktor stilled. "Is someone here? Right now?" He turned with delight toward the door and dropped into a formal court bow. "Greetings, Wise Spirit. Have you traveled far beyond the veil to visit with us this night?"

Julien swatted at his brother, silencing his antics. "Who is it, Miss Thaumas? Do you know her?"

I ignored them, reaching out for Constance as if my touch could somehow secure her to the room. "Constance, can you hear me?"

To my surprise, her brown eyes drifted up to mine and nodded. A look of grave concern crossed her face. "What am I doing in here?" She froze, noticing the brothers. "Who are they?"

"They can't see you," I assured her. "Or hear anything you say."

Julien cocked his head, as if straining to reach out and listen to her thoughts. After a moment, he gave up, frowning.

Constance glanced about the sitting room. "We were just in the kitchen, weren't we?"

"No." My voice was gentle, willing her to remember.

She sighed and her figure flickered heavily, an open flame tugged by a strong draft. "I'm so very tired," she admitted. "I keep thinking I'll slip off to sleep. But there is no sleep. Not here."

She winked out.

And then was back, pacing restlessly in front of me.

"Here. Here. Why am I still here?" She stopped and attempted to take my hands.

A horrible bout of unease filled me as her transparent fingers pawed uselessly at mine.

"I don't understand why I'm here. I did everything right in life. I prayed to the gods. I gave them offerings. Why are they keeping me here?" Her sob was broken up into chunks of ragged sound as she faded in and out of sight.

"Care to let us in on what's happening?" Viktor called out, reminding me of their presence.

Before I could answer, Constance was back, flaring into a moment of solid form, just as I'd seen her look that night in the storm room. "The seeds," she gasped. "I need the sacred seeds."

"Sacred seeds. What seeds?"

From behind me, Julien cleared his throat. "The People of the Petals bury their loved ones full of seeds, stuffed into the bodies. It aids in the decomposition process, helps the dead return more quickly to the earth. Then from their death . . . new life."

It was a lovely sentiment, so different from the People of the Salt, casting our dead to the sea, their spirits at peace deep in the Brine.

"She thinks she needs the seeds—so her spirit can move on." I turned back to her. "Where are you buried, Constance?"

She wandered over to the terrace windows, wavering. When she tried tapping on the glass pane, her hand went straight through it. "Near the side garden, on the south side of the house."

"The mounds," I murmured, remembering the day Alex had shown me the peacocks. "Gerard's rose maze."

Constance's face grew grim. "There's far more than roses in that soil."

There'd been so many mounds lying across the meadow. How many girls had Dauphine harmed? I crossed to Constance, peering out into the dark night. "Are there others with you?"

"I don't know," she admitted. She stilled, as though piecing something together. "Did you see my babies?"

I nodded.

She grabbed my hand, wrapping her icy fingers through mine with a strong urgency. A sharp wave of vertigo washed over me. My knees felt weak. "He intends to do all that to you. Do you see now? Do you understand?" She disappeared for a moment.

"I think so," I said when she returned. "I won't let him."

Constance looked uncertain. "He's too powerful to be stopped."

"I'll find something . . . something that shows everything he's done," I promised. "And we'll tell everyone. We'll tell—"

"The study," she murmured dreamily, cutting me off. "You need to get into the study."

"What's in the study?" I asked, excitement rising up.

"It's locked," she said unhelpfully, winking out. It took her a full seven seconds to reappear.

"I can get in. There are keys," I explained to her. "Two other keys."

"Keys?" Viktor echoed with interest, and I wanted to curse. My mind felt like a buoy caught in a rough storm, lurching back and forth on its tether. I couldn't think well enough to keep track of so many conversations. "We don't need the passageways?"

Julien was silent but I could almost feel him within me, riffling about for information.

"We don't, but she doesn't know where they are," he confirmed.

"Did you ever see them, Constance?" I pressed. I could feel her hand leaving mine, her form nearly gone, and I was desperate to eke out whatever information I could before she vanished once again. "Constance, do you know where they are?"

Her brow furrowed, as if dredging up the words took considerable effort. "No. But he'd use the plants. Their secret messages. You just have to—"

She disappeared.

I waited for a beat, certain she'd sputter back into view, but a minute passed by. I could hear the room's clock tick off every second. Nothing.

The room felt too silent.

When I turned back, I noticed Julien had twisted all the way round, leaning against the back of his chair, his mouth set in a firm line as he studied me. Viktor remained frozen behind the settee, eyes blazing with wonder.

I glanced back and forth between the pair of them. It would be impossible to keep them away now. "How well do you know your flowers?"

༄

"There's nothing here," Viktor whined, pacing back and forth along the length of wall.

"It's the last room in this hall. There must be something."

We'd started searching the rooms closest to Gerard's study, assuming he'd want to keep a spare key close by should his go missing.

The first had been a small parlor overrun with towering trees in marble pots and chairs so spindly they reminded me of spider legs. The next had smelled of dust and neglect. Its walls were papered over with peeling pastels and the woolen rug was full of divots made from furniture now long gone. There was a room full of chairs left in odd arrangements, another with a harp and music stand. We'd searched every room in this wing, even going back into my own, and had found nothing.

"Julien, what about your side?"

His shoes clicked across the tiled floor. "Not a single geranium, dragon's tooth, or porcelain flower to be found."

We'd made a list of every flower we could think of that was used to protect or conceal.

Thorn apples and white roses. Foxgloves and tansies.

"I don't think your spirit knew what she was talking about," Viktor said with a sigh.

"She's not my spirit," I snapped.

He listened at the door for a moment before carefully opening it. Dawn was only an hour or two off and servants would be starting to stir within the house once more. After a moment's pause, he left.

"There's nothing here," Julien agreed before slipping through the door himself.

I scanned the room one last time, disheartened. It had taken us hours to search through those few rooms. Trying to find the right flower in a house devoted to them felt impossible. I'd sooner be able to persuade Gerard to hand over the key from his own neck.

In the hall, Viktor and Julien stood outside my rooms. I couldn't make out their actual words but I could tell they were bickering over something. Every muscle in my body ached, weary for sleep. A sigh escaped me as my eyes rolled up, begging Pontus for fortitude.

I'd had about all I could stand of the Brothers Laurent for the night.

The candlelight flickered, catching on the patterns of marble leaves tracing across the ceiling, and I stopped in my tracks.

Ignoring the brewing argument, I made my way down the hall, back toward Gerard's study.

Directly across from its door, a tree vaulted up the wall, jagged bark and twining branches. It was a hawthorn. Clusters of berries hung among the stony leaves but the twigs were riddled with wickedly sharp spikes, some inches long.

The perfect protection.

I turned toward the boys. "What if Constance didn't mean a flower?"

My question ended their spat and Julien drifted closer, studying each tree as he passed by.

"That's a—"

"A hawthorn," I said, running my hands along it, searching for any place in the carved bark where the marble held any give. At the base, where the trunk separated, its roots digging into the floor, there was a slight variation in the stone, almost imperceptible.

I pushed it and, on the other side of the trunk, a hidden box sprang open, revealing a small, silver key.

Julien's breath hitched. "Well done, Miss Thaumas," he murmured begrudgingly.

36

WITH A SNAP OF VIKTOR'S FINGERS, A SERIES OF CANdelabras flared to life, brightening the study as we entered. I shut the door behind us with a hasty click.

The room was so unlike the rest of the manor. The walls were all wooden paneling, dark and heavy. There was a gallery wall of botanical paintings. A massive desk in black walnut dominated the back of the room. Twin chairs of leather and wood sat poised in front of it. The rest of the study was lined with tall shelves, housing books, pressed flowers, and jars of specimens floating in liquids too murky to see through.

A cloying scent saturated the air.

Formaldehyde, I guessed distantly. With a touch of resin and decay.

"So many books," I murmured, turning around to count them. "There must be hundreds of volumes here. How are we ever going to—"

"Here we are," Julien announced, kneeling at the side of the desk. His fingers ran over an unnoticeable lip, picking at it.

Viktor and I watched as he grabbed a rose-gold letter opener from Gerard's stationery set and used it to pop open a hidden compartment with ease.

"How did you know that was there?" I asked, stepping forward to see what the space contained.

"I don't have many memories of Chauntilalie," he admitted, leaning in to investigate. "But I do remember Papa hiding away a bottle of absinthe so Mother wouldn't know. He let me take a sip of it."

Viktor looked impressed. "Father gave you spirits? As a *child*?"

Julien's nose wrinkled. "Vile concoction. It tasted of soured licorice. But it burned the memory in deep so I suppose I'm somewhat grateful for it."

The first thing that came out of the hidden compartment was a bottle of liquor, a brilliant shade of green. Viktor immediately removed the cap and sniffed at it, then wandered over to the bar cart. Julien removed several leather dossiers and a thick journal, stuffed with loose papers.

"Ladies' choice," he said, spreading the finds across the desk.

I picked up the folder nearest me and settled into one of the armchairs. Viktor rejoined us, bringing over heavy crystal tumblers, filled nearly to the brim with the absinthe. He offered me the first, all but foisting it into my hand.

"Papa is going to notice that much missing," Julien hissed, pushing his away. "And you've not even properly prepared it. There's meant to be burnt sugar and water added."

"It's amazing you've spent so many years exiled from Chauntilalie and yet here you are, sounding just as arrogant as Father," Viktor mused, grabbing at the journal. He flopped into the other chair, throwing his legs over its arm. "Bottoms up," he instructed before throwing back a great swallow of the green spirits. Viktor glanced at me. "Oh, Ver. You're not to be like old fussy Jules, are you?"

I brought the tumbler up. "It smells like stale perfume."

Viktor took another slug, the glass now half empty. "And tastes like ambrosia. Why shouldn't we drink like gods? Oh go on, Ver."

Rolling my eyes, I took the smallest sip I could, wincing. Julien had been right about the taste. It was all anise and fennel but I found it dark and intoxicating.

"May we please focus on the task at hand?" Julien snipped. "The last thing we need is for Father to stroll in, catching us unaware and soused."

Viktor winked and polished his whole tumbler off before opening the journal.

For a time, the room fell into silence as we read.

My ledger was full of loose papers. There were strange botanical renderings, labeled in words I almost knew but didn't. I turned the paper sideways, trying to understand how the plant was meant to grow. There didn't seem to be any roots or leaves.

"Fundus," I murmured to myself. "Myometrium."

Julien looked up from his papers, his eyes like daggers. "What are you muttering about over there?"

"Just reading."

"Can we all agree that's an activity best undertaken in silence?"

From behind his diary, Viktor made a face at me, then sprung from his chair, too restless to sit still. He swiped Julien's cup, then leaned against the back of my chair, peering over to see what I was reading.

"Arina's *burning heart*," Viktor cursed, dropping the journal to the floor. It skidded beneath my chair, striking my heel. He snatched the paper from my hands and slammed it down in front of Julien. "Look at this."

Julien peered at the diagram. "Give me the rest of that."

Before I could protest, Viktor grabbed the folder and tossed it at the desk. Sheets of paper scattered across the top. Julien flipped through them, his eyes darting rapidly back and forth. He sucked in a breath.

"Can you read it?" I asked.

He made a short, insulted noise. "Of course."

"Does it say what kind of plants they are? What he intends to do with them?"

Slowly, Julien glanced up, blinking at me as though I was extremely dim-witted. "These aren't plants. They're anatomical renderings."

I looked over the drawings I'd been studying with fresh eyes, still unable to guess what organs they were meant to depict.

"The female reproductive system," Julien clarified, flipping the paper around as though it would help.

It still looked like a flower to me.

"What do his notes say?"

"They're lists of trials, apparently," Julien said, so absent-mindedly engrossed in the reading, he sounded eerily similar to Gerard. "Specimens used, ratios and dosage amounts. Drugs, extracts." He flipped to another page. "He lists out all of the women. . . . I think I've found your Constance." He cleared his throat. "Constance Devereux. Twenty years old. Blond hair, brown eyes. Biological father, Aukera. No discernable gifts."

"Translate, please," Viktor said, running his fingertip around the rim of the tumbler. His eyes had taken on a glassy sheen. "Not all of us have your eidetic memory."

Julien glanced up. "Aukera. Lord of mirth and god of chance. One of Vaipany's sons."

"Constance's father was a god?" I asked.

"Papa believed so . . ." Julien scanned more of the trials. "This subject was a granddaughter of Acacia . . ." He trailed off as though trying to recall which goddess that was.

"Pontus's daughter," I supplied, feeling pleased to know something he didn't. "She controls the waves with waterspouts."

Julien nodded. "Papa injected a combination of hydrophytes directly into the mother's womb. The babies were born with gills."

I drew in a sharp breath. "He was experimenting with women who came from gods."

Frowning, Julien returned to the papers. "It would appear so, though I don't understand what he's attempting to produce. He tried a variety of bloodlines—Seland, Oberonin, Arius, Versia. There's even a weak line descended from Vaipany himself. Six women. Six gods."

An uneasy sense of déjà vu crept over me. This story was so familiar somehow.

The memory hit me.

Alex had told me it, when I'd first arrived at Chauntilalie.

Dauphine was meant to have a bit of the divine within her, running straight from Arina's progeny. These boys. Alex. They had holy blood within them.

I opened my mouth but Julien continued on, stopping me short.

"Here's a list of medicines used. . . ." He whistled through his teeth. "Poisons, actually. Salvia, mescaline, hyoscine. He crushed up betel nuts, extracted opium poppies. . . ."

I froze, remembering the tea Gerard had given me.

"He even laced the candles in these women's rooms with oil of *Brugmansia*." He glanced at me as if knowing I wouldn't understand. "It's a trumpetlike flower. Very poisonous."

"Their candles," I echoed. "He put poison in their candles?"

Julien nodded.

"And these flowers . . . what color are they?"

"They come in a variety of shades," Julien said. "Yellows, whites, even oranges. But the most powerful of them are a deep pink—much like those candles over there." With a grimace, he gestured to a series of unlit tapers gracing a sideboard. "Don't even think about lighting those, Viktor."

They were the same shade as the pink candles in that cursed nursery. The hallway outside my quarters. Resting beside my bed.

Who knows how long I'd been breathing in their poison.

Gerard had been drugging me, ever since I'd arrived. Lulling me into a state of complacency. Compliancy. Numbing me so I didn't notice all of the strange things within the manor that weren't right.

Viktor clicked his tongue thoughtfully, unaware of my discomfort. "Why would Father be giving babies hallucinogens?"

Julien pursed his lips, musing. "Perhaps to ensure they'd be born in a perpetual state of seeing . . . things."

"Ghosts?" I whispered hopefully.

"Gods."

A chill ran down my back.

Viktor sat on the edge of the desk, his second glass nearly empty. "The gods are everywhere. Why go to such complicated lengths to communicate with them?"

Julien set down the papers, musing. "There are many who don't travel between the worlds anymore, the ones deep in the Sanctum. The forgotten ones."

When I was a child, Annaleigh's husband, Cassius, loved to terrify me with stories of those fallen deities, the Denizens, so long unremembered they'd grown shapeless and too large, morphed into hulking beasts of clay and hungry maws. "I can't imagine why anyone would wish to speak to them."

Viktor chewed on the inside of his cheek. "Maybe Father wants to hear what *they* have to say."

Julien glanced to Viktor. "Did you find anything about it in the diary?"

Remembering it had fallen under my chair, I reached down to pull it out.

"Ver, don't!" Viktor warned, grabbing for it. His movements were slower than they should be, his accuracy impaired by the spirits.

But I had the journal open, already scanning the pages. Unlike the notes filed in the folders, this book was written in Arcannian. I understood it all.

"Oh."

There, scrawled out in Gerard's tiny handwriting and favored evergreen ink, was my name.

My name, written out across the page three times.

Partnered in three combinations.

Again, three.

Always, three.

A small part of me had held out the impossible hope that Julien's theories were wrong, that it was all some terrible and unlucky coincidence that I found myself here, with this family, in this situation.

But there it was, the unmistakable proof.

Gerard had brought me here on purpose, had selected me, had choreographed every moment since my arrival like a well-executed dance.

Alexander and Verity, the first entry read. A series of symbolled notations followed, ending in his final verdict: *Advantageous*. He'd ringed the entire section with a circle of approval.

"'Julien and Verity,'" I said aloud, skipping over the bits of shorthand I didn't understand. "'Potentially favorable.'"

Julien snorted dismissively and I wasn't sure if I should feel offended or flattered.

"'Viktor and Verity,'" I read the last paragraph aloud. The entire thing had been crossed out with a definitive slash of ink, rendering Gerard's judgment nearly illegible. "'Too volatile.'"

Viktor shook his head, downing the last of the glass. "As if he knows anything about us, Jules." He clasped his brother's shoulder, squeezing it tightly, but I sensed he was the one looking to be comforted and consoled.

Julien brushed aside the reassurance with a twitch. "It seems he knows much more than either of us thought. I'm starting to believe we weren't forgotten, dear brother. Just . . . transplanted."

"And yet still found wanting," Viktor muttered, grabbing the diary once more.

The fireplace behind Julien flared to life, the logs igniting as flames shot high up the flue. Startled, I jumped from the chair, a cry for help on the tip of my tongue, before I realized it was only Viktor blowing off steam.

"Some warning would be appreciated," Julien said, teeth clenched. He opened another dossier, ignoring his brother's outburst.

"That man," he spat, flipping through more of the diary. Along the wall, the gas lamps' flames danced, swaying dangerously. "We're not fit to remain at his estate. We're deemed too unseemly to be recognized as his own sons, but he couldn't just give up everything he'd worked for with us. 'Julien's intellectual aptitude grows by leaps and bounds,'" he sneered, his voice mincing. "'Each letter from Sheffield astounds even my wildest hopes for him.' Good for you, Jules. You're not welcome at family dinner, but you've gone and impressed Father."

Julien pressed his lips together. It wasn't exactly a smile, but I could sense his pleasure all the same.

"'Viktor,'" he began reading, then stopped short. After a moment's pause, he ripped the page from the book and crumpled it in his hand. When he unfurled his fist, all that remained was soot.

"Is there anything more on Alex?" I asked, hoping to defuse Viktor's anger, but also wanting to know what Gerard thought would happen once he paired me with his youngest son. I'd never seen Alex do anything like his brothers could. But if Gerard went to the trouble of bringing me—of bringing my *talents*—to Chauntilalie, there must have been something specific he hoped to achieve.

"Pages," Viktor replied darkly, thumbing through the diary, his face taut with rage. "Pages and pages and pages. Whole chapters on the golden one's life. And you know what they all say?"

I shook my head, unable to find the courage to voice an answer.

"Nothing! Not a damn thing." He pitched the tumbler into the fireplace and the heavy glass shattered. "There's not a single thing about our brother that makes him special. Not one. He's completely normal. Completely useless. The exact opposite of whatever it was Father was trying to achieve. Not like me. Not like Jules. But *we* were cast off. *We* were sent away. We—" His words died in a snarl, hands trembling.

It took me a moment to realize the journal was smoking.

"Stop that," I said, snatching it from him and fanning it back and forth. There were singed marks across its edges, blackened shadows where his hands had been, but the book was otherwise unscathed.

Viktor crossed back to the bar cart, muttering to himself as he grabbed the absinthe with an elaborate swipe. He flopped down hard in the chair once more, kicking up his legs over the arm and drinking straight out of the bottle.

"Are you just going to sit there and get drunk?"

He glanced at me, his face drawn and exhausted. "Have you a better suggestion?"

"Let him be, Miss Thaumas," Julien spoke up, his nose still buried in the documents, unconcerned. "He's likely to burn down half the manor in his mood."

Viktor raised the bottle toward his brother, saluting him before taking another swig.

With a sigh of disgust, I thumbed open the diary and began to read.

The first entry was dated twenty years prior. Dauphine had just confided she was with child. Several lists of roots and extracts followed after. It seemed as though Gerard initially began dosing her teas. For days he documented how many ounces she drank and the side effects she experienced. A week later, he added powdered tinctures to her meals. Later on, salves and lotions, applied directly to her burgeoning belly. Then, shots.

My own stomach clenched as I imagined a thick needle plunging within me.

It said she suffered from terrible nausea, that she would often black out after treatments only to sob uncontrollably in her sleep. Gerard wrote she spent whole days in bed, speaking to things, to beings, he could not see.

Her stomach grew and so did the amounts of drugs he foisted upon her.

Dauphine must have realized at some point that these procedures weren't regular. Why had she gone along with it? Had Gerard told her there was something wrong with the babies? That he was attempting to fix them?

I desperately wanted to believe she'd not willingly subjected herself to his mad schemes.

With a fit of disgust, I slammed the diary closed and tossed it upon the nearest bookshelf, unwilling to keep hold of the dreadful things inside it for any longer.

As the diary fell heavily onto the shelf, the entire bookcase swayed back and forth.

I blinked, certain it was an optical illusion, a trick of the light in the dimly lit room.

But no.

The bookcase was swinging, back and forth as if . . .

As if it wasn't really a bookcase at all.

I threw a swift glance back at the boys, wondering if they noticed what I saw. Julien was absorbed in a new notebook, his nose just inches from the page. Viktor's eyes were closed and his head listed against the armchair, the bottle of absinthe nearly falling from his loosened grip.

With wonder and dread, I pressed tentative fingers to the shelves, gasping as the entire behemoth shifted, moving to the left. Just above me, I spotted a piece of tracking disguised to look like trim work.

The bookshelf was a false front, nothing more than a mask hiding in plain sight.

With an *umph* of effort, I pushed the bookcase to the side, revealing another set of shelves behind it. But these shelves held no books on them.

Instead, they were filled with jars.

Rows and rows of large jars.

Wet specimen canisters.

Artie had a small collection of them. He was forever bringing home deceased creatures found washed up onshore, caught in tide pools. He loved examining them and would stick the animals in jars full of formaldehyde. The dark liquid preserved the creatures in a state free of decay.

My throat clenched as I wondered what things Gerard could possibly be keeping in his.

I leaned in to examine the closest shelf, right at my eye level, and twisted one jar round.

At first glance, it was an animal of some sort. It was pale and long dead, its surface strangely pliant and waxy. Elongated limbs bent backward, curled and compressed to fit within the confines of the jar.

A pair of animals, I guessed, counting eight appendages.

It bobbed in the formaldehyde, turning on an invisible axis.

My mouth fell open as the head came into view.

Heads.

It was then that I realized this thing in the jar, not the hidden cache of papers, was the reason Gerard kept the study locked up so tight.

The bodies—body, I mentally corrected, spotting the band of flesh that knitted all three chests together—were small. They'd been born prematurely, that much was clear. Their features, vague and flat in the liquid suspension, didn't look finished, a piece of clay abandoned by a disinterested sculptor.

Even still, the features were wrong, so very wrong.

The triplet on the left side of the mass had a perfectly round head, without ears, and a gaping circular mouth that reminded me of the buckets of lamprey eels Cook would bring to Highmoor, fresh from the docks. Rows of serrated teeth puckered its edges.

The middle triplet's face was a blank canvas. Thin membrane

stretched across the plane where eyes should have been. Its skin was mottled with a network of purple veins.

The baby on the right had no mouth and stared out at the world through a single engorged eye, directly in the center of its face. The pupil was oblong, like a goat or sheep. Its upper appendages ended in stumps, more flipper than arm.

I knew these babies, these things, were dead, but a trick of the light played over the cyclops's eye and I could have sworn it focused upon me.

Wordlessly, I backed away from the jar, from the monsters it contained, and stumbled into Viktor's armchair. Mid-sip, the pungent alcohol sloshed down his chest, staining his shirt the same sickly hue as the pickled babies.

"Ver—"

His protest ended as I sank my fingers into his shoulder, nodding toward the shelves.

"You might be mad about being exiled away to Marchioly House," I said, drawing Julien's attention from the dossiers. "But at least you didn't end up in a glass jar."

Viktor sprang from his seat, eyes narrowed as he approached the bookcase.

There were dozens of those jars on the shelves, some nestled in sets of three, other larger ones tucked between leather-bound volumes, and while I had no desire to examine them further, I would have staked my life each contained the remains of an experiment.

Like moths to a flame, the boys were drawn in, turning jar after jar round as they looked through their cursed half siblings. I found my remaining absinthe and downed the tumbler in one hasty, trembling gulp. It was a poor choice. My bloodstream boiled and every time I shut my eyes, I saw the gaping mouth, the sightless face, those rounded limbs.

"Versia's *stars*," Viktor whispered, hoisting a specimen up. "Are those . . . fronds?"

"Fronds?" I whispered. "Like . . . like a fern?"

Viktor held the jar out and my stomach flipped over as I caught sight of the figure within.

"I've seen that baby before," I admitted, my voice cracking as hot bile threatened to slosh up my throat. "That's one of Constance's."

I gnawed at the inside of my cheek, struggling to put together the bits and pieces of everything I'd guessed at and weighing them against what I actually knew.

And it didn't make sense.

Constance had been viciously murdered. Such an attack wasn't something that could have been easily cleared away. It was laughable to imagine Dauphine in the secret tunnel, on her hands and knees, cleaning up the bloody aftermath, dragging Constance's body out of the manor to toss within a grave she'd dug herself.

And the babies.

If Dauphine had killed Constance, she would have undoubtedly gone after the children as well, wanting to make it appear as if Gerard's mistress had simply taken her children and fled.

But the babies were here.

In Gerard's study.

Here, preserved for further study and speculation. To be analyzed and puzzled over.

By Gerard.

"Ver?" Viktor asked. "Are you all right?"

Slowly, I shook my head. "Gerard killed her," I murmured, my mouth feeling impossibly dry. "Constance. He killed her and them." I gestured to the jars lining the bottom shelf. "Those babies weren't like the others. . . . Look how big their jars are. They'd been born. They were alive. Until . . ." My throat caught and the words wouldn't come.

Viktor paled, looking up at all of the other jars. "Where do you suppose all the other mothers are now?"

"The gardens," I guessed. "Buried somewhere in those rose mounds."

"He needs to pay," Julien murmured quietly, tracing his fingers along the lip of a jar. The formaldehyde within was blessedly too murky to see through. "We have enough evidence, more than enough evidence. The diary . . . these babies . . . whatever is buried out in the mounds . . . We need to go to the authorities and let them deal with it all. Deal with *him*."

Viktor nodded, uncharacteristically subdued.

"But . . ." I stopped, my head roiling. "But you can't . . ."

Both brothers' eyes fell upon me.

"You're not about to justify all this, are you, Ver?" Viktor asked sharply, at my side in a flash. He held up Constance's baby. The little tendrilled arms swayed in the sloshing liquid.

"No, of course not! Gerard absolutely needs to be held accountable—he needs to be stopped—but . . . but before you do that, before you tell anyone else, we need to tell Alex," I decided firmly, blinking hard to keep the room from spinning. "He needs to know this. To know about you and Julien. To know everything Gerard has done. Alex deserves to hear it from us first."

The boys studied each other and I had the uncomfortably distinct impression they were speaking to one another without words.

"Fine," Viktor spoke first. "But somewhere outside the house. You never know who could be listening in."

"Of course . . . What do we do with all this?" I asked, glancing at the papers, the diary, the shards of glass in the fireplace.

"I'm taking the documents with us," Julien decided, crossing back to the desk. "I want to make sure we've not missed anything."

I pushed the false bookcase over, blessedly covering the specimens, then looked around, trying to decide the best way to help. I felt adrift, like a forgotten fishing net, tossed about on waves and gathering up sea debris until the weight of everything pulled me under to a silty burial. I longed to crash into bed but knew sleep was unlikely to come.

I feared I'd never be able to sleep again.

Before Viktor put the absinthe bottle back into the hidden cache, he spit into it with sullen spite. "Gods, why did I drink so much?"

"I've been wondering the same thing myself, brother," Julien said, straightening the papers in an ordered pile. "You've no idea how it feels to be living with either of your thoughts right now. It's like wading through waist-high shit."

Viktor's lips stretched into a deeply amused, wicked smile. "Hearing you say that will be worth tomorrow's hangover, I'm sure."

Their easy banter made me think of my own sisters and I was struck by a sudden longing for them.

Mercy, Honor, Annaleigh.

Even Camille.

Especially Camille.

My throat swelled and I realized I was very close to tears. Julien noticed immediately and I caught the pained look he shot Viktor, clearly beseeching for an intervention. I wiped my face, quickly trying to push the overwhelming thoughts aside. "Gerard said he had messages from my sisters here." I sniffed. "Since we're taking everything else, could I get those as well?"

The desk was bare, save for the fountain pens lined up at the side, a trio of fanatical tidiness. Julien pulled open the middle drawer and rummaged for a moment. "Here," he said, foisting a stack of correspondence toward me.

I took it, puzzled. There were far more than the three RSVPs Gerard had mentioned.

"He's been keeping mail from me," I realized, flipping through the stack. There were envelopes written out in Mercy's swirling cursive, Honor's blocky lettering, Annaleigh's careful printing, and even Camille's copperplate.

Eagerly, I opened one of Camille's, but her wax seal was already broken, the letter gone.

I pawed through all of the envelopes. Every one of them was empty. "Where are the letters?"

"He probably burned them," Viktor said, glancing back at the fireplace longingly.

I blinked in disbelief. "Why would he do that? What good are my letters to him?"

Julien made a face, looking as if he'd swallowed back a heavy sigh. "After all the trouble it took to lure you to Chauntilalie, Papa certainly wouldn't want you to leave. If he cut you off from your family, making it seem that none of them missed you, that none of them expressed any concern for you, you'd feel as though you had nowhere else to go." He licked his lips. "I doubt any correspondence you wrote made it out of the manor either."

I frowned, a spark of anger rising up my spine, as hot and biting as if Viktor had kindled it himself. My hands balled into fists. The nails dug in deep. "He needs—"

"Ah, ah, ah," Julien said, holding up a finger to stop my outburst. "Save it for tomorrow, Miss Thaumas. Save it for when it counts."

37

WHEN FREDERICK OPENED THE DOOR TO ALEX'S ROOM the next morning, his face long and grim, I knew the day was not going to go as I'd planned.

I'd fallen asleep with dreams of whisking Alex down to the lake, away from the prying eyes and ears of Chauntilalie, to tell him everything.

But Frederick loomed over me now, filling the doorframe without an offer to step aside.

"I'm sorry, Miss Thaumas," he began. "Master Laurent is indisposed today."

"Another fit?" I guessed, my heart falling as I pictured Alex in pain once more.

He nodded solemnly. "He's resting now. I know he wouldn't want you to see him in such a state."

"He's had so many of them lately," I observed.

Frederick nodded again, offering no further insight.

"Could I just . . ." I trailed off as he crossed his arms, an impassable mountain too formidable to argue with. "Could you let him know I came by? Once he's awake?"

Frederick promised he would and silently shut the door before I could muster any other request.

I stared at the door, memorizing the woodwork, and tried to process my next step.

We were supposed to tell Alex today.

Everything that was meant to happen today hinged on Alex knowing everything we did.

With a sigh, I left the south wing and made my way down to the first floor. I was too restless to return to my rooms. Too nauseous to attempt breakfast. I could feel the weight of every secret I learned last night pressing down on me, compelling me to act, but there was nothing to be done. Not now. Not without Alex.

I turned down hall after hall without purpose.

I passed by the same set of mirrors three times before I realized I was pacing in a circle, trapped in a hazy loop, just like Constance.

I needed to do something. Anything.

My thoughts were a tangled web of half-understood truths, half-formed plans, and layers of questions that had no answers.

Julien's revelation about Gerard's selected women ate at me.

It was clear Gerard was attempting to coax out some sort of power, some strain of divinity from the women's bloodlines and pass it along to his altered progeny. But how did I fit into that plan?

I was different from most people, that much was true.

But I was not like those women.

There were no gods in my family tree, however many

generations removed. The Thaumas line, for all its proud nobility, was wholly ordinary. I didn't know why I could see what I did, but it wasn't because of some sordid, secret tryst with the divine. I was mortal, through and through.

So why had Gerard chosen me?

And what did he hope my children might do?

I remembered Viktor's musing from last night, that Gerard might be trying to speak to the gods. The older ones, long tucked away into the deepest parts of the Sanctum. The Denizens.

Why would anyone go to such lengths to speak to them?

He'd dosed expecting mothers with mixtures of poppies and betel nuts, water plants and funguses. Things grown in the depths of his poison garden.

Things like the laurel plant that had so affected me . . .

I remembered the wicked grin of the weeping wraith. How she'd moved. How she'd spoken.

I stopped my pacing, nearly tripping over my own feet, as I was struck with the conviction that she'd not been a hallucination after all.

She'd actually been there with us.

I was just the only one who could see her.

A goddess.

Or something like it.

I licked my lips, considering what this might mean.

The gods knew all.

The gods saw all.

She would know more about me. About my gift.

She would have answers.

I was certain of it.

The ground was damp and warm as I spread a blanket out in the Garden of Giants later that morning. It was the only place in the entire estate where I knew I wouldn't be found. When Alex and I had come on our picnic, the soaring statues had been surrounded with tall grasses and brush left to grow in wild tangles.

No gardener would stumble across me.

No one would oversee anything I was about to do.

My hands trembled as I unpacked my satchel of gathered contraband.

A flask of poppy tea, brewed twice as strong as I'd normally prepared it.

A pink candle.

Matches.

And a sprig of laurel leaves, cut from a branch poking through the fence of the poison garden, just moments before.

I'd waited until Gerard had wandered away for tea before making my move and immediately wrapped the snipping into a handkerchief, hoping it would hold the toxic fumes until I was ready to use them.

The full magnitude of what I was about to do swept over me.

I was going to knowingly poison myself in an attempt to summon an otherworldly entity.

I winced, remembering the flash of her pointed gray teeth.

Not a ghost. Something far, far worse.

Releasing a shaky breath, I lit the candle. Its scent filled the air, making me want to heave now that I knew its truth.

I uncapped the flask and took a deep gulp of the tea. Then another.

I paused, waiting for something to happen.

"Hello?"

My voice was weak with uncertainty.

I closed my eyes, trying to recall everything about the weeping woman. Her dark, swirling hair. Her long, ragged nails. The cruel angle of her grin. If only I knew her name.

"I . . . I don't know if I'm doing this right but . . . are you there?"

I opened my eyes.

All around me, the colors of the trees were wrong. It was as if I'd looked directly into sunlight, burning my retinas until the whole world was cast into a different hue. Everything was in shades of blue. Deep navy and cerulean. Swirling galaxies of lapis and cobalt.

The trees seemed to multiply.

But I saw no wraith.

I took another swallow of the tea, then unwrapped the handkerchief and breathed in deeply.

The scent of the laurel's sap tickled at my nose.

I felt faint.

There was a sharp sound of movement behind me.

I turned in time to see one of the garden's statues pick itself up from the earth.

It was almost a giraffe, a great hulking beast, teetering on spindly, knobby legs. Each footstep shook the ground like thunder. Thick spikes ran down its spine. Its muzzle was too long, like a crocodile. It had eight eyes.

They scanned the garden with a horrible, cunning intelligence and when they caught sight of me, I wanted to sink into oblivion.

Despair overwhelmed me as I cowered before the creature.

I watched as its jaw unhinged like a snake, readying to devour me whole.

Unable to run, unable to move at all, I closed my eyes, praying for a quick end.

But nothing happened.

When I opened my eyes, the statue had returned to its spot, nothing more than stone.

"It was just the poisons," I tried to reassure myself. I breathed in more of the laurel.

Magenta blood rained down from the trees, staining my flesh. I could feel the hot substance sink into my skin, tainting my insides.

"I don't want to be here anymore," I murmured as the pond began to boil, festering with swarms of unseen beasts. A strange hum reverberated through the clearing and I swore I could see the air around me shape into waves.

I fell to the ground, unable to stop the shivers racing through me.

It was cold, so very cold. Wind whipped by me, laced with snowflakes. They grimaced at me, their impossible faces filled with rage. The trees lashed out their arms, like drowning men flailing to be saved.

I tucked my knees up to my chest, trying to make myself as small and unnoticeable as possible. The wind's howling stopped, though the trees still danced in its madness.

Then there was a new sound.

Footsteps approaching from behind. Soft as a silken whisper, they tiptoed through the grass, making their way closer to me.

I scrunched my eyes shut.

If this was my end, I did not want to witness it.

Cool fingers cupped my cheek and a gentle voice murmured soothing sounds of comfort.

"Oh, come here, dear heart." The voice was as familiar as the hands that scooped me up, stroking my hair with fingers long dead.

With an incoherent cry of gratitude, I threw my arms around the ghostly form of Eulalie and wept.

38

"YOU'RE NOT REAL. YOU CAN'T BE REAL," I REPEATED, my cries muffled in her layers of nightclothes. Eulalie had died in the middle of the night, falling off the cliffs beyond Highmoor and smashing into the surf below.

She *looked* like a ghost, soft edged and illuminated with an inner glow. Her coloring had been drained away and she existed only in shades of gray, flickering oddly in the now-moonlit forest, like a cuttlefish struggling to remain camouflaged as a predator approached.

"I'm as real as you need me to be," she said, tightening her hold on me.

My heart pounded in my chest so hard that it felt bruised and raw.

"Eulalie isn't a ghost," I protested. "She's been in the Brine for years."

She cupped my face with mottled hands, silencing me. "I hated being trapped anywhere in life. Why should death be any different?"

Her easy smile took my breath away.

I'd forgotten how beautiful she was.

Little bits of memory fluttered in my mind, almost remembered but flitting away before I could fully grasp them.

"Oh, my littlest sister," she cooed, pressing a kiss to the top of my head. "What a mess you've gotten yourself into."

It felt so good to be held, to be comforted like this. I hadn't realized how crushed and wilted I'd become until my sister wrapped her arms around me. I nestled closer to her, my forehead against her neck, as I would have when she was alive, when I'd been so much smaller.

The memory of this sensation nearly swept me away, a riptide pulling across time.

I knew what this was supposed to feel like.

I'd done this before and I remembered it . . . almost.

"Why can't I remember you? Why can't I remember that year?" I bit my lip. "Why am I the only one who sees what I see?"

Her sigh was long and soft, the gentle swell of sea-foam reaching the shore. "A lot of things happened back then. None of them particularly pleasant."

"Tell me," I insisted. "Please."

She twirled her finger around one of her loose ringlets, carefully considering her words. "There was a very cruel woman who wanted to reach out and hurt others as much as she'd been hurt herself . . . and she used the gods to do it."

"The gods?" I echoed. "That's who I wanted to talk to. That's why I did all this." I gestured to the spilled flask of tea, the now-crushed laurel leaves. "I need to find out more about why we're connected. Why I can do all . . . this." I waved my arm about the clearing. Rainbow prisms as large and as tangible as butterflies danced in the air. "Are we . . . are we somehow related to—"

"Oh, littlest sister," she interrupted. "There's more than one way for a god to touch you." She tapped at my forehead meaningfully.

It was as though I'd been peering through a pair of binoculars set improperly. The world had been blurry and indistinct until Eulalie reached out to adjust the focus and suddenly everything crystalized into place. The images were crisp and sharpened with color.

I saw everything.

I *remembered* everything.

My mind felt like a sketchbook caught in the wind, flipping through pages of the past, each memory an illustration drawn out in my own hand.

Papa remarrying.

Eulalie's funeral.

Piles of slippers, sparkling and lustrous at first, then tattered to sad bits of spent leather.

Rosalie and Ligeia, their eyes frosted shut, mottled blue, and never to wake.

Bare feet spinning on point, over and over, without music, without partner . . .

I gasped as the last page of the book was revealed.

Her.

The wraith.

Black tears streaming down her face even as her lips curled back, making us dance to her own tune.

"Kosamaras," I whispered.

Eulalie nodded sadly.

Kosamaras.

Sister to the goddess of the night. Harbinger of nightmares and madness. The bringer of delusions, illusions, tricks of the mind, and despair.

I had not been touched by the divine.

I'd been assaulted by the uncanny.

Kosamaras had taken my sisters and I captive, holding our thoughts in her twisted hands, making us see what she wanted, what we feared.

Eulalie's grip on me tightened, her pale eyes impossibly sad. "You don't need to remember this, Verity. Some things aren't worth it."

"But . . ." I sorted through the memories. The night of the fire. Papa's death. Cassius saving me, seeing me when no one else could. "It ended, didn't it? It's over. Annaleigh, she saved us. Somehow . . . Why am I still seeing things?"

She pressed her lips together. "You've always seen things differently. It's what makes you such a good artist. But when Kosamaras touched you . . ." She tapped at the center of my forehead again. "It opened something up. Something that didn't go back together as it should. That's why you're here now." She glanced back through the woods as if she could make out the glowering shape of Chauntilalie. "He chose you."

"I know," I confirmed. "Do you know what he's trying to do? What it is he wants from me—from my children?"

The words felt so wrong. I didn't have children. Not yet.

"It doesn't matter. You just need to get out. Go back to Highmoor. You can't stay here, Verity. You can't stay with these people."

"But what about Alex? I love him."

Eulalie shook her head. "He doesn't matter. Only you do. You need to leave. Today. Can't you feel it? There's danger all around you. Creeping. Lurking. Lying in wait. Even the air in that house is poisoned," she said, nodding toward the pink candle. "You need to leave. I'll help you. It's why I came all this way."

Her last word drew out long and lingering and its tone reminded me of something. Something worrying and wrong.

I sat up, slipping free of Eulalie's embrace. "Why *did* you come?"

"I just told you. I'm worried about you, Verity. That house is evil. That man is—"

I shook my head. "That's not what I meant. Why are *you* the one here? I've not seen you since I was six. I can barely remember you. If you wanted to send a warning, why not use someone else, someone I know, someone I trust? Hanna. Why is Hanna not here now?"

Her tongue ran over the back of her teeth. "Not many are strong enough to leave the Brine."

Warning bells rang in my mind and my eyes narrowed. "But you are?"

She nodded.

"How?"

Eulalie's face remained flat and expressionless. "I can't tell you that. That's not how it works."

"How does it work? How exactly? Tell me, Eulalie."

She backed away, expanding the space between us as she realized things weren't going as she'd planned. "Why are you being this way? I'm here to help you."

"Maybe so, but you're not my sister."

Her head cocked to the side, eyes wide and wounded. "Of course I am."

"My sisters are in the Brine."

"I know that. I said that—"

"Hanna is at Highmoor. Hanna has always been trapped at Highmoor."

"To . . . to watch over you," she fumbled.

"You said she was in the Brine. Who are you?" I squinted at her, seeing everything for the first time. She *did* look just like Eulalie, an exact replica of every portrait I'd ever seen, down to the fine lines lacing over her skin, like cracks in oil paint.

Her eyes grew bright, filling with tears. "I don't understand. Why don't you believe me? Why don't you—"

As the tears welled up and spilled over her cheeks, they ran black, leaving lines of pigment slick as tar across my sister's crackled skin.

"Kosamaras," I murmured darkly.

It had worked.

I had brought the Harbinger to me.

She smiled and her teeth grew into sharp points. She stretched and Eulalie's façade fell away, revealing her true form. Kosamaras appraised me with those bottomless black eyes and laughed.

"I truly did not know what I was getting myself into all those years ago, little Thaumas girl." She *tsked*, her voice raspy as the husks of dead beetles. "You see through everything. It would be quite impressive if it didn't create so many annoyances for us."

"Us."

She raised her fingers, swishing them through the air as if to indicate a place beyond the forest, beyond Chauntilalie, beyond anything here in our world.

"The gods?" I guessed. "They care what's going on here?"

"They care," she said simply. "We all care."

I snorted back a laugh. "*I* brought you here. I was the one who poisoned myself and then you come with all these theatrics—"

Her face hardened with scorn and the air between us crackled with power. "You couldn't handle me without my theatrics, Thaumas girl."

I did not doubt that.

"I suppose I could have selected a better ruse than your long-dead sister, but my message remains the same: Go. Now. Get yourself as far from this manor, as far from that monster as you can."

Though everything inside me was aquiver wanting to cower before the presence of something so much more than myself, I tilted my face with an imperiousness I did not feel. "It's funny to hear you call someone else a monster."

She snorted. "Don't press your luck with me, little Thaumas."

"Why did you go after my family all those years ago? Two of my sisters are dead because of you. My father. My stepmother."

She shook her head vehemently. "I had nothing to do with him. With her. That was all *him*."

I could hear the distinction she imparted the word. "Who?"

"Viscardi," she hissed.

I shuddered.

A Trickster. The god of bargains and lord over the People of the Bones.

She shrugged. "That's neither here nor there, though."

"But it is, isn't it? Whatever happened to me *then* is why I'm at Chauntilalie *now*. You did something to me."

She stood up and paced the clearing, her gray gown wafting from her like smoke. "An unfortunate mistake."

"Unfortunate," I echoed, following her every move.

The Harbinger stopped beside one of the Menagerie statues and let out a sigh, sounding bored by the conversation. "I didn't know."

"Didn't know what?"

"What you are."

My mouth fell open in alarm. "What do you mean? What am I?"

"Stop parroting back everything I say," she snapped.

"Then say something that makes sense!" I was on my feet in an instant, charging toward her. My fear had been replaced with indignation, anger licking up my spine. She'd tormented my family, sent two of my sisters to cold, icy deaths, and altered some essential part of my very being. The absolute least she could do was give me a straight answer. "What did you do?"

"I beguiled you. The same as your sisters."

"Not the same. They stopped seeing things long ago. I haven't."

"You . . . you were different," she mused. "Usually when someone is beguiled, they see what I want them to." With a flick of her wrist, her fingers erupted into fiery blue flames. I could hear the crackling. I could feel the heat.

"Stop it," I said, ducking as she swiped her hand close to my face, laughing.

She lowered her hand and the flames burned out. "When the bargain ended, so too did the beguiling, but you still saw things.

Things not of my creation. Things not here, but there . . ." Again, she made the little gesture indicating the air around us.

"Ghosts," I guessed.

She nodded.

"Echoes of the past."

Another nod.

"Why?"

"I don't know. Honestly, I don't," she added quickly. "There's just something in there, Thaumas girl." She poked at my temple. "Something different."

Her words sent a shiver down my frame, gooseflesh crawling over my skin. But an idea flickered over me and my heart leapt high. I reached out, grasping her hand. Her skin was oddly textured, like toothed watercolor paper, but I held on fast. "Make it stop."

She squirmed out of my fervent hold. "There's nothing I can do. The door was already open. The beguiling just propped it wider."

"Then shut it!" I cried. "You're a god. If you don't have the power, then who? Pontus? Viscardi? Bring Vaipany here right now and make it stop."

She shook her head, black locks swaying limply down her back. "Perhaps if you . . . if you were to leave here—right now—something could be done."

A mirthless burst of laughter bubbled up within me, as loud and off-putting as a bullfrog's croak. "You want me to make a bargain?"

She shrugged elegantly, the lines of her shoulder blades rising in sharp points. "It never hurts to ask."

I stalked away from her, acid biting hot at the hollow of my throat. "I'm not leaving. I'm not doing a single thing you ask of me. Not until you fix this."

Her face hardened, turning brittle and ugly. "I could snap my fingers and send you back to Highmoor this instant."

"Then do it," I taunted her. "If you're so terribly powerful and potent, do it. Send me back. Compel me to leave. Beguile me all the way back to Salann."

Her fingers balled into tight fists and her nose wrinkled to a sneer. She hissed out words in a language I did not know, finishing off the phrase with a triumphant shout.

All around us, the forest spun, trees and brush bleeding and swirling together in a catastrophic hurricane of color and noise. I felt as if we flipped over several times, strange forces pushing and pulling us, though I was almost certain my feet never left the ground. When it stopped, we were standing in the middle of the Blue Room at Highmoor and I wanted to crumple to the floor to vomit. This was worse than any seasickness I'd ever suffered.

Outside, enormous waves crashed to shore, tossing giant boulders against the rocky cliffs as if they were little more than marbles. Salt hung heavy in the air, coating my tongue with its brackish hold.

My mouth fell open, stunned she'd actually done it. I thought I'd called her bluff, challenged her to something she could not do, but I was back, my sister's heavy woolen carpets beneath my feet.

I spun around, wondering where Camille was. Everything looked exactly as the night I'd left. Not a thing was out of place or altered. Nothing except a lit candle gracing an end table beside my favorite brocaded settee.

My eyes narrowed.

The candle was pink.

Just like the one I'd left in the Garden of Giants.

"It's a remarkable facsimile," I said, looking up at the vaulted ceilings of my ancestral home. Long tentacles, brilliant with silver gilt, trailed down from its zenith and I felt a surprising burst of homesickness. "But it's a fake. We're still at Chauntilalie."

Kosamaras snarled and instantly we were back among the statues. "Wretched girl."

"Why on earth was I so afraid of you?" I wondered, daring to advance toward her.

She stepped back, unfamiliar with being the one on the retreat. "Verity . . . I'm on your side in all this. Forget my past indiscretions and listen to the facts at hand. You are in grave danger. You need to leave Chauntilalie and you need to leave it now. It may already be too late."

"What's going to happen?"

I hadn't thought she could turn a more ghastly shade, but she paled further, visibly shaken. "They're going to use you—use your children—as a key. A key for terrible things."

"Tell me," I insisted. The smaller and more wretched she looked, the more powerful I felt.

"I can't."

I bristled. "You can't do much of anything, can you? We're taught as children to fear you, to fear the Harbingers and cower before the gods, and why? I've seen through every one of your illusions. I'm not scared of you. I'm not scared of Gerard's plans.

But *you* are," I said, watching her face carefully. She looked absolutely terrified. "Whatever you think is coming has you breaking into a cold sweat."

I wanted to laugh at the absurd turnabout.

"And it should you too, little Thaumas," she hissed, her bravado slipping. "You and that boy will create things, terrible things. Things terrible enough to bring down even the gods."

I blinked with surprise at the first bit of actual information she'd given me. "What boy?" My stomach lurched, remembering the vicious line of dismissal striking through Gerard's observations. "Viktor?"

Too volatile.

There were jars and jars of creations Gerard had made and not blinked twice at. Babies with horns. Babies with tentacles. Babies with too many heads and not enough eyes.

Gerard had made those things without a pause of doubt.

And yet he so feared whatever Viktor and I could spawn—

Too volatile.

"Leave," Kosamaras insisted, grabbing at my arm, her face contrite, beseeching, even as her nails raked my flesh. "Leave now while you can."

"He'll just keep making more children. Finding more women."

"None like you. You are who they fear."

Her words struck me like a battering ram to the sternum.

The gods feared . . . me.

"Me?" I sputtered, indignation broiling my middle. "It's not *me* who needs to be feared. It's him. *He's* the one who needs to be stopped."

"Stupid girl. Just go."

"I'm staying," I said, my mind made up, resolution flooding through my veins and rooting me here, to this place, to Chauntilalie and the Laurents. I would see this through. It was the only way to make sure Gerard was stopped.

The wraith's face twisted with rage. "I tried to warn you. I tried to stop this. Whatever perdition you bring upon this world, I hope it eats you first!"

A giant bolt of lightning, wide and white and sizzling with ozone, struck the giraffe statue. The answering thunder punched a hole in my chest, tearing the world apart. I covered my ears, cowering against its force.

When the air calmed down, I opened my eyes.

Sunlight had returned.

The clearing was empty.

Kosamaras was gone.

But there, at the top of the hill, watching from the boardwalk, was Alex, his mouth hung open in horror.

39

"ALEX," I CALLED UP FEARFULLY.

What had he seen?

What had he heard?

He backed his chair away, retreating from me, confusion written across his face.

I sprang into action, racing up the grassy embankment. "Wait. Alex! Please wait!"

He wheeled past one of the Menagerie animals, an almost-butterfly with tentacles instead of legs, and I lost sight of him. When I rushed around the great stony mass, I saw he'd stopped, frozen in the middle of the boardwalk, his back to me.

"Alex?"

I heard my voice rise with uncertain hope. Maybe this wasn't really Alex. Maybe this was still part of the poisons I'd consumed. Maybe he wasn't here at all.

But when he whirled his chair around—whole and him, without a trace of otherworldly tint—I knew such luck was not mine.

"What *was* that, Verity?"

I licked my lips, buying time. "What . . . what exactly did you see?"

His eyebrows furrowed together. "I don't know. You were in the middle of some sort of . . . fit. You were screaming and . . ." He shook his head and a strange light flickered over his features as he studied me. "What's wrong with you?"

I bristled against his insinuation. I'd known there was a strong chance he'd react like this. It's why I had held my secrets so closely all this time. But it still stung to hear him say it aloud. "There's nothing *wrong* with me. I was . . . I was speaking to someone."

Alex scanned the garden in disbelief. "There's no one here. Just you."

"There was," I insisted.

"I saw no one."

"But I did . . ." In a hasty sweep, I knelt beside his chair, putting us both on the same level. "I . . . I see things."

"Things," he repeated.

"Ghosts," I admitted softly.

"That's not possible."

"It sounds fantastical, I know, but it's true all the same." I took his hands in mine, as if I might somehow tangibly impart my confession. "I've seen them my whole life. Ever since I was a girl. I don't . . . I don't always know they're ghosts. My nursemaid, Hanna . . . she's been with me my entire life. She was always there—kissing skinned knees, telling me stories before bed. She held me when I cried, she made me laugh. She was everything to me . . . The night I left Highmoor, I found out that she had died when I was very small. But she'd stayed behind, to look after me." My eyelashes were wet with tears. "All that time, she'd been a ghost."

Alex's face softened by degrees. "Why didn't you tell me this before?"

"I didn't know what you'd think. Or rather . . . I did and I didn't want to see that. Most people who hear you see ghosts think there's something *wrong* with you," I said, throwing back the little dagger he'd flung. It was oddly satisfying to see him wince.

"So . . . just now. Down there. You were talking to a ghost?"

"Not exactly." I looked away. This was the moment I'd been waiting for—I was going to tell Alex everything, confess all that I knew, and there would be nothing left between us. But now that the time was here, with all of my secrets right on the tip of my tongue, it felt impossible. I scrunched my eyes shut and let everything fall loose in a heated rush. "It was a Harbinger. Kosamaras. I summoned her because something terrible is going on at Chauntilalie. Your father . . . your father's experiments . . ."

"Father's experiments," he repeated, and I dared to open my eyes. "The flowers? What about them?"

I let out a deep, shaking breath. "Flowers aren't the only things he's been experimenting on."

Slowly, painfully, I told him everything.

Alex remained silent as I explained how I'd met Constance, how I'd assumed her to be one of Gerard's mistresses, how I'd learned she was a ghost. He stayed still as I told him of her strange children, of the diaries and folders, of the lists of other women. Only when I mentioned the jars in the study did he stir.

"I . . . I can't believe it," he murmured slowly. "It's too terrible to be true."

I pressed my lips together, wishing I could spare him from further painful truth. "There's more."

Alex's eyes rose, meeting mine. I'd never seen him look so exhausted. "How could there possibly be more?"

"Yesterday . . ." I paused, squirming. "Yesterday, I met your brothers."

Alex opened his mouth but nothing came out. He tried again. "I don't have any brothers," he said carefully.

"But . . . you do."

From deep in the woods behind Alex, there was a stir of movement. Viktor poked his head around a tree, offering me a little wave. Julien stepped out from behind a bush. They must have followed Alex to the garden. They'd been watching him, listening in on our conversation. Waiting until the moment was right before revealing themselves.

"Two, in fact," Julien spoke up, startling Alex.

He turned and stared dumbstruck at the approaching figures. "Is this some sort of joke?" He glanced at me. "Who . . . who are these people, Verity?"

I stood up, unable to respond.

"There's no reason to look so horrified." Viktor leaned over the chair, invading Alex's space as he studied him intently. "Incredible."

Slowly, as if entranced, Alex reached out and touched Viktor's face. "You look just like me," he murmured.

"*You* look like *me*, little brother. And *we* look like *him*."

Alex shifted his attention to Julien, who hung back, watching the reunion play out with flat, impassive eyes. "Triplets." His voice was awed and wondrous.

"Alex, this is Julien and Viktor," I said. "Your brothers."

"I don't understand. If they . . . if you," Alex self-corrected, looking back to include the interlopers. He shook his head as the words dried up. "I don't remember having brothers. How could I not remember?"

"We were little more than boys when Papa sent us away to Marchioly House," Julien allowed. "Just after the accident." He looked at the chair meaningfully.

"Marchioly House?" Alex blinked. "No one has been there for years. . . ."

"There was a reason for that," Viktor said in a singsong voice. "Us."

"But why? Why would Father have sent you away?"

Julien and Viktor eyed one another and I could feel their hesitation.

"Just show him," I said, ready to have everything out in the open. "We said we were going to tell him everything."

With a sigh, Viktor clapped his hands and the walkway in front of Alex's chair burst into flames. Alex let out a startled cry and the wheels struck the railing as he tried to back away from the blaze. Without reaction, Julien stamped the fire out. A small circle of soot and ash remained on the wooden planks and an acrid tang charred the air.

"What was that? How did you—"

Julien knelt beside the chair, fixing his stare on Alex. "Papa's experiments. Miss Thaumas told you about them, yes?"

After a moment, Alex nodded.

Julien's jaw tightened. "We were the first of them."

Undeterred, Viktor ignited a series of cattails along the edge of the pond. Their downy heads crackled with every flick of his fingers.

Alex watched in horror before turning to Julien. "So . . . you can do that too?"

"Of course he can't," Viktor snapped. "I'm one of a kind. *He* senses what others around him are thinking. A mind reader."

Julien's eyes narrowed, clearly peeved to be so easily reduced to a title. "It's admittedly not as impressive as being able to set the world aflame, but it's quite a useful trait to have. I must confess, I find myself most curious about you, Alexander. About what sort of gift you possess."

Alex looked stricken. "I can't do either of those things . . . nothing like that."

"Your talent might not be as flashy but there's something there, all the same. Miss Thaumas's presence confirms it."

"Miss Thaumas?" Alex's eyes darted over, pinning me in place with his stare. "Verity, what is he talking about?"

My hands knotted together. "Julien thinks—"

"Julien *knows*," he said, cutting me off through clenched teeth. "Papa somehow learned of Miss Thaumas's abilities to communicate with the dead. He brought her here to pair with you. Whatever you can do must be quite impressive for him to have done all this for."

"Pair?" Alex echoed dully.

Viktor sighed. "Surely we don't have to explain the birds and bees to you, do we?"

"No!" Alex's cheeks burned. "But you make it sound as if Verity was a mail-order bride. It's not like that. None of it is like that. We . . . we love each other."

Julien stifled back a sigh. "Of course. Yes. How fortunate you must be, falling in love with the one other animal in your cage."

"Julien!" I snapped, aghast.

He raked his fingers through his hair, mussing it. "You've no idea how exhausting I find his thoughts, Miss Thaumas."

"Then why don't you leave us for a moment," I said, keeping my voice firm. It was not a question.

With a groan, Julien walked away, taking the boardwalk toward the water's edge. Viktor followed, snickering. Alex waited until he was out of range before speaking.

"I don't understand what's happening, Verity." His eyes were fixed on something in the distance. "I have brothers? And Father . . . Those things they're saying . . . that *you're* saying . . . those horrible things . . ."

"I'm sorry. I'm so sorry. I've wanted to tell you—for days I've wanted to tell you but . . . you've heard everything now. It sounds mad. And then they showed up . . ." I paused, my stomach churning.

Fat tears of gratitude fell down my cheeks as he slipped one hand around mine.

"I want to say I don't believe it, but there they are, proof that something isn't right, proof Father is hiding something." He glanced at Viktor and Julien, who now sat on a fallen log, studiously trying to appear as though they weren't watching us. A slow hiss escaped through his teeth. "And Mother . . . those are her sons. She couldn't not know of them."

"Just because she knows part of the story doesn't mean she knows it all," I said, trying to salvage any hope of finding a silver lining in this storm breaking over us.

Alex let out a painful laugh.

"Julien and Viktor want to go to the authorities. With everything we found in the study last night, they'll have to imprison him." I wasn't sure if I meant it as a piece of information or a warning.

Reluctantly, he nodded.

"I'm so sorry," I said in a rush. "I . . . I can't imagine how you're feeling right now."

"Disgusted," he allowed. "Heartsick. Betrayed. I . . ." He ran his fingers over his face. "I don't know what to think. What to feel. Who to trust." He stared at his brothers for a long moment. "I don't . . . I don't think Mother knew about . . . about the others."

I bit my lip. "I'm sure the police will—"

"No," he said firmly. "I don't want her finding out like that. From strangers. Strangers who think her guilty of all . . . of all *that*. Verity, you can't truly believe she would have stayed here, stayed with Father, if she'd known."

"No," I admitted, pushing back the memory that I'd feared she'd killed Constance herself.

He nodded, relieved.

"So what do you want to do?"

He sighed. "There must be a way we can find out what she knows before they . . . before they tell everyone." His gaze lingered on Viktor uneasily.

"We could get her away from the house. Talk with her. We're supposed to go into town tomorrow," I mentioned slowly. My hands twisted into a tangle so tight my fingers tingled. "My last dress fitting."

Alex's eyebrows rose hopefully. "Do you think . . . do you think you could try to see what she knows? What she'll admit to?"

"Don't you want to confront her yourself? Hear what she has to say?"

"Father would think it odd if I were to come with you for a dress fitting . . . and she might be more open, more honest with you." He took my hands in his, rubbing the feeling back into my fingers. "Please, Verity."

I paused, unsure of how to go about uncovering such a well-kept secret, but Alex looked so painfully vulnerable, I couldn't say no. "I . . . I'll try."

For a long, silent moment, we watched the waves dance across the pond.

"Brothers," he finally said with wonder. "I have brothers."

"Perhaps we should go over and get to know them more."

Alex nodded but didn't move. I stayed in place, willing to wait for as long as he needed.

"I feel as if I'm on the precipice of a cliff," he murmured, keeping a careful eye on them. "The ground is starting to give way and it's already too late to do anything. If I push myself back, it will just cause the plunge to happen sooner. But staying in place won't save me either."

"Then we fall together," I promised.

"I'm sorry about before. I didn't mean to suggest there's something wrong with you. I just . . . This has caught me so completely unaware. I wish you had told me about it sooner. I don't want us to ever keep secrets from one another."

"I was worried what you'd think. It sounds mad."

"The world is full of madness," he responded, his eyes resting uneasily on his pair of brothers. "And if what they say is true . . . it's far worse than I ever would have guessed." He glanced at me. "It must be terrifying to see."

"It is," I said, recalling Kosamaras, her black tears, her gray fangs. Then I thought of Hanna, her cups of tea, her warm embraces. "And it isn't. I'll tell you more about it. I'll tell you everything, I promise. Just . . ."

"After," he supplied, then let out a laugh absent of amusement.

I brought his hand up to press a kiss across his knuckles. From his spot down the hill, Viktor watched on with dark, hooded eyes.

Alex was watching too. "I suppose we shouldn't keep them waiting any longer. Shall we?"

Nodding, I followed after him.

"You're going to talk to Dauphine?" Julien summarized after Alex and I had told the brothers our plan.

We were on the banks of the pond, Julien and Viktor still sitting on the fallen log while I stood next to Alex and his chair. A horse creature towered over us, its mane made up of fiery swirls. Gigantic scorpion-like pinchers jutted from its chest and a forked tongue slithered down, just feet above Viktor's head.

I nodded. "We need to find out how much she knows. What exactly it is she's culpable of."

"And then?" Alex asked, looking back and forth between the two boys for a plan.

"And then we make them pay," Viktor snarled.

"And then we go to the authorities," Julien said, overriding his brother's theatrical bloodlust. "We go into Bloem. We show them the evidence. They'll have to search the house. They'll find the jars. And whatever remains in the hedge maze."

"And what comes after that?" Alex persisted. "If Father is imprisoned . . . *when* he is . . . he'll no longer be duke. Will you stay here?"

"I doubt it," Julien said.

"But you're the oldest, apparently," Alex murmured.

I'd never seen him look so uncertain. His entire life had just been upended, his place in the world—once so sure and planned out—gone.

"I've no interest in that title, in this estate, or that house," Julien said, casting a scornful eye back at Chauntilalie.

"But you can't just abandon it," Alex protested. "The ducal seat can't be left open."

"I can," Julien insisted flatly. "What do you think an abdication is?" He studied Alex curiously, as a scientist might a strange, new insect. "I'd make all the provisions for the estate to transfer to you first, naturally."

Viktor's mouth fell open. "Now wait just a minute—"

Julien didn't shy away. "I can't imagine a worse candidate for a duchy than you. With your mood swings? With your . . . accidents? Alexander has been preparing for this role his entire life. Are you up to date on the trade agreements with the other provinces? Do you know what percentage of taxes are meant to be levied for the king?"

"Well, no, but—"

"He does," Julien continued briskly. "You'd hate being

restricted to such a confining position and if you truly stopped to think it through, you'd be the first to admit it. The title goes to Alexander."

Viktor shut his mouth, his features wounded. "Fine, but I want my share of the inheritance. A man can't wander the kingdom without something in his pockets."

"Of course," Alex agreed quickly. "And you as well, Julien. Both of you would always be welcome at Chauntilalie. I . . . I know we don't know much of each other, and the circumstances are befuddling at best, but . . . this is your home. These doors will forever be open to you."

Viktor appeared temporarily mollified. "So. If that's settled, apparently," he added, throwing a dark look to Julien.

"So," Julien said resolutely. "You speak with Mother tomorrow."

"I will do my best," I promised, sounding braver than I felt.

"Why would you attempt anything less?" Julien blinked at me. "You've something in your hair," he said, staring off to the side of my face, just above my ear.

"What?" I asked, reaching up. Something squirmed against my fingertips and I jerked them away, recoiling. "What is it?"

"*Eucorysses grandis,* if I'm not mistaken. Allow me?"

Without waiting, he reached out and flicked the offending bug, stunning it. His touch felt strange. He didn't handle me as if I was a person of flesh and blood, only a problem to be solved. When he pulled away, I saw a cream and black beetle. Its shell was all sharp angles, like armor.

Julien brought it up for a closer glance, peering at it with concern. "Yes, it is. You ought to take care, Miss Thaumas."

"What do you mean?"

He held out his hand. The bug crawled over the curve of his palm, displaying a set of gruesome markings. With its angles and spots, it looked like a grinning, grimacing skull.

"Some think these beetles portend a terrible death."

"What a ghastly creature," Viktor murmured, leaning in and brushing against my shoulder. He didn't make a move to shift away.

Alex stretched as tall as he could in his chair to catch a glimpse of the cursed insect. Grimacing, he flicked it with a snap of his wrist, sending it off into the undergrowth. "Old superstitions. Nothing more." He offered me a smile but it looked wan and worried.

I took a step to the side, backing away from my close proximity to Viktor. "Of course. I've never even heard of such a warning before."

Julien's gaze landed on me, sharp and quizzical. "You wouldn't, I expect, coming from such a nautical clime. Regardless, I'm glad it wasn't my head it landed upon."

A chill ran down my spine and I desperately wanted to chalk it up to the damp morning air.

"Utter nonsense," Viktor agreed. "And in any case, it last touched our little brother. I'd hate to be in your shoes right now."

"Really?" Alex said, a flinty edge coloring his voice. "It seems my shoes are all you've dreamed of getting into."

Viktor's jaw hardened and I could sense the retorts building up between them, like water wearing down a dam. I wanted to step in, to somehow ease the rising tension. They might not have grown up together, but they were still brothers, flesh and blood. My heart ached as I thought of my own sisters, at how much I missed them. I opened my mouth, ready to speak some truth, deep and profound, but every possible offering felt clichéd and small.

After a dreadful, long moment, Viktor shook his head and stalked away.

"Ignore him," Julien advised as Viktor tossed a handful of rocks into the pond, trying to make them skip. "I always try to."

"You mentioned accidents," Alex said, watching his middle brother with care. "With . . . his fires?"

Julien nodded. "He's always had a terrible temper and the flames only exacerbate it. One little tiff can lead to a blazing inferno. You need to be careful with him."

My cheeks reddened as I remembered the other type of fire Viktor was capable of igniting. When Julien's eyes fell on me, I stilled, forcing the thoughts away.

"I think I'm going for a walk," I volunteered, wanting to flee from Julien and his all-too-knowing gaze.

"You don't have to," Alex protested, but I'd already set off, fixing my direction on a statue at the other end of the pond.

It was smaller than the others, a culmination of stripes and claws, a feathered tail and leathery wings. I sat down—the creature's catlike paws made a surprisingly comfortable seat—and watched the brothers. Alex and Julien had fallen into deep discussion while Viktor poked about for more rocks.

My eyes felt heavy and I blinked drowsily, breathing in the cool, green air. I leaned back against the beast's leg, letting my shoulders relax. All of the secrets I'd kept clutched to my chest, a mass of tangled, twisted knots, were out in the open now.

Alex knew everything and we had a plan, a course of action, a united front.

For the first time since I'd arrived at Chauntilalie, I felt at peace. As I drifted toward sleep, I dared to believe that good would triumph and that Alex and I could prove even the gods wrong.

40

MY EYES SNAPPED OPEN AS I HEARD A SOFT RUSTLING approach me.

Viktor stood yards away, near the water's edge. He swooped down to pluck a sprig of pretty little flowers from the tall grasses, then offered it to me.

Reluctantly, I slid from the statue and bridged the gap between us. "What is it?" I asked, spinning the stem between my thumb and fingers. The cluster of blooms looked like a lady's skirt twirling about a ballroom.

"White dittany. Smell it."

I brought the stem closer to me and caught a strong citrus aroma. "Oh." My eyes watered at the unexpected surprise.

"Pleasant, isn't it? They're quite special, actually."

"Are they?"

He nodded. "The oils on their leaves are uniquely flammable," he mused, studying the dozens of tall plants dotting the shore. "You can set them on fire . . . set a whole field of them aglow, but they themselves will not burn."

I had the sudden premonition he was about to ignite them, just to show me. "Don't," I said, reaching out to stop him.

Our hands brushed, just a whisper of skin against skin, and the air between us changed, charged with electric anticipation.

I glanced uneasily at Viktor as Kosamaras's words echoed through me.

You and that boy will create things, terrible things. Things terrible enough to bring down even the gods.

There was a moment, one short breath, where I could have pulled away, hastily retreating as though nothing had happened.

The moment came.

The moment passed.

My fingers closed around his.

"What are you doing, Ver?"

His voice was warm with amusement, pleased, as if he knew exactly what I was doing, even though I did not myself.

Wordlessly, I reached up, cupping the back of his neck, running my fingers into the thick waves of his hair. He made a soft, surprised noise but I pressed my lips to his, silencing him.

Viktor responded in kind and I arched forward as his hands snaked up my spine, drawing me against his chest. I opened my mouth, running my tongue over his with a brazen audacity that could not be checked.

With a soft, appreciative growl, he stepped forward, causing me to step back, and my ankle caught on a rock. I fell backward, landing on a bed, high with silken pillows and velvet throws. It had not been there before, I was certain of it, but I stretched out anyway, savoring the wanton comfort.

Viktor followed after.

With deft movements, he laid me across the mattress like the main dish of a banquet, an offering spread over an altar. His hands ran down me with ardent reverence, a supplicant bowed low with resolute devotion.

The sky above us was a void of night blue and shimmering stars, swirling closer than I'd ever seen before. Trails of cosmic dust swirled and sparkled, landing on Viktor's naked back, illuminating my bare lengths. I could feel it soak into me, a foreign energy, shaping and shifting my essence, making me something new, something other. It was like witnessing the birth of our world, our galaxy, our very existence.

But then the sky was gone, blocked out by Viktor as he bent over me, pressing kisses down the length of my throat, down my sternum, on each of my breasts. His skin was feverishly warm. Our breaths grew ragged, filling the air with dark wants, deeper needs.

I ran my fingers along the muscles of his chest, exploring the planes and shapes of him, so different from me. His hands guided mine lower, dragging down the ridges of his abdomen, stroking over his length. Our bodies were damp with desire as I pulled him over me, closer to my wanting, covering myself with his heat.

I ached for him, driven almost mad by an incessant need for more, more of him, more of his touch and all the wickedly wonderful things it brought. It burned in my veins, licking up my toes as they curled, setting me ablaze with hunger.

Viktor's fingers dug into my skin as he left a trail of fiery kisses over the swell of my hip bone and I gasped, eyes flashing open.

We *were* aflame.

The fires were real, crackling and dancing with a hypnotic pull.

My blood sizzled as his scalding hands worked their way even lower, clutching my thighs, marking me with his mouth as decisively as a brand, but there was no pain, only that unfillable ache, that impossible insatiability.

You and that boy will create things, terrible things. Things terrible enough to bring down even the gods.

I pushed aside the Harbinger's warning as my nails raked down Viktor's back, eliciting a feral growl from him that made me want to bare my own teeth, howling to the stars.

The stars.

They were even closer now, their place in the universe in peril as we spun new energies, pulling them in to watch the start of something—

Terrible.

—*Rapturous.*

Terrible enough to bring down even the gods.

A tremulous quiver began to grow within me, shimmering and brighter than the stars now surrounding us, spinning ever closer. It pulsed white hot and consuming, setting my body aglow in its radiance. Viktor's eyes roamed over mine and they too were filled with that light.

That beautiful, terrible light.

Terrible.

"Viktor," I murmured, trying to find a way to stop this, even as every bit of me screamed for it to continue.

"Ver," he groaned, pulling me closer, and the light shifted, tingeing as pink as the blush of first love, as a peach ripened in the heat of the summer sun. Then red, bright as poppies dancing in a field, a spool of scarlet thread.

I imagined that thread tying around us now, slipping over our entwined limbs, binding us as one as he thrusted forward, removing all space between us.

"Yes," I gasped, slipping into its hazy, heady depths.

I could not tell where he began and I ended and I did not care. We two were one and it felt so good, so right. Even the stars shimmered with agreement.

But their light changed again, going darker as we fell deeper. As dark as a splatter of blood, a jagged wound, a silent scream.

And I could hear the screaming then.

So many screams.

As if every person in Bloem, in Arcannia, in the whole of the world had opened their mouths and released their deepest terrors. They cried out for relief, for release, for it all to end.

A great tremor rumbled beneath us, shaking the bed, shaking the ground, shaking the world apart.

And Kosamaras's words again rippled through me.

Whatever perdition you bring upon this world, I hope it eats you first!

It was coming. It had started.

"We have to stop," I sobbed, breathless.

We couldn't stop.

Not now.

Not when we were so close.

When *it* was so close.

So . . .

Close.

So . . .

A soft knock snapped me from my slumber and I opened my

eyes, gasping as if I'd just run from the maws of death. My heart pounded, thudding in an unfamiliar cadence.

I'd been so surrendered to the dream, so blissfully, horrifically saturated within it, I couldn't at first remember where I was.

I sat up and the world came rushing back to me.

I was in my sitting room.

Lying on the velvet settee.

After spending the day in the Garden of Giants, I'd feigned a headache before dinner. I knew I'd be unable to stomach sitting in Gerard's presence, pretending everything was fine.

The room was dark now, washed in shades of midnight blue and starlight.

Save for Viktor, poised on the threshold of the open secret passage, illuminated by the glow of a single yellow taper.

Viktor.

My body sizzled as I recalled the way his touch had raked over me.

Not him.

It had only been a dream.

But my middle ached with the echoes of that ecstasy all the same.

He frowned, looking guilty. "Were you sleeping?"

"I . . ." I pushed back a strand of hair, feeling fluttery and flustered. "I was but . . . I'm glad you woke me. I was having the most—"

Sensual.

Shameful.

"—shocking nightmare," I concluded, my chest rising and falling as if I was out of breath. I swallowed hard, trying to stop the quiver in my voice.

"No dreams of me, then?" he asked playfully.

Deep inside, I felt the way his feral groan had reverberated in the deepest, most secret part of me. I stifled back the urge to press him up against the wall and demand he take me then and there. "Afraid not."

"What a pity."

He stepped inside, crossing over to the settee, and I nearly fell off it, struggling to distance myself as he sat.

"You look unwell," he observed, setting the candle down on the table in front of us.

"Just a headache," I said, repeating my earlier lie.

"I shouldn't wonder, sleeping with all those clips digging into your scalp."

With a flick of his wrist, he grabbed the combs holding my waves in place. They came toppling down my shoulders, streaming long and loose, and a flush crept over me, burning as bright as a fever.

This was too intimate.

Too undone.

Too . . .

"Beautiful," he murmured, his eyes dancing over me.

I buried my hands in the fullness of my skirts, my mind full of impossible wonderings.

What if I held his gaze a moment too long? What if our hands brushed, just a touch?

Would we truly spark the world's destruction?

Alex, I thought fiercely, dragging him to the forefront of my mind. It slapped like a cold wave, dousing the treacherous desire coiling through me.

I'd never betray him. I knew that with all my heart.

But oh, how the deep, wicked wondering parts of me wanted to.

"You seemed upset earlier," I said, carefully slipping from his brazen touch. "In the statue garden. When Julien said he'd give the dukedom to Alex."

Viktor shrugged. "It makes no difference to me if he wants to give up the title and all its trappings but I would have thought he'd at least inquire if I'd like them. He's right, though, I suppose. I haven't the faintest idea how to run a place like this, do the things I'd be expected to. . . . Still. No one ever thinks to ask what I want."

"What *do* you want?"

It was a simple-sounding question but heat stole across my chest as his gaze fell on me. As I realized how he might construe my meaning. As I wondered if he'd *want* to construe it.

He ran his tongue over the sharp edges of his teeth, considering. "Right now?"

My mouth opened but no words came out.

"A walk with you?" Viktor suggested.

"A walk?" I repeated. "It's so late. . . ."

His lips rose. "What better time? It's not as though I could take you out for a stroll in broad daylight. What would the staff think—Alexander suddenly springing from his chair just in time to waltz you down the aisle?" His eyes shifted downcast to his lap.

"What are you doing here, Viktor? Truly?"

He shrugged, his lightness dimming. "Truthfully . . . I couldn't sleep. Every time I closed my eyes, I saw Father's notes, written across my mind as sharp as a brand. *Too volatile.*" He swallowed. "I feel as though he summed up and discarded my entire life in just two words."

"He might have written it down, but it doesn't make it true," I murmured hesitantly. It was clear he was hurting but I hadn't the slightest idea how to go about comforting him.

He *was* volatile; it was impossible to pretend otherwise.

But that didn't make him expendable, dismissible.

Viktor's eyebrows furrowed together. "It's so strange . . . I've spent my life being angry at him. Being angry and hating and loathing him. Railing against our imprisonment, dreaming up ways to make him pay, to make him sorry. But when it comes down to it, when it really matters . . . I still want his approval. Isn't that ridiculous?"

Carefully, I laid my hand over the top of his. "Not ridiculous." I wanted to say more but my words felt too jumbled to lay out in a clean line. "Come on," I finally said, standing up and pulling him after me. "Let's go for that walk."

He smiled, but it wasn't the sly grin of triumph I'd expected. Instead, he stooped down to grab the candle before gently tugging back toward the passageway.

I paused, envisioning our bodies vying for space in the narrow tunnel, each accidental brush and bump stoking my inner fires until I pushed him up against the wall, pressing my mouth to his while my hands roamed, claiming every inch of him for myself.

The echoes of the world's scream rang out in my mind, stopping me.

"You first," I instructed. In the pit of my stomach, I knew I was making a terrible mistake.

"As the lady commands," he said, disappearing into the darkness.

I made the shutting of the panel into a bigger business than it warranted, anxious to put additional space between us.

These were temporary feelings, I reminded myself. Lust not love, desire not destiny. This wanting would pass, as would Viktor's time at Chauntilalie. He'd be gone and my equilibrium would return. It was momentary madness, nothing more.

"Did you lock it?"

He turned back as he noticed my absence. The candle threw strange shadows across the slatted wooden walls as he returned for me and I'd been right. The space was too small for the both of us. His scent filled the air, heavy and green and strange, like a stormy summer night, just before the lightning began to fall.

Before the stars fell . . .

"I did," I insisted, pressing myself against the beadboard in an attempt to keep my distance from him.

"Careful," he warned, gesturing to the candle. "You don't want to get burned."

I wondered if he knew how much truth his words held.

"Come," he said, gesturing for me to follow him.

The passage was narrow and it was hard to see much of anything with such limited lighting, but the floor was smooth and flat. I pushed aside any imaginings of daintily twisted ankles rescued by strong, embracing arms. One less thing to worry over.

We came to a fork and after a moment's pause, Viktor turned to the left.

"Do you know where we're going?"

"I think. Mostly. I told Julien we ought to be leaving little markings in chalk for ourselves but he insists we leave no trace of our presence 'upon such cursed grounds.'" He mimicked Julien's disaffected cadence with eerie accuracy.

I traced one hand along the wall and my fingertips came away coated in a dusty grime. "Does he truly think the house is cursed?"

He snickered. "Have you met Julien? I've never known a more scientifically driven mind. If you slit open his veins, reason and logic would bleed out all over your best carpet." He sighed. "You've no idea what it's like living with such a dullard. Though," he added, considering, "you *have* been with Alex."

"He's not dull," I defended.

"His bedside table is littered with books," he said with a snort. "Stacks and stacks of them."

I tucked a lock of hair behind my ear. "There's nothing wrong with reading."

"They'll probably smother him one night in his sleep. Maybe you as well. You really ought to call the wedding off." He glanced over his shoulder, quickly, as if trying not to show his interest.

"I'm not calling off my wedding over a stack of books."

"Stacks," he corrected.

"Not even then."

We went up a short series of steps, five high, then down a long length to another set of them, climbing ever higher in the house. "What *would* make you call it off?"

There was an odd strangled quality to his voice, as if it strained him to sound so careless.

I hesitated. "Nothing."

Viktor snorted. "Are you . . . are you not in jest?"

I shook my head even though he couldn't see it. When he came to another junction, he stopped, looking back. I'd never seen such a serious expression on his face before.

"You're not truly going through with it, are you?"

"Because of . . . Gerard?" I wasn't sure how to phrase everything we'd learned in the last day.

"Among other things."

I'd been pondering this since the plan had been laid out in the Garden of Giants. If Gerard's crimes were exposed, if he was arrested and taken away, there was no longer any danger to me, to Alex, to the two of us. My situation had not changed, nor had my feelings. I wasn't going to turn tail and run.

"Alex had nothing to do with any of that."

"Didn't he?"

"Of course not. You saw him today. He was wholly shocked. You can't fake such surprise so convincingly."

Viktor shook his head with swift disagreement. "That's exactly how someone who had something to cover up would respond. Too over the top and theatrical."

"It was genuine. Earnest. Everything that Alex is."

He snorted. "You sound as though you love him."

"I do." There was no hesitation now.

"It's just me here, Ver. There's no need for pretending."

"I'm not." My words were sharp, the head of a match hungry for a flame.

Quick as a wink, Viktor stepped close, pinning me between him and the wall. "You said he's never kissed you as I have."

I could feel the warmth of his breath on my lips, enticing and tempting me to tilt my head up, bridge the distance, and lose myself in the promise of those kisses once again.

I placed my hands on his chest, fingers spread wide, and he smiled as if he'd won. With gentle but firm pressure, I pushed him back, giving myself space away from him, from the dark twinkle in his eyes, from the danger of his beguiling grin.

"Love is more than just kissing. So much more."

"That sounds like the feeble excuse of a girl who's not been well kissed."

"I'm choosing Alex." I squirmed, uncomfortable with the way he still towered over me. "I've chosen Alex," I corrected with emphasis.

He stared down at me, his face painfully unreadable, before turning and continuing down the passage. I hung back, surprised he'd given up so easily. He paused, listening for my footsteps. "Coming?"

Warily, I followed after him.

"So you've chosen Alex and Alex has chosen you and all of that is so very well and good, but what about children? Have you factored that into your decision?"

"Children might not be in the cards for us," I said, trying to keep my voice even and expressionless.

"And if they are? Can you imagine raising little copies of everything you saw in those jars?" He shuddered.

I shrugged. "That wouldn't happen. Whatever it is Gerard wants to achieve pairing us together . . . it won't happen. Alex isn't like the two of you. He can't do anything like what you do."

Viktor threw an impish glance over his shoulder, raising his eyebrows with brazen suggestion. "We already have that well established, Ver."

He reached out as if to trail his fingers over my bodice, making his intention clear, but stopped just short of touching me. An embarrassed flush of heat rose up over my chest, burning my ears. Everything I wanted to convey felt too big to be cut up into neat, tidy little words. My feelings were too messy and smattered.

"Oh, Ver," he said pityingly. "The things I could show you."

"I don't need you to show me anything," I snapped, irritated by his tone and cavalier assumptions.

I pushed past him and stomped up the stairs, heedless of the dark and unfamiliar ground. The thirteen steps ended at a door and I fumbled for its handle, pushing it open without caring about where we were. Night air rushed down the stairwell, carrying with it the tickling scent of jasmine and orange blossoms. The world was all deep indigoes and inky blues. Twinkling stars spun in slow dances across the scope of sky, dazzling in their far-off beauty.

"The rooftop garden," I murmured, remembering my first glimpse of the entryway's spangled skylight.

It was in front of me now, so much bigger than what it appeared from the ground. Its glass plates jutted up at sharp angles, sleek and silvery in the moonlight. Thick lines of leading held the masterpiece together.

The rest of the roof was full of potted ferns and palms, bursts of flowering bushes and beds of night-blooming buds. Serpentine benches were nestled throughout the botanical splendor, the perfect spots for hidden assignations and the whispering of sweet nothings.

I heard Viktor's footsteps behind me as he treaded up the stairs.

"Starlight," he announced, sweeping his hand across the expanse with pride as if he'd engineered the entire thing himself.

"It's beautiful," I said perfunctorily. I crossed away, leaning against the railing while studiously avoiding any glance toward Viktor or those wicked little conversation benches.

"You're mad at me."

"Irritated," I admitted.

He hummed, wandering toward the opposite end of the roof. "I probably deserve it."

"You do."

"Just . . . consider your options, Ver. All of them. You've been stuck on that chain of islands for far too long. You need to get out, experience the world before settling down. Explore its facets. Satisfy your curiosities."

I turned and blinked at him incredulously. "You almost sound as though you've not been trapped in a rotting manor the whole of your life. 'Experience the world,'" I mimicked, lowering my voice in an attempt to match his baritone. "What world have you seen?"

"I've seen things," he insisted. "I've done things."

"I'm sure you have," I said, making it clear I didn't believe him.

"Tutors weren't the only sort of attendants Father sent to Marchioly. There were girls." Viktor's lips rose in a half-smile as he remembered something. "Beautiful, beautiful girls." He sniffed. "Julien wanted nothing to do with them, obviously. Just meant more for me . . . The things I did there would curl your toes, Ver."

"I take it all back," I said with a lofty, unimpressed air. "You're an absolute connoisseur of sophisticated pleasures. A denizen of decadence and vice. I marvel at your worldly ways."

His countenance fell and for a moment, his vulnerability reminded me of Alex.

"Where do you think you'll go? After . . . everything? With the whole world before you?"

He shrugged and meandered over to the seat nearest the skylight. The glow from the inner foyer lit his face with a strange radiance, drawing me to the other end of the bench, despite myself.

"I don't *want* to go anywhere," he admitted. "All through my childhood, there was always this idea of Chauntilalie in my mind, like a beacon, a mecca, a perfect bright light on the horizon. Something to dream of, to reach for. It seems mad to just abandon it."

"Will you stay with Julien, do you think?"

Viktor shook his head. "We've been together for so long it seems impossible that we could ever be separated, but the thought of spending another day with only him for company is unbearable. He's so . . . empty, but not. So full of thoughts—his own and everyone else's. All thought and no emotion. It's like living with the shell of a human being, staring at half a painting, only hearing the left hand of a piano solo. I can't do it anymore." He dragged his fingers through his hair. "We're this odd set of bookends. Julien feels nothing but I feel *everything*. The world's pain, the world's rage. Every bit of it seems amplified and magnified until it all comes bursting out of me like—" He threw his hand away as if something scalded him and down on the terrace far below us, a brazier suddenly ignited. Its flames shot skyward, lighting the night with a flash and flare of orange.

"And I've never known why," he snarled, his hand now clenched. I could just make out a phantom trail of smoke escaping from the tight fist. "Do you know how terrifying it is to grow up with these things inside you—to be laid so open and exposed to it all, to know you're different, to know that no one else feels what you feel, knows what you know—but to never know why? Or how? Or . . ." He dissolved into dark laughter. "Of course you do . . . and you don't. You grew up completely different from anyone around you . . . but you *didn't* know it and everyone else did." His laughter grew. "Oh, Ver, we're so much alike, you and I. So terribly, terribly alike."

He reached out and cupped my chin, gently, as if holding on to something precious.

"You don't love him." It was said definitively, a statement decided, not an inquiry of doubt.

"I do," I insisted, even as every fiber in me yearned to lean into Viktor's caress, longed to reach out and touch him as well.

"Not like you could love me," he said, brazenly rubbing his thumb across the swell of my cheek. "Not as I know I could love you. People like us—we burn brightly, Ver. We burn and we sparkle, like moonlight over your beloved waves. Alex is nothing. He's earth and loom and soil and clay and he'll smother you. He'll cover that sparkle and squelch it out forever."

"Fire never fares well with water either," I reminded him, drawing up the resolve to turn from his grasp and failing miserably. I tried recalling the terrifying rumble from the dream—that awful booming noise that promised to herald in the end of the world—but here, in the glittering night, it seemed insignificant, a passing fantasy, nothing more.

"Did you know there are islands on the far side of the world created when fire and water meet?"

"No," I admitted, clasping my hands together to keep them from reaching for him.

"You'd think the sea's embrace would be the fire's demise, but together they form something new and radiant. Steam and islands and life. Together they create an entire realm of their own. That could be us, Ver," he murmured, bringing his face near, his lips just scant inches from my own. "Think of the worlds we could create, you and I."

"Viktor, I—"

It began as a protest, I will forever swear that it did.

But then his mouth was on mine, or mine was on his, or they'd somehow moved at the same time, meeting each other, together and insistent. There was a groan. I couldn't tell if it was his or mine, or if again, it was both of us.

The thought rang sharp and ill-pitched in my mind.

Us.

There was no us.

Even if my body screamed for his. Even as I wanted to draw him down on top of me, sprawled out beneath the glorious weight of him, a thousand stars watching on above us.

The stars . . .

The stars we would pull down . . .

The stars we would set spinning to our own tune . . .

There was most definitely no us.

"No," I said, pulling away. "This isn't right."

"Keep on kissing me and I'll show you how right it can be." His voice was low and husky and I had a sudden jolt of desire to bite his lip, just to hear him moan.

"No," I repeated firmly, for my benefit as much as his. "Viktor, stop."

I turned my head to avoid his lips—his stunning, full, and ravenous lips—but he pressed them to my throat instead. I could feel my heart race against them, could feel a coil of heat in my belly, an ache that cried out to be filled. But still I pulled away.

He grasped at me, his fingers tangling into my hair, twisting me back toward him with single-minded persistence.

"I said stop!" I cried out, stumbling over my feet as I stood and backed away, eager to put as much distance between us as I could. I was no longer scared I would change my mind and succumb to his temptations. I was scared he wouldn't listen to my refusal, no matter how loudly it was given. "Too volatile," I reminded him. "Maybe Gerard was right."

With a cry of frustration, he struck the bench, a bolt of lightning sizzling through space, and his hand left a scorch mark emblazoned across the pale marble. Again and again, he pummeled the seat, his hand glowing with an unnatural fury.

The plants around him began to wither, their magnificent leaves shriveling into dry husks in a matter of seconds. I could feel the heat building from where I was, hot and dangerous, a tinderbox showered in sparks, ready to ignite.

Julien's warning rang in my mind, its echoes sending a chill through my core. Being careful wasn't enough. I needed to get away, needed to go now.

"Good night, Viktor," I said with finality, turning for the main door, off to the side of the garden. To hell with the secret passageways. I couldn't imagine a worse place for me to be, with him like this now, focused on me with such indignant, seething rage.

"Ver, I didn't mean—"

I slammed the door shut behind me before I could hear whatever hasty, panicked half-apology he was to offer.

41

"KEEP YOUR EYES CLOSED," DAUPHINE INSTRUCTED, taking my hand and guiding me through the shop. I cringed as her fingers folded around mine and hoped she didn't notice.

I'd been dressed in a room tucked in the back of the atelier, without a single mirror to aid me. Dauphine had wanted me positioned upon a little pedestaled tier in the front of the salon so that when I first saw myself in the completed wedding gown, I would experience it in its full wonder.

Part of me felt cheered as she went through such elaborate steps for the wedding—surely that must be a sign she was as in the dark as Alex believed her to be. If our union was only meant to be the next step in a series of mad experiments, why such fanfare? There were ways for Gerard to accomplish what he wanted without spending thousands of florettes on table settings and puff pastries.

Dauphine helped me onto the platform, holding my hands for balance. I moved slower than I normally would have, flinching at every sound I couldn't determine an immediate cause for. Since racing away from Viktor last night, my imagination had run wild, concocting up terrible scenarios where Gerard would burst out of hiding from secret panels, carrying vials of unknown poisons and medical instruments, demanding a line of progeny.

What would Dauphine do? Would she scream and knock away the tinctures or pin me down as he administered them?

What was going on behind those green eyes of hers?

I could feel her fuss with the gown, fingers skimming over the netting of my sleeves, before fluffing out the skirt.

"Now," Dauphine said, pleasure evident in her voice.

I opened my eyes and felt my lips part—saw them do so in the reflection in front of me—but no sound issued forth.

"I've never seen a lovelier bride-to-be," Dauphine murmured, squeezing my upper shoulders. "You were absolutely right about this gown. I'm glad I listened to you."

The dress had been the only part of the wedding that I'd staunchly refused to budge on. When gown designer Madame Fujiwara learned I was an artist myself, she'd delightedly told me they could produce lace in any pattern I'd dare to dream up. I'd immediately set to work, drawing out a sketch in the salon that day, determined to have one small part of the ceremony that was Alex's and mine alone. She'd added in her suggestions and together we'd created something meaningful and symbolic.

The bodice was sheer lace and had a high neck and elbow-length sleeves, with three vertical lines of alyssum flowers slashing down the front and filled in with diagonal lines of tiny waves, washing away from my center. The back repeated the pattern and had a long row of tiny buttons trailing down my spine. The geometric lines of the top were cinched with a matching belt before falling into a long, flowing skirt of pleated chiffon.

Dauphine had said it customary for Bloem brides to choose a

vibrant hue for their gowns, then use that shade as their signature color for everything from stationery to bedsheets.

But Salann brides wore white and the silk threads I'd chosen reminded me of the salty kisses left on our black sand beaches by adoring waves. It sparkled with a radiant luster and made my skin glow.

It wasn't the big, show-stopping creation Dauphine had wanted, massive pilings of tulle and organza. There was no elaborate beading or patterned paillettes. Its beauty lay in clean, simple lines, well-executed and precise.

I loved it.

The design was perfect, a glorious merger of both Alex and myself. Behind me, the mirror showed ropes of greenery hanging from potted baskets around the shop and dozens of tiny tea lights that glowed in happy clusters, releasing a soft perfume of basil and mandarin. I could almost believe that today was my wedding day. That I was about to walk down the aisle and pledge myself to Alexander.

I held on to that feeling as long as I could, remembering the happier times before Viktor and Julien had crashed into my life, shattering my vision of what the future held.

"My darling . . . are those tears?" Dauphine asked, stepping forward to get a better look at me. "Do you not like it?"

"I love it," I whispered. "It's . . . perfect."

"Then they're tears of joy?"

I nodded, lying.

I was crying for all the things I'd thought I'd understood but didn't. Crying for all I'd hoped for that wouldn't be. A cold, cruel light had been cast upon Chauntilalie's beautiful façade.

It was not a happy, perfect family I would wed into.

It was family with pasts even darker than my own.

There was horror within those gilded walls.

I watched Dauphine's movements through the mirror, wanting to believe she was as much a victim as we were, wanting to believe we'd have another ally to bring Gerard's crimes into the light.

Kosamaras had told me to run.

Julien and Viktor had said to stay and seek.

What did I want?

I stared at my reflection, seeing all of the details and meaning and care I'd sketched into a dress I wasn't sure I'd ever get to wear again.

My fingers skimmed over the gauzy silk layers.

I *did* want to wear it again.

Even knowing all I did. Even knowing what was said to come.

I wanted to marry Alex.

Viktor's fervent kisses couldn't change that.

Nor Kosamaras's warnings or Gerard's mad plotting.

I let out a short puff of breath, centering myself.

I would stay.

I would seek.

I would fight.

Fight for the truth. Fight to drag every secret and scheme out of hiding, letting the chips fall where they might.

I wanted to fight for the boy who *was* innocent in all of this.

The one who held my heart with tender, earnest hands.

The one I'd fallen in love with.

"I think we're ready," Dauphine said, calling Madame Fujiwara over to begin her final inspection.

I squared my shoulders and set my chin high, resolution steeling my frame.

Yes, I certainly was.

∽

"I think I spotted a patisserie on the corner," I mentioned casually as we stepped out of the atelier. All of the brothers had agreed my confrontation needed to happen away from Chauntilalie. "Would you like to stop for a little treat before heading home?"

Dauphine's eyebrows rose in surprise. "Verity—that was a final fitting. Even the great Madame Fujiwara won't be able to take that dress out if you gain an ounce before the wedding day."

"Just tea," I promised with a winning smile. "I was hoping I could speak with you about something . . . outside the house."

She checked the clock tower looming over the square. "Not today, I think. Our to-do list is nearly as long as the Menagerie itself."

I grabbed her hand before she could indicate to the carriage driver that we were ready to depart. "I was thinking of . . . a gift . . . for Alex. A wedding gift. I just . . . I don't want to chance him overhearing anything."

Dauphine grinned wickedly. "My dear, *you* are meant to be his gift." She twisted her lips thoughtfully. "Which reminds me, we ought to look through your trousseau next. You'll want to have new nightgowns . . . chemises . . . silk stockings . . ."

"A physical gift," I clarified, feeling my ears burn.

"Alex won't be expecting it."

"All the more reason for it, yes? A happy surprise."

She studied me, her resolve wavering.

"Actually," I began, wracking my mind to think of anything to tip the odds in my favor. "I wanted to speak with you about . . . about certain things . . . for the wedding night," I stammered. "As you know . . . I didn't grow up with a mother, and my sisters are all so far away. . . ."

She let out a soft sigh of understanding. "Ah, yes. Of course. Of course we can talk. But not there . . . That sort of conversation requires privacy and the baker's wife is such a gossip. Half the town will know your secrets before you've finished your first macaron." She glanced down the street, brightening. "There's a tavern around the corner that Gerard likes to visit. They've a little area set aside, just for him, can you imagine?"

"Being the duke comes with many privileges," I murmured, hoping I captured the right amount of awe.

"And so does the duchess," she said with a grin, tugging me down the promenade.

42

THE DUKE'S PRIVATE ROOM WAS SURPRISINGLY RUStic, and yet perfectly suited for Gerard's tastes, making me wonder how often he visited, whiling away his hours while we all assumed him in the greenhouse.

The room was made of exposed timber beams and stucco walls. Detailed botanic illustrations hung on either side of a small fireplace. A stack of books rested on the mantel, along with glass cloches protecting dried flowers and strange rocks. Two chairs in dark leather resided at the planked table, giving the room a decidedly intimate air.

Dauphine took in the surroundings with wide eyes, drinking in all of the details. "I've never actually been here before. Gerard says he enjoys his privacy while he works. . . ." Her gaze fell to the second chair I now resided in, lingering uneasily upon it.

I studied the renderings on the wall. One showed a diagram of a pomegranate, split in two and revealing its fleshy, seeded innards. Another was an orchid blossom, petals spread open wide. They reminded me uncomfortably of the illustrations I'd seen in his secret dossiers and I squirmed at the oddly explicit feelings they evoked.

Before we could order, a barmaid brought in a bottle of wine, held upright in a woven basket, and two goblets. Her skin was heavily freckled, her hair dishwater blond.

"Oh no," Dauphine said. "Just tea."

The serving girl stopped short. "But the duke always wants this wine when he arrives. Especially when entertaining such fine ladies." She smiled, revealing a mouthful of missing teeth.

"He won't be coming today." Dauphine's voice clipped sharp as her worries were not only confirmed but also said aloud, in such a casual manner. "It will only be the two of us."

The maid blinked, her confusion evident. "But I've opened the wine. . . ."

"Use it for someone else," I intervened, eager for her to go away. The sooner I could uncover Dauphine's secrets, the sooner we could leave this disagreeable room. "It looks quite busy in the dining room. I'm sure it won't go to waste."

"But this is the duke's wine." She hugged the tray to her chest, eyes as wide as the black wraith flowers protecting Gerard's gardens.

Dauphine sighed. "Then we'll take it." She poured my glass, then hers, then paused. "Where's the third glass?"

"Ma'am?"

"If you thought the duke was coming, where's his glass?"

The girl squirmed uncomfortably, cowering beneath Dauphine's all-seeing gaze, before fleeing the room without answer.

Dauphine rubbed at the center of her forehead as if warding off a headache. "He chooses the oddest places for his patronage." She shook herself from her reverie, glancing back to me. "No matter. What shall we toast to?"

I frowned, considering my options. I needed something that would steer our conversation in the right direction. I raised my glass, suddenly inspired. "To the Laurent men."

She let out a surprised burst of laughter but touched her goblet to mine. "To the Laurent men. May yours only ever vex you in all the best ways." She took a long swallow, then made a face.

The wine was bitingly tart and acidic.

"This can't have come from our cellar," she mused, holding the glass up to the window's light.

The door swung open again as the barmaid returned, carrying a basket of bread and a dish of olive oil, garlic, and cracked black pepper.

"Are you certain this wine was just opened?" Dauphine asked, freezing the girl with her green stare.

"Yes, milady. I did it myself."

She took another sip of it, pursing her lips.

The serving girl seemed poised to take flight, frozen on the tips of her toes, ready for any other demands the duchess might make. "Is there anything else I can get you, milady?"

"Nothing for now."

She hurried off.

I took a small sip, swishing it in my mouth as I mulled over what tactic to take. The bright flavor coated my teeth and I picked at the bread, hoping it would offset the bite. "Does he really vex you? Gerard?"

Dauphine tore a bread slice in half, dipping an unladylike portion of it straight into the oil. She chewed for a moment before answering. "It's hard to imagine now, but you'll find that all men—even the good ones—will come to vex you more days than not as the years go by." She sipped the wine again and followed it with another bite of bread. "It's our lot as women to bear . . . But this is dreary talk for a bride-to-be just days before her wedding! We've years and years to commiserate over this."

I nodded, trying to be as agreeable as I could. "Even still, I'm sorry. He spends so much of his days tinkering—"

Dauphine's laughter cut my sentence in half. "You don't know the half of it. He never stops working. Even when you pry him out of the greenhouse, he's still thinking, still writing. Do you know how many notebooks he goes through in a year, writing and drawing and musing?" She shook her head, swirling the wine around in the goblet.

"Where does he keep them all?"

Julien had guessed there was a laboratory secreted somewhere in the estate, far from the greenhouse, where Gerard did the majority of his experiments. Would Dauphine give it away?

Her bracelets clinked down her arm as she scooped up another slice of bread. "What an odd question."

I bit my lip. "I only . . . I know how hard it is to store my canvases and supplies. . . . I just wondered."

Dauphine shrugged, settling back into her seat in the most relaxed stance I'd ever seen her. "It's a large house. I wouldn't know. . . . These chairs are surprisingly comfortable. I wonder if we should get something like them for Chauntilalie. In the Lilac Study, don't you think?"

"And all that work, all that time . . . all over plants," I poked, hoping it would keep her on track, prompting further revelations.

She offered me a small smile. "Oh, but I know Alexander won't be that way. He's always been such a considerate boy. Even as a child. It's such a shame he . . ."

"What?"

She shook her head. "It's silly to want for things that can't be, but sometimes I find myself wondering about what he'd have been like if he'd not . . ." She pressed her lips together.

"Fallen?" I supplied.

"Fallen," she agreed. "Has he told you about that day?"

I nodded.

"How he remembers it?"

Her phrasing struck me as odd. "He said he was running on the stairs and fell." I noticed her glass was almost empty and leaned forward to refill it for her.

"Oh, Verity, I shouldn't."

"I won't tell if you don't," I said with a quick wink, happy when she laughed. "How *should* Alex remember that day? Did something else happen?"

She raised the glass to her lips again, stalling.

"They're awfully steep," I said carefully. "I can see how a little boy would have trouble climbing them."

"You said you wanted to talk about the wedding night," she said, briskly changing the subject, and I could sense it was unwise to press her further. "Surely you know a little about what is meant to go on then."

"I . . ." I watched her take a large gulp of the wine as if to prepare herself for the conversation to come. "A bit."

Dauphine nodded. "Well . . . I suppose . . . there might be . . . difficulties, at first. What with Alexander's injuries . . . I'm honestly not sure how it will go between you two." Her finger circled the rim of the goblet. I'd never seen her so flustered.

If I made her uncomfortable enough, perhaps she'd switch to a more useful topic . . .

"Alex warned me it might not be possible to fully . . . consummate . . . our relationship."

Dauphine's cheeks burned. "Oh . . . I'd never considered that."

"No?" I pressed. "I would have thought—"

She cleared her throat, then took another sip.

"We just hate to disappoint either of you."

"Disappoint?" she echoed.

"We'd never have any children," I said, sinking the dagger in. If she had known Gerard brought me to Chauntilalie for any other purpose than painting that portrait, this would be her greatest fear. "The Laurent line will end with Alex."

"Oh." Her face softened and she reached across the table to place her hand over mine.

"I know what a letdown that would be to you. To Gerard. And my sister has already written, expressing concern about all that." The lie rolled easily from my lips.

A strange light flickered to life in her eyes. "Has she?"

I nodded. "She said it was the single most important task for any duchess—issuing the next heir." Dauphine frowned and my heart hurt, knowing I'd opened up one of her old wounds. "I'd just hate for you or Gerard to think we weren't taking our responsibilities seriously," I said in a rush, trying to smooth it over.

She took a swallow of wine, musing over my words. "Verity. I'm touched you're concerned about that . . . but you needn't worry. If you want children, there are plenty of ways."

I took a deep breath.

This was it.

She was about to spill all of Gerard's secrets, implicating herself in the process.

"Are there?"

Dauphine nodded. "Of course."

As if seeking fortification, she drained the last of the goblet before motioning to refill mine. When I waved her off, she poured the last of the bottle into her glass, filling it nearly to the brim.

"It's a bit unconventional, but adoption is certainly an option."

My eyebrows rose in surprise. "I would have thought that . . . that Gerard . . . would only want a true Laurent as heir."

The room was silent for several terrible heartbeats.

Dauphine's eyes darted toward the door, assuring herself we were alone. "What exactly do you know?"

"Know?" I echoed, trying to buy myself time as my insides scrambled. The ground beneath me felt impossibly treacherous, ready to give way with any wrong step. If I admitted to everything I knew and she'd been working on Gerard's side, she'd go straight to him and they'd act before Julien and Viktor could ever get to the authorities. But if I played dumb, it was unlikely she'd freely volunteer any useful information.

I took a steadying sip of wine before remembering how sharp it was.

She pushed the bread basket forward, then took another sip herself.

I eyed her glass.

The wine had already loosened her behavior—she was all

but slouching in her chair, ripping chunks of bread from the loaf, looking more like a peasant than the esteemed Duchess of Bloem.

Perhaps it might also loosen lips . . .

I took another swallow, just enough to nearly empty the glass—I couldn't let *my* wits run wild from me—and pushed it to the center of the table, where she was sure to notice.

Ever a gracious hostess, Dauphine picked up the bottle before remembering it was empty. "We need more wine!" she called out, her voice growing loud enough to call for the barmaid. "More bread. More wine."

Her tone was strained. Her skin was flushed and glistening with sweat.

"Are you feeling well?" I asked.

Dauphine's head bobbed. "I'm fine. I'm actually feeling so . . . fine."

I dabbed my napkin at the corner of my lips, hiding my smile.

My plan was already working.

The girl returned, an open bottle in one hand, another bread basket in the other.

Dauphine clapped like an excited child as her glass was refilled, then grabbed hold of the bottle and shooed the serving girl away. With an unsteady hand, she filled my goblet, drops of wine spilling onto the table like blood splatter.

I studied it, remembering the blood on Gerard's apron the night of Constance's murder.

How had I ever thought it was beet juice?

I pushed the extraneous thoughts from me but they bobbed persistently back, buoys at sea. No matter how I tried not to think of Gerard's apron, of the dark lines of black and red staining his nails, I couldn't force the images out of my mind.

I set the glass away, resolving to drink no more of it. The wine, for all its bite, was strong.

I wiped my upper lip, feeling a sheen of dampness across it. Despite the empty hearth, the room seemed overly warm.

"Perhaps we should get some water," I mused, my tongue dry and sticky. "But . . . we don't know her name. Dauphine . . . we don't know the serving girl's name!"

She stared at me, her face twisted in curious amusement. "Why would we need to?"

I blinked, my eyelids feeling heavy. It seemed terribly important to me that we did but I couldn't express why. "For the water . . . or the wine. What if we need more wine?" I let out a short gasp. "Or bread?"

She laughed and it sounded like a snort, which made me laugh too. "Do you want to know a secret about being the duchess?" she asked, gesturing me close as though she was going to whisper in my ear. "When you're duchess, you never have to remember anyone's name. You just need to speak very loudly. More wine!" she shouted, showing me, and then broke into bawdy laughter.

I covered my mouth to catch my snickers, my thoughts circling loosely through my mind. There'd been something I'd been trying to get at, before all the talk of barmaids and wine. Something important . . . I brightened. "I think you were about to tell me something."

Dauphine trailed her finger over the rim of her glass, making the crystal sing. "Was I?" She studied me thoughtfully. "You're so pretty," she confessed in a rush. "I can see why he wants you so badly."

"Alex," I said, my heart warming as I pictured him. The man I was going to marry. My Alex.

Dauphine's smile dimmed. "Yes. Yes, of course."

"I'm not as pretty as you are," I said, worried she needed some sort of assurance, some bit of bolstering. "You're so strong and beautiful."

She looked touched, running her hands over her dress. "You really think so?"

I nodded fervently. "And kind. You've both been so kind to me."

Dauphine waved off my praise, swishing her hand as though swatting at a fly. "No. No. I could have been kinder."

"No!" I gasped, my head swaying back and forth with vehemence. I wanted to take all of the warmth flooding through my chest, all of the affection and gratitude I felt, and give it to her. It felt vitally important that she knew how much I appreciated her. "You've done so much . . . bringing me here and helping me with . . . with everything."

"You . . ." Dauphine looked as though she were about to burst into tears. "You are far kinder than I'll ever be, but . . . you'll be so mad when you find out."

I leaned forward, patting at her arm. "Find out what?"

She shook her head, hiccupping back a sob.

"Dauphine," I said, pawing at her, mussing the rows of pleated ruffles slashing across her bodice. "Tell me. You can tell me anything."

"It's about . . ." Another hiccup. "It's about the babies."

Alarm bells clanged in my mind, cutting through the strange haze that had settled over me and setting my heart to an uneven patter. "The babies. . . . The babies in the jars?"

I froze, realizing what I'd just done. Realizing what I'd just given away.

But she nodded, seemingly unaware of the mistake I'd made. "The jar babies."

"You know about them?" I asked carefully. It wasn't until after I swallowed that I was even aware I'd picked up my glass. The wine's tart aftertaste lingered on my tongue. With a flinch, I pushed it from me.

"Oh yes," she confirmed after a moment of painful silence. "I know," she said, tapping at her temple. "I *know* all about them. How they were designed. How they were made. But I don't *see*. He wouldn't let me see them."

"Gerard," I asked, needing confirmation.

She nodded.

"Gerard makes them. The babies in the jars."

"He tries," she said with a laugh, even though there was nothing humorous about the conversation.

"I saw them."

Dauphine grasped my hand, my arm, clutching on to me as if I were a life preserver. "You have? You saw the babies?"

I think I nodded.

"Can I tell you a secret?"

I leaned in as she gestured for me to come closer.

Her breath was hot and wet in my ear. "I'm the reason they're in those jars."

"What?" My gasp rang out in the quiet room as sharp as a slap.

Dauphine had confessed.

She'd confessed to it all.

She *knew* of the experiments.

She'd *helped* with them.

She'd helped Gerard in their messy aftermath . . .

"I mean, I didn't put them *in the jars*," she clarified, her hands restlessly drumming against the table. "But I was the one who kept them . . . kept them from being born."

I recalled how small many of the babies had been.

"What did you do?" I whispered, feeling sick.

She blinked, her eyes impossibly large and glassy. "I tried to stop him."

43

"STOP HIM?" I ECHOED. "YOU WANTED TO STOP Gerard?"

Dauphine nodded, her earrings swaying back and forth with fervor. "Of course. I couldn't stop him from finding the women—all those golden, golden women—but I could stop the babies. Just—" She made a slashing motion. A pair of scissors snipping thread. "Before they could draw breath." She pushed back a wave of hair, as if seeking to right herself. "He's not the only one who understands what plants can do."

"Does Gerard know?"

She shook her head, then rubbed at her forehead as if warding off a dizzy spell. "Of course not. He never can see the whole picture, only the pieces that interest him. He blamed the women. He thought them too weak. He never could see that I . . . that I . . ." She trailed off as if unable to admit exactly what it was she'd done, even to herself.

"You poisoned them?" I confirmed.

"Most of them." She licked her lips. "There were so many golden women."

"The women were golden?"

My head ached, feeling impossibly sluggish. Words I knew held no meaning. My mind was a jumble of nonsensical ideas.

"Their blood. Golden. Just like yours."

I struggled to follow along. "If you didn't want those babies being born . . . why did you write to me? Why did you bring me to Chauntilalie?"

She took another sip of the wine and I placed my hand on her forearm, stopping her from draining the glass. The tears that had grown in her eyes spilled over now, falling down her cheeks, her remorse palpable. "Gerard wanted you for his experiments, I can't deny that. But I . . . I wanted you for Alexander." She rubbed at her cheek. "He's so content and . . . stagnant. I don't want him to remain at the estate, forever alone, forever waiting to take on the next step of his life. I want him to find love, to find a partner who will see the world with him, open up his life in ways I never could. My letter to you wasn't a lie, not all of it. I *am* friends with Mercy. When I was at court, she told me so much of you and I knew—I just knew—if Alexander could meet you, he'd love you." She let out a deep sigh. "I suggested bringing you to the estate for the portrait, and Gerard . . . he'd heard the rumors about your family. About the things that had happened to you when you were a little girl. About the things happening to you now, I guess."

Her voice was soft, careful.

"You knew all of the things he wanted to do to me, and *you still brought me here*," I accused, my stomach sloshing. A wave of anger trembled through me. "How could you do that?"

Dauphine's lips rose in a painful smile. "Because I knew

that nothing would come of it. Alexander's injury . . . I knew he wouldn't be able to have children." She nodded earnestly and I couldn't tell if she meant to reassure me or herself. "And even if he could, he's nothing like—"

She stopped, catching herself just in time.

"Like Julien," I supplied. "Like Viktor."

Dauphine took in a sharp breath. "How do you know about them?" She frowned. "Gerard's diary. You found Gerard's diary?"

"I've met them."

Her eyes grew large. "Where?"

"At the house . . . in the secret passages. They . . . they're at Chauntilalie."

The glass fell from her grasp, shattering on the table.

"That's not possible. No." Her denial was hushed, a plea for contradiction.

I nodded. "They've been there for weeks."

Dauphine closed her eyes, her breath shaking, as the serving girl came back into the room.

"I thought I heard . . . Oh, oh, let me clean that up," she said, crossing to the table, hands fluttering.

"Leave us," Dauphine instructed.

"It won't be a moment," the barmaid said, picking up the biggest pieces of glass. "I'll just—"

"Leave. Now!" The order came barking out of her throat and the serving girl jumped. All of the pieces she'd gathered scattered across the floor as she scurried away.

Dauphine's eyes opened. "We need to get back to Chauntilalie. Alexander is in terrible danger."

"From them?"

She nodded.

"No," I disagreed, even as I remembered Viktor smashing his smoldering hands on the bench. "They're not . . . They're angry, yes, but they're not dangerous. They want to put a stop to everything, to hold Gerard accountable." I brightened, relief easing the ache along my sternum. "You can help us. You can explain what he's done to the authorities. You can verify everything."

"And admit what I've done? Admit what I allowed him to do? To those girls—to me?" She shook her head. "No, Verity. No." She grabbed the bottle and took a long swig directly from it.

"Why *did* you let him?" I asked quietly. "You must have known all those medicines, all those shots . . . they weren't normal."

Dauphine hummed in agreement. Her skin, normally so lustrous, had a slightly green pallor to it and her eyes were vague and unfocused. "I knew," she confirmed. "I knew everything he was doing and I let him." She swallowed back a cry. "I let him because I was a stupid, young girl and I believed in him. I believed in everything he was doing, everything he sought to achieve." She let out a short laugh. "I was so, so stupid."

"But what *is* he trying to do? We found some of his papers. We know he wants to talk to the gods, but why?"

She stared at me, a look of disgust crossing her face. "He's not trying to talk to the gods, Verity. He's trying to *create* one."

My stomach lurched, remembering the babies in the jars. The gills. The horns. "That's impossible."

"Not for Gerard. Not with all those golden women. He just needed to find the right combination." She looked at me meaningfully.

A shudder ran through me and I finished off the last of my

glass, wanting to slip into the wine's hazy embrace and let it dull everything into muted shades of apathy.

This was all so much bigger than I feared. Bigger than I could handle.

I wanted to get back to Chauntilalie.

Back to Alex.

I didn't want to be the only one with this knowledge.

"Gerard had a little sister. Did you know that?" Dauphine asked, her voice sounding dreamy and distant.

"I didn't."

"Emilee." She continued on as if my answer meant very little to her. "His father was a very devout man. Allister worshipped Arina with single-minded reverence. To him, the gods were without fault and could do no wrong. For all his piety, he was a very cruel man. He turned a blind eye toward the suffering of others. He said it was their fault, that if they'd only been more devout, more pious, sorrows wouldn't plague them."

"What happened to Emilee?" I asked, cringing from her answer even before Dauphine spoke.

"She was born without hands. Rather than let the people in town wonder what the great and mighty Allister Laurent had done to displease Arina, Gerard's father drowned Emilee in the koi pond before she was a week old. She's buried down by the lake, in the grove where Gerard planted the red buds. He said their blooms reminded him of her little pink cheeks."

"That's horrible," I whispered.

"Gerard stopped praying to the gods that day." Dauphine sipped the wine with a glassy stare. "He saw them as flawed beings, neither omnipotent nor infallible. He noticed all of the ways our world—the world that *they* created—was wrong. And he wanted to right it."

She set the wine bottle on the table.

"He started small, tinkering with plants, making little changes to improve their faults, then moved on to bigger things. He met me when I was just sixteen." She sighed with a smile, somehow still remembering those days happily. "He was so dashing and charismatic. I adored him. I would have done anything he asked." Dauphine paused. "I *did* do everything he asked . . . and it worked. We had three sons and . . . you should have seen them all when they were born, Verity. They really were golden. They glowed with importance. You could see that these were beings who were going to change the world."

"But you banished them. You sent Julien and Viktor away."

She nodded, looking ill. "You can say you want to bring down the stars, but you'll never understand how their fires will burn until you do."

She picked up the bottle and drank from it. One swallow. Another. Another after that.

"Bring down the stars?" I echoed, squirming as memories of my dream—my nightmare—rushed over me. A flush of shame burned through my cheeks, as blazing as the fires Dauphine mentioned. "We need to go," I decided. I'd learned all I cared to and wanted to be done. "We need to go now."

"There's no more wine," Dauphine said, tipping the bottle upside down. Not a drop spilled from it. "We never did learn that girl's name. Hello?" she said, raising her voice. "Hello out there. Oh, where is she?"

I tried to stop her as she pushed her chair from the table,

kicking shards of glass underfoot, but her arms were slippery. Slippery and sweaty and I supposed my hands were too. When had it become so hot?

When Dauphine tried to stand, she crashed back with an ungainly thud. "Oh. That didn't work right." Lines furrowed her brow, and for a moment, she looked as ill as I felt. "This . . . this isn't working right." But then she licked her lips and broke into a fit of giggles, her laughs pitched too high, too loud, too much, and then cried out, "Hello? Yes. In here! We need . . ."

"Help," I murmured, supplying her with the right word, before the walls tipped all the way over, swallowing me whole. "Help us. Help . . . me . . ."

She snorted, shushing me. "We don't need help. We need more wine!"

44

ALEX'S BED WAS MASSIVE, SPRAWLING OUT TWICE AS wide as it was long and topped by a coverlet in charcoal velvet. It felt sinfully luxurious as I made my way across it, crawling over the tufted peaks as though I were an intrepid adventurer, climbing an uncharted mountain. Picturing myself outfitted in olive drab gabardine and goggles, I giggled.

Alex stirred.

"Verity?" he whispered, his voice fuzzy with sleep. "Where have you been all day? We thought you'd be home hours ago."

"I was with Dauphine," I sang, as beautiful as any nightingale. "We tried on my wedding gown." Another giggle. "Well. Not we. Me. *I* tried on *my* wedding gown and she helped." I hiccupped. "Alex, it's so pretty. It's so pretty and long and white and pretty and you should see it. You will. You will see it."

He sat up, scratching his hair. It was deliciously rumpled. "Are you . . . are you drunk?"

"No! No. I don't think so. Well. There was a bottle of wine. Two. Maybe three? But that was hours ago. I think. What time is it?" The world floated around me, feeling too large and unwieldy to properly focus open. I fixed my eyes on Alex, letting the rest of the room fade into dizzying chaos.

He adjusted the bolster pillows behind him, propping himself upright. "Can you open the curtains? I can't see the clock from here."

"It must be late. It feels terribly late," I decided, doing as he bid. I nearly crashed into a wingback chair that suddenly sprouted up from the floor like a flower. When I pulled open the drapes, rays of sunlight raced into the room, blinding me. "Oh. Or not."

"No," he agreed, squinting. "I waited for you and Mother to return all morning. I've been so anxious to see what she said."

"She said," I repeated. "She said . . . you're in bed." I giggled at my rhyme.

Dark lines creased his forehead. "Another round of muscle spasms."

"Oh, Alex." I stumbled back over to the bed to sit beside him, taking his hands in mine. "Are you all right?"

"Better now that you're home and in one piece . . . mostly. What did Mother say?" He patted at the pillows, beckoning me to join him.

"We went to the most marvelous tavern," I announced, crawling over his frame and collapsing into the downy softness. "Your father has excellent taste in wine."

Alex cocked his head, worry shining in his eyes. "Father was there?"

"Was he?" I fretted. "I didn't see him! He'll be so upset we didn't say hello."

Feeling wonderfully rid of inhibitions, I nestled next to him, snuggling my head against his chest. He smelled so . . . green. Like fresh-cut grass and sun-dappled leaves, a summer rainstorm and a forest hike.

His breath audibly hitched. "Tell me what Mother said. I haven't seen Julien or Viktor at all today, and then with you gone for so long—I almost began thinking I'd dreamed everything about yesterday."

The bed was impossibly comfortable and my eyes fluttered shut in a drowsy haze, lulled to relaxation against the warmth of Alex's side. His fingers tickled at my waist with annoying persistence.

"Yes, yes. Your mother . . . Your mother . . ."

"My mother," he prodded.

"She . . ." My mouth fell slack as sleep fought to claim me.

"Verity," Alex murmured, his lips close to my ear.

"Hmm?"

He poked at my shoulder, pulling me away from blessed unconsciousness. "You know, I imagined our first time in this bed a bit differently."

"So has your father," I muttered. My stomach clenched, flipping over with a nauseous ache, and sweat broke across my scalp. My mouth felt thick and fuzzed over. How much wine *had* I drunk?

I vaguely remembered Dauphine calling for a third bottle but I didn't think I'd had any of it. But she had. She'd tossed the empty vessels into the fireplace, cackling like a fool as they smashed in green shards. Bastian had rushed in shortly after, gathering us out of the tavern and into the coach. I struggled with what happened next. It seemed much easier to shut my eyes and forget it all.

"Verity Thaumas!" Alex exclaimed, his voice snapping me out of my daze. "What happened today?"

I pushed myself up before leaning heavily on a corner of his stack of pillows. I rubbed at the back of my neck, attempting to keep myself awake and present. "Water, please."

He reached over to the side table and poured me a glass of water. "An excellent idea. Drink that, then another."

I nodded, gratefully downing it all in a long, thirsty gulp.

He refilled it once, then twice, before setting the pitcher aside. "So?"

As I tried to focus, the room swam about, tipping and turning. "She knows."

Alex bit his lip, looking grim. "You're certain?"

I nodded. "And . . . there's more . . ."

His eyebrows furrowed. "How can there be more?"

I paused, unsure of how to explain every revelation that had come to light in that tavern. "She knew about the experiments . . . on the women and her. She knew Gerard was trying to shape you all into something . . ."

Golden.

". . . greater than you'd be."

He frowned. "What do you mean?"

I licked my lips. "He's trying to create a new sort of person. Not . . . not even a person, really." I took a long sip of the water. "He's trying to create a god."

Alex scoffed. "That's impossible."

I wanted to agree but could not. "You didn't see the babies. . . . They had things about them that were so different. So wrong. So . . ."

Golden.

I shrugged helplessly.

"But if . . . if Father selected women with this special blood, with these divine parents or grandparents or second cousins or whatever it was . . ." He raked his fingers through his hair, struggling to get a handle on his thoughts. "Why are all the babies dead? Julien and Viktor and I . . . we lived. Why did all the others die?"

"Dauphine," I murmured unhappily.

"Mother?"

"After seeing the powers that Viktor and Julien had . . . she changed her mind. She no longer supported what Gerard was doing. So she . . . she did what she could to stop him." I took a deep breath. "She said that Gerard wasn't the only one who knew what plants could do."

Alex looked sick. "You think she poisoned the women? Their babies?"

"I'm certain of it," I said, queasy.

"And Father didn't know."

It was a statement. Not a question.

"It's why he keeps tinkering, trying out new mixtures, new bloodlines. He knows he did it right once before. He doesn't understand why he keeps failing now."

"Will Mother tell the authorities? Will she help us put Father away?"

"I think she could be persuaded." I glanced up. "By you. She's sleeping now, I'm sure. I think Bastian helped her to her rooms. But once she's awake, talk with her. She loves you. So much. I know she'd do anything you asked."

Alex nodded, not meeting my gaze.

"Is everything all right?"

He let out a bark of dark laughter.

"That's a foolish question. Nothing is right, I know, but—"

"How long did you know about them?"

A shiver of alarm raced through me. "Julien and Viktor? Only, only a day. Not even that."

He winced, clearly hurt. "How could you keep something—something so big—from me, for any time at all?"

"Alex, I wanted to tell you. I did. I promise." I took both his hands in mine.

"He likes you, you know," Alex said, his voice small and pinched. He still hadn't looked at me. "Viktor. He flirts with you—so openly. Is that . . . is that why you didn't tell me?"

"No," I said, and I couldn't tell if my answer was too hasty, giving off an air of guilt. "No, of course not."

He blinked, his eyes distressingly bright. "I saw him standing beside you, walking beside you, and I just . . . I saw this picture of what we could have been like if it wasn't for this chair. If I hadn't fallen. There're so many things we could have done, Verity. So many things I want to do and . . ." He wiped his hand over his face, pushing back the surge of emotions. "I'm jealous, I'm afraid. Bitterly jealous."

I ran my tongue over the back of my teeth. It felt thick and heavy and incapable of expressing what raced through my mind. "I promise you, with all of my heart, there's no comparing you two." I cupped my hands to his face. "Viktor may have walked alongside me for an afternoon, but you'll be with me all our lives. I'm so sorry you ever doubted you're enough for me."

"I feel like such a fool."

"You're not. But if you need to hear me say it—Alex, I love you. With all my depth and breadth. You're the one I want. You're the one I'm going to marry."

His lips rose a fraction. He still looked so sad. "Even after all this, after everything my family has done . . . you want to marry me?"

"It's not your family I'm marrying," I promised him. "It's you."

Still, his gaze did not waver.

"Alex," I murmured softly, scared the sudden fluttering within me would startle away, a butterfly precariously perched atop a flower.

His eyes met mine.

And then I kissed him.

For a moment, he remained still and unresponsive and I worried I'd somehow made everything worse. But then I felt him move against my lips, warming and coming to life.

My hesitation and wariness were gone. I no longer worried about what I ought to be doing with every individual part of me. I closed my eyes and enjoyed exactly what this was, what a kiss was meant to be like, with him. When Alex pulled away, I felt breathless, giddy and radiating with happiness.

"Would it . . . would it be all right if I stayed with you, a little while longer?"

Alex pressed a kiss to my forehead, nodding. "Please."

I settled onto the mattress, resting my cheek to his chest. When I dared to steal a peek at him, his eyes were closed, his face relaxed and dreamy. I studied him, my eyes traveling fondly over the length of his nose, the curve of his eyebrows.

This felt . . . good.

Right.

I could see our years stretching out from this point forward, Alex and me, together against the world. On the day he'd proposed, I knew I loved him—cared for him with a deep appreciation and affection—but today, in this moment, I fell *in love* with him. More than I'd ever dreamed possible.

I pushed myself up on one elbow, leaning over him, and kissed him softly, tentatively, wonderingly. His eyes flashed open, meeting mine.

"What's that for?" he asked, and his lips brushed against mine as he spoke, sending the most delightful bubbles fizzing into my bloodstream.

"Because I could," I said, joy swelling in my throat. "Because I wanted to. Because I love you."

"I love you," he echoed, unaware of the revelation crashing through my heart.

And that was all right.

It was enough that I knew it. That I'd been changed.

I kissed him again, my breath catching as his arms wrapped around my back, enclosing me in the sweetest embrace. He moved his mouth across mine slowly, as if he had all the time in the world, as if we had a lifetime to explore every bit of the other.

And we did.

"You feel like the sea," I murmured, my fingers trailing sinuous patterns over his chest, fluttering up his face, and sinking into his dark hair. I'd never felt peace like this outside the consuming embrace of the waves. It was as if I were floating now, face toward the sun, nestled in the cool grasp of the water. It held me, covered me, surrounded me with a constant security, setting everything inside me at peace.

He paused, looking amused. "The sea? I'm as rooted to the earth as a person can get. I *am* a root," he reflected, his hands splayed across my back, drawing me closer. "One root in a very large system, all holding up the same twisted, rotting tree. But you," he said, and I let out a soft gasp as he nibbled at the underside of my jaw. "You are the rain."

His tongue slipped inside my mouth, tracing and teasing. This, *this* was how I'd always hoped his kisses would feel, sending me aloft in shimmering spirals of wonder. I was too giddy to breathe and, even though it pained me to, I broke away from him, flopping on my back as I tried to draw in deep enough gasps of air.

Carefully, he rolled himself to his side, pressing the length of his body against mine. His skin felt feverishly warm and I wanted to pull him on top of me, losing myself under his weight, absorbing every bit of him into me.

He showered my face with little bursts of kisses, covering me with reverence and awe. "You're like a summer storm that came crashing into my life, soaking the ground and bringing me to life. I mean it, Verity," he said, stopping his ministrations. "I was a seed planted too far into the ground, waiting for my life to start. I had all these ideas of what I would do and be like when I grew up, when I took over my father's title. But you . . . you made me realize I could be that man now. I don't have to wait. I don't have to wonder. You made me grow into the person I want to be. So you see—earth," he said, pressing a hand to his chest. He ran his fingers along my lips before leaning down into a crushing kiss. "Water."

I lost myself in the rapturous haze of his mouth moving over mine, his hands opening parts of me I never knew existed as our gasps and sighs filled the room.

"It's more than that," I murmured as his teeth dragged down the length of my neck.

"More?" he echoed, his voice full of warmth and want.

"More," I agreed, crying out. "Oh yes, more."

༶

The soft click of the door swinging open stirred me back to consciousness.

For a moment, I didn't know where I was, didn't know the time of day.

My body felt long and limpid with bliss, like a dot of sealing wax stamped across a spread of thick and creamy parchment. I flexed my toes, stretched my shoulders, and took stock of my surroundings. I felt the soft rhythmic movement of Alexander's chest as he breathed in and out. Through the slit in the curtains, I could see the sky had turned a vibrant shade of lilac, streaked through with golden peach clouds.

I was in Alex's room.

It was sunset.

A lazy smile warmed my lips as I remembered the moments before we'd drifted to sleep, tangled together in a joyous embrace. Those moments had put to rest so many of the questions Alex feared.

I dared to picture a new future with him, one with children of our own. Children with my dark hair, his green eyes. They wouldn't be the extraordinary golden beings Gerard hoped for, but they would be wholly ours. Wholly perfect.

I gasped as I spotted a figure peeking into the bedchamber and struggled to free myself from Alex's limbs, heavy in sleep.

"Frederick?" I guessed, squinting in the darkened room.

Beside me, Alex sighed, his eyes fluttering open. He spotted me and his smile was wicked and full. "Morning."

"Evening," I corrected.

I no longer felt intoxicated but my head ached, throbbing with every syllable I uttered. I looked hopefully at the pitcher of water on Alex's nightstand, but it was empty.

"Master Laurent," Frederick said, drawing attention as he turned the gas lamps on, brightening the room. "I'm so sorry to barge in on you . . . and Miss Thaumas . . . like this."

"What is it, Frederick?" Alex asked, pushing himself into a sitting position.

"I've come to get you."

Alex glanced at his clock. "For what?"

The manservant's gaze fell to the ground, his lip trembling. "You need to come with me, sir."

"Tell me," Alex persisted. "Whatever it is, you can say it in front of Verity."

He clasped his fingers together, wringing them bloodless. "It's your mother."

Dauphine.

The tavern.

"If she's awake, we should go speak with her," I murmured to Alex. "As soon as possible."

He nodded. "Could you bring the chair over for me, please, Frederick?"

Frederick sprang into action. I pushed myself from the opposite side of the bed, straightening my skirts and finding the sparkling slippers I'd kicked aside earlier. I jammed my toes into the golden leather, ready to be off.

"Your mother . . ." Frederick opened his mouth but the remaining words refused to fall.

He'd bent over to adjust the chair's footrest. Alex reached up to touch the valet's shoulders. They were shaking.

Alex frowned. "Frederick? What's wrong?"

"It's Lady Laurent . . . She . . . I'm afraid to tell you . . . she's dead."

45

"DEAD?" ALEX AND I GASPED, RESPONDING AT THE same time.

"What do you mean?" he continued.

"That's not possible," I said, speaking over him. "I was with her . . . just hours ago. She was fine."

Not fine.

Not exactly.

But not . . .

Dead.

My mind reeled, trying to remember the last moment I saw her. Everything was so hazy. She'd drank more than I had—had she slipped going up the stairs, as Alex had as a boy?

Frederick started to say something but then shook his head, mind changed. "Lord Laurent needs to see you."

Alex nodded, his face unreadable, even to me. "There must be some sort of mistake. We'll get to the bottom of it. Thank you, Frederick."

"I think . . . ," the giant murmured, grief etched sharply into his face, "I think the duke would prefer if it were only you, sir."

Our eyes met and fear spiked through my middle. I didn't want Alex facing Gerard by himself. What if Dauphine had told him of my questions at the tavern before she'd . . .

I could see it playing out with painful clarity.

The wine would have loosened her inhibitions, freeing the thoughts she normally kept in check. What if she'd told him she'd poisoned all those women?

The glint of gardening shears stabbed into Constance's chest flickered in my mind.

Had he killed Dauphine too?

She's not dead, hope insisted fiercely within me. *It's a mistake. It must be.*

Alex shook his head. "Verity is part of this family now. He will see us both."

The hallways felt longer than usual, the floorboards sprawling out over miles as we made our way to the north wing. We seemed to pass by a thousand windows. Each sparkled so brightly I knew Frederick was wrong. Chauntilalie couldn't continue in such splendor without the lady of the house here, orchestrating it all.

Dauphine was not dead.

But every footman we passed had red-rimmed eyes. They bowed their heads respectfully as we raced by. Some had already changed into darker versions of their uniform. Seeing the inky wool brought back visceral memories I'd long forgotten, growing up as a little girl in black bombazine dresses and jet jewelry, mourning a mother I never knew and sisters who had died far too young.

"Alex," I said, reaching out to touch his shoulder, trying to stop him, trying to stall him before this awful moment came crashing down.

"I'm sure it's fine," he said, taking on the role of comforter, as if it weren't his own mother in questionable peril.

I tried to see that as a good sign.

If Dauphine really was dead, Alex would have to feel it somehow.

His disbelief spurred my heart toward optimism.

Alex came to a stop, facing the door of Gerard's study. He glanced at me, his expression apprehensive.

"It's going to be all right," I murmured, trying to offer solace against the unknown. "She can't be . . ." I trailed off, never wanting to finish that sentence.

"Do you think he knows?" Alex asked, his voice measured and hushed. "That we know? Do you think . . ."

I heard the words he did not say.

Do you think he killed her?

"I . . . I'm not sure," I whispered.

Alex swallowed, looking slightly green, then stretched out to tap on the door. "Father?"

"Yes. Come in." The door muffled Gerard's voice too much to be certain of his tone.

I pulled it open for Alex, allowing him to enter first.

My eyes instinctively looked toward the bookcase holding the specimen jars. The false front was rolled in place, hiding away all traces of Gerard's experiments.

Gerard sat behind the desk, his palms spread across its surface. His eyes were dry but his lips had settled in a grim line. A roaring fire crackled behind him, filling the air with a heat so powerful it was hard to breathe.

He glanced up. "Verity."

I held my breath, listening to the grandfather clock tick, counting the seconds of silence that went by, wondering how he was going to handle this, waiting for it to all break loose, like a summer storm, pure madness and fury.

Gerard's face remained a placid mask, revealing nothing of his inner thoughts. The longer the silence went on, the greater my desire to let out a scream and demand answers became.

He sighed, as if the awkwardness of the situation pained him. "I need some time alone with my son, Verity. I think perhaps it best if—"

"I want her here," Alex said, his hand clasping mine with resolution.

Despite the firm confidence of his voice, his fingers trembled and I folded my other hand over his, aching to offer support however I might.

Gerard's eyes flickered from his son, to me, and back to Alex again. "Very well." His voice was brisk and businesslike. "There is no easy to way to say this, but Dauphine is . . . dead."

Hearing it a second time was no less a shock. I wanted to ask questions, but the sudden absence at my side stalled me.

Alex's hand had dropped free of mine.

I knelt beside the wheelchair, pulling him into a swift embrace. I tried to remember condolences given out after Papa's passing. Though Kosamaras had unlocked that missing section of my life, allowing me to recall everything in crystalline detail, there were none. None that mattered. Grief so terrible can't be soothed away by words whispered in haste.

Alex stifled back a sob, covering his mouth as tears spilled down his face like rain. "No."

"I . . . I'm sad to say it's true." Though Gerard seemed determined to keep a stiff upper lip for Alex's sake, his lower one trembled. For one awful, sympathetic moment, I didn't see the monster I knew he was. I only saw the man, small and alone. For all his faults—and there were many—he had truly loved Dauphine, in his way.

I sat back on my heels, unsure of what to do. "Gerard," I began. "I'm so sorry. This is shocking news. I was with Dauphine only hours ago. She seemed fine and happy and . . ." I remembered the bottles shattering in the tavern's fireplace with a wince. "What happened?"

His lips twisted, as if he was sucking at a piece of food wedged tight in the corner of his teeth. "She was poisoned."

My gasp was loud enough to break through Alex's misery, stirring his attention.

"What? That can't be right. Who would want to poison Mother?"

Gerard traced a whorl on the desk with his thumb. "Apparently, while in Bloem, the girls visited a tavern."

My mouth fell open.

I felt Alex's eyes fall on me, rounded wide with concern.

Gerard glanced up, studying his son first, then me. "Someone tampered with the wine you were served."

Trying to recall the afternoon was like wading through a thick sludge. The acidic taste of the alcohol still lingered in my mouth, coating everything with a tart sharpness.

Poisoned.

"The wine?" Alex echoed, piecing things together more quickly than I. "When Verity came in this afternoon, she was . . . not herself. Spacey and giggling and just *wrong*. I thought she and Mother had only gotten tipsy, but if the wine had been drugged . . . how much did you drink?"

"I had a glass," I murmured. "Maybe two. I didn't like the way it tasted . . . the way it made me feel. I thought it was just very strong wine. . . ."

The duke swallowed, his stare severe. "And Dauphine?"

"The rest of the bottle . . . and another," I admitted, cringing. "Maybe more?"

He let out a sharp sigh, shaking his head.

"We never ordered it," I remembered suddenly. "The serving girl just brought it to us. She said it was from your special stock."

Gerard froze.

"This was at the Adler's Crown?" Alex guessed. He shifted toward his father. "You keep a room there. Everyone in Bloem knows that. Anyone could have slipped something into your vintages. It would have been so easy. But who would want to hurt Mother? Or Verity?"

Gerard's gaze landed upon me, swift and terrible. I could see a lie forming on his lips.

Alex, lost in thought, didn't notice. "You don't think . . ." He ducked his head close to mine, his voice hushed. "Could it have been *them*?"

"Them?" Gerard repeated, catching his son's words, his ears as sharp as a bat.

I started to shake my head, denying it. Julien wouldn't have, I was almost certain. He was so set on righting wrongs and going through proper channels. He was protocol and reason, meticulously rational and by the book.

But Viktor . . . His anger, once sparked, could blaze out of control. And he was so very angry. The unexpected speed with which he reacted made him terrifying, but also an unlikely choice for a poisoner.

Poisoning took time and skill. It was methodical. It required so many steps.

It was not a process I could see Viktor undertaking, he who flared hot and bright and fast.

"No," I decided. "Not them."

Alex looked unconvinced.

"Alexander," Gerard said, poised at the edge of his chair. "Who are you talking about? If you know someone who might have hurt your mother . . . who might have hurt Verity," he added after a slight hesitation, "you must tell me."

"Must I?" A dangerous current rippled beneath the two short words, and when Alex glanced at his father, his eyes were dark. "Must I tell you things, Father?"

Gerard looked taken aback. In all my time at Chauntilalie, even at his angriest, I'd never seen Alex so hostile.

"There are all sorts of things you've never told me."

He licked his lips. "What do you want to know?"

"Why don't you start with my brothers?"

Gerard had the audacity to feign confusion. "You . . . you don't have any brothers, Alexander. You know that."

"Viktor and Julien's presence suggests otherwise," I said, ready for his game to be at an end.

As their names were said, Gerard paled, sinking back into his seat as if I'd physically struck him. "They're here?"

I nodded.

"I should have known they'd make their way to Chauntilalie after that fire. Arina's heart!" Gerard struck the table in self-reproach. "It's not safe for you here, Alex. It's not safe for any of us." He shifted his attention to me. "You need to get Frederick to order the three of you a carriage and get away from here. I will deal with the pair of them as I should have years ago."

"I'm not going anywhere," Alex said, bucking his father's plans. "Mother is dead. We have to"—he swallowed—"send out an announcement, call in the Sisters of the Ardor. We need to prepare her body with seeds, return it to the earth. We have to—"

"I know the order of mourning," Gerard snapped. He raked his fingers through his hair, tugging at the ends with a growl of frustration. "None of that matters now."

"Because of them?" Alex questioned, his voice sharp as a blade.

Gerard nodded.

"Because of who?" he persisted. "Tell me. I want to hear you say it."

Gerard let out a pained sigh. "Your brothers."

The two men stared at each other in heated silence but I could feel the words each wanted to say, to scream, piling up on either side of the desk.

"Brothers," Alex finally spat out. "I have brothers. Brothers you kept from me."

"Brothers I kept *you from*," Gerard said, emphasizing the difference. "I can't imagine how angry you are at me, Alexander—especially having only heard their version of the story—but I did the right thing. I will always swear I did the right thing."

Alex barked out a burst of bitter laughter. "The right thing? You sent your sons away. You exiled them. Children."

"Monsters," he amended.

"They were boys!"

Gerard turned to me. "You've seen what they can do?"

Reluctantly, I nodded.

"Then you know what I did was right. I was right!"

"But you made them," I began, trying to stop the rising tension from drowning us all. "If you think them monsters . . . why did the experiments continue?"

"Experiments?" he echoed innocently, sweat beading across his brow.

"I was in that nursery. I saw those babies. And Constance," I added with grim finality.

Gerard's eyes darted to Alex, registering his expression. When he finally spoke, he kept his voice carefully restrained. "I took care of that before she ever got to you."

"I saw them."

"You did?" A wondrous smile crept over his lips and my insides tightened, feeling sick. I'd just confirmed he'd been right about me. I was as every bit as different as he'd hoped. As he'd dreamed.

I wanted to wipe the look of reverenced awe from his face.

Before I knew it, I was on my feet and across the room.

"I've seen this too," I snarled, pushing aside the false bookshelf and revealing the rows of jarred babies.

The room fell silent.

"What . . ." Alex cocked his head, trying to understand what he was looking at. "What is that, Father?"

He pushed himself toward the shelves.

"Alexander, don't!" Gerard protested. He stood but made no further motion to approach his son.

Alex picked up one of the jars, gently turning it around until the baby inside faced him. I saw a flash of teeth and too many eyes before looking away.

A noise of disgust escaped from Alex. "How could you do that, Father? How could you do any of this?"

Gerard's face fell, smoldering with disappointment. "If I'd not *done that*," he replied, echoing Alex's tone, "I wouldn't have you."

Alex tucked the jar back into the case, shaking his head. "I'm nothing like that. Nothing like any of these."

"You're right. You're more. So much more." He pushed back the waves of his hair. "You are my greatest achievement, Alexander. And you don't even know it."

I shook my head. "No. Julien. Viktor. They have their talents. Alex has—"

"Alexander has it all," Gerard said. "It's hard to explain what you were like as a child, my boy. You were so . . . so very . . ."

"Golden," I muttered as my stomach heaved, thick and queasy.

"Yes!" Gerard nodded emphatically. "He was—he still is—so golden!"

Alex glanced down, as if trying to spot some sort of difference between him and us.

"Golden and strong and resilient. I created the perfect specimen—a mind full of kindness and infinite capacity, a heart of goodness and love, a body of persistence and power. I created a better god than any that reside in the Sanctum!"

Alex looked horrified. "Father!"

Gerard's blasphemy echoed sharply in the room, sending a shiver down my spine. I could hear Kosamaras as clearly as if she'd just whispered into the curve of my ear.

You and that boy will create things, terrible things. Things terrible enough to bring down even the gods.

I thought back to only hours before, when Alex and I had

been nothing more than a tangle of limbs and ravenous hungers, gasping, grasping, and crying out with need and ecstasy. Desires filled. Appetites sated. My mouth now tasted of ash.

She'd meant Viktor.

Not Alex.

Not Alex, who had no trace of power within him.

Not Alex, who was warm and mine and so very human.

Pontus *please*, not Alex.

Alex held up his hand, studying its lines, as if they might show him exactly who he was. "But . . . I can't do anything like my brothers do. What power am I meant to have?"

Gerard glanced at his legs meaningfully.

"What?"

"You lived," he whispered breathlessly. "You don't remember that day but . . . haven't you ever wondered how far you fell?"

"A handful of stairs, only two or three. Mother said I just landed wrong, so very wrong and—"

Gerard shook his head. "Alexander, you went over the balcony."

Alex blinked in disbelief. "That's not possible. That's at least—"

"Forty feet. Forty-two, actually. I measured it myself. Forty-two feet onto the marble floor below. I saw it happen. You were like a meteor plummeting to earth. We had to cut away the section where you landed. It had smashed to bits."

"The Laurent crest," he murmured with understanding.

I recalled the rose-gold chips that made up the large mosaic in the entryway. It stood out starkly from the cool gray marble, as if it hadn't been part of the original design.

It hadn't.

"We couldn't find any stone that matched just right, so I told the contractor to make something beautiful in its place. Every time I walk over that crest, I'm reminded that my son is alive. Wonderfully, *impossibly* alive. Because of me. Because of what I did." He swallowed, beaming with pride. "I created a god. An immortal."

The air in the room had taken on a hushed, reverent quality.

"And what of Julien and Viktor?" I asked, daring to break it. "What did you create there?"

Gerard had the decency to look away, ashamed. "Something different entirely, I'm afraid."

"Different?" Alex whispered skeptically.

"Julien never cried as a baby. Not once. He would just stare about the room with those giant, expressionless eyes. I can't tell you how many nursemaids we lost, unnerved by his unblinking gaze. Only when Viktor pitched himself into a fit would Julien stir. It took me longer than it should have to understand what was going on. No one ever expects their children to have such . . ."

"Variations?" I suggested.

"Deviations," he corrected. "On his own, Julien is harmless, but with Viktor . . . they spur each other on toward madness."

"What do you mean?" I remembered how they often seemed to communicate without words, one entity sharing two bodies.

"Viktor has always been rage and wrath, quick to fits of anger and violence. Once, he set the nursery curtains on fire. We'd thought one of the maids had been clumsy with a taper but it was only Viktor, wanting a bit more milk before bed." Gerard wiped the back of his hand over his forehead.

I pictured my nephew Artie. He was not much older than the boys when they were cast out. When he didn't get his way, his howls could be heard halfway across Highmoor. "He was a child. Maybe you should have taught him that it was wrong to use his . . . gifts," I said, mindful to choose a word that wouldn't further upset Alex, "in such a manner."

Gerard stared at me, deadpan. "He was six weeks old. He nearly burned down half the manor. After that, we kept the pair of them from Alexander. It was too risky to keep them together."

I remembered Viktor on the rooftop garden, the look of fury, of being just heartbeats away from losing his grip on everything.

Any desire I had to defend him dried up.

"I shouldn't have lumped them together," Gerard admitted. "It forever changed Julien. Having Viktor's thoughts—those terrible thoughts—constantly saturating his mind . . ." He shook his head. "No one should be forced to live that way."

"Do you truly believe me the monster in this story?" a voice asked from the back of the room.

My head whipped around. Viktor stood on the threshold, arms folded across his chest. He wore dark navy pants, a white shirt, and a gray vest, an exact match of what Alex had on.

"Who was the one who sent poor little Julien away to live with such a madman?" He stepped into the study, locking the escutcheon behind him with a casual flick of his fingers.

A hidden door at the side of the room swung open and Julien stepped out, dressed in the same clothing, making them a perfectly identical trio.

Constance was wrong. There'd been a secret passageway all along.

He crossed over to sit on the edge of the desk, dangling his legs back and forth with a strange childishness as he stared down at his father. "Hello, Papa. Remember me?"

Gerard swallowed, his Adam's apple bobbing heavily. He nodded. "Ju-Julien."

"Very good," he said. His lips rose, showing off a line of teeth. It looked more of a grimace than a smile.

Viktor's eyes wandered about the room with unchecked curiosity. "I always thought this room was so large and important, the seat of Father's power and might. Now it just looks"—his gaze fell on Gerard and he grinned—"terribly, terribly small."

Gerard's nostrils flared, anger flashing across his face as he studied the son he hadn't seen in fifteen years. "Verity, I want you to take Alexander away from the study. Get him out of here. I will deal with these two on my own."

I felt rooted to the floor, unable to move as I glanced from Gerard to each of the boys.

Even still, Alex swatted in my direction, keeping me at bay. "I'm not going anywhere."

"Bravo, little brother," Viktor commended, slowly clapping his hands together. He sank into one of the armchairs. "Finally showing Father your spine." He made a face, crossing one leg over the other. "Poor choice of words, my apology."

"He's not actually sorry, you know," Julien confided. "He's laughing quite a bit in there."

Gerard studied his oldest son with awe. "What wonderful things we could have done had that one not ruined your mind." He sighed. "What an absolute waste."

Julien's stare was flat and chilling. "Don't talk to me of waste. It's my mind. My life. You were the only person who could explain what was going on within me. You knew I was different. You knew *how* and you knew *why* and you still sent me away with *him* and all that *he* thinks."

"There was no saving you," Gerard said sadly. "No saving him. It was *his* fault you were sent away. Remember that!" He whirled round on Viktor. "Every angry impulse, every selfish thought, your envy and hate, your rage and wrath. They consumed you whole, bursting out until the rest of the world suffered as much as you have. I should have smothered you the second I realized what I'd created."

Viktor leaned forward, irises all but aflame. "But you didn't, did you, Father? Does that thought fill you with shame and despair? Do you ever think how the world would be, if you had? Does your conscience keep you up at night, wondering what sort of glorious things the golden boy would have achieved had it not been for me?"

Alex's eyebrows furrowed together. "What . . . what is he talking about?"

Viktor rolled his eyes. "Did you know that yours was the only birth they ever celebrated? Who could blame me for stealing out of my chambers? I just wanted to share in my brother's special day. The golden child's golden birthday." He doffed the back of Alex's head, ruffling his hair.

Alex ducked, trying to free himself from Viktor's grasp. "Father!"

"Father," Viktor mimicked, pitching his voice too high. "Help me. Save me!" He pantomimed something falling from a great height before smashing into the ground.

My blood ran cold as I realized his meaning.

"Alex didn't fall from the balcony, did he?" I asked Gerard. "He was pushed over." I turned to Viktor. "By you."

"Julien helped too," Viktor admitted as Alex's mouth dropped open.

"Only because you were so angry." Julien glanced back to Gerard. "You've no idea how persistent he is in here," he said, tapping his forehead. "It's like being pulled about on puppet strings. Even when he's far away, I can feel the cords tugging at me, slicing up all my insides and soft matter."

"You could have killed me," Alex said, aghast.

Viktor rolled his head about, stretching his neck. "That actually *was* the point. We didn't know you were so . . . hardy. He still is, too, you know, Father? We've been dropping all sorts of things into his teas, his nightcaps, but nothing has stopped him yet."

"The muscle spasms he's been having," I gasped, realizing what they'd done. "You've been drugging him?"

Viktor grinned.

Alex's fingers dug into the arms of his chair. "Why? Why would you— What have I ever done to you?"

"It was never you. It's always been to punish us." Gerard sighed. "After the first fire, Dauphine and I sent away the nursemaids, the extra hands. We told everyone Viktor and Julien had stopped breathing in their sleep one night. We presented you as a single child."

"There it is," Viktor said cheerfully. "They only had eyes for you. The unproblematic favored son. The bright, shining light of the Laurent family. Arina, how I hated you." He brightened. "But no longer. Now I see, now I understand. Now I know exactly who's responsible for everything. You"—he pointed to Gerard—"and that woman."

"Mama is no longer with us," Julien reminded him.

A funny little laugh fell from Viktor's lips. "Oh, yes. I almost forgot—my deepest condolences on your recent loss, Father. But

I suppose you've no need of coaching on how to grieve the death of a lover. You've gone through so many over the years."

"You . . . ," I murmured, finding my voice. "You were the ones who poisoned the wine."

"Sadly, no. Someone beat us to it." Viktor's head swung to Gerard, his eyes sparkling and sly. "Any thoughts on who could have done something so heinous?"

I felt like a battering ram had struck my sternum, knocking every bit of breath from me. I stumbled to the second armchair, sinking into its tufted leather.

Alex's eyebrows furrowed together, impossibly wounded. "Father, what are they saying?"

"It . . . it was an accident," Gerard said, his voice stripped bare and strained. He'd been so stoic before, riding out his pain behind a hardened façade, but it crumbled now as Viktor and Julien blew it apart, one crack at a time. "Verity, you must believe me. That wine was never meant for you. Or Dauphine. I swear it upon my very life."

46

THE ROOM FELL INTO STUNNED SILENCE.

Gerard had drugged the wine.

Gerard had poisoned us.

Poisoned Dauphine.

Murdered Dauphine.

I tried to wrap my mind around it. Around that afternoon. "If the wine wasn't meant for us, who *was* it for? It was there for someone, already poisoned . . . for who?"

Julien tilted his head. "Yes, Papa. Who?"

Gerard took a shaky breath. "That's a very long story."

Viktor held up his hand, gesturing about the room. "And yet, we've nothing here but time. Tell the Brothers Laurent a good tale. Shall we cuddle under some blankets and douse the lamps?"

Beside me, Alex remained silent, staring at his father with a look as sharp as granite. I could feel the waves of fury radiating from him.

"The wine . . ." He cleared his throat, trying again. "That wine, at the tavern, isn't poison. Not exactly."

"You added something to it, that much is clear," Julien said.

Gerard nodded. "A bit of . . ." He swallowed, looking queasy. "A rather large bit of valerian root. It's a sedative. It's not meant to kill anyone, just—"

"Render them unconscious," Viktor jumped in. "Just long enough for you to abscond the lady in question back to Chauntilalie. I'm curious, Father. Would you have your way with her once she stirred or would she wake up already in the family way?"

"Is there any water in here?" I interrupted, my stomach churning. The combination of heat cast from the blazing fire and the cool recitation of Gerard's crimes left me close to swooning. "I feel faint."

"Of course," Gerard said, motioning to ring the little bell on his desk.

"Stop," Julien said, covering the brass bauble and sliding it neatly out of Gerard's grasp. "It's a bit crowded in here already, wouldn't you say?" He glanced at me. "And you wouldn't really drink anything that man gave you, would you?"

He had a point, I thought, swallowing miserably.

"So Mother was simply a victim of gluttony," Viktor mused. He *tsked* as if it saddened him before a snicker burst free.

Alex pressed his hand over his mouth. I saw the line of his throat contract, as if holding back his urge to retch and knew this was becoming too much for him. Dauphine's death, Gerard's admissions, it was all too much. He looked like a thread overwound and about to snap.

"I never meant anything to happen to her. You must believe me, Alexander." Gerard reached across the table, trying to connect with him, but Alex's eyes were unfocused. "I would have never hurt her."

"But you did mean to hurt Constance," I said, grabbing at his attention. "You murdered her." Hot bile sloshed in my gut, threatening to come up as I remembered the gardening shears. "But I don't understand why. I saw those babies. She gave you exactly what you wanted. She—"

"She was going to tell you. Tell everyone. Everything. The babies . . . they grew to full term, they made it through the births, yes, but they . . . they weren't developing as they should. They were weak, fussy. Constance begged me to fix them, to save them. She loved them, she truly did, but there was nothing to be done. When they died, she said it was a sign. My experiments, my creations, were doomed to fail. She threatened to warn you, Verity. She didn't want you to go through what she had. But I . . . I couldn't let that happen."

Gerard shrugged as if he'd been completely helpless in the situation. As if he'd only followed the most reasonable course of action. He blinked innocently, his eyes cold and without remorse.

Alex murmured something, too low to catch at first.

I reached out to him, squeezing his shoulder. "What did you say?"

Slowly, painfully, he glanced up, meeting Gerard's gaze. "I said he's mad."

"I'm not," Gerard insisted. "I know exactly what I've done. I understand how it looks to you, how you must think it is, but . . . you don't see what I do. . . . You don't understand that some sacrifices must be made for the greater good."

"Good," Alex repeated. "What good could possibly come out of any of this?"

"If you . . . if you all could just understand . . ." Gerard buried his face in his hands. "My father was . . . an intensely religious man. All my childhood, I was brought up worshipping the gods. Not just Arina—all of them. I could tell you every one of them, however old, however forgotten. I knew every Harbinger, every half-god spawn. We celebrated their festivals; we honored their ways. When he became duke, I watched Papa dismantle my grandfather's beloved ballroom and turn it into a shrine. For . . . them," he said, casting his hand into the air in a gesture that reminded me uncomfortably of Kosamaras.

Viktor shifted in his chair. "Oh poor Father, how terrible your youth must have been." His face hardened. "We know nothing of what that must be like."

"Dauphine told me about your sister," I said, cutting off his theatrics. "How she was born without hands. How your father killed her because of the imperfection."

Gerard nodded. "That was the day I stopped praying to the gods. I saw them for what they were—beings of preternatural powers, certainly, but at heart, no different than you or I. They weren't blessed with divinity. . . . They were just the next step in our own evolution." He rubbed at his chin. "The problems in our world showed me that their powers were not without limit. I knew I could improve upon that, distill that essence that makes them different from us. And then I would perfect it, create my own god. One who would fix the messes they made for us. When I met Dauphine Armella, I was certain she would be the woman to help me achieve all my goals."

"Why?" Julien asked, head tilted.

Alex let out a soft, ragged breath. I reached out to entwine my fingers with his, happy when he didn't pull away.

"The Armella tree is riddled with half gods and secret assignations. Her genetic makeup couldn't have been more perfect."

"And you loved her too, of course," Viktor said, all but sneering.

"We did grow . . . terribly fond of one another," Gerard said, twisting his lips and looking almost guilty. "And I was right. She gave birth to the three of you. When we saw how mixed the results were, I wanted to try again but Dauphine refused. The treatments had taken a toll on her body. . . . It was just too much for her to do again."

"So you brought in a bit of help," Viktor guessed snidely.

Gerard nodded. "I tried again so many times. But it never . . . I never could quite replicate the experiment. The women always died before the babies could be born. They weren't strong enough." He shook his head as his face colored in disappointment.

I opened my mouth, about to tell him of Dauphine's meddling. I wanted to shout her deception from the rooftop but stopped short. She'd committed terrible acts but had done so to thwart a madman. Spilling her secrets now wouldn't bring the women back; it wouldn't undo Gerard's crimes. Some secrets ought to be taken to the grave.

"That's why it was so important to find the right partner for Alexander," Gerard continued. "It's paramount *his* genes continue on, paired with someone equally special. Someone who has the strength to carry the new gods, to birth them, to raise them to their destinies. When your sister told Dauphine the story of the cursed Thaumas sisters, I knew you were the right girl for Alexander."

I felt the weight of everyone's eyes fall upon me.

The room felt so dry, the fire scorching and bright. It was almost impossible to think straight. "We're not going to have anything to do with this perversity," I spat at Gerard. "Alex, come on. We're leaving."

His eyes were watery and so heartbreaking. "I . . . I don't know what to do. This is all . . . so much. Too much. I . . ."

"We'll go away. Get away," I promised him, cupping his cheeks, trying to make him look at me. "We can sort through it all later. But first we have to get out of here. Get away from him. From Chauntilalie."

"And them?" he asked, glancing toward his brothers.

"And us?" Viktor echoed, peering at me with a smirk.

"Do whatever it is you want. Drag him to the authorities, turn him in. Take the house for yourself. It's all yours. Alex, we're done here."

"No," he protested, tugging me back. "I'm not running away."

"Please. We need to go. I need to go. I just need . . . I need some water." I was gasping now, panting like a dog on an insufferable summer day. Rivulets of sweat dripped down my neck, soaking my bodice. My head felt too heavy to hold up.

Gerard removed his cravat and unfastened the top buttons of his shirt. His face was flushed and blotchy. "It *is* too hot in here." He glanced at Viktor, his eyes unfocused and listless. "You. You're doing this."

"Doing what?" he asked innocently.

Visible waves of heat radiated off his body.

"You see," Gerard said, fanning himself as he panted. "You see now. I should have . . . should have never have . . ." His hand fell heavily on the table, reaching for the rose-gold letter opener in the tray before him.

"Julien, do it, now!" Viktor ordered, his voice cutting through the swirling, sweltering confusion.

A light dawned in the oldest Laurent brother's eyes. He leaned over Gerard, peering down like a stone gargoyle, Viktor's rage etched across his face.

With a quick motion, he grabbed the back of Gerard's head and slammed it forward, cracking his skull against the polished edge of the desk.

Gerard's forehead split down the center like a melon grown too big and too soft.

"Father!" Alex said, lunging his chair toward the desk before Viktor sprang into action, pulling him back. They tussled for a moment, and I feared the wheelchair would topple.

Gerard fixed his gaze—now cross-eyed—upon me. "Get my son out of here," he pleaded, before Julien struck again.

I turned away, screwing my eyes shut, powerless to stop the burst of violence.

But I still heard the sounds.

The sharp smacks of bloodied flesh.

Julien's grunts of exertion.

Alex's raspy breaths of horror.

Finally, the dull thud of a body falling to the floor.

Then, silence.

Silence wide and yawning.

Silence so big it felt as if we'd been swallowed into its void.

The air brightened, cooling quickly as tempers subsided.

"What have you done?" Alex whispered.

I dared to open my eyes.

Gerard's body was blessedly hidden away behind the desk but its surface was covered in blood and other things I did not want to acknowledge.

Julien remained perched on its edge. His chest rose and fell heavily. He was wrung out, but his face was blank once more as he studied the mess left behind.

Viktor gripped the handles of the wheelchair, as if preparing to hold his brother back but any trace of fight had left Alex. He stared at the scene, eyes wide, mouth open with surprise.

"What was needed," Viktor murmured.

I'd expected him to sound triumphant. He'd wanted this revenge. He'd wanted to make Gerard suffer as he and Julien had.

But his voice sounded hollowed out, as empty as Julien's expression.

"He was picking up the letter opener. You saw him do it. He would have hurt Julien. He would have hurt me. Ver," he snapped, bringing me into their morbid tableaux. "You know what he was capable of. You know he would have done it."

From his seat on the table, Julien silently turned his hands over, as if just now noticing the spray of blood across them.

"But not like that. Not like any of—" Before Alex could finish his sentence, he turned to the side, throwing up.

Viktor's nose wrinkled in disgust. "He was a monster. He was *the* monster in our little story, and in fairy tales, the monster must always be slain."

He stepped out from behind the wheelchair, crossing to the desk. He leaned across it, studying Gerard's motionless form. After a moment, he nodded.

"You did what you had to," Viktor murmured, pressing his forehead to Julien's, squeezing his arm with commiseration. He turned back to us, drumming his fingers against the desk, careful to avoid the congealing puddles. "Long live Duke Laurent."

"Long live the duke," Alex recited vacantly, his words nothing more than a flex of muscle memory.

I noticed the tip of Gerard's shoe sticking out from the side of the table, saw drops of blood spattered across the patent leather. "How are we going to explain this?"

"We say exactly what happened," Viktor said, as if it were the most obvious of answers.

"No one will believe us," Alex murmured, sounding small and lost.

For the first time since the attack, Julien stirred into motion, turning to stare at us. His eyes were too wide, too unblinking. "What did you make me do?" He rubbed at his forehead. "Your thoughts. Those images. They were so loud. . . ." He scrubbed furiously, as if trying to wipe away the memory. A red welt rose across his skin. "I couldn't hear anything but you."

"Julien, stop," I said, reaching out to still his fervor.

He smacked my hand away, the slap stinging. *"What did you make me do?"*

"Calm down," Viktor instructed, and Julien's hand fell back into his lap, still once more. "It was only ever self-defense."

"Was it?" Alex asked.

"Self-preservation," Viktor continued, nodding, convincing us. "And no one can fault you for that, dear brother. For protecting your life, your security and sanctity, and defending it, using whatever means necessary."

"I suppose, but—" I began, then gasped as Viktor took up the letter opener himself and plunged it into the hollow of Julien's throat.

47

EVERYTHING SEEMED TO SLOW DOWN INTO IMPOSSIbly long seconds that stretched and expanded, allowing me to see every detail of the horrifying action.

Julien let out a strangled, airy sound as he struggled away, flipping himself from Viktor's grip. The letter opener went flying, spinning madly through the air like a sparkling baton. It landed at Alex's feet, its edge slicked red.

Blood—droplets, then a stream, then a torrent—followed after as Julien crashed onto the desk. His eyes were open wide but flatter than usual, his life already ended.

Viktor stood over his brother, dispassionately watching the blood pour from his throat. It came in spurts, pushed by a heart wild with shock, before tapering to a slow ooze.

"Long live Duke Laurent," he muttered again, a dark grin lighting his face. With a painful slowness, his eyes left Julien's body, rising until they met our horrified gaze. "Now," he mused, settling his attention on Alex. "What to do about you?"

I sprang into action, grabbing at the handles of Alex's chair. There was no time for words, no time to beg for mercy. We needed to leave. Now.

"The lock! The lock!" Alex cried as I pushed him across the study. I barely paused as he flipped it to its side and flung open the door.

"We need to get to the lift. We need to get to a carriage," I sobbed, racing us down the hall. Everything about me felt so small. My lungs had collapsed in on themselves, unable to draw enough breath. Black spots danced in the corners of my vision. "Help!" I called, my voice weak. This hallway had been full of footmen. Where were they now? "We need help!"

"Why isn't he following us?" Alex demanded, his head wrenched back, looking over his shoulder. "What is he doing?"

At the chair's front, one of the smaller wheels wobbled, its caster spinning loose, and I struggled to keep Alex from careening into the windows. "It doesn't matter. We have to get to the lift."

"Oh, little brother," a voice sang out. Viktor's words echoed down the hallway, unseen. "You can run but you can't hide."

"Frederick!" I shouted. "We need help.... We need... Help!"

"Frederick! Johann!" Alex tried. "Anyone!"

Viktor's laughter followed after us.

"Where is everyone?"

Alex shook his head mutely.

We turned left, fleeing down the short hall as fast as I could push the shaking wheelchair. My arms ached, muscles burning. When we reached the lift, I wanted to burst into tears. It was parked on the first level.

I slammed the button to start its ascent.

Nothing happened.

I struck it again.

Everything stayed still.

The lift remained motionless.

No steam grumbled up through the pipes. From deeper in the house, I could hear the slow, methodical click of Viktor's shoes along the wooden floorboards.

"The latch," Alex said hoarsely, realizing the problem. "Whoever used it last didn't flip the latch."

"Alexander . . . ," Viktor called. "Come out, come out wherever you are . . ."

He paled visibly.

"You need to hide," I whispered. "By the time I get downstairs and the lift makes its way up, he'll be here. It'll be too late. Find someplace safe to hide. I'll send up the lift and try to draw him elsewhere. Listen for the lift."

Alex shook his head. "I can't let you take that risk. I need to—"

I grabbed him with a sudden fierceness, fingers trembling as I pressed a kiss to his lips. "I need you to stay safe. For me. For us. I love you, Alex. *Hurry.*"

His face muddled with contradicting emotions but then he pushed away, disappearing down the nearest corridor.

"Alex, the lift is jammed," I said, raising my voice, making it impossible for Viktor not to hear me. "We'll have to take the back stairwell instead."

I raced away in the direction opposite Alex, making my progress as loud as possible. I needed Viktor to know exactly where I was.

I did find a little staircase, eventually. It was steep and narrow, coiling round and round, built to take up the smallest amount of space within the manor, not intended for a swift descent.

Halfway down the rickety thing, I tripped, smashing the

back of my calves along the iron treads and landing hard against the railing. My head struck the curved metal and for a horrible second, I could picture the bolts giving way, plummeting down, as I crashed into a broken heap upon the landing.

I paused, waiting.

The railing had held.

For now.

My vision was blurry and I struggled to focus. I could feel a warm wetness trickling into my slippers but there was no time to stop and assess the damage.

I pushed forward, however shakily.

"Ver?" Viktor's voice was at the stop of the stairwell. "That sounded like quite a tumble. I hope you didn't hurt yourself."

"Alex, we need to hurry!" I hobbled my way down the last of the steps. My voice sounded funny and I wondered how hard I'd hit my head. When I pushed back a loose curl of hair, my scalp felt sticky with blood.

A great booming laugh rebounded down the stony walls. "Do you really think me so stupid? How on earth are you meant to be carrying the boy? On your back?"

He laughed again and I stopped on the landing, wincing. He'd seen straight through my ill-conceived plan. I could only pray the feeble attempt to divert his attention had allowed Alex enough time to find a safe hiding spot.

Viktor's footsteps clanged down the metal steps, then stopped. I glanced up and saw him peering over the edge.

"Ver . . . what are you doing?" He took a step down, forcing me to retreat farther, keeping the space between us the same. "Drop the heroics. Let's find the boy, finish him off, and be done with all this."

"You're mad."

He shrugged.

"Why are you doing this?"

"Because," he answered, his tone even and reasonable. "I can. Because I want to. Because everything that boy has ever had was meant to be mine. And I want what's mine."

"It was meant to be Julien's," I said.

"He never wanted it. He was going to just hand it over to that little fool."

"You killed him." He snorted as if it was of little importance. "Your own brother. Your closest friend."

"He was in the way. Now he's not. And soon dear little Alexander will be out of your way and it will just be us."

"There is no us," I insisted, falling back another step as he advanced forward. "The two of us together—"

"Think of it, Ver. Think of what we can create. We will bring new gods into this world, shaping it in our image. You and me."

"No," I said flatly, retreating down two stairs now.

His eyes roamed over me, tangible and unwelcome. "We'll see how you feel. After."

"After?" I echoed, worry creeping in.

He offered out a carefree wave of his fingers before disappearing behind the railing. His footsteps were softer now, ascending the spiral.

"The lift," I muttered to myself, setting out toward the back of the house. "Fix the lift."

The house was strangely empty as I stumbled through it. I'd never noticed just how many servants the Laurents employed until they were all absent, stilling the manor to silence. Chauntilalie seemed bigger without them, a living thing with its eyes now fixed upon me, its sole entertainment.

I took a wrong turn, lurching down a corridor with doors on both sides and not a window to be seen. My vision swam before me and I leaned against a door, listing heavily. It pushed open, revealing Marguerite. She cowered behind a sofa, the drapes hastily drawn and the gas lamps lowered.

With enormous eyes, she peered at me in the darkened space. "Is that you, Thaumas girl?"

"We need to get out of here, Madame Laurent. There's been a terrible . . . *so* many terrible things."

"Dauphine," she said, nodding, making a little sign over her heart, with three fingers raised.

"And . . . Gerard as well."

She stilled. "Which one of them did it?"

"Julien, sort of— But, wait. You know about them? That they're here now?"

She looked at me with obvious disdain. "Why do you think I'm in here, hiding in the dark, wretched girl?"

"The staff is missing—"

"I sent them away . . . for help," she added as I blinked uncomprehendingly. "When I saw him here, Viktor, outside my son's study, I sent for help. I've known those boys all their lives. I've seen what my son accomplished. . . . Believe me when I say we'll need all the help we can muster."

"Alex is hiding upstairs. The lift was left down here and without Frederick, he's been trapped."

She tutted in dismay. "Whatever you plan on doing, those boys will stop you at every turn. Viktor is ruthless and Julien—"

"Julien is dead," I cut in. "Viktor killed him."

Again, she made the gesture over her heart. A ward of protection, a prayer for a departed soul.

"And you're certain . . . you're certain that my son . . ."

I nodded. "I'm so sorry, Madame Laurent."

Her sigh was steeped in resignation. "He made many terrible mistakes, that son of mine. I always knew those boys would be the death of him, one way or another." She shook her head sadly, her carefully pinned curls swaying.

I wanted to reach out and comfort her. The lines across her face seemed deeper, etched with a grief that had not yet fully emerged. As if sensing my thoughts, she pulled away, hugging her arms across her chest, a crumbling tower of solitude.

"You stay here and I'll send the lift for Alex. . . . Surely there's a carriage left. We can take that and get away."

"And how do you propose my grandson get into said carriage? Without that giant of a manservant, he'll be just as stuck out there as he is here."

"There's the lift, down at the docks, to lower him to the rowboats. We'll go out into the lake and wait till the servants return with help."

"I . . . I suppose we might try that." She stood up on shaking legs, gripping the back of the sofa, fingers dug in deep.

I glanced about the room. It was full of flower vases, little golden statues of Dauphine's beloved peacocks. Everything was too small, too delicate. I spotted a set of tools near the hearth and brightened.

The heft of the brass poker reassured me. Little lines of flowers wound their way to its pointed tip but I wouldn't let their beauty be a distraction. I would use this weapon if I had to. To save myself. To save Alex.

I practiced swinging it through the air, feeling ridiculous with Marguerite's eyes upon me.

"You look almost intimidating," she said appraisingly. "I suppose it's the best we have. Where is Alex? Exactly?"

"Upstairs, somewhere. I told him to come when he heard the lift. We won't have time to come back this way for you. Head for the boat now. We'll meet you there."

She sighed, pained to be taking orders from one who so annoyed her. "Very well. Bring me one of those rods. If you're going to leave me here to fend for myself, I too would like to be armed."

I selected the dustpan for her. It was lighter than the poker, but its scoop would make an effective weapon if required.

She tested the weight and nodded approvingly.

Now armed, we made our way to the exit on tiptoe. I took a deep breath before turning the doorknob, certain Viktor would be lying in wait for us.

The hall was empty, seemingly deserted.

My frame trembled as I peeked out to check the corridor.

A chill of alarm prickled through me as I felt something grab hold of my collar and I nearly screamed, but it was Marguerite, her clawed fingers squeezing me.

"Take care of my grandson," she said before pushing past me to make her way down the corridor.

I watched her turn a corner before I raced off in the opposite direction, heading for the atrium.

I could tell from the sharp curses and grunts of pain that I was already too late.

High above me, up on the balcony, Alex and Viktor struggled with each other, exchanging blows. Blood ran down Alex's face from a cut at his temple and his nose looked broken, smashed beyond recognition. Viktor's shirt had ripped and his movements were ungainly, as if one of his legs had been injured during their scuffle. Both sported fresh, swollen bruises and split knuckles. The unmistakable odor of singed hair and burnt flesh filled the air.

I wanted to cheer as I watched Alex ram into his brother's side with his chair, knocking him off-kilter. Viktor's hand reached up, pulling the chair over and tipping Alex free. The ceiling above me shook from the crash and bright embers drifted down to the marble floor.

"Alex!"

"The latch, Verity, get the latch!" he shouted before the sound of a fist striking flesh rang out and he groaned.

Stumbling toward the lift, I stepped on a piece of broken pottery and slipped. The atrium was littered with shards of shattered vases and strewn flowers, fallen over the balcony as the boys fought.

My teeth sank into the side of my tongue as I landed hard on the unfeeling stone floor and a burst of blood filled my mouth. Spitting it out, I crawled toward the lift, then ducked as a small wooden table smashed to the ground, inches from me. I flipped the latch and pulled the lever, preparing the lift for ascent. The steam sounded like a rumble of thunder as it worked through the pipes.

But before I could pull myself inside and hit the button to start it, I was wrenched backward and thrown across the floor.

"What happened— Marguerite?" I asked in disbelief, squinting as twin sets of her filled my vision. They moved together in unison, stepping forward and swinging the fireplace scoop high.

Stars clouded my mind as she struck me and I collapsed, writhing.

"You're far more clever than I gave you credit for, little Thaumas girl," she hissed, kicking at me with her pointed shoes.

I managed to roll over, protecting my middle, but she landed a hard strike against my spine. I groaned.

"Verity!" Alex howled, and from my vantage point on the floor, I saw him pulling himself up to peer over the balcony, looking down in horror as his grandmother attacked me. "Grandmère, you must stop. You must—"

He never finished what she must do because Viktor reached up and cracked his head against the railing. Alex fell out of sight as I screamed.

"Why are you doing this?" I cried, flipping to the side to avoid the brass dustpan. The quick movement caused my head to spin and for a moment, the world pitched black.

"He's my grandson."

"Alex, Alex is your grandson. Viktor's a monster."

Marguerite frowned, her lips downturned as if she was declining a second cup of afternoon tea. "Viktor was who I was promised. Alexander . . ." She shook her head. "Alexander is broken. Weak. Your union would have amounted to nothing. All of my son's research would have been in vain."

"You knew? You knew what Gerard was doing?" I wanted to sit up but a sharp pain hitched at my side. "Why didn't you stop him?"

"Stop him?" She tittered. "I did everything in my power to *help* him."

She raised the pan above her head and I was too dumbstruck to move in time. The brass scoop came down across my left shoulder. I curled into myself, clutching my injured arm to my chest.

"Do you think I would have ever bowed down to Arina after what my husband did? She could have stopped it, she could have let my daughter be born flawless and whole, but instead she went to the opera that week. She dined at the best restaurants, surrounded by her court of chevaliers, and do you think she spared one single thought for Emilee? For me? My years of devotion meant nothing to her. Everything we do for them—the prayers and festivals, the sacrifices and offerings. They mean nothing."

Marguerite shook with indignation.

"When Viktor Laurent was born, I rejoiced. We were one step closer to bringing them all down. But for all his brilliance, my son failed. He was scared, frightened by the power he'd created. He threw in his lot with the runt of the litter and told himself it was better that way. But I knew . . . I knew."

The clamor on the balcony rose and I couldn't make out who was shouting, who was groaning. More debris went sailing over the edge. I prayed something would strike Marguerite but she ducked away, moving easily.

"The day Gerard told me he'd found the right partner for Alexander, a girl who would truly help herald in the new golden age, I knew I needed to act and act quickly." She pressed her thin lips together. "That first dinner at Chauntilalie, I could see you were special. I knew you were meant for Viktor. . . . I never went to the family flat in Bloem. I headed instead to Marchioly House."

"You helped them escape," I said, seeing everything clearly.

She nodded. "No one ever suspected it was me. I set the fire. I found the boys and I brought them here." She let out a sigh. "It's a shame my son will never see the fruits of his labors." She shrugged. "I suppose it's a blessing the family crypt is so large. So let this, let all of this"—she pointed to the chaos upstairs—"play out, Thaumas girl. And when it's over, you and Viktor will be together. And the real work can begin."

My stomach lurched and I turned over, sputtering up a mouthful of bile. As I spat it out, I spotted my poker. It had been kicked aside during her first volley but it wasn't far, a little more than an arm's length away.

I stretched, grabbing for the poker, then screamed as she brought the dustpan down upon my arm. I flipped over, knocking her back in the process.

She howled, grabbing at her hip, and I took the moment to launch myself at my weapon. My entire body railed against the motion. I wanted to curl up as small as I could, make myself into a space so little there would be no room for the pain. But my fingers closed around the brass rod and I whirled around, staggering to a stand as I pointed it toward Marguerite.

A wicked smile bloomed over her face, her wrinkles stretched manically long.

"Verity!" Alex cried out, hidden behind the balcony. His voice didn't sound right. It was too thick. Too wet. "Send the lift! Please!" His entreaty trailed off to a garbled end as a bone-shattering crunch filled the air.

With a gasp of frustration, I turned, limping toward the iron doors. Before I could take another step, pulling myself inside the cage, something large fell over the lip of the balcony. A dark form sailed through the air and crashed onto the atrium floor with a horrifying thud.

The body did not move again.

My entire being froze as I stared at the fallen figure, willing for it to twitch, willing for there to be some sort of life in the splayed, spread limbs.

"Alex?" I whispered.

No response.

From the body.

Or upstairs.

I took a tentative step toward it.

Toward *him*.

He was still a him.

He still might be a him.

Not . . . it.

"Alex?" I breathed, leaning over the broken body. A sob welled within me. It was him. It had to be him. I couldn't imagine a world where it was not him. "Please," I begged anyway, beseeching Pontus, Arina, any god who cared to listen. I wouldn't be particular. "Please don't be Alex. . . ."

I turned his face toward mine and the tears broke. His features were soft, swollen beyond recognition. His nose seemed two sizes too big, his jaw lumpy and undefined.

One eye remained half open, staring with an unfocused, lopsided gaze at the skylight above. Red starbursts had exploded like fireworks over his iris, seeping into the white.

There was blood.

So much blood.

"Alex?" I asked, taking his hand in mine. There was no muscle response. No grip. No grasp. His soul, his essence, whatever it was that had animated him and made him whole and human and mine, was gone.

No.

No, no, no.

I shook at his frame, spurred on by the insane hope that Gerard had somehow been right.

That he had made him immortal.

That Alex was still alive.

"Please," I whispered, my voice small and tight.

Nothing.

Not even a twitch.

A sob ripped through me, tearing my heart in two.

"Verity! Look out!" a familiar voice cried.

I glanced up and my mouth fell open as, through a vision of tears, I spotted Camille.

She was standing at the threshold of the atrium, pointing behind me.

"Camille?"

I turned just in time to see Marguerite's dustpan swinging at my head.

48

I WOKE WITH A STARTLED GASP, AS IF BEING SHAKEN awake.

The room was too dimly lit to be familiar. Long gray drapes were pulled over the windows and the gas lamps were lowered to a ghostly glow.

I couldn't move at first, my body swaddled in a series of bandages and dressings. A cast plastered over one wrist, hard and heavy, and I could feel gauze wrapping around my middle, but there was oddly no pain.

Not yet, though I was certain it would soon come crashing upon me.

With my free hand, I reached out, searching for water.

There was a sharp intake of air from deeper in the room. Then, from within the gray void, movement.

"Verity? Are you awake?"

The mattress pressed down, as if someone now sat on its edge. I struggled to see who was there and when I did, my heart broke.

"Camille?"

She nodded, taking my uninjured hand in hers. "I'm so happy to see you," she said, pressing a kiss to my fingers.

"Am I . . . am I at Highmoor?"

She shook her head. I'd never seen her so out of sorts before. Her hard duchess shell had chipped away, her hair plaited loosely down her side, and circles smudged dark beneath her eyes. "We're at Chauntilalie, in one of the guest rooms. There wasn't a good way to move you upstairs after . . ."

"What are you doing here?" It hurt to ask. My throat was impossibly dry and felt as if it had not been used in days.

"I . . . I found you. During the attack . . . don't you remember?" She pushed back a wisp of hair from my face, her amber eyes dancing over me as she took in every wounded detail.

It seemed impossible to shake my head. "I thought I was seeing things. Why would you ever come to Bloem?"

She looked hurt. "Your wedding. I . . . I came a few days early. I wanted to . . . help you, however I could, and I wanted . . . I wanted to apologize and set things right between us." Her fingers flexed around mine, holding tight as if to impart every bit of earnest truth she felt.

My eyes were far too heavy to remain open and I closed them, certain I was dreaming. There was no way Camille was here. There was no way Camille would be here, feeling remorseful and wanting to set aside our differences.

"I'll let you go back to sleep," she murmured, withdrawing her hand from mine, and my eyes flashed open.

"Are you really here?"

Her eyebrows drew together. "Of course I am."

"You never sent a response."

"I did! I did the second I received the invitation, I promise. They were beautiful," she added, as though it mattered now. "I'd never expected you to choose something so elegant."

"I didn't pick them," I admitted, and she let out a little laugh, surprising us both. "Could you get me something to drink?" I asked. "I'm so thirsty."

She was gone for a moment, then returned with a pitcher and a crystal tumbler. The sound of the water spilling into the glass was the most beautiful thing I'd ever heard.

Camille helped me sit up, positioning pillows beneath my bruised back to help keep me upright. The pain began then—not a slow creeping of awareness, but a bolt down the spine, a series of tremors racing along every nerve. My fingers balled into fists so tight Camille had to hold the glass for me, slowly pouring that blessed water into my mouth as though I were a baby bird.

"I'm glad you're here," I began, sinking back into the bedding. Sitting up, even for a short moment, proved too taxing. "Where's Alex? Where is his . . ." I trailed off before I could say the horrible idea aloud.

Camille ran her fingertips over my face and my stomach tightened at the gentle touch. It all but confirmed what I feared.

"He's in the next room, resting."

My heart skipped a beat; certainly I'd misheard her.

"His body?"

She shook her head, frowning.

"But . . . I saw him fall. There was no way he could have survived that. No way he could have—"

"That wasn't him on the floor. He was on the balcony."

"He's alive?" I asked, needing clarification, needing to hear her say the actual words aloud, as if they were some sort of magic spell binding him here, assuring his continued existence.

"He's alive," Camille repeated, and tears pricked at my eyes.

"So Viktor..."

He'd been the one to fall.

Alex had somehow, wonderfully, impossibly survived.

She bit at the corner of her lip. "The boy on the ground? Or the other one in the study? The authorities don't know what to do about them. No one knows who they are."

"Alex's brothers. They're... they *were*... triplets. Julien and Viktor."

She licked her lips. "They're dead too."

I nodded.

Camille touched my hair again. "What happened here, Verity? When I arrived, there were no groundsmen to open the gates, no footmen to greet us once we made our way through. I came in and found that horrible old woman standing over you, about to... She was about to kill you, Verity. If I'd been just seconds later..." She swallowed and shook her head, the sentence too painful to finish.

A flash of red echoed through my mind as I remembered Marguerite's confession.

"What happened? To Marguerite?"

"There was a poker on the floor. I picked it up and... struck her."

I inhaled sharply, pain spiking along my ribs. "You killed her."

Camille looked away uncomfortably. "I... I did what I had to do."

Her words and tone reminded me so much of Viktor, I felt sick, the room swimming before me with a queasy ache.

"More water?" she asked, and I nodded.

"How long have I been asleep?" I asked after several shallow sips.

"Almost a day. The healer said you broke your wrist and cracked two ribs, but she was able to set everything. It will take time, obviously, but you'll recover."

"Where . . . where are they all? The . . . bodies."

"They were taken to the crypt. Beneath Chauntilalie. I don't fully understand the People of the Petals' traditions for burial, but I'm told the Sisters of the Ardor are handling all of the necessary arrangements. Everything will be properly done."

"And Alex—does he know all this? Is he . . . awake?"

She nodded.

"Can I see him?"

She hesitated. "I don't know how we'd get you to his room."

"There's no shortage of wheelchairs in this manor," I offered, trying to smile.

Her lips rose in a half-hearted echo. "He's not in the best of shape right now, Verity. He needs lots of rest. As do you."

"I know. I'm sure of that, but . . . I need to see him."

She smoothed out the cotton duvet covering me, running her fingers over the embroidered vines stitched across its hem. "You really love him, then?"

I nodded.

"I wasn't sure, when I first received the wedding notice. I wondered if it was some sort of arrangement."

"It started that way, as far as his parents were concerned.

But . . . I love him. And he loves me. So, so fiercely. He's a good person. I know we'll both take care of one another, make each other so happy."

Camille mulled this over. "I thought perhaps you were trying to punish me, trying to show you didn't need my approval, my input." She let out a slow sigh. "I'm so sorry for how I acted before you left . . . how I've been acting, for years. I don't know if I will ever be able to fully explain it, if I'll ever be able to make you see . . . I truly was doing it all for you, Verity. I wanted to protect you. I wanted to keep you safe."

I lifted my hand, indicating the cast. "It does appear that you had good reasoning to worry. This isn't exactly how I dreamed my first trip from home would go."

Her smile was small but there. "Will you forgive me?"

I stared at her for a long moment, taking in the dark circles beneath her eyes, the lines of worry pinching at her face. "Will you forgive *me*? Running off in the middle of the night—all those things I said to you before I left . . . I didn't . . . I just didn't know how else to do it. To take hold of my life."

"I'm sorry I made you feel as though that was the only option out."

Tears bit at my eyes. "I was mad at first. So mad. But then . . . scared." I took a deep breath. "I'd play out all these conversations in my head. . . . I'd start and stop so many letters to you. I was so scared I'd broken something between us. Really, truly shattered it. I knew you hated me and I knew you were right to do so."

She pressed a careful kiss to the top of my forehead. "You're my sister, you goose. Even on our worst days, I could never hate you. I'll never not love you. Never," she repeated firmly.

"I love you."

She studied me for a long moment. "You really want to go see Alexander?"

I nodded fervently, even though it made my head feel strange and disjointed.

Camille squeezed my hand before pushing herself off the bed. "I'll see what I can do."

∽

Alex's room was just down the hall from mine, but as Camille slowly pushed me there in a borrowed wheelchair, the journey felt miles long.

My heart ached as I spotted a familiar figure approach us, shuffling in and out of visibility.

"I thought I heard something," Constance whispered, caught in another of her loops, unaware of anything but the past. "I think someone's following us."

She flickered out of sight, only to reappear at the end of the corridor, retracing her steps.

"I thought I heard something . . ."

"When the Sisters of the Ardor come," I mentioned, reaching my hand up to still Camille, "you need to make sure they put seeds on the rose mounds. Their sacred seeds. At the side of the manor. It's very important."

". . . I think someone's following us."

Camille followed my gaze as I watched Constance play out her final night again. I knew she couldn't see her but noticed the hairs on my sister's arms rise, her flesh goose bumped.

"I will," she promised. "Verity . . ." She eyed the empty corridor uneasily. "Are you ready to see Alexander?"

I nodded and she opened the door.

"Verity?" he murmured as we entered the darkened room and approached the bed.

The only source of light was a single taper candle on the far side of the room—its wax blessedly a soft shade of amber. I could barely make out his huddled form within all of the sheets and pillows. The healers had warned of his injuries before allowing me to visit, saying they thought it better to be well prepared.

The list was long and painful—a shattered nose, scorched flesh on both his hands and across his neck. Several of his wounds required stitches and the black thread made his face resemble a gruesome patchwork quilt. There'd been damage to his eyes and though I didn't understand everything they spoke of—iris distortions and corneal abrasions—I knew he needed to remain in a safe, dark environment if they were to heal.

"I'm here," I said as Camille pushed the chair alongside his bed for me. She gave my arm a sympathetic squeeze before slipping from the room and closing the door behind her.

Once we were alone, I took his hand tenderly in my good one, mindful of his injuries beneath the thick gauze. "Are you all right?"

His laugh was soft. "No. Not really."

"Have they given you any medication for the pain?"

I think he shook his head. It was hard to tell with all the dressings and wraps covering his face. "I've been so worried about you. I was certain you'd been killed. The last thing I saw before I blacked out was Grandmère . . ."

"I'm here. I'm all right," I promised.

"I can't believe . . . I still don't comprehend what happened. I've been lying here, thinking everything over, and I just . . . It doesn't make any sense to me."

"I don't understand it all myself," I confessed. He'd lost his entire family in one horrible day. His mother, his father, his grandmother, two brothers he'd barely even known. "But we'll make our way through it. Together."

His fingers slackened against mine, loosening his hold. "About that . . . Verity."

A cold, hollow spot bloomed beneath my sternum.

"I . . . I can't imagine you'd want to remain here, not after . . . everything. You've been poisoned and drugged, lied to and assaulted. I'd understand if you wanted to flee and forget everything about this place. Forget about me. Forget that we ever . . ." He let out a shaky breath. "Know that I won't harbor any anger or resentment toward you."

"For what?" I asked, unable to discern his meaning.

"For breaking off the engagement," he clarified as if it were obvious.

I was surprised by how much his words stung. "Is that what you want?"

His sigh offered no indication one way or the other.

"Alex?"

"No," he whispered, his voice quavering and on the verge of tears. "I don't. But I . . . I didn't go through everything you did. No one was trying to use me for . . . for . . ." He stuttered to a stop, a sob breaking. "For all of that."

"But they were. He *was*. You were as much a victim of that

as me." I wanted to reach out and cup his face but I couldn't see how to do so without causing pain, so I stroked the top of his arm instead. "I fell in love with you, not your family, not your title. I fell in love with the boy who makes my heart happy, who showed me a new way to watch the rain . . . All of the things that happened—those awful, terrible things—they haven't changed that. That love hasn't gone anywhere."

The room was filled with a weighted silence and the longer it lasted, the greater my doubt grew.

"Ver—"

My stomach dropped, hearing Viktor's favored nickname wet on Alex's lips.

For a moment, Viktor was all I could hear, his laughter ringing out in the stairwell.

He struggled to sit up, breaking the word in two. "—ity, I can't."

I stilled, frozen in place. "Oh."

I'd misunderstood.

I'd been so concerned with showing him how much I still cared, proving my devotion, that I hadn't stopped to worry if he felt the same way. I'd never questioned if it all had been too much for him. If I'd been too much.

I released my hold, rocking the chair back, ready to flee the room, flee him, flee the boy who no longer loved me.

"I can't," he repeated, licking his lips. "I can't."

"I understand," I murmured, choking back tears.

I needed to get away from him. I couldn't bear for him to hear me cry.

He sighed. "It just . . . It makes me feel so weak."

I paused my retreat, looking over my shoulder. "What does?"

"I should let you go, I know that. It's the proper thing to do. The right thing to do." Alex swallowed. "But I can't."

"You can't?" I echoed softly.

He shook his head. "I can't imagine my life without you, Verity. Or . . . I could, but I don't want to. I don't want you to go. I don't wanted to be apart and I . . ." His voice cracked.

"You love me?" I asked, returning to the bed.

"I do."

"And you still want to marry me?"

"Arina help me, I do."

He reached for my hand and pressed a kiss softly onto my palm. In my mind's eye, I saw him as the boy I'd first met upon my arrival at Chauntilalie, sitting outside the manor, waiting for me with sparkling eyes, a dazzling grin.

I remembered the mornings spent tracing out those eyes, that grin, over and over, filling pages.

The picnics by the lake, his laughter bright in the air.

The look of hope on his face as he asked me to marry him.

The way we'd held on to each other before everything had fallen apart.

The way I wanted to keep holding on to him now.

"Good," I murmured. "Because I can't think of anything I want more than you."

"You do?" he whispered in disbelief.

"I do." I brought his hand to my lips, mimicking his gesture, sealing my words with a fervent promise.

He let out a sigh, his fingers wrapping round mine in a tangled knot, impossible to break. "I do."

49

EVERY BELL IN BLOEM RANG OUT AS I MADE MY WAY down the flower-strewn aisle to marry Alexander Laurent.

I was pushed there in a wicker wheelchair by Camille, smiling proudly. She'd decorated it with rock-roses and gardenias in the softest shades of pink we could find.

The healers had wanted us to wait, had begged and pleaded for us to hold off for a few weeks, but as Alex once said to me: when you know you've found your love, you act on it. Life is unpredictable, so you need to seize hold of what you love and cherish every moment together.

So just three days after the attack, we wed.

One of the sleeves of my dress had to be sliced open to allow for my cast, and Alex wore large spectacles with black-tinted lenses to protect his eyes, but when all was said and done, we were married and together, exactly as we'd wanted.

"This certainly isn't how I'd envisioned our wedding night," Alex admitted once we were brought into his chambers, after an intimate, subdued dinner with family and friends. Most of our invited guests had already begun their travels to Bloem on that terrible day, not realizing they would witness a wedding, then remain for five funerals.

The services were set for tomorrow.

Alex had decided both Viktor and Julien would be buried in the family earth, their remains joining generations of Laurents, accepted in death as they had not been in life.

"No?" I asked, stumbling from the bathroom toward the bed. I ought to have been nervous for him to see me so exposed in my new nightdress—a beautiful gown of thin lawn cotton, bedecked in ribbons and dainty stitching—but my ribs ached too much to worry on it.

Frederick had already moved Alex out of his chair, propping him up on a mound of pillows. He'd pulled the bedsheets over his chest and was looking in my general direction.

"It's too dark to even see you," he complained, removing the tinted glasses and squinting against the light of a single candle.

It was one of Annaleigh's candles. The staff had taken pains to remove each and every one of Gerard's pink tapers from Chauntilalie, burning them all—and every last canister of poppy tea—in a bonfire far from the house.

"I know, without a doubt, you must be a ravishing sight, but it would be nice to have confirmation of it as well."

I eased myself into the bed. My wrist throbbed, and I'd never been more exhausted in all my life. I collapsed onto the pillows beside Alex.

"You ought to rest," I said, and pressed a soft kiss to his lips, pushing the glasses back up the bridge of his nose.

"I know many people say to begin as you mean to go forward,

but I promise you this, Lady Laurent, not every night of ours will end before ten o'clock."

"No?"

"Oh, no." He kissed my forehead and I curled alongside him, careful not to bump against his injuries. "I promise you here and now, our nights will be long and lovely. Full of kisses and starlight."

Stars...

My dreams that night bordered on nightmares. In them, I ran through the deserted halls of Chauntilalie, searching for Alex. The air was filled with the cries of the babies and peacocks, and above it all, the triumphant cackle of Viktor, believing he'd won at last.

I tried escaping into the secret passages, tried running down stairwells and corridors.

Everywhere I turned, he was there.

I startled awake with a gasp, sodden and sweaty and blinking with confusion at the soft gray light of the room. A ray of morning sun had managed to slip through the heavy velvet curtains, illuminating the space enough for me to see that I was in bed alone.

Curious, I sat up, peering about the space.

I spotted Alex laid out on the chaise, attempting to read a book. Frederick must have come and gone while I dozed. Alex angled the book toward the window, catching the pages in the meager light.

"I thought you were meant to be resting," I said, greeting him, my husband. A thrill wriggled through me at the thought. *My husband.*

"It's amazing what a good night's sleep can accomplish," he said before lowering the book to look at me. His smile was warm and bright. "Good morning, wife."

My lips rose, warm and content. "Good morning, husband."

His dimples flashed before he returned to his reading, absentmindedly crossing one ankle over the other.

Epilogue

DRIP. DRIP.

Drip. Drip. Drop.

Far beneath the bones of Chauntilalie, rainwater trickled down the walls of the Laurent family crypt. The door opened and five women dressed in gauzy blush-colored robes and spangled headdresses entered, carrying with them baskets of seeds. Even at the height of spring, their breaths puffed frostily in the chilly air.

They were the Sisters of the Ardor, postulants of Arina, come to deal with the bodies of the dead.

Each deceased was laid out on a slab of marble. The polished stone trapped the cold temperatures of the crypt, helping to slow down the unpleasant realities of the decomposition process.

First Dauphine, her naked form hidden beneath a piece of silk dyed a soft lavender hue. Once the sisters had prepared her body, anointing it with oils and packing it full of sacred seeds, the fabric would be knotted around her, acting as a sort of chrysalis for all of the changes to come. The roots from the sacred seeds would have no trouble tearing through the thin silk, seeking deeper soil.

Roots were very good at trailblazing their way into the world.

Beside her lay her husband, Gerard Laurent. The Sisters had prepared a special blend of seeds for him, making sure to include dozens of *Euphorbia marginatas*. Already, the new duke had removed nearly every trace of snow-on-the-mountains from the grounds of Chauntilalie, heralding the start of his reign with a bower of *Dictamnus albus*. The white dittany blooms were everywhere around the manor, and the new ducal motto of "Perfected Loveliness" had already been warmly received by the citizens of Bloem.

Next was the old woman. Marguerite Laurent. Her life had been long. Her death—if indicated by the contusions that bloomed across her body—painful and swift.

After her came the two mysterious figures. They were both obviously Laurents, spitting images of the new duke himself, but no one could claim to know exactly who they were or how they'd come to be at Chauntilalie.

The first had died a terrible and gruesome death, and the Sister assigned his remains packed the gaping wound at his throat full of seeds, whispering a cycle of prayers over it with a visible shudder.

The last body had obviously taken a horrible beating but there was a peaceful stillness in his reposed form. The last Sister, the youngest and only a week out of her novice robes, had been assigned him.

She pulled back the silk sheet and said her first prayer.

Next came the oils, to the head, the hands, the heart.

As she traced her holy patterning over the body's chest, she thought she felt something beneath the skin, a movement subtle and soft. She glanced toward the Sister next to her, wanting to ask guidance but scared to look foolish.

He was to be the first body she had ever prepared and she wanted to be seen as a competent custodian.

She picked up her basket of seeds and prepared to start planting them.

But as she took up her first handful, ready to strew them across the long lines of his naked form, she dropped everything.

There on the table, on the funeral slab, the dead boy's fingers moved with a small but unmistakably alive twitch.

ACKNOWLEDGMENTS

Writing a book is very much like planting a garden. You start with a little tiny seed of an idea, and with lots of water, sunshine, and care, amazing blooms begin to sprout.

I'm so thankful to have Sarah Landis cultivating my ideas and helping them grow. Never once have you ever thought my plots were too wild, and I'm forever grateful for your belief in me. You deserve an entire greenhouse full of *campanulas* (constancy, gratitude).

I owe the grandest bouquets of light red dianthus caryophyllus (deep admiration, thanks) to my entire team at Rock the Boat for championing my books and tending to them with such diligent care. Shadi Doostdar—you and your entire team are the most marvelous, hardworking humans, and I'm so insanely lucky to call you colleagues and friends.

So many people have early-read and cheered on Verity's tale. *Acacia* (platonic love, friendship, repels ghosts!) to Kirsten Miller, Erin Hahn, Jeannie Hilderbrand, Elizabeth Tankard, Kaylan Luber, Melanie Shurtz, "Lord" Ekpe Udoh—who unknowingly let me borrow his name!—Jessica Olson, Kendare Blake, Megan

ACKNOWLEDGMENTS

Shepherd, Lauren Blackwood, Courtney Summers, Stephanie Garber, Shea Ernshaw, and all my incredibly talented Team Landis family. A special arrangement of *moluccella laevis* (ardent gratitude) to Jamie Sumner for your insightful sensitivity reading. You are incredible.

Amaranthus (endless love, fidelity unwithering) for Hannah Whitten. You gem. You treasure. You are my forever ride-or-die. I could not do this job without you. Thank you for letting me steal your name and give it to a ghost.

A million *helianthuses* (constant warmth) to every reader who has picked up one of my stories from the shelf. I've adored meeting you at bookstores and festivals, on school visits and Zoom calls. Your enthusiasm and love make every bit of this process a joy. I'm wildly grateful to you.

Extravagant bundles of *lonicera caprifolium* (I love you, steadfast and generous affection) to all of my family and friends. You've taught me to dream big and work hard and have given me the gift of so many stories. I would not be here without you. Extra sprigs of *calendula officinalis* (fidelity, adoration, helps with seeing the fairies!) for Mama, Daddy, Tara, and Carol.

Paul. No love interest I write will ever come close to you. *Kalanchoe* (eternal love, lasting affection, persistence) and top-shelf ramen for you. Always.

And Grace. You've helped me plant every seed in every one of our gardens. You sing to the sprouts, tell the flowers how brave they are, and cheer as they grow. I love you more than you'll ever know. Pink *dianthus caryophyllus* (a mother's love, always on my mind) for you.

ALL GIFTS COME WITH A PRICE.

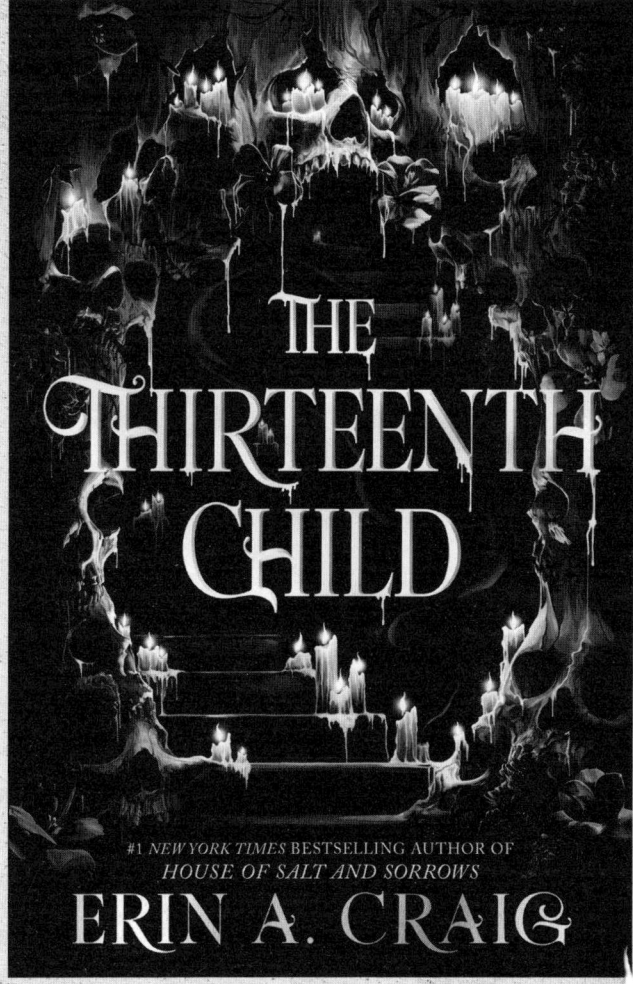

"Haunting and deeply romantic.
I was enchanted from the very first page."
—Ava Reid, #1 *New York Times* bestselling
author of *A Study in Drowning*

ERIN A. CRAIG is the #1 *New York Times* bestselling author of *House of Salt and Sorrows*, *Small Favors*, *House of Roots and Ruin*, and *The Thirteenth Child*. After getting her BFA in Theatre Design and Production from the University of Michigan, she stage-managed tragic operas filled with hunchbacks, séances, and murderous clowns, then decided she wanted to write books that were just as spooky. An avid reader, an embroidery enthusiast, a rabid basketball fan, and a collector of typewriters, Erin makes her home in West Michigan with her husband and daughter.

ERINACRAIG.COM